PRAISE FOR THE NOVELS
OF *NEW YORK TIMES*
BESTSELLING AUTHOR
DALE BROWN

"Brown puts us in the cockpits of wonderful
machines and gives us quite a ride."
New York Times Book Review

"The novels of Dale Brown brim with violent
action, detailed descriptions of sophisticated
weaponry and political intrigue. . . . His ability to
bring technical weaponry to life is amazing."
San Francisco Chronicle

"A master at creating a sweeping
epic and making it seem real."
Clive Cussler

"His knowledge of world politics and possible
military alliances is stunning. . . . He writes about
weapons beyond a mere mortal's imagination."
Tulsa World

"A master."
Larry Bond

"Nobody does it better."
Kirkus Reviews

DALE BROWN
AND
JIM DeFELICE

A DREAMLAND THRILLER

WHIPLASH

HARPER

An Imprint of HarperCollinsPublishers

This is a work of fiction. Names, characters, places, and incidents are products of the authors' imagination or are used fictitiously and are not to be construed as real. Any resemblance to actual events, locales, organizations, or persons, living or dead, is entirely coincidental.

HARPER

An Imprint of HarperCollins*Publishers*
10 East 53rd Street
New York, New York 10022-5299

Copyright © 2009 by Air Battle Force, Inc.
ISBN 978-0-06-171300-2

First Harper paperback printing: November 2009

Visit Harper paperbacks on the World Wide Web at
www.harpercollins.com

10 9 8 7 6 5 4 3 2 1

Dreamland: Duty Roster

Lieutenant General (Ret.) Harold Magnus

Magnus once supervised Dreamland from afar. With Colonel Tecumseh "Dog" Bastian as its on-the-scene commander, the organization succeeded beyond his wildest dreams. Now as Deputy Secretary of Defense, Magnus hopes to repeat those successes with Whiplash. His hand-picked commander: Bastian's daughter, Breanna Stockard.

Breanna Stockard

After retiring from the U.S. Air Force to raise her daughter and help her husband's political career, Breanna found herself bored with home life. She was lured back to a job supervising the development of high-tech wizardry under a combined CIA and Pentagon program. But will she be happy behind a desk while her agents are in trouble?

Jonathon Reid

Reid's official title is Special Assistant to the Deputy Director Operations, CIA. Unofficially, he's the go-to guy for all black projects, the dirtier the better. He knows how to get around agency politics. More important, he knows where all the agency's bodies are buried—he buried half of them himself.

Colonel Danny Freah

Fifteen years ago, Danny Freah won the Medal of Honor for service far beyond the call of duty. Thrust back into action as the head of a reconstituted and reshaped Whiplash team, he wonders if he still has what it takes to lead men and women into battle.

Nuri Abaajmed Lupo

Top CIA operative Nuri Lupo is used to working on his own. Now the young CIA officer has to adjust to working with a quasi-military team—at least half of whom he can't stand.

Chief Master Sergeant Ben "Boston" Rockland

Boston finds himself shepherding a group of young CIA officers and special operations warriors across three continents. To do it successfully, he has to be part crusty old dog and part father figure.

Hera Scokas

Despite her ability with languages and the black arts of special operations, Hera Scokas hasn't been able to climb the CIA career ladder as quickly as she wished. Now that she's been given her greatest opportunity, she faces her greatest challenge: taming her personality to get the job done.

John "Flash" Gordon

Six years as an Army Special Forces soldier taught Flash two important lessons: keep your head down when the shooting starts and never volunteer. Too bad he can't follow his own advice.

Carl "Tailgunner" McGowan

Recruited to Whiplash from a SEAL team, McGowan is always ready with an irreverent putdown. He's also the guy you want watching your back when things get nasty.

Clar "Sugar" Keeb

Raised in Detroit, Sugar stands just shy of six feet, but that's the only thing shy about her. The CIA paramilitary officer could flatten any man in the unit—and will if they get in her way.

March 2012

———

1

**Termini train station
Rome, Italy**

NURI ABAAJMED LUPO STEPPED OFF THE TRAIN FROM
Naples and turned left, walking up the long platform toward
the central terminal area. He was a short, solid man, five-
eight, 170 pounds, though his trim waist made him appear
lighter. He generally walked with a bit of bounce in his step,
though this afternoon he was keeping the bounce very consciously in check. Gray daubed into the close-cropped hair
at his temples made him appear two decades older than he
really was, Nuri's jeans and open collar shirt were nondescript enough to make him appear European, if not quite
Italian—an irony, since all but one of his grandparents had
come from Italy, and he still had relatives in Sicily and the
Italian section of Asmara in Eritrea.

His shoes gave him away as an American. It was not so
much the manufacturer—Merrell, which, though American,
sold its wares all over the world—as the fact that they were
hiking boots, rarely worn by native Italians except for the
specific purpose they were intended.

Nuri found the shoes particularly comfortable, and today,
being identified as an American did not bother him. His
features were mutable; depending on the circumstances, he
could pass as a European, an Arab, a Persian, a South or

Central American. He'd even once been mistaken for Filipino, though in that case he had been aided by some strategic makeup and a prosthetic device. Such variability was a result of his genes and his background, but it was an important asset to Nuri's profession.

He was, to use the old-fashioned term, a secret agent. A covert officer. A spy.

In general, his job called for much less drama and danger than might be implied from watching James Bond movies or reading an old Le Carré novel. Today, however, it would have given its fictional counterparts a good run for their money. Already he'd survived a bombing, which was all the more disturbing because it didn't appear to have been aimed at him.

Nuri wrapped his right hand around the strap of his backpack as he came to the large doors at the end of the platform. He glanced downward, avoiding the gaze of the two sub-machinegun-toting carabiniere, and moved to the center of the large hall, turning back as he reached it as if to get his bearings. He stared at the signs, pretending it was all new to him.

Not counting his childhood, Nuri had been in the terminal no more than five dozen times. Most of these visits had been made the night before, in a virtual reality program that had allowed him to familiarize himself with Rome while sitting in a hotel room in Alexandria, Egypt. The program was extremely realistic, right down to the notoriously unscrupulous taxi drivers.

"Subject approaching from platform," said the Voice in his headset.

"Which door?" muttered Nuri.

"Center door."

Nuri adjusted his headphones. They looked exactly like a pair of Apple iPod phones, a year or two out of style. He watched the door, waiting for Rafi Luo to come through.

Though he had been following him since Egypt, Nuri hadn't gotten close enough to him to actually see him in the flesh.

He'd seen photos and even spoken to a three-dimensional computer model of him, but he had not come within five hundred meters of Luo since he first began tracking him two days before.

He hadn't had to. Luo had been tagged with a biomarker that allowed him to be tracked via a satellite network to virtually anywhere on the planet. There were dead spots in large buildings and underground—subways were a particular problem—but since most people came out eventually, there was literally nowhere in the world Luo could hide.

Assuming, of course, that he stayed alive.

So far, he had—though the bomb that had missed Nuri had almost certainly been meant for Luo. A car had blown up on a street in Alexandria right outside the hotel where he was staying, seconds after he'd turned from the front door to return the room key he'd forgotten to hand in. Nuri had been walking down the street at the time. The force of the blast, funneled by the large buildings on the block, had thrown Nuri to the ground, but left him and the hotel unscathed.

Luo had noticed, of course. But the way things were in Alexandria these days, he couldn't be sure that the bomb was meant for him. And in any event, his profession invited all manner of dangers.

Nuri spotted him striding into the station, head high, looking more like a movie star on vacation than a vital cog in an illegal weapons ring. Luo bounced through the crowd, arms and hips swinging as if he owned not only the terminal, but the continent it was built on. His slicked-back hair glowed black. His chiseled face was a magnet, drawing stares even as his smoked glasses imposed a certain distance from the common rabble.

Luo was fully aware of his looks. He'd used them since he was thirteen or fourteen, breaking the hearts of countless girls and women. Many of them could recognize his type from the distance, knowing he would use them and leave them without remorse, yet still they found themselves attracted to him, driven as if by genetic imperative. This had fanned Luo's disdain, not just for women, but for much of the world. He was more than selfish and vain; he wanted and felt entitled to any desire that happened into his mind. Sex, of course, but lately money had become its very near rival. No corporate titan lusted after material rewards more than Luo did. And none had less regard for anyone who stood in his way.

He pulled his glasses down, scanning the wide indoor terrace of Rome's train station. Luo had a vague notion that he was being followed. It was a notion that was always with him, a paranoia important to success in his profession. But as he scanned around he saw nothing to tip him off that he was actually being watched. He did not see Nuri, and even if he had, the tourist would not have registered as a potential threat.

Nuri, drifting behind a surge in the crowd, lamented that the Italians did not believe in take-out coffee. He didn't have time for even an espresso.

"Subject proceeding toward western doorway," said the Voice in his ear.

Nuri began to follow, girding himself for the inevitable squabble with the taxi driver. While in theory the fare should not have made a difference to him—he had an ample supply of euros, not to mention a stack of Egyptian and American bills—it nonetheless stung him to be cheated. And he would have to account for his expenses to the accounting department eventually. They always paid particular attention to the small items like taxi fares, which were impossible to document.

Luo turned left outside the door, ignoring the queue for the taxis, which were lined in a chaotic, Italian-style jumble at the edge of the plaza. He walked along the stone sidewalk and out along the Piazza Esquilino, more an extended bus stop than a traditional Italian piazza. For a moment it looked to Nuri that he was going into either the cinema or the five-star hotel at the corner near the Piazza della Republica; Nuri would have welcomed either stop, since he wanted a chance to get a coffee and maybe something to eat. But instead Luo continued down Via Nazionale, moving easily among the throng of tourists and local residents.

It was a clear day, pleasantly warm for March. A bright blue sky arched over the city, and the sun seemed to brush away the dust and grime from the facades and storefronts along the street. Via Nazionale had its share of hotels, but most of the shops here catered to residents, clothing and shoe stores butting up against a bookstore and the occasional tobacco store.

"Am I being followed?" Nuri asked, muttering to himself. He was wearing a pair of video bugs attached to the back of his collar, scanning the area behind him.

"Surveillance has not been detected," replied the Voice.

Nuri's heart began beating faster as Luo continued down the street in the general direction of the Imperial Forum. Luo wasn't a tourist, and the course was too direct to have been plotted merely to see if he was being followed. He must be meeting someone.

Nuri quickened his pace and closed to within a half block. Luo crossed through the traffic near Villa Aldobrandini, then went down the narrow hill to a little street just above Foro di Augusto. Ruins spread out before him, Rome's ancient past pulling itself from the dust. There were many lessons a man might draw from such a sight—the fleeting nature of wealth and power first among them. But Luo drew none, his mind far from the ruins.

Realizing he was getting too close, Nuri stopped in the middle of the parking lot near Trajan's Column. The column was a majestic, impressive sight, undiminished by the fact that it stood in front of a building and square undergoing renovations.

"Who is that at the top of the column?" he asked.

"Trajan's Column," replied the Voice. "Colonna Traiana."

"Is that Trajan at the top?"

There was a pause before the voice answered.

"St. Peter."

"St. Peter? How'd he get there? Isn't that a Roman column?" This time the pause was longer.

"The answer is not immediately available," said the Voice,

indirectly announcing the limits of its network memory. "Do you wish the matter researched?"

"Negative."

The Voice's admission of its limitations cheered him a little, making up for his lack of caffeine. Nuri walked along the parking lot, pausing to hear the pitch from a man selling picture books. He wanted ten euros. Nuri shook his head and started to walk away.

"Five euro," said the man, in English.

Nuri hesitated, thinking the book would be decent cover.

"Quatro," he said, turning back. "Four."

The man said in Italian that he was driving too hard a bargain for a wealthy American.

Nuri shrugged and started to walk away. He was a little annoyed that the man had responded in English rather than Italian; he felt his accent had been perfect.

"Four euro, *si,*" said the man, holding the book out.

Nuri stopped and reached into his pocket for some coins. The man began telling him a story as he counted the change, explaining in English that he lived in the area. Some years before he had been a woodworker, but his hands no longer cooperated: a fact obvious from their violent shaking as he took Nuri's money.

The man knew a great deal about the ruins, more than what was in the books. He offered himself as a guide, but Nuri merely shook his head and took the book. Turning to go, he remembered his question about St. Peter on the column.

"Ah, the pope—1587," said the man. He pointed at the book. "The story is there. The legend—when Traianus was taken up, yes? From the vault below, his skull was there. It told the story of his release from hell."

The explanation confused Nuri, but now Luo was getting too far away. Nuri thanked him.

"I can tell you the entire story—if you want a guide—I am here every day," said the man, calling after him.

Up the street, Luo was nearly to the Coliseum, his pace as jaunty as ever. A long line stretched around the side of the amphitheater as visitors waited to get in. But he had a pass that allowed him to avoid the lines, and he walked through the group entrance, stepping through the metal detector without pausing to empty his pockets. The detector found nothing.

Nuri headed toward the end of the line. As he reached it, a young man with a British accent stopped him and asked if he'd like to join his tour.

"Twenty euros, and you beat the line," said the young man. "You get right in. And you get a full tour."

"I beat the line?"

"Yes, you come right in with me. Twenty euros."

Nuri unfolded a twenty from his pocket. The young man grabbed it hungrily—generally he had to bargain down to ten or fifteen this close to tour time—and directed Nuri toward a short, dark-haired woman standing near the entrance. Nuri went over, starting to get a bit anxious—if Luo was meeting someone inside, he wanted to be close enough to hear what was going on, or at least see who it was.

"We can go right in?" he said to the woman.

"*Si, si*," she said. "We are on our way. Come."

Nuri started toward the gate with a dozen other tourists, a hodgepodge from Britain, Japan, and China. Tour groups were given special privileges at the Coliseum, and in fact at most of the attractions in Rome and Italy. If you were in a group, you could jump ahead of the line, entering at a pre-scribed time—or perhaps immediately, depending on the arrangements the group's sponsor had made with the authorities.

"Direct me," he muttered to the Voice as he passed the metal detector.

"Proceed twenty paces straight ahead."

Nuri walked down the main corridor, passing the displays of ruined bits of columns, mortuary plaques, and statues. He went through an arched opening—*vomitorium* was the proper name—and came out onto the main aisle circling above the arena area. He walked forward, pretending to look at the ruins, but in fact scanning for Luo.

He couldn't see him.

"Direct me," he said.

"Reverse direction," said the Voice.

Confused, Nuri followed the directions to a door just off the main corridor inside. The Voice told him to open the door and go down the stairs inside, but the door had an alarm on it, apparently not included in whatever schematic the computer had accessed.

Nuri reached into his pocket for his key chain. On the chain was a small card that looked like the sort of tag one held against a credit card reader when making a purchase; not coincidentally, it carried a Visa logo to reinforce that impression. Pressing his thumb firmly against the middle, he slid the card along the doorjamb, waiting to hear a buzz in his headset. As soon it buzzed, he pushed through, the alarm temporarily deactivated.

The corridor opened onto a darkened staircase. Nuri found a banister at the right and descended slowly, listening as he went.

"Turn left," said the Voice, directing him down a tunnel-like corridor. A dim blue glow of natural light shone toward the far end, where it met another hallway at the right.

Nuri paused, considering whether he should proceed. While he wanted to know why Luo was here and who he was meeting with, being discovered following him would be counterproductive, and very possibly fatal.

Being detained by the museum security people wouldn't be helpful either.

Nuri opened the book he'd bought, paging through until he found the Coliseum. He folded it open, and glancing at the illustrations, began walking forward through the corridor, pretending he was somehow following the book. He was in the center area of the Coliseum, the basement beneath the arena where animals and gladiators waited before the games. You didn't have to be very superstitious to think the place was thick with ghosts.

He heard voices as he approached the first corner. He

stopped, folded over the page in the book, then plunged forward, holding the tour guide out as if he were using it to relive an ancient scene of life and death.

There was no one there. The voices echoed against the thick stones of the massive structure. The sounds were odd and distorted; he couldn't tell what the language was, let alone pick out individual words.

He started walking again. The corridor opened up—

"Direct me," he told the Voice.

"Proceed forward twenty yards."

Nuri took two steps, then stopped, considering how much distance he should keep from Luo, and whether he might not be better off circling around. The ruins were a maze of small rooms and alleyways; he could probably slip very close to him without being seen.

He turned and started down a small passage just behind him. Nearly two thousand years before, the passage had held the cages for lions brought back from Africa especially for the anniversary games held in honor of Rome's founding. A winch and pulley located on the wall just behind him had been used to haul the cage up to the level just below the arena floor. There, its open third side allowed the animal to escape. Sensing freedom, the lion would trot up a ramp into the open air, confronting a pair of terrified Christians, who were promptly torn apart by the starving beast for the amusement of the crowd.

All of this was recounted in the book Nuri was holding in his hand, but he had no chance to contemplate it, or even read it. For as he walked down the passage, two gunshots, very close together, echoed loudly through the stone archways of the Coliseum's basement. He spun and dropped to his right knee, watching as a figure ran past in the corridor.

All he caught was a fleeting glimpse. He rose, his instincts telling him he should follow. But as he took a step, another instinct took over; he jerked himself backward, diving around the low, ruined wall to his right. As he hit the ground, the shadow that had passed returned, pumping two shots in Nuri's direction. The bullets missed, but their ricochets sprayed stone splinters and dust. There was a scream above, and another shot. Nuri dove through an opening on his right, rolling into a small room as the figure with the gun ran into the passage where he'd just been.

Nuri leaped to his feet and ran from the room. He turned left, running toward a stage that had been erected opposite the gladiators' entrance to the arena.

The shooter followed. Nuri ducked to the right, into another small alley connecting the rows of rooms, flattening himself against the wall. The footsteps continued, then suddenly stopped.

Nuri looked up and saw a half-dozen tourists standing on the ruined steps opposite him, staring down in horror. He slipped to the ground and turned the corner, hoping to catch a glimpse of the gunman as he ran off.

He saw him, or rather, her—a young woman dressed in baggy green khaki slacks, with a wide top and a knit cap pulled over her head. She wasn't running. She had stopped and was looking directly at him.

She started to pull the gun out from the holster beneath her shirt where she'd just tucked it.

Nuri jerked back into the corridor, about to run—only to realize that his escape was blocked off by a wall. He'd turned into a dead end.

2

Washington Metro

AT ROUGHLY THE SAME TIME NURI LUPO WAS SCRAMBLING in the dust of the Coliseum, Colonel Danny Freah was scrambling down the platform at the Alexandria stop of the Washington Metro, heading for the train that had just stopped and opened its doors.

The car was crowded. He slipped in next to a tall woman in a powder-blue pantsuit a few feet from the door, trying to squeeze himself into the tiny space as more passengers crammed in behind him. The doors slapped shut, then opened, then closed. The train started with a jerk, and he just barely kept himself from falling into his neighbors.

The people around him, all on their way to work, barely noticed him. The lone exception was a black woman about half his age, who thought he reminded her a little of her father, albeit a slightly younger version.

Danny, who had no children himself, might have been amused had he been able to eavesdrop on her thoughts. His own, however, were much more practical. It had been a while since he'd been in D.C., let alone since he used the Metro, and he wasn't sure if he'd gotten on the right train.

"I can get to the Pentagon from here, right?" he said, looking at the woman in the powder-blue suit.

"You would have done better to figure that out before getting on the train, wouldn't you?" she answered.

"Then I would have missed the train."

"Wouldn't you have been better off in the long run?"

"Maybe yes, maybe no. I have a fifty-fifty chance, right? Assuming I found the right line."

The woman looked him up and down.

"Most colonels are not gamblers," she said. "They tend to be conservative by nature."

"There's a difference between gambling and taking a calculated risk," said Danny. "This is taking a calculated risk."

"I suppose."

Danny laughed. "Is it the right train?"

"I suppose."

The train arrived in the sculpted concrete station a few minutes later. As the crowd divided itself toward the exits, Danny spotted several people in uniform and followed them toward the restricted entrance to the building. As the crowd narrowed, he found himself behind the woman in the powder-blue suit.

"So I guess this was the right stop," he told her.

"I didn't say it wasn't."

"You said you 'supposed.' Like you had some doubts. But you work here, so you knew."

"You 'suppose' I work at the Pentagon," she told him.

Danny looked for a smirk or some other sign that she was kidding with him. But she wasn't.

Mary Clair Bennett did not have much of a sense of humor. She had spent the past twenty-two and a half years working for the Defense Department, and if she'd laughed at a single joke in all that time, the memory of it had been firmly suppressed.

In the days before titles were engineered to replace pay raises, Ms. Bennett would have been called an executive secretary. Her personality fit the words perfectly, combining efficiency with more than a hint of superiority. Ms. Bennett— she was a particular stickler for the title—had always felt that being a little chilly toward others enhanced her position with them. While her two nieces might have argued passionately on her behalf, few people would have called her a particularly warm person. Even her sister, who lived out in Manassas, found she had very little to talk to her about when she came for her biweekly visits.

"Well, thanks for getting me here," Danny said as they reached the security checkpoint.

Ms. Bennett rolled her eyes. He smiled to himself, amused rather than annoyed, and joined the line for visitors.

The line led to a sophisticated biometric scanning and security system, recently installed not just at the Pentagon, but at most military installations around the country. More than a decade and a half earlier, Danny had presided over the system's precursor, developed and tested at the nation's premier weapons test bed and development lab, the Air Force's Advanced Technology Center, better known as Dreamland.

That system had essentially the same capabilities as the one used here. It could detect explosives and their immediate precursors, scan for nuclear material, and find weapons as small as an X-Acto blade.

The system checked a person's identity by comparing a number of facial and physical features with its stored memory. The early Dreamland version had been somewhat larger, and tended to take its time identifying people; it would have impractical dealing with a workforce even half the size of the Pentagon's. In the fifteen or sixteen years since then, the engineers managed to make it smaller and considerably faster. The detectors were entirely contained in a pair of slim metallic poles that rose from the marble foyer floor; they connected via a thick wire cable to the security station nearby. Each visitor walked slowly between the poles, pausing under the direction of an Army sergeant, who raised his hand and glanced in the direction of his compatriot at the station. The station display flashed a green or a red indicator—go or no go—along with identifying information on the screen.

One couldn't simply visit the Pentagon; his or her name had to be on a list. Even a general who didn't have an office here needed a "sponsor" who made sure his or her name was entered into the system.

"Please wait, sir," said the sergeant as Danny stepped up to the posts. "We have to recalibrate periodically."

The more things change, the more they stay the same, thought Danny. Such pauses had been common at Dreamland.

Then, the process could take as long as half a day. Now it took only a few seconds.

"Please step forward," said the sergeant.

"Good," said the second sergeant at the console, waving Danny through. Then he caught something on the screen. "Whoa—hold on just a second."

Startled, Danny turned around.

"Um, uh—you're, uh, Colonel Freah." The soldier, embarrassed by his outburst, stepped awkwardly away from the console and snapped off a salute.

It was unnecessary, since they were inside, but Danny returned it.

"This here's a Medal of Honor winner," said the sergeant, turning to the other people on line.

Now it was Danny's turn to be embarrassed. One of the civilians spontaneously began to applaud, and the entire line joined in. Danny put his head down for a moment. He always choked up at moments like this, remembering why he had gotten the medal.

More specifically, remembering the men he couldn't save, rather than those he did.

"It was . . . a while ago," he mumbled before forcing a smile. "Thank you, though. Thank you."

"Yes, sir. Thank you, sir," said the sergeant nearest him.

"You all have a good day," said Danny, turning and starting down the hallway.

It had happened a very long time ago, more than a decade, during his last assignment with Whiplash—his last assignment at Dreamland, in fact. Colonel Tecumseh "Dog" Bastian had just turned the base over to a three-star general, officially completing his mission and restoring the base to its former glory after an infamous scandal had threatened its closing. Danny, who'd come on board with the colonel, was due to be reassigned when the mission came up.

Just one more job before you go, son. Can you do it?

The irony for Danny Freah was that if he had to list all of the action that he'd seen under fire, the mission that led to his medal would only have ranked about midway to the top. Five minutes of sheer hell wrapped inside days of boredom—the usual lot of a soldier, even a member of Whiplash—at the time, the ultraelite Spec Warfare arm of Air Force Special Operations, assigned to provide security and work as Dreamland's "action" team. They had deployed all around the world under the direct orders of the President. Colonel Bastian had worked for the President himself, outside the normal chain of command. They'd accomplished an enormous amount—and burned bridges by the country mile as he went.

Those days were long gone. Danny was a full bird colonel now, his life as boring as that of a life insurance actuary as he tried to get in line for a general's slot.

In a perfect world the coveted star would have been presented to him on a velvet pillow, thanks to his service record. But the world was far from perfect. The enmity that Dog had earned throughout the military bureaucracy also extended to those closely associated with him, including Danny Freah. Dog's successor—who liked and helped Danny, though he wasn't a particular fan of Colonel Bastian—hadn't exactly won a lot of friends either. And then there was Danny's record itself. Jealousy played a much more important role in the military hierarchy than anyone, including Danny, liked to admit. The fact that he was neither a pilot—a "zippersuit"—or a graduate of the Academy also hurt him subtly, denying him access to networks that traditionally helped officers advance. His closest friends and associates tended to be the enlisted people he'd worked with, and as loyal as they might have been, they had zero juice when it came to the promotion boards.

Still, professional back-biting, petty rivalries, and old boys (and girls) clubs wouldn't have amounted to much of a block to Danny's career during ordinary times. Even two or three years before, he would have made the general's list without too much trouble. But the world's economic troubles had made the times anything but ordinary.

The new administration had come into office the previous year by promising to both balance the budget and hold the line on taxes. Other administrations had made similar promises. The difference was that this President, Christine Mary Todd, actually meant to keep her word. Every area of the budget had been cut, including and especially the military. The Air Force was looking to cut the number of generals on its rolls in half.

The man Danny was coming to visit had been a victim of those cuts, though in his case he hadn't done too poorly. Harold Magnus was the deputy secretary of defense, a position he'd stepped into just a few months before after retiring from the Air Force, accepting the fact that earning a fourth star was highly unlikely.

General Magnus had briefly served as Colonel Bastian's commanding officer; though technically responsible for Dreamland, the general's responsibilities were mostly on paper. A reshuffling had soon taken him out of the chain of command, and he'd had almost no contact with Dreamland or its personnel since.

"Actually, I was looking forward to getting some serious fishing in, and maybe improving my golf," Magnus told Danny as he ushered him into his office. "But I got suckered into this. Primarily because I've known the Secretary of Defense for thirty years."

Magnus winked. Though in his late sixties, he still had the look of an elf about him. Or maybe Santa Claus—the years had added several pounds to his frame, which had never been svelte to begin with. Known as a firebrand during his early days in the Air Force, Magnus had gradually softened his approach. He now came off more like a grandfather than a whip-cracker. He was, in fact, a grandfather, and a rather proud one, too, as an entire table's worth of photos near his desk attested.

"Coffee?" Magnus asked Danny.

"No thank you, sir."

"I'm going to have some, if you don't mind."

Magnus pressed the button on his phone console. His secretary knew him well enough that she didn't have to ask what he wanted, appearing with a tray inside a minute.

"So how's your wife?" Magnus asked Danny.

"I'm afraid we divorced a number of years ago."

It was five, to be exact. The marriage had floundered long before then.

"I see. I'm sorry to hear that."

Magnus stirred his coffee. Married to the same woman for nearly forty years, he was a little baffled by marital discord. He never knew exactly what to say when confronted with it. He could count on one hand the number of times he'd had a disagreement with his wife in all that time. But he knew it existed, and realized it wasn't a character flaw. His usual strategy when the issue was raised inside his family—one of his daughters and son-in-law had been having troubles for over a year—was to stay silent for a moment, offering the other party a chance to speak if they wanted. If nothing was forthcoming, he always changed the subject.

"See the old Dreamland crew much these days?" Magnus asked when his internal time limit had passed.

"No, not really," confessed Danny. "I still see some of my men occasionally. Ben Rockland's a chief now, out at Edwards."

"Rockland—I think he may have been after my time."

Danny nodded. The general was being polite. He'd had no dealings with the enlisted members of Whiplash, and thus had no reason to know Rockland—whose nickname was Boston—let alone any of the other team members.

"What about the scientists?" asked Magnus, sipping his coffee.

"The scientists, not really," said Danny. "Ray Rubeo invited me to his birthday party two years ago. It was an interesting affair."

"Some estate, huh?"

"You can tell he doesn't work for the government anymore."

Rubeo had been the chief scientist at Dreamland for several years. He left after falling out of favor with Dog's successor. He was now the owner of a portfolio of companies in the alternative energy field; his biggest had recently won a contract from the government to build an orbiting solar power station. Rubeo's birthday party, his fiftieth, had lasted two weeks and featured a Venice night, a Cairo night, and a Taj Mahal night, all in the actual places. Danny had caught the Taj Mahal celebration.

"You don't see Jeff Stockard anymore?" asked Magnus.

"Zen? Oh yeah, I see him every so often. Couple of times a year. A little more if I'm around. We'll go to a ball game or something."

"Really? I've been spending a fair amount of time with Senator Stockard myself. He likes to take my money."

"You don't play poker with him, do you?"

"I'm afraid I do. Though it's more like work."

"You can say that again." Danny shook his head. "I'd never play cards with Zen. Much easier just to give him my wallet."

"Some people think he might run for President next time out," Magnus said.

"Oh?" Danny hadn't heard that.

"Some people think he'd be perfect. He wonders if the voters could deal with a guy in a wheelchair. Roosevelt was in a wheelchair, but no one knew it."

"I think if anybody could convince them, Zen could."

"I agree with you there, Colonel."

Magnus glanced at the clock on his desk. It was early in the morning, but he was already running a little late. "I suppose you must be wondering why I asked you here," he said, putting down his coffee. "Actually, it has to do with Breanna Stockard."

"Bree?"

"You know she's working for the Office of Technology, right?"

"Uh, yeah, she might have mentioned something like that."

Breanna had left the regular Air Force to help Zen when he ran for Congress twelve years before. After that, she'd stayed at home for a few years to raise their daughter, Teri. But even a rambunctious preschooler wasn't enough challenge for the former Megafortress pilot, and Breanna had begun examining her options soon after Teri learned how to count.

Her husband's job as congressman complicated things. Zen was borderline fanatic about avoiding even the appearance of a conflict of interest, which ruled out working at any company that did business with the government—a surprisingly large range of firms, especially in the Virginia area where they lived. Though Breanna was still in the Reserve and flew C-5s and C-17s part-time a few months a year, returning to

the Air Force full-time was out of the question because of
Teri. So she'd gone back to school for a law degree.

That wasn't without its potentials for conflict, either, considering how many law firms had dealings with the government. She'd held several posts, including civilian jobs with
the Air Force, and had last worked for the U.S. Satellite
Agency, a quasigovernmental concern responsible for putting
and maintaining satellites in orbit. The Office of Technology
was a Defense Department entity that had largely taken the
place of DARPA—the Defense Advanced Research Projects
Agency—the military's central research organization, during
the last administration.

"We're putting together a special project out of that office,"
Magnus said. "And we'd like you to be part of the team."

"I see."

"Breanna suggested you for the position. I immediately
agreed."

"It's a civilian job?"

"Not exactly. You'd still be a member of the Air Force,"
said Magnus. He was hedging, because he couldn't tell
Danny too much about the job unless and until he actually
agreed to take it. "Your responsibilities—let's say they would
be multidisciplinary. And in keeping with some of your past
experience."

"I see."

Danny leaned back in the chair. He had suspected there
would be some sort of job offer, of course, but he had been
hoping the assignment would be something more traditional—a base command would be ideal. He'd already done
two stints at the Pentagon and hadn't particularly liked either.
From everything he had heard, a staff position was unlikely
to help him get promoted, unless he worked directly for the
Joint of Chiefs of Staff.

"You're worried about your career," said Magnus, deciding
to be blunt.

"Well, a little."

"You should be in line for a promotion, but with the freeze

on, you know the odds of getting a star on your shoulder are pretty slim."

"I've heard slim and none."

"None may be an exaggeration," said Magnus. "But I think you're right as far as the immediate future goes. I don't see any additions being made to the list of generals this year, or next. It's tough. They're encouraging people to retire."

"I know."

"This team would be outside the normal route to promotion," admitted Magnus. "In fact, it might make it harder for you to get to general—at least in the *traditional* way."

"Is there another way?"

"There's always another way," said Magnus. "This job could lead to other things. But it won't help you become a general, not by itself. I'd be lying if I told you that."

"What is it?"

"You'll understand that I can't go into too many details," said Magnus. "But it's very similar to the job you had at Dreamland. Part of that job, anyway."

"Part."

Magnus decided he had to give Danny more information if he was going to win him over.

"We want to resurrect Whiplash," he said. "Only this time, it'll be even better."

3

Coliseum, Rome, Italy

NURI'S HEART DROPPED A BEAT AS HE STARED AT THE SOLID stone wall cutting off his escape. He threw himself to his right, pressing against the wall as a bullet flew next to him.

Stone flicked from the wall, hitting him in the forehead. Unhurt, he threw himself down out of desperation, crying out as if he'd been hit by the bullet itself.

"There! There!" people were yelling above.

"Look out!"

"Watch!"

"There's been a murder!"

"That man has a gun!"

Nuri heard footsteps running toward him. He collapsed facedown on the ground, pretending he was dead.

The shooter hopped over the wall and saw him. She pushed him over to his back, extending her arm toward his heart and firing twice. Then she raised her aim for his forehead and pulled the trigger.

Nothing happened. The pistol, smuggled past the metal detectors by an accomplice she'd never met, was empty.

Nuri looked dead. Ordinarily, the woman wouldn't have taken a chance on looks alone, but she had no choice. She was out of bullets, alarms were sounding, people were watching. She dropped the gun on his prostrate body and fled.

The bullets that hit Nuri in the chest had bruised his chest and trachea, but he was otherwise okay, thanks to the thin-layer protective vest he wore under his shirt. The Teflon and carbon polymer vest had diverted most of the energy from the small caliber bullets, saving him from death, though not pain.

He rolled over, trying to get back his breath. With great effort he forced away the black shroud around the edges.

Scumbags, that hurt. Damn.

Nuri pushed up to his knees, his whole body trembling. He couldn't hear anything—there was sound around him, echoes of noise, but nothing his brain could process.

He got up and stumbled into the next passage, saw someone's legs moving ahead to the left. He leaned forward, using gravity to help him move. Disparate sounds began to emerge from the incoherent cacophony. People screamed and shouted in panic as they tried to funnel through the Coliseum's narrow outer passages.

I have to get close to her, he told himself. *Close enough to get a marker on her.*

He reached into his pocket for the vial of marker liquid and held it. A wave of pain hit him as he reached the hall where he'd entered the arena area. Feeling faint and nauseous, he put his free hand against the wall, steadying himself while waiting for the pain to pass. It didn't, though, and finally he lurched off the wall, heading toward the steps.

There were so many other alarms and sirens sounding that if the alarm went off when he pushed through the door to the main level, no one noticed. He walked into the main hall, then took a step back as a flood of panicked tourists rushed by, running toward the exit despite the pleas of one of the guards for them to stop.

"Which way?" he asked.

"The subject is below," replied the Voice. "He has ceased to move."

"The shooter?"

"No data."

Of course not; the system had no information to use to follow her. Nuri pushed out into the corridor, weaving left and right as people fled. He went to the archway, looking out on the stone path below. But he didn't see her.

It was too late now to go back to Luo. His best bet would be to get outside, take a wild shot at finding the shooter or maybe someone supporting her. If that didn't work—and it almost certainly wouldn't—he would find someplace to catch his breath, then start figuring out what had happened.

People were still running toward the exit. Nuri took a few steps with them, his chest heaving but his legs sturdier now. He felt a sting in the top of his thighs and pushed harder.

The woman had been wearing khaki green pants, with black running shoes. The detail crystallized in his mind as he reached the exit. He tried working his memory toward her shirt. It was some sort of print T-shirt, over another T-shirt.

Italian, maybe. A soccer team?

No, some sort of slogan. Not in Italian. French, he thought.

Maybe one of the cameras had seen it.

Her face?

Nuri pressed his memory but it wouldn't yield an image. He turned in the direction of Piazza del Colosseo, the street at the end of Via dei Fori Imperiali. There was a truck there, selling water and other drinks. The alarms were still sounding in the Coliseum, but the people milling around didn't know what was going on. Most thought there was some sort of fire, or a false alarm.

Nuri quickened his pace, his stomach queasy but the rest of him feeling stronger. Adrenaline buzzed through his body, making his ears ring. He saw a woman with green pants eyeing him in front of the truck. He glanced at her shoes and saw that they were black. But she was wearing a red silk blouse, and her hair was long. The shooter's had been short.

A wig.

He stared at her face. The woman turned abruptly, walking up the hill. Nuri glanced around, making sure there were no other likely suspects, then started to follow. But as he did, a girl nearby began to yell.

"There he is! There he is!" she said in English, pointing and screaming. "There! There!"

The girl had seen him in the ruins and thought that he had been the one shooting. Everyone nearby turned, and one of the men near Nuri reached to grab him. He pushed the man away, then saw a pair of policemen running toward him from the Coliseum.

The last thing he wanted to do was end up in police custody. Nuri spun and ran across the street, dodging past a tourist bus to run into the Metro stop. Leaping over the turnstile, he ran toward the down escalator, pushing people aside and then squeezing past a pair of old women. His stomach felt as if it was going to explode.

A train was just arriving. Nuri ran through the doors and found a seat, then closed his eyes as he waited for it to move again. The doors shut. The train lurched forward, then stopped. Nuri pushed his eyes closed further, worrying that it wouldn't start, afraid he'd been caught. But then the train began to move again.

He leaned his head back against the window and contemplated his next move.

Two stops later he got off at Termini, hoping it would be easier to blend into a crowd there if anyone was looking for him or following him. He decided he would find a hotel where he could see to his wounds and perhaps monitor the news. He walked up and around the piazza, down the block, then back, and finally across to Nationale. He chose one of the hotels a few blocks from the station that he had passed earlier.

The desk clerk squinted at the disheveled man who stood before him. Most of their clientele, especially at this time of year, were Italians in Rome on business. The man before him looked too disheveled to pay the bill.

Nuri gave him an American Express card for the reservation. The clerk made sure to check his signature on the register against the blurry script on the back. It matched, but that didn't satisfy his doubts.

"I need your *passaporte*," he said.

It was a standard request in Italy, where technically visitors were required to be registered with the local police. Nuri hesitated, unsure whether to hand over his "regular" passport or the diplomatic one. He decided the diplomatic passport might raise too many questions, and gave the man the normal one.

The clerk saw the hesitation as one more bad sign, and might have called his supervisor or even decided to claim they were full had not a large family come through the doors. Just in from Modena for a visit with an ailing grandmother, there were three children under six in the party, and the small lobby suddenly felt as if it were under assault. The clerk processed Nuri's credit card, then promised to have his passport ready within the hour.

"Your bags?"

"The airline lost them," said Nuri. "I'll deal with it later."

Upstairs, he pulled off his top shirt and undid the vest,

which looked like a tight-fitting, waffle-style sports T-shirt. The sides were hooked together, and Nuri had to hold his breath to undo them. Pain shot through his entire chest as he pulled the vest apart. The spots where the bullets had hit were dark purple and black. Bruises in the shape of spiderwebs ran out from them. His nausea returned. He stood over the toilet, dry heaving for four or five minutes. He ran a warm bath, laying with some difficulty against the side of the tub as the water slowly filled it up.

The bath didn't do much to relieve the pain. The beer in the minifridge, Stella, made only slightly more headway.

The bruises were nothing. The real pain came from the fact that he had permanently lost Luo, and would now have to start from scratch on the Jasmine Project.

JASMINE WAS ONE OF THE CODE NAMES USED BY A RING OF smugglers who worked primarily in Africa. As these things went, they were relatively small fish. Their main wares were flowers—they got them in and out of different countries cheaply, sometimes legitimately, but more often without applying for the proper inspections or paying government fees, thus allowing them to be sold more cheaply. Low-priority smuggling of this nature was common, especially following the collapse of the Free Trade agreements at the start of the decade.

But if you could smuggle flowers, you could easily smuggle drugs. If you could smuggle drugs, you could easily smuggle weapons.

Actually, the flowers tended to be relatively lucrative, especially when the risks for everything else were figured in. But most of the organizations involved in smuggling didn't have risk analysts on the boards of directors.

Jasmine had attracted the CIA's attention after it sold machine guns to a notoriously abusive warlord in Somalia. The Agency didn't mind the sale—the warlord was fighting against an even more notoriously abusive warlord. But it raised Jasmine's profile in the Agency, which soon realized that the network—actually more a loose organization of contacts with a variety of benefactors—was very active in the Sudan. Still, Nuri might never have been assigned to check into the network had it not acquired a variety of finely milled aluminum tubes and small machine parts some months before.

Aluminum tubes might have any number of uses, depending on their exact dimensions. In this case, the tubes happened to be of a size and shape suited for the construction of medium-range missiles—a particularly potent weapon in the Sudan, since they would allow rebels to fire against urban centers from a considerable distance.

The tubes could also be used to construct machines useful in extracting uranium isotopes from "normal" uranium. That seemed unlikely, given that they were bound for the Sudan, but just in case . . . Nuri was given the assignment to find out what he could about Jasmine.

He'd spent months wandering in and out of eastern and northern Africa, getting the lay of the land. He had help from the NSA, which provided him with daily summaries of intercepts and would give him transcriptions on the hour if necessary. And he had an array of "appliances" to help— most importantly, a biological satellite tracking system that could locate special tags practically anywhere on earth, and the Massively Parallel Integrated Decision Complex, a network of interconnected computers and data interfaces that constantly supplied him information via a set of earphones and a small control unit that looked like a fourth generation Apple Nano. Called the MY-PID by the scientists, Nuri referred to the system as the Voice, since it primarily communicated through a human language interface.

But mostly Nuri was on his own. He didn't mind. He'd always been a bit of a loner, not antisocial, but willing to rely on his own wits and abilities. The only child of expatriate parents who spent most of their adult lives moving through exotic countries, he was used to that.

By the time Nuri reached the Sudan, the aluminum tubes had been delivered. Jasmine had not had a similar deal since.

In fact, the network seemed to have fallen into a bit of a lull, without any large deals for some months, if the NSA intercepts were to be believed. But he'd managed to track down Luo in Turkey two weeks before, following a credit card trail. He'd missed him in Istanbul, but found him in Alexandria, where he was able to have him "tagged" by an unsuspecting masseuse working in an unlicensed bath.

At least the sign claimed it was a bath.

His surveillance and NSA intercepts made it clear that Luo was expecting some sort of big payoff from a deal being cooked up in Italy.

But now all that work had been flushed by a woman with a gun.

NURI POPPED THE TOP ON ANOTHER BEER, SIPPED THE OVERflow on the top, then sat down to talk to his CIA supervisor. The Voice network had a separate communications channel, but he used his sat phone; Jonathon Reid wasn't typically on the Voice network.

"Hey, Bossman," Nuri said to Reid, "how's it shaking?"

"Poorly," said Reid. "Was that your subject who died at the Coliseum?"

"Word gets around fast."

"It's on the news."

Nuri reached over and flipped on the television. It was, in fact, on the news. The reporters didn't know the dead man's name, let alone the fact that he was an arms smuggler. But they did have his picture, courtesy of several tourists. They also had a reasonable description of the alleged shooter: Nuri Lupo.

"I didn't shoot him," said Nuri, watching the homemade video on the screen. The legend at the bottom said it had been posted on YouTube.

"That's good to know," said Reid. "I was beginning to lose faith."

Jonathon Reid's official title as special assistant to the Deputy Director Operations, CIA, covered a myriad of responsibilities and not a few sins. Reid was a throwback in many ways, an old-school line officer who had been exiled from the Agency following a very bad case of "red butt" two decades before.

"Red butt" was a term veteran officers used to describe how someone in the field reacted when someone in the bureaucracy told them how to do their job. Someone with red butt typically began telling that person what he or she could do with their advice. The general result was termination of some sort—usually by reassignment rather than firing, though the latter was not completely unheard of. A red-butt-induced reassignment was both mind-numbing and career ending. Usually it resulted in something that made counting paper clips in Fredonia look exciting, and the usual result was early retirement.

Reid had ended up in Fredonia, though he didn't count paper clips there. The small town in upstate New York had an outpost of the New York State university system. Granted a job as a permanent visiting professor—red butt or not, the Agency took care of its own—Reid had used his position to work behind the scenes, writing and lecturing on national security and technology issues, and quietly advising a number of politicians and government officials. One of his main themes was leveraging technology to help men and women in the field do their jobs more effectively. A year ago he'd been brought back by the new CIA director.

Reid had actually been offered the position of deputy director, an extremely powerful post whose responsibilities included overseeing the Agency's covert action programs. But he had declined for several reasons, the most important that he thought he would be a lightning rod for controversy, since he had made many more enemies since leaving the Agency.

The fact that he had just celebrated his seventy-eighth birthday had nothing to do with the decision.

Alerted to the shooting, Reid had arranged to obtain information from the Italians on the investigation. An FBI liaison officer had been dispatched to the local headquarters. The FBI agent worked routinely with the CIA on terrorist cases, and had been instructed to forward updates to Reid.

"The shooter was a woman," said Nuri. "Short hair. MY-PID didn't get enough to ID her."

"Yes, I've checked. But you might look at some of the online video sites and see if you can get a better image."

"Good idea."

"You looked pretty scared in the images, Nuri. It shakes my confidence in you."

"I wasn't scared. I'd just been shot in the damn chest at point-blank range."

"Your bulletproof armor did its job."

"How many times have you been shot in the chest?"

The answer was twice, but Reid, realizing he'd pushed a little too hard, said nothing.

THE YOUTUBE VIDEO SHOWN ON THE NEWS DID NOT INCLUDE a good image of the actual shooter, but a search of similar videos turned up three other videos of the same incident. Nuri, looking at the images in the hotel's business center, forwarded the information to the CIA's technical people via a blind e-mail address. By the time he got over to the embassy to follow up, they had sent the image to the FBI liaison in Rome, who managed--with some difficulty—to persuade the local prosecutor to let her compare the image to those captured by various security cameras around the Coliseum. Only about half of the possible cameras had been working, and only a half dozen of those were connected to computer systems that the carabiniere could easily access. Fortunately, one of them was the Metro system, which provided a good image of the woman getting on the same train Nuri had taken.

Nuri shook his head. The next time she saw him, she'd aim for the head first.

The woman had gotten off at the next stop, Cavour.

Nearly six hours had passed since then, but Nuri had decided to stay in Rome at least for another day, and if that was the case, he might just as well take a shot at finding her. So he went over to the Metro stop and began placing small video bugs, hooking them into the MY-PID circuit and hoping that the video would catch a glimpse of the woman. The bugs were about the size of a small bead on a woman's bracelet. They attached to a wall or other surface with a tiny piece of a gumlike sticker. The small size meant their integrated batteries lasted only a few hours, and they needed a larger transponder to pick up their signals and upload it to the satellite network. But they were nearly invisible, and provided video quality on par with the typical laptop or cell phone camera.

From the Metro stop, Nuri bugged a number of hotels, then left bugs on lampposts and buildings. Hungry, he was about to go across the river to a Sicilian restaurant he remembered from an earlier visit when the Voice told him it had a possible match.

"How possible?" he asked. His stomach was growling, and he could almost taste the *caponata di patate*.

"Facial bone structure matches. Height is within five percent. Hair is different."

"That could be a wig," Nuri told the computer.

"Assumption cannot be tested."

"No kidding."

He walked over to the area where the computer had spotted the woman going into the Hotel Campagnia. It was a mid-level place, used by foreigners mostly, about evenly split between business people and tourists. He scattered a few more bugs around, and contemplated whether it would be useful to call the FBI liaison and try for a list of the guests. As he did, the Voice warned him that the subject was coming down into the lobby.

Nuri went across the street to a café and ordered a glass of wine. The woman paid her bill, then had the clerk call her a taxi to take her to Fumicino, better known to Americans as Leonardo Da Vinci International Airport, which was just outside of Rome.

He might have called the FBI liaison then, to get her name, but even if the Italians cooperated—an iffy proposition—it would have taken hours. Instead, he took matters into his own hands, swiping the pocketbook of the woman sitting next to him as her back was turned.

He slid it under his shirt and crossed the street.

"Sfortunate!" he yelled, rushing in. "The lady dropped her pocketbook."

"C'e?" asked the clerk.

"The woman, who just got in the cab."

"Who?"

Nuri described her. "Where was she going?"

"The airport."

"Did she have a cell phone?"

The clerk looked baffled.

"I could call her," Nuri explained.

The clerk bent over to the computer and pulled up the registration. "There is no cell phone."

"What's her name?" Nuri asked. "I can page her."

He pulled out his sat phone quickly, fearing the clerk would want to do it for him.

"She was pretty, wasn't she?" added Nuri.

"Ah, yes. Margaret Adamoni."

"Her name was Margaret Adamoni," said Nuri, repeating the name for the Voice. "Did she say which terminal?"

The clerk couldn't recall.

"Check the wallet with me," said Nuri, "so we can't be accused of stealing money."

The clerk agreed, and in short order they discovered that the wallet belonged to someone else entirely. Nuri, pretending to be embarrassed, made a quick exit, then grabbed a taxi to the airport.

There was no Margaret Adamoni registered on a flight out of Fumicino, but the MY-PID tapped into the international flight registry, which used computerized passport IDs to screen for possible terrorists and other suspicious persons. Discarding people traveling in groups and examining flight profiles, it found three possibilities. After buying a ticket, Nuri checked two out at the gates. He missed the third.

That, of course, turned out to be his subject: Bernadette Piave, who'd just gotten on her plane for Athens, Greece, when he reached the gate. He went back to the ticket area, bought a ticket for the next plane, and booked an Alitalia flight two hours later.

It was only as he was waiting that the Voice turned up an interesting tidbit from a file maintained by Interpol: Bernadette Piave was believed to be a pseudonym for a woman named Meg Leary. That was the extent of the file there.

The CIA had its own file on Leary. It was restricted; not even the Voice could access it. So Nuri had to get help from Reid.

Meg Leary had been born in 1969 in Belfast, Ireland, the daughter of a convicted Irish Republican Army bomb maker and a woman from Dieppe, France. A short time afterward, Meg's mother disappeared, and she was raised by her father's family, shuttling back and forth between different uncles, aunts, and grandparents as the family members spent time in prison for their alleged roles in the Northern Irish "troubles." Given her family history, it was not surprising that she had her first run-in with authorities at age thirteen; she was arrested for allegedly spraying a Protestant home with submachine gun fire. The Protestants in question were prominent "provos"—essentially the Protestant equivalent of the IRA— though that didn't prevent Bernadette from serving jail time. Her rap sheet grew from there to include armed robbery and a variety of weapons charges, all before she was eighteen.

She was arrested a few days before her eighteenth birthday on suspicion of murder—a member of the family she'd first shot at when thirteen—but the evidence against her proved insufficient. That was the last time the British criminal justice system had anything to do with Ms. Leary. Officially, at any rate.

Reports from the various agencies charged with dealing with Northern Ireland stated that she had "apparently reformed." There were rumors that she had been drummed out of the IRA, or that she was never a real member in the first place. In any event, she hadn't received so much as a traffic ticket in the twenty-five years since.

"That's all the file has?" Nuri asked Reid.

"That's it."

"The implication is what?"

Reid sighed. "Don't jump to too many conclusions."

The implication was that she worked, or more likely *had* worked, for the Agency in some capacity.

Like maybe an assassin.

"Can you get somebody to watch for her in Athens?" Nuri asked.

"I don't think that will be necessary," said Reid.

"Why not?"

"She's a freelancer, Nuri. She works for the highest bidder."

"So you do know her."

"Not personally. But you'll be wasting your time in Athens."

"Not if I can figure out who hired her."

"Do you think you can do that by following her?"

Nuri leaned back against the thin airport lounge seat and thought about it. Someone like Leary was unlikely to lead him to an employer; she might not even know who had hired her in the first place.

"We didn't hire her?" he asked Reid.

"Of course not."

"You're sure?"

"Reasonably sure."

"Who? A competitor? The Sudanese? The Egyptians?"

"Unfortunately, your guess is as good as mine. When will you be able to return home?"

"Home?"

"Here. We have some new arrangements to acquaint you with. It will make starting over with Jasmine considerably easier."

Months of work, down the drain.

"Get me a flight, and tell me when it leaves," Nuri told Reid. "I'm already at the airport."

4

Pentagon

DANNY FREAH'S INITIAL REACTION TO GENERAL MAGNUS'S offer was thanks, but no thanks.

Magnus's limited description made the assignment sound a lot like his job at Dreamland, without the security component. Eventually, the unit would be bigger than Whiplash, which at Dreamland had never numbered more than a dozen people, at least not while he was assigned to it. "Wing size, potentially," Magnus said, though he added that it would start out much smaller.

Commanding a unit that large would be a definite plus in his plan to advance to general. But Magnus had made it clear that the job was outside the normal Air Force structure, and that wasn't going to help him at all.

The detour on the road to general wasn't the only thing bothering him. Magnus was undoubtedly right about how limited the opportunities in the near future were, so taking this job might not hurt at all. But Danny couldn't articulate, not even to himself, the other reasons that made him hesitate.

Everything had bored him after Whiplash and Dreamland. There was no way it couldn't. He'd traveled across the world, saving people, at times even saving entire countries, or at least good portions of them. No assignment that followed could ever come close in terms of excitement or gratification.

Yet, he didn't want to go back.

He was . . . afraid.

The word came at him like a train in a tunnel exploding in a sudden rush.

Afraid.

Was he?

Yes.

Afraid of what? he wondered.

Not death. Danny had learned that when you were in danger—when it was actually a possibility—death was not something you tended to think about. There was too much else to do. It was only later that it hit you, if it hit you at all.

His fear was of something else: Not being able to measure up to what he had done before. Of proving unworthy of the Medal of Honor he'd been awarded. Of disgracing himself and everyone who believed in him or looked up to him, like the sergeant at the gate that morning and the others who had applauded.

Danny realized this on the way back to his hotel, as the Metro came to his stop. He got out of the car and walked slowly toward the exit. Outside, he took out his cell phone and called a cab to take him to the hotel. He was annoyed with himself, unnerved at the waves of introspection that consumed him.

This wasn't what a leader did, Danny thought. And he was a leader. There was no question about that.

The taxi was just arriving when his cell phone rang. The number didn't look familiar, but he decided to answer it anyway as the cab pulled to the curb.

"Freah."

"*Colonel* Freah?"

"Yeah?"

"Please hold for the senator."

"Danny, what the hell are you doing in town without calling?" said Zen Stockard, his voice booming out of the clamshell speaker on Danny's phone.

"Hey, Zen. I just came in for a quick meeting."

"That's no excuse, Colonel."

"Hey, hold on a second, OK?" Danny got into the cab and told the driver to take him to his hotel. "Still there?"

"What the hell are you doing staying at the Alexandria Suites?" asked Zen, who'd heard the destination.

"It's nice and not too expensive."

"I don't care—you should be with us. Teri loves your bed-time stories."

Danny laughed. The last time he'd stayed with them—a year before—he'd told her fairy tales for half the night, all variations of things his grandmother had told him when he was little.

"What are you doing for dinner?" asked Zen.

"There's a nice restaurant about two blocks away. I figured I'd walk on down."

"Forget it. The Yankees are in town to play the Nationals. You and I are going to the game."

"Uh—"

"Listen, buddy, I'm not taking no for an answer," said Zen. "A senator outranks a colonel by a hell of a lot."

"Sir, yes, sir," laughed Danny.

When he'd been in the Air Force, Zen played down the fact that his family was wealthy. He'd banked nearly all of his trust proceeds, never took money from his father or uncles, and with one exception had never called on them for help. That exception had been during his fight to get reinstated on active duty after the crash that cost him the use of his legs.

Now that he was older, however, and had clearly set his own path in the world, he took advantage of the conveniences his family's money provided. A driver and a van specially adapted to his wheelchair were the most obvious. There were others, though—like open invitation to use the owner's suite at the Nationals.

Zen arranged to pick up Danny at his hotel an hour before the game. He grinned as his old friend spotted him and trotted out to the van.

"Danny," he said, as Freah pulled open the sliding door at the rear. "How the hell are you?"

"Is a U.S. senator allowed to use profanity?"

"Only if his daughter isn't in the car. Jeez, man, you're looking good."

"You don't look too bad yourself. You put on a little weight."

"Too many fat cat lunches," said Zen.

It was a joke. Among his strictest rules was that he always paid for lunch.

"So how's Bree?" Danny asked.

"Good."

"Teri?"

"Ready to run for princess. She's taking tap dancing lesson now, besides the ballerina stuff. She's amazing. Must get it from her mom."

Zen rocked back and forth in the wheelchair, which was fitted with a special brace holding it in place in the van. The brace was similar to the one he had used in the Megafortress years before. The driver's side had a similar arrangement, so he could push the regular seat back and use hand controls to drive himself if he wanted.

Too much beer drinking at a baseball game for that, though.

"Hear much from your father-in-law?" asked Danny.

Zen felt himself flinch. "No one hears much from Dog those days," he said. "Not even Bree."

Danny nodded.

"So don't tell me that you're rooting for the Yankees tonight," said Zen, anxious to keep things cheery.

"I *am* from New York."

"Buffalo is not in New York. It's Canada, isn't it?"

Danny did, in fact, root for the Yankees, though very discreetly. Zen was anything but discreet as the Nationals took a 6-0 lead into the sixth inning. But then the Nationals' pitching crumbled and the Yankees mounted a comeback, tying it at 6-6 in the eighth. The visitors went on top by a run in the ninth, the home team scored one, and the game went into extra innings.

It wasn't until the top of the tenth that Zen told Danny that he knew he'd been offered the new Whiplash job.

"I figured there was an ulterior motive here," said Danny.

"Actually, my ulterior motive was to get to a baseball game," said Zen. "If it weren't for you, I'd be listening to some State Department dweeb telling me about how China's going to blow up next week. You were my excuse to the staff to blow it off."

"Uh-huh."

"So what about it?"

"What about what?"

"You taking it?"

"I don't think so."

Zen pushed his chair up closer to the open window of the booth. The Yankees' best hitter had just struck out.

"Hey, it's no reflection on Bree at all," said Danny.

"I didn't think it was," said Zen. "This guy's going to whiff, too."

He didn't—he sent a long drive to the warning track in center field. The Nationals fielder needed every inch of his six-nine frame to catch it, jumping high at the wall to bring it down.

"If you take it, we'll see a lot more of you," said Zen when the crowd had quieted down. "I hope. Got a couple of dates lined up for you."

"Thank you, Mr. GoodDate.com."

The Nationals manager had seen enough. He came running from the dugout waving his right hand, asking for a new pitcher.

"How come Breanna didn't ask me herself?" said Danny.

"She doesn't want to talk you into it," said Zen. "She's afraid you'll take it just as a favor."

"So she sent you?"

"Actually, no. She doesn't know you're at the game with me. She'd probably be pretty mad if she found out. So don't tell her, right?"

"I won't."

Zen hadn't learned of Danny's candidacy from Breanna. He found out originally from Magnus, who'd consulted him not just because he'd served with Danny, but because Zen was a member of the Senate intelligence committee. The new Whiplash concept had been championed by the committee, and Magnus was a smart enough backroom politician to keep his allies well-informed about what was going on. He also suspected that Freah would need some convincing to take the job.

Danny stared down at the ball field. He was sure plenty of other people could do the job.

"I can probably come up with a whole list of people for her if she wants," he told Zen.

"Well, why don't you then? Give her a call. Tell you're thinking about it and you want to talk to her."

"So she can talk me into it, right?"

"She won't."

"You didn't have to take me to a baseball game to get me to call her, Zen."

"Hey, I told you—the job's just an excuse to get out of the reception." He pointed toward the field. "Watch now. This guy's going to strike out, too."

THE BATTER DIDN'T STRIKE OUT—IN FACT HE HIT A HOME run, and when the Nationals were set down in order in the bottom of the tenth, the Yankees won the game.

Zen was a reasonably decent sport about it when he dropped Danny off at his hotel. Breanna was a reasonably decent sport the next day when Danny called her at her office.

"I understand General Magnus spoke to you yesterday," she said when she came on the line. "So, have you made up your mind?"

Danny hesitated. He had, but he knew it wasn't the decision she wanted to hear.

"You don't have to take the job, Danny," she told him. "It's all right."

"I want to—"

"Great!"

"No, no, I mean—I don't know, Bree. I just . . ."

"It's a tough job, I know." She tried to hide her disappointment. "We can't really ask you to keep making the same kind
of sacrifices you made when you were younger."

"It's not my age—"

"I don't mean it that way."

"I do want to be involved. It's just . . ."

"You don't want the job. It's OK," she told him. "Don't
worry."

"Can we have lunch?" Danny asked. "Or coffee or something?"

THEY ARRANGED TO MEET ON THE MALL THAT AFTERNOON,
not far from the Lincoln Memorial. The day turned chilly,
threatening rain. Danny, dressed in a civilian T-shirt and
jeans, found himself rubbing his arms for warmth as he
crossed from the reflecting pool. Breanna, coming from a
meeting on Capitol Hill, had already called to say she was
running behind, and he took advantage of the delay to walk
around.

He stared up at Lincoln, seated not on a throne but on a
simple chair.

Lincoln was a man who knew the costs of war, who suffered them personally. How many mornings had he risen feeling he had gone as far as he could, yet continued, conscious
not just of the burden, but of the necessity of his mission?

He should take it, he thought. It was his duty.

And he wanted to. But still, he was afraid—not that he
couldn't do it, but that he wouldn't measure up to who he'd
been.

Fear was a terrible reason not to do anything. Fear only
held you back.

He *should* do it.

Danny felt his pulse rate kick up as soon as he saw Breanna walking from the direction of the Vietnam Memorial.
Two bodyguards trailed behind at a respectful distance as

she strode toward the monument where they said they'd meet.

She spotted him and waved.

"Hey there," he said as she stood on her tiptoes to kiss his cheek in greeting. "You allowed to kiss the hired help?"

"It depends on whether they kiss back," she countered. "How are you, Danny?"

"I'm good. Yourself?"

"Busy, unfortunately." Breanna took a step back, comparing him in her mind's eye to the younger version she'd known a decade and a half before. He looked a few pounds heavier, though not overweight by any means. His face seemed more relaxed, the space beneath his eyes smooth. She remembered his eyes were always puffy from lack of sleep. He'd always looked a few years younger than he was, and that remained true. A casual acquaintance might guess he was in his late twenties or early thirties.

"I don't mean to play Hamlet," he started.

"I kind of know what you're thinking," she told him. "After my—after our crash, when Zen and I were lost on that island off India. When I was laid up. I went through—it was an awful experience. I wouldn't want to go through it again. I don't. With Teri, now—I've taken my risks."

"No, that's not it," said Danny. "I guess—well you know, one of the things is, I am in line, I want to be in line, to be general. And that was one of the things on my mind."

"There's not going to be a list this year, Danny. And probably not next year."

"Yeah. But listen, forget all that—I want the job."

Having expected that Danny would reject the offer, Breanna was surprised—and then apprehensive. "I don't want to talk you into it," she said.

"No, that's OK. I've made up my mind. I'm doing it."

"It's a tough job."

"You trying to talk me out of it?" He smiled, but there was an edge in his voice. Her reaction did make it seem as if she had changed her mind.

"No," said Breanna. "Not at all."

"When do I start?"

"Monday. Sooner if possible—as soon as we can get the paperwork settled. Whatever time you need for your assignment now. The sooner the better."

5

Tehran, Iran
One day later

THERE WAS NO GRAND FUNERAL FOR RAFI LUO, NO FINE oration or long march to the mausoleum trailed by weeping women and bereft children. Like the majority of people who had died in the Coliseum, his body was eventually dumped in a potter's grave, unmarked and unremembered. The Rome authorities would never know who he was, let alone why he had been killed. As far as they were concerned, his death was an insult and an expense, nothing more.

His demise did not provoke a great deal of emotion from his business associates, either. Many of them did not even know he was dead for quite some time. Only one of his partners was aware that Luo was bound for Italy, and his initial reaction was both selfish and completely in character: profit would have to be shared one less way.

Luo's demise did, however, provoke the interest of one man. His name was Bani Aberhadji, and he had never met Rafi Luo, though he was Luo's greatest benefactor and even, in a sense, his protector.

Bani Aberhadji drew a paycheck as a low-ranking functionary in the Iranian ministry responsible for motor vehicles, ostensibly helping to oversee the registration and inspection of trucks in the port city of Bushehr. Unlike many of his co-workers in the ministry, Aberhadji came to work every day, and could usually be found at his desk immediately following morning prayers. This made him a singularly punctual motor vehicle clerk, and not just in Iran. In fact, Aberhadji was unusually precise and efficient in his duties. A person with a registration problem could not expect him to bend the law, but he could at least receive a prompt answer to any request. He would not have to proffer a bribe to receive it; in fact he would find that a bribe would neither be welcomed or accepted.

Aberhadji's official duties consumed perhaps thirty minutes of his time on the busiest days. The rest of his office hours were spent on his second job—coordinator of special projects for the Iranian Revolutionary Guard, and as a member of the Guard's ruling council. He was also the commanding officer of Brigade 27. It was in this capacity that he had dealt with Rafi Luo, though never directly.

The Revolutionary Guard—or Pasdaren—was established following the overthrow of the Shah in 1979. The Guards' role in the country's vanguard had been cemented during the 1980s war with Iraq, when thousands of volunteers defended the country against Saddam Hussein. Its political influence, however, had begun to wane over the past few years, until many in government considered it completely irrelevant.

The government's recent signing of the nuclear disarmament treaty was seen by many, even inside the organization, as the ultimate sign of its fall from influence. Aberhadji had a different view. To him, it showed just how necessary the group was. The Revolutionary Guard was the country's—and Islam's—last hope against the encroaching Western forces of decadence and apostasy.

It was critical in these difficult times for members of the organization to adhere strictly to the tenets of their religious beliefs, to perform all of their duties as effectively as possible, and to appear as model citizens in all ways. These requirements suited Aberhadji perfectly. He had been pious from the womb. Many called him imam, or teacher, though in fact he was not formally attached to any mosque and did not, as a general rule, lead prayers when he attended. Piety was simply part of his being.

The people he generally dealt with were anything but pious. Brigade 27 did not have a regular base or even regular members. It was concerned with spreading the Revolution beyond the geographical boundaries of Iran. Its forebears had funded and encouraged movements among Shiites in several places, most notably Palestine, Lebanon, and the Horn of Africa. Today, its most successful project was in the Sudan, where the long-running Revolution showed signs of spreading to Egypt, long a goal of the deeply committed.

Luo was one of several dealers whom Aberhadji had funded, through middlemen, as part of the general campaign to help the Sudanese Brothers, the umbrella organization of the Shiite freedom fighters. But his interest in Luo's network had gone further than that. For Aberhadji had made use of his network in his other capacity as head of special projects.

Secretive even for the highly secretive upper echelons of the Guard, Aberhadji's project had a singular goal: the creation of an Iranian stockpile of nuclear weapons to replace the ones being signed away by the government.

This, of course, was forbidden by the agreement the government and the Grand Ayatollah had signed. But Aberhadji and others among the Guard's elite believed the agreement was illegal, and they had evidence that the Ayatollah himself wanted them to proceed. There was no question that the agreement had been signed under duress. Iran was suffering from the worst depression in its history, with famine rampant thanks to an embargo on oil sales that made it impossible for Iran to sell its petroleum at market prices. It still sold, of course—China was more than willing to break the embargo if the price was right and the transactions were carried out in secret—but the severe discounts forced on the country hardly made it worth pumping from the ground. The United States, the Satan Incarnate and the Revolution's traditional enemy, had engineered the boycott, changing its own energy policies to dramatically reduce its dependence on oil and make it possible.

Luo's demise did not directly threaten Aberhadji's project. His organization supplied only a very few of the many items required, and it had been months since Aberhadji used them. Many people would have cause to kill Luo, including his own associates. But Aberhadji immediately began making inquiries.

Aberhadji's main agent in Africa, a slightly disreputable yet ultimately reliable Guard member named Arash Tarid, had checked into the murder only hours after it happened. He believed the Egyptian secret service had been involved. But that belief appeared to be based only on rumors.

Aberhadji decided that he would take the opportunity to visit his deputies involved in the special project. He was due to make his rounds within a month anyway; doing so now, to make sure everything was secure, would put his own fears to rest. He'd pay special attention to the posts in the Sudan, even visiting the facilities personally.

And so he went to see his superior at the motor vehicle bureau to ask for unscheduled time off.

Like many in the ministry, Rhaim Fars had gotten his job because he was related to someone in the central government, in his case an uncle who was close to the Iranian president. That president had left office nearly a decade before, but Fars retained his position for several reasons, not least of which was his generosity and benevolence toward those he suspected had better political connections than he did. Still, Aberhadji's request for an indefinite leave tested his goodwill.

"Perhaps we should put a limit on it," said Fars, gesturing to his underling to have a seat. He poured him some water, then took a sip of his own. Fars did not know that Aberhadji was even a member of the Revolutionary Guard, and would have been surprised to find out how important he really was.

"I am not sure how long my business will take," said Aberhadji.

"And it's of a personal nature?"

Aberhadji said nothing. He would not lie, but he would also not say anything that would reveal either his position or his interests. Obtaining the vacation time was merely a matter of being persistent.

"We are approaching our renewal time," said Fars. "There will be demands for our paperwork."

"Mine are in order."

The true issue for Fars was not the paperwork, but the inspections that followed; the minister liked to see the entire staff at his welcoming party.

On the other hand, Aberhadji would not contribute to his "present"—a sizable amount of money that would be presented "spontaneously" at the party. This was little more than a kickback by the employed to maintain their status. To smooth the waters, Fars had made up Aberhadji's share the last two years. And come to think of it, Aberhadji had left very early the year before, so early that the minister surely saw him go—something more noticeable, and therefore more insulting, than his not showing up at all. So Fars reasoned that perhaps it was not important that Aberhadji be there after all.

"You have personal time accrued," said Fars, deciding he would find an excuse that would allow the vacation. "That was my point in asking the question. You have not taken any time to tend to your family, and a man like you, a pious man, has a great deal of obligations, thanks be to the Prophet."

Aberhadji nodded. He had no immediate family and had had none since he was young. His father had died in the war against Iraq, and his mother passed away a year later, mostly out of grief.

"Well then, let us put you down for a week. The matter is decided," said Fars.

"It should be stated as indefinite."

"Yes, well, we will say two. If, at the end of two weeks—"

"It should say indefinite. It may be less than two."

"Well then, two weeks can cover it for the moment."

"It should say indefinite."

Fars could not grant someone an indefinite leave except for a medical emergency. Aberhadji's honesty was a problem.

Fars decided it need not be. He could prepare two versions of the request—one for Aberhadji to sign, the other for the Tehran bureaucrats. Problem solved.

"So, indefinite. And should we put down that the business is a matter of a personal nature? Clearly, you're not going on a vacation. I only have to ask," Fars added, "because you know I have to make these reports each week to Tehran. In this economy, I think they are always throwing problems in to keep us on our toes."

"It is a private matter. Certainly."

"Good," said Fars, choosing to interpret that as personal. "I will take care of it," he added, rising. "Don't worry. Take whatever time you need."

6

McLean, Virginia
Three days later

DANNY FREAH FOUND HIS EXCITEMENT GROWING AS HE made the arrangements to take the new Whiplash assignment. It had been quite a while since he had been involved in a "black" or secret project, and he'd forgotten just how quickly things could move once they had that imprimatur. Breanna assigned one of her assistants as a facilitator, taking care of the paperwork and everything else necessary, even finding him a condo to rent.

"It won't be much," she warned, "but you won't be there very much anyway."

Actually, the apartment had its own terrace and a view of

the river. The bedroom was about twice the size of the living room he had been renting in Kentucky. Best of all, he could afford the rent.

The only problem was that the moving company he'd hired to cart his furniture couldn't arrange to pick up everything and deliver it for several weeks. Danny spent the weekend packing and taking care of last minute arrangements. After a Sunday afternoon good-bye party that stretched well into Monday morning, he hopped in his rental car and drove straight back to Washington, D.C., stopping at a McDonald's to shave and change into his uniform. Parking at the Pentagon without a permit these days was a fool's errand, so instead he returned the car to a rental agency at Reagan Airport and took the Metro. As the train reached the stop, he thought of the prim and proper woman he'd seen the last time he was there. He couldn't help wondering if he'd run into her again.

As it happened, he did run into her—and a lot sooner than he'd thought. For when he reported to Breanna Stockard's office as directed, he found her manning the secretary's desk.

"You're Mary Clair Bennett?" he asked, extending his hand.

"Colonel Freah. Prompt. Very good," said Ms. Bennett, who did not take his hand.

"I, um—we met," he told her.

"I *am* sorry. I do not recall."

"On the train."

"Train?"

"It's not important. That's a great apartment you found me. It's fantastic."

"Naturally."

"I want to thank you for all your help with these arrangements. I don't know what I'd have done without you."

"It is my job, Colonel."

"Ah, Danny, I see you've met Ms. Bennett," said Breanna, coming in from the hall.

"Me and M.C. go way back," said Danny.

Breanna had never heard anyone, including Ms. Bennett herself, refer to her as anything other than Ms. Bennett. She glanced at the secretary, who was glaring at Danny.

He didn't notice, and wouldn't have let on if he did.

"Let's get you situated," Breanna said. "Ms. Bennett, you can reach me via text. I'll be gone for most of the day."

"Yes, Ms. Stockard. Of course."

"Where'd you dig her up?" Danny asked as they waited for the elevator.

"She's wonderfully efficient, if a little stuffy."

"That's like saying the North Pole is a little cold."

"I don't need a friend," said Breanna. "What was with the M.C. bit? I think you better lay off that."

"I'll get her to thaw. You'll see," said Danny. He was already planning to send her flowers as a thank-you for the apartment and everything else. "How long do you think it will take to get a Pentagon parking permit?"

"You won't need one. You're not going to be working here. You won't even have an office here."

"Oh?"

Forty minutes later Breanna presented Danny to a plain-clothes CIA security detail at the entrance pavilion of the CIA's campus in McLean, Virginia. Known as Langley, the headquarters complex was among the most closely watched and guarded area in the world. Despite the fact that he already possessed a high level military clearance, the CIA security people had him sit in a special biometric chair that "read" 114 different biometric aspects, measuring everything from his weight to the size of his ankles. While this was going on, a machine in the corner analyzed the DNA from a scraping in his cheek, and another machine took stock of his saliva.

"So am I who I think I am?" Danny asked when the technician in charge of the measurements told him they were done.

"You are Daniel Freah, according to the computer," replied the technician. "Though I have no idea if that's who you are."

A woman in the next room gave Danny a small bluish-red ring to wear on his right pinky. It fit perfectly.

"That has all your biometric data in it," she told him. "You don't need any other ID while you're here."

The ring had other functions, as Breanna explained while they walked back to her waiting car. An integrated circuit allowed it to be used as an encryption device in a dedicated communication system. It could also be tracked via the same satellites, allowing it to be used as a backup locator. The system would also recognize if it was removed from his body, or if his pulse stopped; while it could still be tracked in that case, it would no longer function as an active ID.

"Basically, we'll know where you are at all times," said Breanna. "There's no escape."

She meant it as a joke, but already Danny was feeling as if he'd gotten into a little more than he'd expected. They drove past the main CIA building, continuing around to a nondescript office building at the far corner of the complex. The building looked as if it dated from the 1950s or perhaps early 1960s, but in fact was only three years old. A single story structure, it had no external markings or any other identification. This was not unique at Langley; anyone who didn't know where he or she was going didn't belong there.

After Breanna and Danny passed through an automated security system in the lobby, Breanna led him to an office diagonally across from the reception area. The guard standing at the door nodded but didn't step aside until the door, operated by its own sensor, swung open behind him.

Danny was expecting to find a standard office inside—his office, he thought. But instead he found an empty room with a narrow staircase to one side. Breanna led him to the staircase, gesturing that he should descend. He did, and found himself staring at a steel door.

"State your name," said a mechanical voice from somewhere behind the door.

"Danny Freah."

"Rank?"

"Colonel."

"What is your favorite color?"

Danny thought of answering that he didn't have a favorite color, but decided he had better play it straight.

"Blue," he said, and the door opened.

"Are you going to ask my favorite color?" Breanna asked, following him inside.

"Just thought I'd lighten things up for the colonel," said a short woman dressed in a black pantsuit as she stepped out from behind the security station opposite the door. It was her voice that Danny had heard. "I watched *Monty Python and the Holy Grail* last night. I could have asked you what the aerial velocity of a swallow carrying a coconut was," she added, pushing the mike of her headset away. "But I was afraid you'd get it wrong. Then I'd have to kill you."

"This is Sergeant Mercer," said Breanna. "She's going to do a weapons check on you, even though that door wouldn't have opened if you'd had a gun."

"Procedure," said Mercer. "Lighten up, Colonel. I promise not to hurt."

Mercer took what looked like a lipstick holder from her pants pocket and waved it around Danny.

"He's clean. Likes the Yankees, though. Might be a problem."

"Your little wand told you that?" said Danny.

"We have our ways, Colonel. Welcome aboard."

The room they had entered was a long, rectangular space that held a security station and an elevator to a lower level. The elevator had no visible controls, nor did it work by voice command. You simply entered and were whisked downward. Danny found that mildly annoying.

"What if I changed my mind?" he asked Breanna.

"Then you get out at the bottom and get back in," she said as the door opened on the lower level. "But I don't believe anyone has ever changed their mind. Come on."

Danny had expected a hallway similar to the laboratory areas at Dreamland, most of which were also located in underground bunkers. Instead the door opened on a wide, open space that looked more like a parking garage than a science lab. Thick steel girders ran overhead, supporting a network of beams and pipes. The floor was cement. Girders punctuated the space at regular intervals.

Cabinets were clustered around the girders at the far end. These were computers, most working as massively parallel units in so-called "cloud" arrangements. Thick cables snaked across the floor, connecting them to different peripherals and in some cases to each other.

Overhead lights came on as Breanna and Danny walked, then faded behind them. Finally a set of spots came up on a black wall. There were no doors or windows in it; no visible opening of any kind. Breanna strode toward it. Danny followed, expecting at any second that the panel would move upward or back, that some hidden opening would appear to allow them to enter. But it didn't.

He stopped a foot from the wall.

Breanna passed through it.

Danny had seen many incredible things at Dreamland—aircraft that flew themselves, blimps that could disappear, controllers that could be manipulated by thought. But disappearing walls was beyond anything there.

He put his hand forward, touching the surface of the wall. It felt solid, as solid as any of the walls in his house. He tapped his fingernails against it, made a drumming sound.

I'm losing my mind, he thought.

"Danny?"

Convinced he was about to wake up from the most involved dream he'd ever had, he took a short step to his left, aligning himself with the exact spot Breanna had used to go through the wall. Then he took a short breath and stepped forward.

Into a well-furnished reception area.

He turned back around. The wall was a solid, a darkish beige color on this side.

"It's nanotechnology," said Breanna. She was standing near him. "It *is* a wall. And an opening."

"Is it really there?"

"Absolutely. Touch it."

"I did," said Danny. He did again, drumming his knuckles this time.

"But you can move through it, if you move deliberately," she said. "And if it recognizes you. Like this."

Breanna put her entire arm through, then turned and smiled at Danny, half in, half out.

"Parlor games are difficult to resist," said a familiar voice.

Danny turned and found Ray Rubeo frowning at him.

"Doc!" said Danny. "You're here?"

"Apparently," said Rubeo. There was a slight bit of gray around the temples, but otherwise very little about him had changed in the past fifteen years, including his frown. "Though in this place you never really know."

Rubeo was no longer a government employee. But several of his companies were under contract to the Office of Technology, and when Breanna had offered him the opportunity to brief Danny Freah on Whiplash, he had decided to take her up on it. Rubeo had always liked Freah and the Whiplash people personally, though he found many of their security procedures annoying. The pinkie rings had been his idea, an easy way of eliminating many of the delays imposed by the security checks and constant surveillance. Like everyone admitted to Room 4—the code name for the basement facility on the CIA campus—he, too, wore one.

"I suppose you want an explanation about the nano wall," said Rubeo.

"Well, yeah."

"Very well. It's a parlor trick."

The wall worked by arranging energy within certain frequencies; to put it crudely, it was as if molecules were iron shavings in a child's Etch A Sketch game, and used to draw a wall. The field could be broken by movement at certain speeds, but not others; the wall could not be penetrated by bullets, for example.

"So it could protect against a missile?" asked Danny.

"Concrete is just as effective." Rubeo waved his hand. "There are perhaps some uses for camouflage, that sort of thing. Or very expensive walls."

It also made a high-quality projection screen.

"Have a seat," said Breanna, gesturing to one of the nearby club chairs. "And I'll show you what it can do."

The wall morphed into a crisp video display, the sharpest Danny had ever seen, demonstrating its prowess with a scene from last year's Super Bowl.

"Another parlor trick," said Rubeo, this time with a touch of pride.

The video ended abruptly, replaced by the seals of the CIA and the Department of Defense.

"The Office of Technology is involved in a lot of projects," said Breanna. "We work very closely with a number of government agencies. Some of us work for the Defense Department, and some of us for the CIA. You might say our responsibilities are intramural."

The CIA still had its own technology department, separate from Breanna's operation. The Wizards of Langley were responsible for a host of innovations, everything from supersonic spy planes to microscopic bugs. But changes in the organizational structure of the intelligence and military communities, along with severe budget cuts, had moved a great deal of their work over to the Defense Department. Some research had always been outsourced in any event, and many of the changes simply meant that the scientists, engineers, and other technical experts simply had a different paymaster.

Whether directly funded by the CIA or through the Defense Department, the problem wasn't coming up with new technology. It was getting it out of the developmental labs and into the hands of field agents. Breanna, with her Dreamland background, had been picked to make that happen. One solution was to simply eliminate much of the bureaucratic infrastructure. Where once layers of liaisons and department managers had fought over turf in both Defense and Intelligence, now a handful of people worked with her and the scientists directly.

"Is Whiplash going to be a CIA command?" asked Danny. "Or military?"

"Neither," said Breanna. "It's more like a hybrid."

"How?"

"We're going to work that out. You're going to help."

"OK."

Breanna glanced at her watch. Reid and Nuri Lupo were due to meet them in a half hour.

"Let's introduce him to MY-PID," she told Rubeo. "We have a meeting soon and I'd like him to be familiar with some of the technology."

Rubeo closed his eyes. He hated the nickname; it was very 1984. "Very well. Come with us, Colonel. And please don't touch anything. It may blow up."

Rubeo was so deadpan that Freah didn't know whether that had been a joke or not.

The scientist led the way down the hallway—more nano walls—to a small room set up like a library. Small armchairs were clustered around a large cube at the center of the room. The cube that was a display unit for MY-PID. Breanna took one of the chairs and pulled it close to the cube. Danny did the same.

"Ray Rubeo, 13-13-13," said Rubeo.

"Acknowledged," said a disembodied voice.

"I need the weather in Moscow. Display it please."

A graphic showing a sun covered by a cloud appeared on the center screen. The temperature, in Celsius and Fahrenheit, appeared under it.

"The weather tomorrow, in Moscow," said Rubeo.

Rain.

Rubeo made a number of other requests for data, all instantly answered by the computer. Danny was used to computers and their ability to quickly produce data from their memory banks. While the cube and its graphics appeared very slick, the system didn't seem to be anything unusual. Even the voice command interface was familiar from Dreamland.

Rubeo produced a small button from his pocket and placed it on top of the cube.

"Locate Colonel Freah and project his image," said the scientist.

Danny's image—captured by the tiny video bug—was displayed on the screen.

"How does it know it's me?" asked Danny.

"Produce positive identification of subject," said Rubeo. The computer complied, displaying a skeletal biometric image next to Danny's face.

Danny still wasn't impressed.

Rubeo took a set of earphones and a small, iPodlike device from his other pocket and handed it to him. Danny put on the device, and heard the computer's voice ask him to identify himself.

"Danny Freah."

"Identity confirmed. Please calibrate voice level."

"It wants to get a feel for how loud you're going to talk to it," explained Breanna. "There are microphones in the wire."

"How loud should I talk?"

"Whatever level you're comfortable with," Breanna said.

"Testing, testing," said Danny.

"Ask it any question you wish," said Rubeo.

"Who won the World Series?" asked Danny.

"Which year?" asked the Voice.

"Last year."

"The Boston Red Sox, four games to two, over the Chicago Cubs."

"Who's going to win this year?"

"Insufficient data."

Rubeo rolled his eyes. He glanced at Breanna, then left the room.

"Locate Dr. Rubeo," said Breanna after he was gone.

The screen moved its schematic, showing Rubeo in the maze of rooms about fifty meters away. He was in a lounge area, making himself a cup of tea.

"It's tied into a satellite system that can be used to track individuals all over the world," Breanna explained. "The system uses biomarkers that can be picked up by the satellites. There are some limitations, but as long as a subject is aboveground, the system can find him. Down here, a separate system is used. The rings. The Voice can plug into a number of different systems, not just its central core here. It's like an automated assistant. The idea is that it will help CIA officers in the field. And Whiplash."

"How close to going operational is it?" asked Danny.

"We've been using it for a little over two months on a special project. You're going to hear about that project in about twenty minutes."

"Where is this MY-PID?"

"It's not in a specific place." Breanna always had trouble explaining exactly how the system worked. "Think of it as a cloud, or even the Internet. The computers you just passed are part of it, but they're not the sum total. The network is scattered around the world, and then there are the different sensors. Different video bugs can be plugged in, and the system can ask to be admitted to some databases and other intelligence systems."

"Who controls it?"

"No one. The Voice is completely automated. It's on its own—just like your laptop would be. Because, that's what it is: a personal computer for field operators."

Danny wasn't exactly sure what to make of that—a computer system that had no one running it? The parallel to personal computers didn't reassure him.

"All right. How does Whiplash fit into this?"

"MY-PID will be one of its tools. The unit itself will work on different projects. We want you to support Nuri on Jasmine—he'll explain that."

"Support?"

"Yes. The whole idea is to get technology onto the front lines. Whiplash is part of that."

"Are we testing, or doing?"

"Both. Just like we were at Dreamland. Whiplash and all of us."

Danny felt comfortable with the parallel to Dreamland, but using a computer system that had no human supervisor sounded impractical. There had been a few automated systems at Dreamland—the robot Ospreys, for example, which were part of his security at the base. But even there, someone on watch was always supervising them, prepared to jump in and override if necessary. Here, there was no supervision.

"I was hoping that we would have more time to build things up, but this situation seems more serious than we thought."

"So what else is new?" said Danny.

7

CIA Headquarters (Langley)
McLean, Virginia

FOR AN OFFICER WHO SPENT MOST OF HIS TIME IN THE FIELD, coming to CIA headquarters was not generally something to look forward to. Even if one wasn't coming home to be called on the carpet, the stay tended toward the onerous. For one thing, it was almost always associated with paperwork: official reports, expense reports, and briefings. Then there were the routine and not routine lie detector tests, dreaded audits, and the even more dreaded physical and psychological fitness exams.

But perhaps the worst thing that could happen to you at Langley, at least as far as Nuri Lupo was concerned, was being second-guessed. Which he expected was on today's agenda in bulleted capital letters. He'd taken it as a particularly bad sign when Reid told him to take the weekend off. Reid himself always worked Saturdays, so a routine pummeling could easily have started then. Anything that had to wait for the work week to begin was guaranteed to be onerous indeed.

Not that there was *really* much to second-guess him on. But of course, that was never the point.

Nuri's only consolation—and it was thin—was the fact that he had found a restaurant with a cute waitress the night before. She'd flirted a bit, and he figured he'd be eating there a lot if he was stuck here for any length of time.

He drove to the parking lot near the main building, parked in one of the visitor's slots, and went inside to meet Reid. He was a few minutes early, and after going through the ID and weapons check—guns were frowned on—he decided to head down the hall and grab a coffee at the Starbucks. Along the way he passed the displays of Cold War paraphernalia. Though put out mostly to impress visiting VIPs, Nuri found the old gadgets endlessly fascinating, and lingered on his way back, admiring the miniature bugs in the cases, huge by today's standards.

Reid, coming down from the other direction, spotted Nuri in the hall. He paused and studied the agent, surprised at how young he looked. He was, in fact, young, though Reid would never hold that against him.

It was nearly impossible for the older man not to draw parallels with officers and agents he'd known in the past, and his mind did so freely in the few seconds that passed before Nuri looked up and saw him waiting at the end of the hall. The young man reminded him of several people, all good men, all dead well before their time. The comparison that came most readily was to Journevale—Reid remembered the agent's code name, not his Christian name, even as he pictured him.

Journevale was a Filipino who'd been recruited by the British to work in Vietnam and at some point was handed over to the U.S. During the time Reid knew him, he'd lived among the Hmong people in Laos, helping organize guerrilla groups that fought along the Ho Chi Minh Trail.

When Reid wanted to check on his status, he had to parachute in via Air America. The flights in rickety airplanes, held together by duct tape and wire, were horribly dangerous; jumping out of the plane at night into the dark jungle wasn't much of a picnic, either. In the days before GPS satellite locators, it could take hours to find a contact in the jungle; Reid twice failed to meet his agent at the landing zone and had to hike several miles to a backup rendezvous point. But Journevale always managed to meet him, even when the pilots had gone far off course. He was good with languages, and cheery, and best of all, he could cook murderously well. The tribespeople worshipped him.

He'd killed himself in a Bangkok hotel room after the war was lost and his people were slaughtered. It was the honorable thing to do.

"Hey, Bossman," said Nuri. "Sorry I'm late. I just grabbed a cup of joe. The coffee I've been drinking's lousy. Everybody wants to put sugar in it."

"Let's go, then."

"Where to? Your office?"

"Yours."

Nuri realized he meant Room 4, the support project headquarters. That was a bit of a surprise.

"I've been doing quite a lot of thinking about Jasmine," said Nuri as they got into Reid's car outside. "I have some ideas on how I can get inside."

"Why would Luo be so important that he had to be killed?" asked Reid.

The tone in his voice told Nuri that Reid already had a theory. But his supervisor liked the Socratic method of quizzing his underlings before lowering the boom.

"Competitor wants the market to himself."

"Possible. Other theories?"

"He pissed off the wrong person," said Nuri. "They got him back."

"Plausible."

"Or the Egyptians killed him. They're becoming more active. They see the rebels as a threat, and want to keep them off balance. You take out Luo, you deprive them of ammo for a few months."

"Also plausible."

"What do you think happened?"

"I have no opinion, really. It's going to be your next step to find out more information. The analysts have finished going over the data," Reid added, almost as an afterthought. "The tubes could not have been used for rockets."

"OK. And where are they?"

"That's the next thing you have to find out."

Room 4 was located on the opposite end of the campus, but even so, the drive took only a few minutes. There was no parking lot there; they had to park near a larger building about fifty yards away.

Reid turned off the ignition but didn't get out of the car.

"We're going to expand your team," he told Nuri.

"Expand?"

"As I told you when you started. The Whiplash concept calls for more people."

"Mmmmm," said Nuri.

"We have a new officer who's going to be in charge."

"In charge of me?"

It was a reasonable—more than reasonable—question. Reid ducked it, though. "Not precisely."

"The operation."

"The operation remains a CIA mission."

"So what's his role?"

"He'll be in charge of the paramilitary component."

"I'm paramilitary."

"In the sense I mean," said Reid, "they are DOD, and you are CIA."

"And independent?"

"No one is independent, Nuri. You know that."

Reid opened the car door. Nuri took a sip of his coffee, then left the cup in the car.

"What's that mean, exactly?" he asked Reid, catching up to him.

"It means Agency and military people work together. You've been there before."

"Generally, there's someone specifically in charge."

"I'm in charge. And Ms. Stockard."

Politics, thought Nuri. They were probably haggling about the real chain of command above him, each agency trying to protect its turf. Generally that meant no one was in charge, a potentially dangerous situation.

"I think you'll like the man we've chosen. He was in the Air Force. He worked at Dreamland."

"Air Force? He's a pilot?"

"No, he was with the original Whiplash. Danny Freah. He's a colonel."

It all fit together for Nuri. Breanna Stockard—a very nice woman, though in his opinion a fish out of water as a manager, far too laid back—was recreating her past glory by surrounding herself with fellow Dreamland alums. Even the name of the project, Whiplash, was the same.

He clamped his mouth shut. There was no sense complaining.

They cleared security quickly. Nuri shivered slightly as they descended—the closed-in stairwell reminded him of the labyrinth beneath the Coliseum.

"Jonathon, good morning," said Breanna Stockard, who was waiting just beyond the nano wall as they came in. "Mr. Lupo, good to see you again."

"You can call me Nuri."

"Nuri, this is Danny Freah. Colonel, Nuri Abaajmed Lupo. He's been overseas for a while. Still jet-lagged?"

"I'm over it," said Nuri. Danny was younger than he'd expected.

Ray Rubeo was standing in the corner, arms crossed. "Mr. Lupo, good morning," he said.

"Hey, Doc."

"I trust the gear is working satisfactorily?"

"You might make the bulletproof vest thicker."

"Resistant. It's resistant, not bulletproof," said Rubeo in his world-weary voice. "Any thicker and you wouldn't be able to wear it beneath your clothes."

"You should work on it."

Rubeo frowned. "I have a few things to attend to," he told Breanna. "Text me if you need me."

"I thought we would begin with an informal briefing on the situation in the Sudan for Colonel Freah," said Reid after the scientist left. "And then Ms. Stockard and I will expound on what we see as the next step, both for the project, and for Whiplash."

"Sure," said Nuri.

"Why don't we go inside?" suggested Breanna. "We'll be more comfortable."

"The Sudan is the incarnation of hell on earth," started Reid. He'd prepared a brief PowerPoint, which the computer system presented on the cube at the center of the room. "The country has been in and out of revolt forever. The various factions have different grievances and aims. Our interests are not directly tied up in any of them. We were drawn there because of an arms selling network known as Jasmine."

Some part of Sudan or another had been involved in civil war since before the country gained independence in 1956. The wars had various causes, though the outcome was uniform: the majority of the people suffered, while a few tribal and religious leaders managed to eke out a marginally better existence. Darfur, in the west, had occupied the world's attention in the first decade of the twenty-first century. Now things were flaring in the eastern borderlands with Ethiopia. The Sudanese government was dominated by Arab-speaking Muslims; the rebels were a mixture of different tribes and ethnic groups. Arabic was their common language; many of the elite and even a number of peasants could manage reasonable English.

Reid turned his attention to the arms dealers who made much of the bloodshed possible. He noted that Jasmine, like many of its brethren, was a loose association of people who moved things around the world, mostly from Africa to Europe. He mentioned the aluminum tubes, and their possible connection to nuclear weapons. Finally he came to Luo's assassination, a professional job that suggested the game Jasmine was involved in had very high stakes.

Nuri, not necessarily convinced of this, wondered if Reid knew something about the assassin he didn't. Meg Leary was a pro, which meant that whoever hired her had a reasonably decent amount of money. Nuri thought it was a rival trying to move in, even though he hadn't seen any evidence of this yet. But it could also be a government.

Had the U.S. hired her? That made no sense to him, but he had to admit it might be a possibility. Reid surely would have told him, or at least hinted more strongly.

Maybe Luo double-crossed the Iranians, who were the source of most of the money the rebels had in the Sudan. Or maybe the Israelis didn't like him for some reason. They tended to do their own assassinations, but weren't above outsourcing when it was convenient.

"Luo's assassination brings us back to square one," said Reid. "We want to take another look at the rebel groups in the Sudan, and possibly find another way into Jasmine."

"Why not track the murderer?" asked Danny Freah.

Nuri smiled. He knew he was going to resent working with anyone, but at least this fellow thought like he did.

"That's impractical," said Reid. "She's a professional. It's unlikely she'll yield much information."

"You're protecting her?" said Danny.

"She wasn't working for us, Colonel. We don't know who she was working for. Nuri has some theories."

Nuri shrugged. "I would have preferred to do it that way, too," he told Danny. "But it didn't work out."

"So what happens now?" Danny asked.

Nuri turned to Reid.

"Originally, Mr. Lupo was able to work in Ethiopia."

"That won't work anymore," said Nuri. "Jasmine used a café in Addis Abba. I bugged the place. But unfortunately, the owner was arrested a few days later and the café was closed down. The smugglers are staying out of there for the most part, because the government's cracking down."

"So we'll have to work directly in the Sudan," said Reid. "And given the situation there, Nuri could use some protection and backup."

"Which is where Whiplash comes in," said Danny.

"That's exactly the way it's supposed to work," said Breanna.

She looked over at Nuri and could tell he was apprehensive. She couldn't blame him. He'd never worked with Danny and didn't know what to expect.

"Do you think you can bug the rebels in the Sudan?" she asked him.

"Yeah, of course," said Nuri. "I've already checked the area out."

He had been through the area earlier. He'd also worked a little with the simulator, which presented 3-D models and conjured situations to practice infiltrating an area. But Nuri had found that real life, at least in the Sudan villages, was much too messy for the computers to model correctly. He'd already decided he wouldn't bother trying to model the next mission there.

"What's the goal here?" asked Danny. "How much is it to test MY-PID, this computer thing, and how much to find out what these Jasmine people were doing with the aluminum tubes?"

"Actually, to find out who got the tubes and what they're doing with them," said Nuri. "Jasmine was just the conduit."

"I'd say, Colonel, that the tubes are much more important than the technology at this point," said Reid. "It's there to help, nothing more. If the tubes are being used to process nuclear material, that's an extremely serious situation."

"Who the hell would process the material in the Sudan?" said Danny.

"That's exactly what we want to find out," answered Reid.

"RELATIVELY PAINLESS, WASN'T IT?" ASKED REID AS THEY drove back to the administration building.

"I guess."

"I think you and the colonel will get along fine."

"He thinks he's in charge," said Nuri.

"Keep your ego in check, Nuri."

Nuri frowned and reached for his coffee. It was still warm.

"Do you want some time off?" Reid asked.

"I don't need it."

"Good. You're booked on a flight out to Paris tomorrow night. You can connect from the there to Egypt."

"Fine."

Nuri began mentally checking off what he'd have to do. They'd need a cover, first of all. And gear. He could get most of it in Alexandria.

"You've done very well, Nuri," said Reid as he parked. "Luo's death was not your fault."

"Thanks."

"One more thing before you go," said Reid. "Accounting needs to talk to you about some expenses."

8

Port Sudan, Sudan
Ten days later

DANNY FREAH PULLED HIS YELLOW BASEBALL CAP LOWER as the boat approached the pier. He stepped up toward the bow, holding his bag tightly against his leg as someone jostled against his side. The small ferry had set out hours earlier from Riyadh, Saudi Arabia. When it left the dock there, the sun was about at eye level over the water; now it was long gone, sunk into the gray mass of Africa.

The passengers crowding Danny were mostly poor Sudanese returning from work. There were a few pilgrims mixed in, devout Muslims who had performed the hajj, or holy trek, to Mecca. The rest were operators, thieves, and pretenders.

Danny fell firmly into the last camp. His passport and papers declared that he was a doctor of paleontology, a claim backed up with several official letters from the Sudanese and Egyptian governments. Each seal had been bought for five thousand dollars cash, a price high enough for him to consider turning them over to a legitimate paleontologist when his job here was done.

Except few legitimate paleontologists would dare travel to the Sudan.

"How's the dock look?" Danny muttered.

"Rephrase question," answered the Voice.

He pushed the earphone in his right ear a little deeper. Though designed specifically for his ears, the plugs didn't feel very comfortable.

"Are there armed men on the dock?" he asked.

"Affirmative. Six guards within customs area. Additional men beyond the gate. One armored car."

"Why do they need the armored car?"

"Rephrase question."

Danny didn't bother. He had been using the M I DID "appliance" for several days, but it still felt uncomfortable. Nor had it been particularly useful. He knew where he was going and what to do. The Voice's contribution to his mission so far had been to tell him how warm it was and how unlikely it was to rain.

He squeezed his eyes together, fighting off fatigue. He'd flown from Cairo via Rome with barely an hour stopover, and from there to Saudi Arabia. Immediately on landing he'd rented a car and driven halfway across the country to the ferry. All told, he'd spent roughly eighteen hours traveling. He'd napped for a little less than four hours during the first flight. Those were the most he'd had in a row since starting his new assignment.

Searchlights flashed on above the pier as the ferry closed in. Through the glare, Danny saw men armed with automatic rifles waiting for the ship to dock. Behind them was the armored car the Voice had mentioned.

Danny gripped his bag as the ferry bumped against the dock. A deckhand sprung across, tying the ship to the wharf. Another removed the spar from the rail and stepped back. People began jumping across. Danny waited until it was clear that the boat wasn't getting any closer, then leapt as well, crossing over to the worn wooden planks.

The rickety dock was bisected by a metal fence that enclosed the customs and passport control areas. To get into Sudan, a visitor or resident had to queue in the single line that started at the center of the fence and spread willy-nilly in front of it. Occasionally, a customs officer or one of the soldiers guarding them attempted to form the wedge-shaped mass into order, but it was hardly worth the effort; as soon as one person moved forward, the order collapsed, and the crowd once more jockeyed for position.

Like nearly everyone who'd gotten off the ferry, Danny was black. But his fresh, Western-style clothes and confident manner stood out from the others as sharply as if his skin had been green. One of the customs officers waved at him, calling him around the press of the line. He had Danny walk to a chained gate at the far end of the pier. One of the soldiers accompanied him, glancing backward every few seconds to make sure none of the other passengers followed.

They didn't. While a few were jealous that a foreigner would be allowed to cut in line, they also knew the reason. The foreigner represented money, to both the customs agent who would expect a "fee" for the convenience, and to the country, which collected for an instant visa whether he had one already or not.

The natives watching, on the other hand, were merely a nuisance.

"Papers," said the customs officer.

Danny reached into his pocket for his passport. He'd been well-schooled on the procedure; inside the passport was a crisp hundred dollar bill.

The bill disappeared into the agent's palm so quickly Danny thought it had been vacuumed up his sleeve.

"What is your purpose here?" asked the man in English.

"I am on a dig," said Danny. "We're looking for dinosaurs."

"Hmph." The customs agent could not have been less interested. "That bag is all you have?"

"Yes, sir."

"Open it, please."

He gestured toward a table nearby. Danny had been told that once he gave the official the bribe, he would be waved through. Now he started to feel apprehensive. He had no money for a second bribe.

The customs agent stood over him as he unzipped the small black case. He was not looking for additional money, but rather, doing his job. In his mind, the hundred dollar bill was a tip from a beneficent westerner, accepted custom rather than corruption. It would not influence him one way or another. If he found any contraband—literature against the regime, a gun, drugs of any sort, including prescription medicine—he would arrest the American.

The bag contained a change of clothes, extra socks, and two pairs of sunglasses. Nothing illegal.

"You are listening to an iPod?" asked the official, pointing to the headphone.

"It's off." Danny showed him the control unit. He worried for a second that the officer would take it, but he merely frowned at the device.

"Go," the man said, dismissing him with a wave.

Danny made his way off the pier, ducking his eyes from the glare of the lights. The rotten fish smell of the seaside gave way to the scent of rotting meat. Crates of goats were stacked along the path that ran from the pier into the start of the city. The animals bleated and moaned, hoping they might convince someone to let them roam the port. Peddlers huddled near the end of the fence, selling various wares. Anything that wasn't on display, said a crude sign in Arabic, could be obtained.

A stocky black man in a long Arab robe approached Danny from the cluster of people milling near the entrance. Danny saw him from the corner of his eye and tensed.

"Welcome to the hell-hole capital of the world," said Ben "Boston" Rockland as he took Danny's elbow. "Our ride's this way."

"How you doing, Boston?"

"Good. I was beginning to think you'd never get here."

"Me, too."

"Don't use too much English around here. The natives are pretty restless as it is."

Boston had been in Port Sudan for several hours, more than enough time to form an impression of the place. He had seen two muggings in that time, one by a police officer. There surely would have been more, but most of the people in the city were too poor to bother robbing.

"The thing is, this is the good part of the Sudan," he told Danny, leading him toward the bus they had leased.

DANNY AND BOSTON HAD FIRST MET AT DREAMLAND SOME fifteen years ago, when Boston replaced one of the original members of Whiplash who'd been killed during an operation. Though the sergeant had an impressive record, he also had what some of his superiors politely termed "issues with authority." He'd seen action in the first Iraq war, where he served as a pararescuer. He'd also done time as a combat air controller and was "loaned" to the Marines under a special program that put combat veterans on the front lines with other services. But Boston had also nearly come to blows with at least two officers in the past three years, one of whom pressed but then dropped formal charges against him.

"A misunderstanding," said the captain on the record. Off the record, the captain called Boston a hothead but said he'd also saved three men in combat the day after the incident, and so the captain decided to forget the matter out of gratitude.

Serving with Danny and Colonel Bastian had changed Boston's perspective considerably. He still thought most officers were jerks. But he also knew that there was an important minority who weren't. That knowledge had helped Boston advance after Whiplash was disbanded. He was now a chief master sergeant, a veritable *capo di capo* in the military's chain of command.

It hadn't been easy wresting Boston away from his assignment, a cushy job as senior Air Force enlisted man in Germany. Not because he didn't want to go—he started packing as soon as Danny gave him the outlines of what he was up to. Boston's commanding officer, however, put a premium on his chiefs, especially those whose extensive combat experience made them instant father figures for the "kids" in the unit. Danny had to get General Magnus involved; fortunately, Magnus had been responsible for one of the CO's early promotions, and eased Boston's transfer as a personal favor.

After the briefest introduction possible to the new Whiplash concept, Boston had shipped out to the Sudan to scout out locations for a base. Danny remained in the States, recruiting more members and arranging for their gear.

"You're going to love this bus," said Boston. "Got a port-a-john and everything."

"As long as it runs."

"Walks more than runs. But it'll get us there. When's the rest of the team showing up?"

"Couple of days."

"Nuri's waiting for us. Interesting fellow."

"Why's that?" asked Danny.

"Just interesting. Knows a bunch of stuff. Pretty good cook."

"Yeah?"

"You should taste what he does with goat and garlic."

"Can't wait," said Danny.

"You're also going to need this."

Boston held out a pistol. It was a large Dessert Eagle, more than twenty years old.

"Got it in town," he said. "Everything else I saw was just peashooters, .22s and revolvers, pretty useless to stop anyone. I figured it would do until we're settled. No spare ammo, though."

Danny took the weapon in his hand. The pistol had a heft to it that made it a clearly serious weapon. Chambered for .44 Magnum, it held eight rounds and could stop anything lighter than an elephant in its tracks.

He slid the gun under his belt, tucking it beneath his jacket.

The bus was an old French municipal bus, converted to private service. It came with a driver, Amid Abul, an Arab who had lived in Derudeb for ten years, occasionally hiring himself out to the CIA as a driver and local "consultant." Nuri had hired him to provide transportation to their base in the hills to the south, and to help in whatever capacity seemed practical.

Nuri had dealt with Abul before, but even he didn't fully trust him; it would have been foolish to do so. Though as the owner of a bus, he was relatively well off, the inhabitants of the war-torn country were so poor that most would gladly give up a relative to a sworn enemy for a year's supply of food and water. Nuri had given Abul a cover story, telling him that his friends were paleontologists. Abul, who knew Nuri was CIA, was smart enough not to ask any questions.

Danny kept up pretenses by asking whether he had ever seen any bones in the sands nearby.

"Plenty of bones, Doctor," answered Abul. "But all of men."

The buildings and houses they passed were mostly black shapes barely discernible in the darkness of the night. They faded as the bus wound its way beyond the city, illusions conjured by a stage manager designed to convince an audience that Port Sudan was a real place.

The landscape, harsh and mostly barren during the day, looked surreal at night, the endless darkness punctuated by black stalks and hulking mounds, silhouettes of gray hills and mountains.

After about an hour and a half, Danny began to relax. There was almost no traffic on the road, though it was the only highway to the south from the coast. It was easy to believe they were the only people left on earth.

The area was warm, but not as warm as he'd thought it would be; the night became more pleasant as they left the moist air of the coast. The mountains and foothills of the eastern part of the country received much more rain than the desert to the west. While the fields and hillsides were hardly lush at this time of year, grass, shrubs, and trees grew in the thin but well drained soil. Here and there farms made a stab at civilizing the land.

Danny felt his eyes start to close. He shifted often, shaking himself, trying to stay as alert as possible.

Boston had no trouble staying awake. He'd been drinking coffee practically nonstop since arriving in Africa, but it wasn't the caffeine that made his muscles buzz. The idea of being back in action after so many years thrilled him.

As far as he was concerned, he'd spent the last few years as a mascot for the Air Force brass. He'd had plenty of responsibility, but responsibility and action were two different things. His job really didn't call for him to *do* all that much. The men and women he directly supervised were mostly chiefs or senior NCOs themselves.

It had been years since he'd really *done* anything. The elite nature of the units he'd served in meant that even the lowest person on the totem pole not only knew his job, but did it in textbook fashion. Boston had sometimes perversely hoped that a screw-up would find his or her way to the unit; it would give him a project.

All of this might have been a tribute to his organizational and leadership skills—or maybe just colossal good luck—but in truth Boston was not comfortable with the role that had settled on him: that of father figure. He had always looked up to the chief master sergeants he'd known; even in the few cases where he didn't respect the men, he always admired the rank. But becoming chief made him feel not so much honored and respected as simply old. He didn't mind the kids at all, and having people jump when you said boo was easy to get used to. But there was also a kind of distance between him and the others that made him uncomfortable. He felt as if he was always on stage, a plastic role model who could not deviate from what preconceived notion the audience had. Inside, he knew he was just good old Ben "Boston" Rockland, tough kid from the streets, snake eater ready for action . . . not the rocking chair.

Being with Colonel Freah—several times he'd come close to calling him captain, as he'd been in the old days—made him a snake eater again. Just being called Boston felt good.

Not that Danny hadn't changed. There was a hint of gray in the hair that curled at his temples. He'd also mellowed, slightly at least, over the years. Danny had always run him particularly hard, trying to prove that just because they were both black, he wasn't cutting him any slack. Now they were more like old friends.

The bus's headlamps caught a black shadow in the road as they came out of a sharp curve. There was a truck in the road.

"Shit," muttered Boston.

Danny, who'd been dozing, jerked awake.

"Can you get around it?" Boston asked the driver.

"I don't know," said Abul, downshifting. He left his right foot hovering over the gas and used his left foot to slow and work the clutch.

"Somebody behind us, too," said Boston. "This ain't no coincidence."

The truck's lights came on ahead of them. It was a military vehicle. Two men with berets stepped in front of the lights, arms raised to stop them. They had M-16 rifles.

"This is the army?" said Danny.

Abul shrugged. It was impossible to know who was stopping them. The reason, though, was easy to predict—they wanted money.

"I see six," said Boston, who was looking behind them. "I think we can make it past them."

Danny leaned forward, trying to see beyond the truck in the road. It was blocking most but not all of the highway. There was a deep ditch to the left. They might make it past, he thought, but they might also fall into the ditch and tumble over. The road curved to the right a short distance beyond the army truck, and there was no way to see what might be there.

"What are these guys going to ask for?" Danny asked Abul.

"Money."

"What if we shoot them?" said Boston.

"Bad, bad. They have many guns. Plus, the army will not be happy."

"Stop the bus," said Danny.

The driver hit the brake.

"Keep the engine running. Be ready to leave. You think you can get around the truck?"

Abul looked at the space. It might be possible, but it would be very tight. "A chance," he said.

"If I say go, you go," said Danny. "No argument."

"What are we doin', Cap?" asked Boston.

"Playing it by ear," said Danny.

Outside, the soldiers surrounded the bus. The two men who'd held up their hands pounded on the door, yelling.

"He wants us to come out," said Abul.

"That, we're not doing."

Danny slipped across the aisle and sat in the first row. Removing his pistol from his belt, he flicked off the safety and held it behind his back.

"Open the door and tell him we're scientists," he told Abul. "Poor scientists. We don't have any money."

Abul glanced at his passenger nervously. "They will just take some money and leave," he said.

"If we let them do that, they'll see us as easy marks," said Danny. "They'll hit us again and again."

Abul disagreed. But rather than telling Danny that directly, he told him he didn't understand what he said. "My English not good."

"They'll rob us again and again," said Boston. "And then probably kill us."

"You can't get away from them," said Abul. "If tonight you escape, tomorrow they will come."

"Tomorrow will take care of itself," said Danny.

The soldiers pounded on the door again.

"Go ahead and open it," said Danny.

Abul put his hand on the handle and pulled it toward him. Robbery was a simple cost of business here; resisting was foolish.

"Out!" shouted the leader of the small band of soldiers. He'd been in the Sudanese army for five years. He was nineteen.

"Tell him," said Danny.

"My passengers are scientists," said Abul in Arabic. "Poor men."

"We will see their papers!" yelled the leader. He pointed his M-16 at the driver. "And they will pay for our troubles."

"They only want to see your papers," Abul told Danny. "And a small bribe will make things right."

"How small?" asked Danny.

Abul asked the gunman how much the inspection might cost. The soldier replied that it was impossible to say beforehand.

"There are only two men, and they are very poor," said Abul.

The number displeased the soldier. Ordinarily a bus like this would carry at least a dozen foreigners and yield a good amount of loot. Ten U.S. dollars would feed his men for a month; a hundred would give them a new store of ammunition, which was starting to run low.

"Tell them to come out," he told the driver.

"He wants you to come out," Abul told Danny.

"We're not coming out. If he wants his money, he's coming in," said Danny.

Abul turned back toward the door, not sure what to tell the soldier. But the man saved him the trouble, bounding up the steps angrily. In the Sudan, the gun was law, and best obeyed quickly.

Danny coiled his body as the bus rocked.

"First one is mine," he muttered to Boston as the Sudanese leader came onto the bus.

The soldier raised his rifle and shouted angrily. Then he fired a three-shot burst through the roof of the vehicle to show he meant business.

As he started to lower the rifle, something hit him in the side of the head, sharp and hard—Danny's fist.

Danny pounded the soldier's temple so hard that he cracked the skull. With his left hand he grabbed the soldier by the scruff of the neck and threw him face first to the floor, scrambling on top of him as his rifle flew down.

"Go! Go! Go!" yelled Boston. "Past the truck! Past the truck!"

Abul needed no urging. He stomped on the gas as the soldier's companion raised his gun. The bus leapt forward. The right fender scraped against the side of the troop truck as Abul fought to keep it on the road.

One of the soldiers leapt onto the back of the bus. Boston turned and fired, pumping three bullets into the door. The man fell off, dead.

Abul jerked the bus onto the road behind the truck, barely keeping it upright as the shoulder gave way on the left. He let off the gas and cranked the wheel desperately, staying with the curve. A man ran at the bus from the side, and Abul lowered his head, hunching over the wheel and praying to Allah to deliver them.

Behind him, Danny quickly frisked the soldier, tossing away a pistol and a grenade, along with two magazines for the M-16. Now that he was on the floor, the man looked small and almost frail. His rib bones poked through his uniform shirt.

"Up," Danny ordered.

The soldier didn't understand. Danny grabbed his shirt and threw him into a seat. Fear gave way to resignation on his face. The man prepared himself to die.

"You're a lieutenant?" said Danny incredulously, noticing the metal pins on the man's brown fatigue collar.

The soldier didn't understand.

"Ask him his name," Danny told the bus driver.

Abul was too busy driving to translate.

"Hey, Abul, who is this guy?" Danny said.

The soldier turned and spat blood to the floor. He worked his tongue around his teeth, trying to see if any had been broken. He'd been shot once when he was seventeen; the punch in the face felt worse.

"Stop the bus," said Danny after they'd gone almost a mile from the other soldiers.

Abul did so, his foot heavy on the brake. His hands were shaking.

"Ask him his name and his unit," Danny told the driver.

"What is your name?" said Abul from his seat.

The soldier didn't answer the question, merely staring at Danny. Never in his life would he have expected a robbery victim to act this way, especially a westerner. It was impossible; the man, he decided, must be a devil.

"Open the back door, Boston," said Danny.

"What are you going to do, Colonel?"

"Get rid of him. He's of no use to us."

"You must kill him," said Abul. He jumped up from his seat. "Shoot him. Shoot him."

"I don't think so," said Danny.

"You will kill him or he will kill you. He will kill me," said Abul.

"You come this way a lot?" said Danny.

Abul had already resolved that he would never drive this way again, but that was irrelevant. The soldiers were fierce and predatory; they would certainly want revenge for this sort of embarrassment.

"Kill him," said Abul.

"I don't know, Colonel," said Boston. "Abul may be right. They aren't going to interpret mercy as a good thing here."

Danny looked into the soldier's face. He fully expected to die.

"How old are you?" he asked.

The soldier had no idea what he was saying.

"Abul?"

Abul translated. The man simply shrugged. He wasn't able to answer the question accurately, and would not talk to a devil for anything. It was one thing to lose his life— everyone did, some more quickly than others—and a much different thing to lose his soul, which he knew would last forever.

"Get the door, Boston," said Danny.

"Mr. Rock," said Abul, appealing to Boston. "To let him go now—foolish."

"So was not paying him," said Danny. He hauled the kid to his feet and pointed the gun toward his groin.

"You remember me. My name is Kirk," he told him, using one of his aliases. "Kirk. You screw with me, next time I blow these off."

He jammed the gun hard enough to make the kid suck wind.

Boston opened the door at the back. Danny pushed him out.

"Go," Danny told the driver. "Get us the hell out of here."

9

Eddd, Sudan

WHILE DANNY FREAH WAS DECIDING HOW TO BEST IMPRESS the Sudanese army that he was not a man to be messed with, Nuri Abaajmed Lupo was another two hundred and some miles to the south, doing his best not to be noticed by one of the army's most ferocious opponents, a rebel by the name of General Mohamed Henri Wani—Red Henri, in the local slang, because of his red hair and his unusual French given name.

Nuri had traveled to a village some fifty miles west of the base camp, intending to be back before Danny and Boston arrived. But talk in town that Red Henri was coming had enticed him to bug the small bar-restaurant-inn that served as the village's main hangout. He'd no sooner gotten the bugs placed when two of Red Henri's bodyguards showed up at the door, effectively sealing everyone inside for the duration of their leader's visit.

As an outsider, Nuri was immediately suspect. He was dressed in the loose white garb worn by nearly everyone else in the village. His stubble beard and swarthy skin made him look Arab, like about thirty percent of the population. But the population was so sparse that locals knew instantly who fit and who didn't, and their glances toward Nuri gave him away to the two bodyguards.

Nuri told them enthusiastically that he had been hired

to help a scientific team looking for dinosaurs in the foot-hills nearby. It was the same story he'd told the café owner and everyone he'd met. The bodyguards—two boys barely fourteen—weren't very impressed.

"Sit there," said the taller one, pointing to a small wooden chair near the side of the room. "Hand over your gun."

Nuri handed over his AK-47. Few men traveled without weapons here, and the rifle raised no extra suspicions from the bodyguards.

The question for Nuri was whether to hand over either of his pistols. He finally decided that he would give up his Glock, and lifted his long shirt to reveal its holster.

"Why do you have a pistol?" asked the tall bodyguard. "These monsters you dig up—they are dangerous?"

Anywhere else in the world, the comment would have been meant as a joke. But the rebels were uneducated and largely naive about anything beyond their limited experience. They also tended not to joke with strangers.

"Yes," said Nuri, his voice grave. "Some men have been killed by them. The medicine is very strong."

"You should have the general protect you," said the body-guard, meaning Red Henri.

"It would be a great honor." Nuri bowed his head. All he could do was hope that the young man would forget the sug-gestion.

Red Henri had gotten his nickname as a young man, when his hair was red. It had since thinned and turned gray, but for many of his victims the adjective remained an appropriate reference to the blood on his hands. Like many of the rebel leaders, he called himself a general, but the highest rank he had held in the Sudanese army was corporal.

After the sun set, Nuri thought the visit would be canceled and they would be let free. But darkness had no effect on Red Henri's itinerary. They all continued to wait, bored and barely awake.

Finally, about twenty minutes after midnight, an ambu-lance siren sounded in the distance. The guards immediately snapped to attention, prompting everyone in the place to rise and stand. The proprietor, a short man with caved-in cheeks and a right ear that looked as if it had been bitten off, rubbed his hands nervously by the door.

The siren grew louder. A blue flashing light stroked the darkness outside. The guttural roar of mufflerless trucks and a heavy bass beat vibrated the walls and floor of the house. Nuri couldn't place the beat until the motorcade pulled up in front. It was the bass line of an American rap song, an obscure Beastie Boys tune more than two decades old.

Red Henri traveled with the core of his army, about two hundred strong, most of them packed into the backs of old pickup trucks. They spread out around the town, posting themselves as lookouts and rousting any of the residents who had fallen asleep after the arrival of the advance party.

All twenty-three of his personal bodyguards—he considered the number, which could only divided by itself and one, a strong omen of success—jumped from the troop truck that rode in front of his Chinese-made Hummer knockoff. They formed a phalanx around their general, who waited for his aides riding in the ambulance at the head of the convoy. As his communication czar approached—that was the man's title—Red Henri pointed at him. The communications czar shook his head and held up his BlackBerry. Red Henri frowned; he liked getting messages on the device, though he never answered them.

Entourage assembled, the rebel leader swept toward the house. The men inside, who'd been standing at attention the entire time, strained to stand even straighter as his first soldiers came in.

The rebel army's dress was a collection of different castoffs. Some wore uniforms purchased from Kenya, a sometime ally. Others wore civilian clothes donated by charity groups in Europe and the U.S. who thought they were helping the needy. The handful of former Sudanese soldiers wore the uniforms they had deserted in.

All of Red Henri's bodyguards dressed in baggy khaki pants and white T-shirts, with red scarves tied around their closely shaven skulls. To a Western eye—an American one especially—they looked more like television or movie "gangstas" or wannabe gang members from a decade before. This was not a coincidence. Red Henri had been inspired by music videos when he established the uniform; he loved American rap, gangsta and otherwise.

At six-ten, Red Henri dominated a room, even a crowded one like the one Nuri was trapped in. The rebel extended his arms as he swept in, greeting everyone as if he was joining a party in progress. The owner of the house cowered at the side, then tried to kiss his hand as he came near. Amused, Red Henri waved him off, asking for something to drink.

Nuri had never seen Red Henri this close before, and while he wanted to stay as inconspicuous as possible, he couldn't stop himself from staring as he made mental notes. Red Henri's face was baby smooth, unmarked by either care or disease. He'd been shot many times over the decade that he had fought, but none of those wounds were visible beneath the white track suit he wore. He had the air of a politician, and the self-assurance a phalanx of bodyguards brings.

The rebel man who had spoken to Nuri earlier about dinosaurs walked over to one of Red Henri's aides. Within moments Red Henri had heard the story and came over to greet him personally.

"You are a scientist!" he said with enthusiasm. He spoke first his tribal tongue, then switched to English.

"Yes, Your Excellency."

"You can help me."

"I'm just a poor man—"

"You will still help us!" Red Henri slapped him on the shoulder happily. "I am glad you are with us."

"I will do what I can, Your Excellency."

"These spirits you are digging up. They are not angry at being disturbed?"

"They have to be handled very delicately," said Nuri. "It is not easy—it can be very dangerous."

"Then you are a brave man."

Red Henri slapped him on the shoulder one more time and walked away. Relieved, Nuri began thinking of what he would eat when got back to camp.

He had settled on salted goat kabobs when the ambulance siren sounded outside, calling the general's entourage back to order. The two members of the advance team nodded at the owner, who fell into a chair from relief as they left. The trucks rumbled to life and the hard beat of rap once more began pounding the ground.

"I wonder if I could have some tea before leaving," Nuri asked the host. "I have a long drive."

The man pointed to a warm kettle on the nearby counter. Nuri went to help himself when one of the rebels came back inside.

"You, there, come," he said in Arabic, pointing at Nuri.

"What?"

"The general wants to see your bones. Come. You'll show us your camp."

"I don't think—"

The aide grabbed hold of Nuri's arm and pushed him toward the door.

"That was not a request. You ride with the general and do as he says."

"I have a motorcycle," said Nuri. "I'll follow."

"The motorcycle in front?" The man smiled. "It will make a fine addition to the cause. It was very generous of you to donate it."

10

Approaching base camp Alpha, Sudan

AFTER THEIR ADVENTURE WITH THE SUDANESE ARMY, NEIther Danny nor Boston had any trouble staying awake.

Danny stayed in the front seat opposite the driver, scouting forward and brooding on what other difficulties might lie ahead. He also told the Voice to warn him of any vehicles ahead, something he realized he should have done earlier.

The computer dutifully informed him that the coverage here was periodic, provided by an orbiting spy satellite rather than a Global Hawk or a geosynchronous satellite specifically assigned to the area.

"Keep an eye on things anyway," Danny said.

"Slang recognized," said the Voice. "Will do."

"How are we doing?" Danny asked the driver after they'd been back on the road for another hour and a half. They still had another three hours to go.

"Oh, very good, very good," said Abul. "Very good time."

"You come from this area?"

"Oh, no. In the north," said Abul. "I drive here for the money."

"Is this a rebel area, or an army area?"

Abul shrugged. "More rebel than army," he said.

The area belonged to whoever happened to be there at the time. It was a mistake to think of the rebels as one united group—there were several, and most didn't like each other. But it was hard for strangers to understand that.

"The rebels ever bother you?"

"They bother only the army," said Abul, fudging.

"We shake you up back there?"

Abul didn't understand, but thought the question required a no, and gave one.

"We heard that it wasn't safe to go around without weapons," said Danny. "So we were prepared."

"I know that you are not scientists," said Abul abruptly. "I am not a fool."

"What else do you know?"

"I know to keep my mouth quiet."

"That's good," said Danny. "There'll be a bonus for the trouble. And the damage to your vehicle."

The offer to pay for the crumpled fender brightened Abul's mood considerably. The additional money would make it possible to buy a second vehicle, and maybe even a third. In the Sudan, that would make him a very rich man.

It also meant he could operate the buses in the north, where things were much more stable.

Neither Abul nor the two Americans spoke for more than two and a half hours, until Boston spotted the burned-out armored car that marked the road up to the hills where they'd made camp. It was an old British AEC armored car, manufactured at the very end of World War II. It had passed through a number of owners, including Yugoslavia and Kenya, before finding its place in the Sudanese defense force. A Russian-made RPG—not quite as old, though itself fairly venerable— had ended its career a few months before.

"There's the turn," said Boston. "Look at that old soldier, Colonel. Older than our grandfathers."

Abul slowed down. Boston put his hands against the window of the bus, watching the sweep of the headlights. He'd chosen the site because it would be easy to defend.

"We oughta give Nuri a call," Boston told Danny. "So he doesn't blast us on the way up."

"Go ahead."

Boston took out his satellite phone to call Nuri. Only Danny and Nuri were hooked into the MY-PID. Danny actually could have made the call himself on the MY-PID channel, but in truth he simply didn't consider it. He still wasn't comfortable with the system, still wasn't thinking about it as a tool that could help him rather than a computer that could foul him up.

"I ain't getting an answer," said Boston.

Now Danny did use the Voice. He went to the back of the bus so Abul couldn't hear or see him. "Where is Nuri?" he asked.

The Voice gave him a set of GPS coordinates.

"Where is that in relation to me?"

"Fifty-two-point-three miles west. He is moving. Speed indicates a land vehicle."

"What's his direction?"

"Due north."

"Not toward Base Camp Alpha."

"Negative at the present time."

Danny stared through the bullet holes. His solution had been the worst of both worlds—he'd pissed off the Sudanese, but hadn't eliminated them as a threat.

A bad move. He was out of practice. Maybe fatally so.

Abul took the turn and drove up into the small camp, which consisted of three small personal tents—glorified pup tents, big enough for someone to sleep in and little else—arranged around an old stone cottage. The building had been used many years before by a shepherd who'd looked after a herd of goats. It had been empty for nearly fifty years; the roof had been gone for nearly that long.

"You can pull the bus up a little further," Danny told the driver. "Which tent is yours?"

"I sleep in the bus."

"Fine. We'll make something to eat."

Boston took a quick tour of the perimeter, making sure they were alone. Nuri had posted sensors all around, but Boston didn't trust them.

Danny took one of the battery lanterns and checked out the building. About a third of the stone partition between its two rooms had tumbled down. Nuri had set up some camp chairs in the front room, along with a small table. A hand of solitaire was laid out on the table, the deck skewed as if the player had tossed it down in disgust.

Most of their gear was still en route and would be dropped via parachute the following night. They had a camp stove, cooking utensils, extra clothes, a tool kit. A backup radio, two GPS units, a pair of AK-47s and spare ammunition were in a small trunk at the side of the back room. Digging gear—picks and shovels, sticks, strings, the finer trowels and tools of the paleontology trade—sat near the front door. There was a dirt bike; Nuri had taken the other one to scout.

Danny looked at the roof. A tarp could easily cover it. But there wasn't much chance of rain at this time of year, and with luck they wouldn't be there long enough for it to matter.

"Nuri made some sort of stew," said Boston, coming in after checking around. Between his light and Danny's, the room was fairly bright. "We can just heat it up."

"Where is it?"

"In that box there."

"Not in a refrigerator?"

Boston laughed. "Colonel, they don't have any iceboxes in hell."

Danny went over to the box. The food was in a covered ceramic pot.

"I think if we eat this, we'll end up in purgatory," said Danny, examining it. "Or at least the latrine."

"I've been eating it for two days straight, and I'm not sick."

"It's two days old?"

"You get it good and hot, all the germs die." Boston picked up the pot and put it on the stove. "What do you think of Abul?"

"I guess he's all right."

"You trust him?"

"You tell me. You've been with him."

"I don't know. Nuri thinks he's okay, but doesn't really trust him. He doesn't trust anybody. He's got that look about him."

"Uh-huh."

"Remember Stoner? The guy we lost in Romania?"

"Yeah."

"You think those rumors about him being alive were true?"

"I doubt it." Danny looked into the pot. It was a bubbling mass of gray, with unidentifiable black chunks floating on top. "I'm not going to eat that crap."

"Suit yourself, Colonel."

"You probably shouldn't call me colonel," said Danny.

"What should I call you?"

"Danny."

Boston made a face.

"Then Doc or something like that," suggested Danny. "Boss. Chief. Anything that's not military."

"I keep wanting to call you captain. Kind of think of Colonel Bastian every time I call you colonel."

"Yeah."

"Funny guy."

"Funny?"

"I mean—*remarkable*."

"Yeah."

Danny heard a sound in the distance. He didn't know what it was at first—it sounded like an airplane very far away. Then he realized it was the sound of a truck.

"Kill the lights," he said. "Let's see what this is."

Boston led the way to one of their lookout posts, detouring quickly to grab the night vision goggles, which he'd left in his pack on the bus. Abul, who'd heard the noise but decided to ignore it, joined them. Danny squatted next to the rocks and pointed the night glasses in the direction of the noise. Red Henri's ragtag armada appeared in the distance, the ambulance leading the way.

"Jesus. It looks like the whole Sudanese army is coming for us," said Danny.

He handed the glasses to Boston.

"Shit—but they're coming from the wrong direction," said

Boston. "This must be another unit—they must have radioed for help."

"Can I see?" asked Abul.

Boston gave him the glasses.

"This is not the army. This is Red Henri," said Abul.

"Who's he?" asked Boston.

"A rebel commander," said Danny. "He's the one that's not attached to any of the religious movements. Right?"

"He is a heathen," said Abul.

"Whatever his religion is," said Boston, "he's coming straight for us."

Danny took back the glasses. Between the pickup trucks and the troop truck, there could easily be two hundred men there.

"What do you want to do, uh, Doc?" asked Boston. Doc didn't sound right, he decided.

"We should hide," said Abul. "Red Henri—very unpredictable. Sometimes nice. Sometimes . . ."

He put his hand to his throat and made a strangling sound.

Danny turned back and looked at the camp. They'd put out the lights; it looked deserted. But they'd have to leave the bus there.

Two hundred versus two? Even with a Megafortress backing them up, the odds would have been pretty long. As much as he didn't like the idea of hiding—it smacked of running away—there was no other choice.

"All right—can we get up to that high ground there?" he asked Boston.

"Yeah, that's what I'm thinking."

"Grab the rifles and extra ammo and let's go."

11

**Base Camp Alpha
Sudan**

LISTENING TO RED HENRI PONTIFICATE ABOUT HOW HE FI-
nanced his campaign in the Hummer, Nuri couldn't decide
whether he was a little crazy or very crazy. He was definitely
crazy, and eccentric besides, but his economic arrangements
suggested that he had at least an occasional attachment to
reality. Such as it was.

Red Henri had built his movement around his control of a
copper mine about thirty miles southeast of Eddd. Though
ostensibly owned and operated by a Belgium consortium,
Red Henri and his troops had more to say about production there than the production manager, let alone the individual stockholders. The company paid him a fee to provide
security—basically money so his troops wouldn't wreck the
place, though in theory they were defending against other
rebel groups and robbers. The company also paid him personally as a "political consultant"—basically a bribe to keep
him from wreaking havoc. But the biggest portion of the
mine-related income came from a "transport tax" that Red
Henri's soldiers collected from anyone going into or out of
the mining area. Miners and anyone who wanted to do any
business with them there had to pay the U.S. equivalent of
three dollars going and coming. The fees allowed Red Henri
to pay his soldiers about twice what the government paid its
forces—when it paid them at all.

The arrangement demonstrated that Red Henri was, if not
smart, at least very clever. On the other hand, his belief in the
supernatural went far beyond that of most of the Sudanese
Nuri had met. Many in the southern portion of the country
clung to the ancient animistic religion, believing in spirits
that their grandfathers' fathers would have prayed to. Like
many of them, Red Henri believed that spirits walked the

earth as men did. He also believed that he could see them. He carried on regular conversations with them—and for about half the ride from the village, he interspersed his comments to Nuri with an animated discussion with two unseen spirits who were sitting in the back of his Hummer.

When he spoke to them, Red Henri used a tribal language so obscure that even the Voice would have been unable to decipher it, had Nuri dared to show the earphones. But Nuri got the most salient parts—the spirits were divided about whether the scientists should be allowed to stay or not. One of the spirits was very hungry, in fact, and thought that the best use of the scientists would be as food.

Red Henri took a neutral position in the argument.

Nuri wasn't sure whether Boston and the others would be back yet, and he certainly wasn't going to call to find out. He assumed they were smart enough to be on the lookout—and to hide if they saw the caravan coming.

The convoy moved with little regard for the highway. The ambulance was accorded the lead, but otherwise each driver vied with the others to move as fast as possible, cutting one or the other off and occasionally coming close to colliding. Some weeks back, Red Henri had decided that the driver and occupants of the last vehicle to arrive at a town he was inspecting would get no supper, and while he had soon relented, none of the drivers wanted to risk their leader's displeasure. They drove fast, and they drove with their headlights off, hopping across the landscape, bouncing on springs and shocks that had long ago stopped dampening any bumps.

"Up this way, yes?" said Red Henri, pointing in the general direction of the camp.

"That's it," said Nuri.

The fact that the rebel leader knew where the camp was surprised Nuri. He hadn't seen them scouting the area at all.

Red Henri picked up a radio and called to the ambulance, making sure the driver knew to turn up the road into the hills. The driver took the direction as an invitation to blow his siren. The wail bounced across the hills, echoing through the desert.

DANNY CROUCHED IN THE ROCKS ABOUT A HALF MILE ABOVE the camp, watching with his night glasses as the rebel leader and his entourage pulled into the camp. Their movements were somewhere between that of a highly polished military unit and a troupe of clouds.

"There's Nuri, getting out of the Hummer," said Danny. He handed the glasses to Boston.

"Brought a few friends home for dinner," said Boston. "What should we do?"

"Too late to do anything but watch."

THE BUS WAS THERE, BUT IT WAS OBVIOUS TO NURI THAT the others were hiding. He nonetheless went to each tent and then to the building, calling for his fellow scientists, and hoping he'd come up with an idea on what to do next.

Red Henri got out of the Hummer. His spirits got out with him, still arguing over whether the scientists should be allowed in the area or not. As the men mustered around him in their usual formation, he saw that no one had come out to greet him. This was a severe breach of etiquette, one that spoke very poorly of his hosts. It was also a strong argument on the side of the spirits, who felt the scientists should not be allowed to dig here—and should, in fact, be eaten.

"Where are your scientists?" Red Henri demanded when he saw Nuri come out of the building. "Why are they not greeting me?"

"I thought they were sleeping, but I guess I was wrong. They may have gone to work in the field."

"Which field?"

"I'm not sure."

"Maybe you didn't have scientists here," said Red Henri. "No friends."

"No, there are two here already, and more on their way. See, they have to dig at night because the spirits—"

More scientists? How many?

Even one would be too many.

Red Henri suddenly understood the spirits' point. These men had not asked permission to be here. Their digging was a severe imposition, not just to the spirits, but to him.

Of course they're not here. It's as I said—they're nothing. They've already run off. My brother came this way this after-noon and chased them down.

Rubbish. Your brother couldn't chase a flea.

"I don't believe there were any scientists," Red Henri told Nuri. "There were no scientists here."

Nuri wasn't sure whether he should agree or not.

"Were there scientists?" demanded Red Henri.

"Of course."

Red Henri unsnapped his holster. Nuri cursed himself for not shooting the bastard when he had the chance. Two of Red Henri's bodyguards were directly behind him; he had no chance of getting his pistol.

"What happened to my scientists?" said Red Henri, pull-ing out his gun.

"They dig at night, so as not to offend certain of the spirits that watch over the bones."

Red Henri began to laugh. Finally, he saw the truth. The men were simply cowards.

"Your scientists ran away, didn't they?" he said to Nuri. "They saw Qwandi's brother and they ran. And Qwandi's brother is the mildest spirit here. So you won't be getting any work done. That's too bad."

Red Henri rocked the pistol back and forth in his hand. He made up his mind that he would kill Nuri. But as he raised his pistol, the first spirit spoke.

You can't eat him if he's a coward. You'll become a coward yourself.

"He's not the coward," said Red Henri.

Of course he is. What man has cowards for friends but is not one himself? It is impossible.

Red Henri nodded at the wisdom of this. "I'll just shoot him and leave him, then."

If he is bringing other friends, you should wait to shoot him, said the other spirit. *They may have money and other things. He had the nice motorcycle.*

Nuri tensed. He didn't have a plan to escape. The only plan he had was to drop down, grab the pistol from his leg, and try and shoot Red Henri. It would be preemptive revenge only, so he could tell himself that he died doing something.

Red Henri pointed the gun at Nuri's forehead. Nuri leaned to his left, ready to dive to the ground. But Red Henri raised the gun and fired, the shot sailing harmlessly into the sky.

"I do not think you are a coward," he said.

"Well, uh, thanks."

"You should not be friends with cowards. When a man is a friend with a coward, he becomes a coward. It is the same as eating his heart—you become a coward. Do you want that?"

"No," said Nuri.

"When your scientists come back, you will come see me. We will have much to discuss. The spirits wish to be asked permission. Some are against you. One suggested you be eaten."

"I'm probably not that tasty."

Nuri started to laugh. But Red Henri didn't even smile as he turned away.

DANNY, BOSTON, AND ABUL CAME DOWN FROM THEIR HID-ing place about a half hour later, after the rebel troop had cleared out. They found Nuri sitting in front of one of the campfire stoves, sipping from a small bottle of scotch.

He hated the stuff generally, but it had a certain medicinal quality and was the only alcohol he'd been able to find during his brief stop in Ethiopia before coming to Sudan.

"There you are," said Nuri. "You missed the party."

"We weren't sure what was going on," said Danny. "We

saw all the trucks and everything. We figured it would be better if we just disappeared for a while."

"Probably. The spirits might have thought you were brave, and eaten you."

Danny gave him a puzzled look. Nuri didn't explain.

"Jasmine hasn't been around for a while," said Nuri. "Henri didn't know Luo was killed. They're starting to run low on ammo."

"Is that good or bad?" asked Danny.

"Good. It means he'll show up eventually."

"So why did you bring Red Henri here?"

Nuri looked up from the stove. This was the problem when you worked with someone, he thought—they were always second-guessing you.

"He wanted to see the place," Nuri said. "And he had two hundred reasons why I figured it was a good idea to let him."

"What did he want?"

"Dinner."

Danny didn't realize Nuri meant that literally, and Nuri didn't say. He just went back to sipping his scotch.

12

**Base Camp Alpha
Sudan**

NURI WOKE THE NEXT MORNING WITH A KILLER HEADACHE and an aching midsection. He didn't mind, figuring the alternative would have been much worse.

Around noon he and Boston went with Abul in the bus to a village about sixty miles south to see what food they might be able to buy, and to add video bugs to the Voice's network.

Danny prepared the camp for the arrival of the rest of his men and the bulk of their supplies.

The original plan called for them to come in via truck convoy from Ethiopia, but that would take several days, and the misadventures with Red Henri convinced Danny that the cover story was less important than reinforcements. He called Breanna on the sat phone around noon, which was six in the morning D.C. time. She was already in the office. Within a half hour Reid called back, telling Danny the drop would be made at midnight.

The hills and trees made the camp difficult to parachute into if the wind kicked up, and not wanting to lose anyone to a broken leg right off the bat, Danny went out and scouted for an easier landing zone. He found a field about three miles to the north that even Ray Rubeo could have jumped into without a problem. The distance from the camp was an asset; if anyone happened to see the drop, it wouldn't necessarily show them where Base Camp Alpha was.

Danny set up automated beacons there and called in to confirm the drop.

"I'm wondering if you could add a couple of dirt bikes to the supply list," he asked Reid.

"Are you practicing for the motocross?"

"Red Henri decided he liked ours," said Danny.

"And you gave it to him?"

"Not exactly."

"I'll see what I can do. Anything else?"

"A few crates of ice cream would be nice."

"Amusing, Colonel."

MUCH TO DANNY'S SURPRISE, REID MANAGED TO PACK some ice cream into the supplies, arranging for a quart of vanilla, chocolate, and strawberry to travel in a special thermal box packed with dry ice when the team and supplies jumped from a specially outfitted 787 that night.

From the outside, the Boeing 787 Dreamliner looked exactly like the several hundred of its brethren in service. Its markings indicated that it was operated by Royal Dubai International Airlines. The name sounded familiar, especially given the near monopolization of air traffic over the past few years by airlines from the oil-rich emirates, but the company was entirely fictional, owned and operated by the CIA.

The interior of the plane had been heavily modified, although the bulk of the cabin was outfitted for passengers. A special bulkhead cut off the main cabin about halfway back. Behind the door was a pressurized cargo compartment where specially sized pallets of equipment could be stored. These were loaded through a special hatchway at the underside of the fuselage. The hatchway could be opened in flight, allowing an automated system to disgorge the pallets at the pilot's command. Targeted by a GPS system, the pallets were then "flown" to the landing zone either by an onboard steering system or by the copilot, who communicated with them via satellite.

The same hatchway was used by CIA paramilitary officers to make high altitude jumps. Fully deployed, the hatchway sheltered the jumpers from the nasty slipstream encircling the Dreamliner's body and wings. The ramp and the aircraft had been designed to minimize any radar echoes that might give away the plane's purpose. If the situation warranted, special parachutes could be used that minimized their signature as well.

The system was not without its limitations. The more gear and people involved in the drop, the harder it was to coordinate and get everyone down in the same place. The crates had to go out first. The jumpers then had only a few seconds to work their way down the ramp and jump. Traveling at 35,000 feet at about 400 knots, with the wind howling around you—it was a lot harder in real life than it sounded during the briefing.

While all four of the new Whiplash team members making the jump were parachute-qualified, only one had used the plane before. That made Hera Scokas the team jumpmaster.

Her role as scold came naturally.

"Yo, get moving," she barked as the last of the three crates began sliding down the ramp. "Come on, Shugee."

"My name ain't 'Shugee,' honey," snapped Clar "Sugar" Keeb, who was going out first. Like Hera, Sugar was a CIA paramilitary officer. A black woman raised in Detroit, she'd served in the Army for eight years before joining the Agency. At five-ten and 200 pounds, she had more than a half foot advantage over Scokas, and would have decked her had she been nearby.

She didn't mind being called Sugar. Everybody used it. Clar's nickname had been applied by an aunt because of how sweet she liked to make her Rice Krispies when she was two, and she'd lived with it ever since. Shugee, though, was out of bounds.

Sugar put her gloved hand against her oxygen mask, making sure it was tight. Then she unhooked her safety belt and stepped off the ramp, pushing her body forward to fall in a frog position.

The sky ate her up. Night jumps at 35,000 feet were not Sugar's idea of fun. The wind seemed to sense that, and crushed the top of her helmet against her head. She slid hard to the left, off-balance. A large arrow appeared in the middle of her visor, pointing to roughly two o'clock.

"Yeah, no kidding," she mumbled, tilting her body back to get on course.

Ten meters above her, John "Flash" Gordon felt the baloney sandwich he'd eaten just before the flight pushing back up through his esophagus. In the six years he'd been in the Army Special Forces, he'd never had a baloney sandwich. He'd also never eaten before a jump, not since an unfortunate experience during an early qualifying jump, where his stomach had revolted at 7,000 feet.

His change in routine had been as inexplicable as it was unfortunate.

Flash clamped his mouth shut and concentrated on the arrow in his helmet. He was right on course.

Hera, meanwhile, was in the plane, waiting for the fourth

member of the team to unhook his safety harness so she could jump after him.

The man she was waiting for, Carl McGowan, was experiencing one of the downsides of the safety strap—the snap on the hook was difficult to manipulate while wearing gloves.

"Yo, Tailgunner, we jumping today? Or next week?"

"Yeah, yeah, yeah. Keep your bra on," muttered McGowan.

The lever finally gave way. McGowan pushed off the side and took a running leap down the ramp, flying forward into the air as if he were diving into a pool.

As he fell away from the plane, it occurred to him that he would much prefer that Hera took her bra off. She had an A-1 body, even if she was meaner than the bastards who'd worked him through SEAL Hell Week a decade and a half before.

DOWN ON THE GROUND, BOSTON SCANNED THE DESERT with his night glasses, making sure that neither Red Henri nor any of his competitors were approaching. A CIA Global Hawk had been detailed into the area for the night, but he trusted his own eyes more than any high-tech sensor. The fact that he was using a high-tech sensor to greatly magnify what his eyes could see didn't change his opinion.

Danny checked his watch. The Voice had announced the launching of each crate and Whiplash crew member, along with its estimated time of landing. If he wanted, he could listen to updates on where each was going to land. But he didn't feel much like listening to a play-by-play, so he told the Voice to alert him only if any of the jumpers or crates was going off course by more than twenty-five yards.

Fifty years before, falling within twenty-five yards of a target would have been considered a reasonable performance, perhaps even an outstanding one. World War II paratroopers struggled with barely steerable parachutes and air crews who often found themselves navigating mostly by instinct. Now the technology was so advanced that packages could be practically delivered to a front door.

Not that skill and human error were completely removed

from the equation. The team members had hit a heavy cross-wind after deploying their chutes, and struggled to remain on course as they dropped over the last 5,000 feet. Danny, monitoring the team communications channel through the Voice, heard the jumpers cursing and complaining as they coped with the wind. Even with the night vision screens built into their jump helmets, the darkness hampered their depth perception.

"Sounds like they've been working together for a while," he told Boston.

The first cargo chute came down about five yards off target, its winglike canopy making a loud *hush* as it fell. The second and third hit precisely on their crosshairs, each twelve and a half yards progressively north, each thumping against their protective bottoms with a satisfying *cru-ump*.

Then came the team members.

Sugar hit first, landing about five yards to the east of her target. Then came Flash, who hit exactly on his target mark, and within .03 seconds of the computed time for landing originally calculated when he left the plane. McGowan came down twenty-two yards from his target, directly due north of Hera's landing spot. This meant Hera had to steer away to avoid a collision. Her corrections sent her roughly fifty yards off the mark, making her jump the worst of the group.

"Hey jumpmaster," said Sugar, "looks like you kinda missed, huh?"

"Whoa," said Flash. "You ain't telling me the jumpmaster with, like, five hundred years of experience, blew her jump so badly she just about landed in the Atlantic."

"All right, let's get moving," barked Boston. "We have to get these crates unwrapped and packed into the bus."

Hera folded her parachute, angry but knowing that explaining why she'd had to go so far off course was only going to bring greater derision.

The crates were designed to be broken down quickly. Still, it took over three hours for the team to get everything onto the bus. They fashioned a rack out of the cargo containers for the roof, giving Abul fits as he worried about the lines breaking the frames on the bus's windows.

"I don't think the motorcycle will fit in the bus," said Boston as they finished. "Maybe we should drive it back."

"And who's going to drive it?" asked Danny.

"Gee, I don't know." Boston smiled. "We could draw straws, or just go by rank."

"Officers excluded?" said Danny.

"Oh yeah. This is strictly an enlisted thing."

"What about those of us who aren't in the Army?" asked Sugar.

"Hey, I'm not in the Army," said McGowan. "So I oughta get dibs."

"I'll ride it back," said Danny, taking the handlebars. "I think Chief Rockland needs a little time to bond with his people."

"Thanks," said Boston.

THE BIKE WAS A DUCATI, REMADE FOR SPECIAL OPERATIONS work under contract to the Technology Office. It had an extra large gas tank, and a heavy duty suspension to accommodate the weight of a soldier with a full complement of gear. It lacked the glossy paint normally associated with Italian motorcycles, and included a few accessories not normally found in street bikes, like a miniature forward-looking infrared radar mounted in the headlight assembly. But it was still a Ducati, and Danny had a blast riding it back to the base, running ahead of the bus. The dirt road was just loose enough to add maneuvering interest as he zipped up the hills.

His fun lasted all of ten minutes, as the Voice announced that a pair of Jeep-sized vehicles were approaching on the road south. The computer calculated that the bus would arrive at the highway within thirty seconds of the Jeeps.

He had the Voice cut into the team radio channel.

"Boston, have Abul stop for a while," he said. "Two Jeeps are heading our way. I don't want them to see you."

"No problem, Cap. How's the bike?"

"It's nice. I'm going to get a little closer to the road and have a look at these guys."

"Roger that."

Danny leaned on the gas, accelerating so he could get near the road well before the other vehicles. The oversized muffler and heat dissipater turned the trademark Ducati roar into a low moan—a sin, really.

He stopped about a half mile from the road and lay the bike down gently in the dirt. Adjusting the infrared image from the motorcycle, he zeroed in on a rise in the road about a mile to the north and waited.

"Estimate time for the vehicles to pass," Danny asked the Voice.

"Three minutes, eighteen seconds."

"Can you identify them?"

"Negative."

"Are they Sudanese army?"

"The army does not operate Jeeps."

"They're real Jeeps?"

"Chrysler Motors, model year 2001."

"Do these belong to Red Henri?"

"Vehicles are not among types known to be operated by East Sudanese Liberation Crew headed by rebel known as Red Henri."

The Voice listed three probabilities: two rebel groups that operated to the west, and an aid organization, which was headquartered far to the north. Danny doubted it was the aid group—even do-gooders knew better than to drive out here at night.

The lead Jeep took the hill at about forty miles an hour, cresting into his view. It carried four men; the rear Jeep held two.

They began slowing, and Danny sensed that they were going to turn up the road toward the camp. Sure enough, the lead vehicle stopped abruptly just past the turnoff, then backed up and began climbing the hill. He had the Voice project the image from the Global Hawk into the control unit, watching as the Jeeps continued on the road toward their camp.

"Nuri, you on the line?" Danny asked over the Voice's communications channel.

"Yeah, I'm looking at them on the laptop."

"Who are they? Do you know?"

"No idea. I'd guess rebels, but that's pretty obvious."

"Maybe you oughta hide up in the rocks."

"Maybe. Let's see what happens."

BACK AT THE BUS, THE WHIPLASH TEAM MEMBERS WERE developing a shared case of cabin fever. They had spent the better part of the last three days traveling, first to report for the assignment and then to get into position to make the jump. None of them, Boston included, liked the idea that they were sitting and waiting in the desert, as if afraid of a couple of locals in old Jeeps.

Hera pushed her feet against the seat back, trying to keep her muscles from going into spasm.

"Hey Chief—when we are we moving?" she asked.

"Soon as Colonel Freah says we're good to go."

"When's that going to be?"

"It'll be when it is," said Boston.

"That's a line of Plato, isn't it?" said McGowan.

"Who's Plato?" asked Boston.

"Plato's that guy in the Popeye cartoons who ate all the hamburgers," said Flash.

"No, you're thinking of Pluto."

"I know who Plato is, asshole," snapped Boston, but no one heard him—they were too busy trying to remember the cast of the ancient cartoons.

BECAUSE THEY'D HAD TO SCRAMBLE TO PULL THE OPERA-tion together, Flash, McGowan, Hera, and Sugar had joined Whiplash as provisional members. There was no question that they were qualified; all had proven themselves in covert operations in the past.

But impressive résumés didn't make a good team great. Boston knew all too well that the opposite could be true. The success or failure of a group depended very much on the chemistry between them, whether they were trying for a pennant in baseball or sneaking behind enemy lines in battle. Even if he had personally vetted everyone in the group, he still wouldn't have been sure how they would all work together in the field.

What he'd seen so far didn't encourage him. They'd pitched in to help secure the gear well enough. But he could tell they were still checking each other out, deciding whether they wanted to trust each other.

"BRUTUS WAS THE GUY POPEYE BEAT UP," SAID BOSTON, in a tone that suggested the conversation should end. "Wally was the hamburger guy."

"You're wrong," said Flash. "It was Bluto."

"It's amazing how grown men can argue about cartoons," said Hera.

"We aren't arguing. We're discussing," said McGowan.

"This is about as intellectual a discussion as those jawbonis can have," said Sugar.

"Who are you calling a jawboni?" said McGowan. "I'm Scots—I don't do jawboni."

"All right," said Boston. Sensing the animosity level starting to rise behind the joking, he decided it was time to act less like a chief and more like a kindergarten teacher. "Who wants ice cream?"

DANNY WORKED OUT A PLAN IN HIS HEAD TO AMBUSH THE men in the Jeep if they went into the camp. But it wasn't necessary. The Jeeps continued up the road without turning off, moving through the hills.

They brought the bus into camp twenty minutes later and began unpacking. The gear seemed to have gained about a thousand pounds in the five miles from the drop. The process dragged as they sorted, stored, and installed. Even Danny grew tired. He kept himself going the last hour or so thinking about Reid's ice cream.

With everything finally squared away a half hour before sunrise, he divided up the watch, then headed to the house and its makeshift kitchen for a prebedtime snack.

Only to find the ice cream gone.

"You always said the troops were the first priority," Boston said when Danny asked for an explanation.

"From now on, they're the first priority on everything *but* ice cream."

13

Sudan desert

THE JEEPS THAT DANNY HAD SEEN DID NOT BELONG TO ONE of the rebel factions. They were actually carrying Bani Aberhadji south to a small village about forty-five miles southeast of the base camp.

The Iranian Guard official was visiting the village, located in the shadow of the hills, as part of his inspection tour. The village was under the control of a Sudan rebel and former regular army officer known as Colonel Zsar. Zsar was a comparatively modest man—he'd been a captain when he deserted the army, and a promotion of only two ranks showed considerable restraint. He couldn't be called humble—a humble man would not have survived here—but he was a devout Shiite Muslim, a minority, if not quite a rarity, in this part of Africa.

Colonel Zsar's force of fighters totaled over five hundred, and when his loose allies farther east were counted, over a thousand. Just as importantly, he was well-armed, with several pickup trucks and even a pair of armored cars supplementing a small-arms arsenal rich in automatic rifles, grenade launchers, and heavy machine guns. Colonel Zsar had a half-dozen light artillery pieces and several heavy mortars. Rumors of these weapons were widespread and one reason the Sudanese army had never attempted even a token appearance in his area of control.

There were several reasons for Colonel Zsar's success. Though not a charismatic leader, he was able to influence followers with a calm and reassuring personal style. Though confident in battle, he did not overreach, choosing battles carefully and, like most of the successful rebels, he avoided major confrontations with regular army soldiers on anything less than overwhelmingly favorable terms.

He also had a strong defensive base to work from, protected by the hills and close to the border. Not only was he far enough from the main centers of government control to make it difficult for them to launch a large attack, he was isolated from most of the other rebels as well.

Like other successful rebels, Colonel Zsar had a steady source of income to pay for his army. But his was unique—the village he controlled was a modest manufacturing center, turning out small wooden and clay bowls, miscellaneous pottery, and wooden shovels. Zsar charged the owners a small tax in exchange for keeping order. Lately he had taken over one of the pottery factories himself, and added two others, both related to agriculture. One skinned cows and occasionally other animals, selling the meat and tanning the hides for use elsewhere. The other processed milk—collecting it and pasteurizing it. By Western standards, the operations were small and primitive. But here they were major sources of employment and veritable economic powerhouses.

It was the economic base that had brought Colonel Zsar to Bani Aberhadji's notice some two years before. And when his emissary in Sudan, Arash Tarid, reported that Zsar was a fellow Shiite, Aberhadji knew he had found the perfect situation.

Tarid was at the wheel of the lead Jeep, driving Bani Aberhadji to the village below Colonel Zsar's fortress headquarters. Colonel Zsar's foray into entrepreneurship had been made possible by Aberhadji's generosity, and he was coming specifically to visit his milk factory.

The colonel had not been notified of the visit. Undoubtedly he would see the Jeeps, realize they belonged to Tarid, and rush to meet them. Aberhadji did wish to see him—the personal touch was important, after all—but first he wanted to see the plant.

"There are no guards?" said the Iranian as they came near the village. It was well-off for Africa, but the ragtag collection of shacklike houses, old huts, and battered trailers and prefabs would have been considered a poor slum in Iran.

"No, they've seen us and recognized the Jeeps," said Tarid. "If they didn't, they would have fired at us by now."

"You're sure of this."

"Yes."

Tarid was not himself comfortable with the level of security, but it was typical among the rebels, even extensive. The lookouts might not even have been awake. But even the most alert would know that two Western-style vehicles did not pose an immediate threat, and intercepting them was far more likely to cause problems than merely watching.

"We have to go through the cow yard," Tarid added. He'd been born and raised in Tehran and had little tolerance for the beasts. "Your boots will be dirty."

"A minor inconvenience."

"Yes, Imam."

Tarid sped up as they neared the village. Here the security was much better, and the lookouts far less likely to be sleeping. Hidden in the rocks above were two watchmen armed with the latest rocket-propelled grenades available from China. Tarid had not only supplied the rockets, but had figured out where they should be placed to provide maximum coverage. They were the first line of defense for the village, meant to give the machine guns nearby ample targets to fire at. Aware of how easy a target he was, he had no desire to linger.

Tarid was roughly the same age as Aberhadji, but anyone looking at the two men would think him a full generation older. Like Aberhadji, he had fought as a teenager in the Iran-Iraq War in the 1980s. But he had been in many more battles, fighting from the very beginning of the conflict to its inconclusive yet bitter end. So many of his friends had died by his side that he often asked Allah, blessed be His name, why he had been spared. Even now he was not sure whether he had been chosen or simply overlooked.

Past the initial lookout points, Tarid hit the brakes and turned into the yard in front of the milk factory, driving past the small sheds toward the barn and processing building at the rear. The two biggest problems for industry anywhere in Africa were power and clean water. Water for the factory, and the rest of the village, came from an underground aquifer at the base of the hills. It was plentiful year-round, and unlike the streams, disease-free.

The village's electricity was not as dependable. It came from two sources: the regional grid, which had power lines running through the area, and a series of diesel engines, scavenged from train locomotives, adapted and used as generators. These were located at the southeastern end of town, near the highway in a fenced lot protected around the clock by Colonel Zsar's best troops. But those sources were not enough for the milk factory; it used two large generators of its own to supplement power. A three-month backup supply of diesel oil from Kenya, paid for by Bani Aberhadji, was stored in a lot behind the farm yard.

A guard peered out from the barn door as the Jeeps drove into the yard.

"Why is he hiding?" said Aberhadji. His voice was soft but his tone reproachful.

"It would be unusual to have a guard watching over the plant," said Tarid. "He is trying to be discreet."

"If that is his goal, he has achieved the opposite. Better to show himself. This makes it look as if he has something to hide."

Tarid avoided arguing with Aberhadji, saying instead that they would have to go through a door at the rear of the building.

"No one challenges us?" Aberhadji asked as they got out of the vehicle.

"The men above and the man here recognize the Jeeps," Tarid repeated. "There are not many vehicles like them in this part of Sudan. They know who I am. To challenge their benefactor would be a great insult."

"They should challenge us," insisted Aberhadji. "For form's sake if nothing else."

Tarid led him around the back of the building. It was difficult for foreigners, especially those who knew the country's history of war, to understand the mores here. Tarid had practically had to install locks on the doors himself. The burglar alarm and closed-circuit video were real novelties.

He put his key in the door, though he knew from experience there was only a fifty percent chance the door was actually locked. Inside, he led Aberhadji down a long corridor toward what looked like a storage area. He paused in front of the restroom, then entered. The light flicked on automatically, powered by a sensor.

At the far end of the bathroom, he opened a closet, revealing an inner door. Tarid pushed it open and stepped inside a narrow hallway that sloped gently downward for about twenty feet. A guard stood at the end of the hall, an AK-47 in his hands.

Tarid nodded at the man, whom he recognized from previous visits. The man stepped back, allowing the two Iranians to pass through a thick metal door anchored in the stone of the hill above.

"Careful of the steps," said Tarid. "The way is not well lit."

The stairs, cut from the rock, ended at a steel mesh walkway, which extended through a natural cave for a good ten yards. Another guard stood on the metal deck near the end of the walk. He, too, was armed with an AK-47, and he too made way for the Iranians.

Beyond the guard was a Sheetrock wall framed with steel studs. The wall was little more than a year old, but already the dampness had eaten into the plaster and lines of mold were starting to appear, black streaks and freckles that popped through the whitewashed surface.

A doorway opened into the room at the right. To gain entrance, Tarid had to ring a bell at the side. A buzzer sounded, and the lock flew back. He pulled the door open, holding it so Aberhadji could enter.

Six men were working at the far side of the room. They were clad in white lab coats. One wore a lead apron and thick rubber gloves. He was using a large set of prongs to remove a small jar from what looked like an oversized metal oven.

The oven was part of a centrifuge assembly. Aberhadji had arrived at an opportune time— the plant had just received a piece of yellowcake uranium and begun processing it. Ordinarily the facility would be empty at this time of day.

"We should not get much closer," said Tarid, holding Aberhadji back. "The material is highly toxic. If there is an accident, breathing it would be dangerous."

In its present state, the refined uranium was not nearly as dangerous as Tarid believed. Nor was it quite pure enough for its ultimate purpose. That would be completed at the next stage of its processing, in a factory in lower Kenya also funded and controlled by Aberhadji. But Aberhadji had no need to go any farther. He had seen all that he wanted to see.

"They work as soon as a shipment comes," said Tarid. "The work is done in a few days now. Then they relax, until the next one."

Aberhadji nodded. He was extremely pleased.

"Let us say hello to Colonel Zsa't," he told Tarid. "Then we must go. I have much to do."

14

Base Camp Alpha
Sudan

THE FIRST ORDER OF BUSINESS FOR DANNY AND THE OTHERS at the fake dinosaur dig was to prepare in case Red Henri or the Sudanese army decided to pay another visit. To do that, defense and intelligence had to be strengthened.

The first was accomplished by mounting several automated weapons around the perimeter. Bullet panels and mines were deployed along the road and hooked to a central control station at the house, a small laptop computer. The bullet panels, first developed by the Dreamland weapons team a decade before, were literally that—panels with projectiles that could be individually fired, or launched en masse at an enemy. As originally conceived, the weapon was nonlethal, intended for crowd control. These panels, however, fired the equivalent of magnum rounds, each capable of stopping a 300 pound man and piercing all but the newest body armor. Boston described them to Sugar as "claymores on steroids."

The mines were meant to make it harder for anyone to launch a flank attack. They were fused to miniature motion detectors, which could be focused by command on specific areas, providing wide or narrow field protection. They could be detonated by radio as well, and included a fail-safe protection circuit "tuned" to the rings the Whiplash members wore. This prevented a Whiplash team member from setting off the mines accidentally—though no one wanted to personally test the circuitry. The mines could also be turned off and on from the central command station.

The rest of the team's firepower was more traditional. They had a half-dozen AK-47s, common weapons in the area, and indeed the world, despite their age. But they also had two heavy machine guns: XM-312s, which fired .50 caliber rounds. The 312s had recently replaced the M2, a machine gun that had

seen service in the U.S. Army longer than any of its operators
had been alive. Among the newer weapon's advantages was its
weight; at forty-two pounds it was about a third as heavy as a
"Ma Two," far easier for a single man to lug.

Each member of the team was also equipped with SCAR-
H/MK 17 assault rifles, originally developed by the U.S. Special Operations Command. There were two versions of the
SCAR, one "light," one "heavy." The MK-17 was the heavy
version, firing a 7.62mm round rather than a 5.56. Most of
the team members, like many soldiers in the field, preferred
the stopping power of the heavier round, though that limited the guns to magazines that contained twenty rounds, ten
less than the lighter caliber. The difference didn't sound like
much, until the middle of a firefight.

The Global Hawk that had been detailed to the team the
night before had gone on to other assignments. In its place,
Danny launched a pair of small hydrogen blimps outfitted
with LED technology that made them almost invisible to the
naked eye. These were the direct descendants of much larger
stationary radar ships developed at Dreamland. They had
to be tethered to the ground and could not be maneuvered,
but together they provided a view that extended roughly fifty
miles around the post.

As a side benefit, the blimps also lofted radio antennas
connected to radio scanners, identifying transmissions in the
area. The frequencies were then transmitted to a National Security Agency network, making it easier for the cyber spies to
sift through the literally billions of satellite transmissions it
monitored and identify the rebels' for decrypting. While the
NSA had started a program to pick off transmissions in the
region a week before, the rebels were sophisticated enough to
change satcoms, frequencies, and encryption methods often
enough to make tagging them a laborious process. The scanners didn't make it instantaneous or foolproof, but the difference was significant.

Short-term reconnaissance of areas far from the camp
could be provided by "Owl" UAVs. These aircraft, with a

wingspan the size of Boston's thick hand, had low-noise engines powered by a bank of batteries and solar electric panels on the top wing. They had two drawbacks: their bodies were black, making them nearly invisible at night, but not during the day, and a relatively limited flight time; in general they could be depended on to stay aloft for roughly four hours. The actual time depended on the wind and other conditions, and in practice most tended to last twice as long, especially when the sun could help provide the charge.

THERE WERE THREE REBEL CAMPS IN THE REGION THAT HAD had dealings with Jasmine. Nuri had scouted them all but not yet bugged them. With the defenses shaping up, it was time to start. He chose as his first target the village controlled by a rebel named Tura Dpap, sixty-two miles southwest of Base Camp Alpha. He saw it as a relatively straightforward job.

Danny wasn't so sure. The village straddled a highway, the only road in or out. Both the northern and southern sides were watched by men in sandbagged positions who stopped any vehicle coming or going, demanding a small "tribute" or tax. They were heavily armed. The satellite photo showed two RPG launchers in the northern post, and it was reasonable to guess that the southern post would have the same.

"There's no way we can get enough firepower down past these guys if there's a problem," said Danny as they reviewed the photos on the table in the "kitchen" and command center they'd established in the roofless building. "That open plain on the north and the hills to the south make it impossible to flank them."

"It's not a military operation, Colonel," said Nuri. He chafed at Danny's objections even more than his mind-set. He'd been on his own long enough now that explaining what he was going to do felt like rolling a heavy rock up a hill. "This isn't an attack. It's the opposite. We're trying to find someone and follow him. If we have to fight, we've already failed."

"I appreciate that. I'm just worried about you getting in trouble. Like the other night."

"That worked out fine, didn't it? That's the way it goes sometimes. You gotta take risks. That's the game."

Nuri got up to refill his coffee cup from the pot on the camp stove at the side. The coffee was bitter and burnt.

"Someone should go in with you to help cover your back," said Danny.

Nuri didn't think that was necessary, but it wasn't worth arguing about. "I'll take Hera," he said. He didn't know her well at all, but she was fellow CIA, could speak Arabic, and most important, was good-looking. "We'll go looking for supplies. It should only take us a few hours."

"Fine," said Danny.

"Don't forget we're supposed to be setting up a dig here," said Nuri. "That has to be laid out as soon as possible."

"I didn't forget." Danny didn't like the edge in Nuri's voice, but he let it pass.

NURI DECIDED IT WAS WISER TO TAKE THE BUS INTO THE village, since it would be more in keeping with the cover story of scientists bumbling their way through unfamiliar territory. This was just fine with Abul, who was chafing at the way Danny and the others were treating him. Even though Nuri had vouched for him, Danny insisted on keeping Abul away from the high-tech gear. With the monitoring station set up in the house, it meant he couldn't go inside to eat.

Hera dressed in a pair of very baggy pants and a pair of man-style shirts, along with hiking boots and a black cap whose peak hid much of her face. Her intent was to appear drab and boring, but Nuri thought she looked like the most beautiful woman he had ever seen.

The only problem with her outfit was her unusual accessory—a SCAR rifle. Nuri had his hideaway strapped to his calf, hidden by his long pants. It was the only weapon he planned on bringing.

Hera had other plans.

"You can't bring the rifle," he told her as she slung the SCAR over her shoulder.

"Why not?"

"Because they may inspect the bus. How many paleontologists go around with military rifles?"

"At least one," said Hera. "Me."

"You can bring an AK."

"That's an old piece of garbage."

"It works."

"Excuse me," said Abul, "but if you want my opinion—"

"We don't," snapped Hera.

"I do," said Nuri.

"It's more dangerous to be armed," said the bus driver. "The movement has been pretty benign toward westerners."

"Benign?" said Hera. "Like Red Henri?"

"I've carried the rifle with me on the bike the whole week," said Nuri.

"I would wager that it has attracted much attention. When people see it, they immediately are on their guard."

"We can't go without protection," said Hera. "That'd be nuts."

"You can hide the guns inside the seats," suggested Flash, who was nearby, listening to the conversation. "Cut holes in them."

"You cannot cut into my seats," protested Abul.

Nuri thought this was just a bargaining position, but the bus driver/owner turned out to be almost fanatically dedicated to preserving the interior of his bus; the most he would allow were slits in the underside big enough to hide ammunition. Looking over the interior, Nuri realized he could hide two SCAR rifles in the space beneath the dashboard, as long as the guts of the blower were removed. This meant doing without the air-conditioning, which hadn't worked all that well to begin with.

"This is a driving inferno," complained Hera as they drove south. "A slow one, too."

Nuri shrugged. He was beginning to regret choosing her to come along.

"The breeze is very pleasant," said Abul. "Imagine if we were in the desert instead of the hills."

"There's plenty of desert around."

"No, no, no. This isn't desert. This is the very nice part of the Sudan."

"It's lovely."

"There is much water the further south we go. Swamps."

"Just like New Jersey."

She meant it as an insult, but since Abul had never been to New Jersey—and in fact didn't know where it was—he took it as a compliment.

The rebel soldiers who guarded the village approach during the day flagged down the bus with the professional boredom of conductors taking tickets on a morning commuter train. One came aboard, glanced at Nuri and Hera, then told Abul that the tax was ten dollars American to pass.

"Ten dollars?" said Nuri in Arabic. "Why so much?"

The soldier glanced at him, reassessing his appearance. He was dressed like a European. More than likely he was one, but if he wasn't, he should be taxed like one for trying to ape them.

And the woman was also foreign.

"Ten," the soldier told Abul.

"Ten dollars is five times what most vehicles pay," insisted Nuri.

At fifteen years old, the soldier had been with the rebels for nearly eight years. This made him a veteran and, by seniority, an NCO. He did not like to be questioned.

Abul, starting to get nervous, asked diplomatically if the tax had recently been raised.

"That is always what it is," said the soldier.

"It was less a week ago," said Nuri. "You think we are rich, so you can charge what you want."

"You are to pay or turn around," the soldier told Abul.

"Tell him if we pay ten dollars, we expect that to cover our return trip," Nuri told Abul in English.

Doubtful that the deal would be accepted, Abul nonetheless made the offer. The soldier surprised him, saying that was acceptable.

"I doubt they'll keep the deal," said Abul.

"They'll keep it," said Nuri.

He pulled the bill from his pocket, held it up, then tore it in half.

"You will get the other half when we come back," he said, passing the bill to Abul.

Abul took it and held it out toward the soldier the way a man might hold a steak out to a tiger. The soldier's eyes flashed with anger, but then he smiled.

"You are very clever," he told Nuri. "Very clever."

"You're pretty clever yourself, Captain."

"Only a sergeant," said the young man. He smiled at him—a broad smile that revealed he was missing two teeth—then left the bus.

"Why did you dicker with them?" Hera asked Nuri as Abul pushed the bus forward. "You were only pissing him off."

"No, I was telling them not to screw with me."

"They had the guns, we didn't. If you made him too mad, they'd shoot us."

"You don't understand the psychology," Nuri told her. "Ten dollars is a huge amount of money. When I came through on my motorcycle, they charged me the equivalent of a quarter, and in the local currency. If we gave in right away, then they would think we had a lot of money. And if we have a lot of money, then we should give them more. They feel if they are the stronger ones, they deserve it."

"All you did was piss them off," said Hera. "If you wanted to show them you were strong, you wouldn't have paid anything."

"That wouldn't have been fair—and might have gotten us all killed."

Hera rolled her eyes.

Roughly five thousand people lived in the village, their numbers swelling it in size to a small city. Most were crammed into ramshackle buildings made from scraps and gathered into distinct hamlets on either side of the highway, which ran through the center of town. About seventy percent were families of guerrillas, and most were related to each other. The faction was a small player in Sudan's revolt, unable to project power much beyond the immediate area, though they had launched occasional forays against the army farther north. The villagers survived on subsistence farming, though their yields had faltered over the past few years, as the nutrients in the soil were not replaced. The situation was similar to that in western Sudan, where steady soil erosion encouraged desertification, which then made it impossible for the people to survive.

Tura Dpap, the village and rebel leader, was an elder in the tribe whose people made up the bulk of the population. He was well-liked, generally called "Uncle" by his followers— many of whom were, at different removes, his actual nieces and nephews. Unusual for the rebel movements, he was an older man, well into his fifties. He had also never married, equally unusual.

The village centered around a church building that had been founded and then abandoned by missionaries nearly a hundred years before. Uncle Dpap had taken over the building and repaired it, painting it bright yellow, a color that had come to be associated with his movement. There was no steeple, but the roof and the cross-shaped facade made its history clear.

The two buildings next to it were used by Dpap and his closest advisors as homes, sheltering not only them and their families, but bodyguards and younger soldiers with no families and nowhere else to stay. Directly across the street were three small stores and a restaurant. The buildings dated from roughly the same time as the church, and had suffered through several cycles of disregard and repair, but were the sturdiest structures around.

Rebel soldiers, most of them in their early teens, milled around the center of town. Every one of them had a rifle;

many wore ropes around their neck with ammo magazines taped to them.

Though she'd seen boy soldiers and worse conditions in Somalia, Hera was appalled by how young the kids were. Some would have been in only third or fourth grade in the States.

"We're taking our pistols with us," she said, slipping her hand under the seat in front of her.

"We don't need them," insisted Nuri. But he didn't stop her from taking one.

The video bugs Nuri was planting were bigger than the ones he normally used. About the size of a quarter in diameter and three quarters thick, the size was a function of the batteries they contained, which would allow them to transmit for as long as six days. They would transmit to a small booster unit a half mile away; the booster would send the signals to the Voice's satellite system.

As he stepped from the bus, Nuri put a piece of gum in his mouth. The gum was the adhesive that held the bug in place. The size of the bugs made them relatively easy to spot, and thus harder to place than the ones he normally worked with. He walked over to the stores, then stopped, as if he couldn't decide which one to go into first. He was actually looking over the facade to see if there was a place to hide the bugs.

He couldn't find a good spot offhand, and with the soldiers watching, decided to move inside the middle building. Hera followed.

A year before, she had been assigned to visit a resistance movement in northern Tibet, living in the mountains for several months as she gauged the seriousness and strength of the movements that were opposed to the central Chinese government. She had not been impressed. The so-called rebels lacked focus and organization. The group here, with the ability to run its own stores, seemed light-years ahead.

Which wasn't saying much.

There were only men in the store. All fixed their eyes on her as she came in, following her as she walked behind Nuri and glanced at the mostly empty shelves. A radio tuned to the government music station played a mix of European techno and African music, the beats changing violently from song to song. The floor vibrated lightly to the music.

Nuri went to the shopkeeper, who worked behind a counter with a small cash box as his register.

"Nuri Abaajmed," he said enthusiastically in Arabic, reaching out his hand. "I am a professor of paleontology at the University of Wisconsin, America."

The word "America" got everyone's attention. The man's smile showed he had about half his teeth. Nuri told him about the scientific expedition "up the road." The shopkeeper told him he could speak English, which he promptly demonstrated.

"Honor to me a visitor here," he said, spreading his arms in a gesture of friendship.

"We need a few supplies," said Nuri in English. The man clearly didn't understand, and he switched back to Arabic. "We could use some blankets, water, and perhaps fruit. Do you have fruit?"

"Usually, we have much fruit, but just now we are out of it. The customers liked it very much," said the shopkeeper.

Fruit was in fact a rarity. The store had had a few dates some months back, but it had taken weeks to sell them, mostly because he priced them so high the soldiers couldn't afford them.

"But here—-beans we have." The man took Nuri around to an aisle and showed him several cans, which had apparently come to Africa as part of a church donation in the distant past. The dust on them could have filled a good-sized litter box. Nuri took one, then a second.

Glancing around the shop, he thought the best place to slip a bug in would be near the window, but two soldiers were using the low ledge as a seat.

Then he had a better idea—the roof.

"Do you have a restroom?" he asked, handing the African his cans.

The shopkeeper showed him through the crowded back storeroom to a cordoned-off corner, where a round hole had been cut in the floorboards for a latrine pit.

"I'd need some paper," said Nuri, glancing around.

The man pointed to some folded yellow sheets, then gave him another toothless smile.

"I'll be done as soon as I can," said Nuri when the man made no sign of moving away. "If you could look after my friend. She's new to the country."

The grin widened at the suggestion. "Yes, yes," said the man, and he disappeared into the front.

Nuri had hoped for a back door, but saw none. There was a window, though, next to the hole in the floor. He pushed at the sash but it wouldn't budge.

The stench from the hole was overwhelming. He held his breath and tried pushing up again. The window still wouldn't move.

He was about to give up and go back inside when he realized the bottom frame was held in place by a painted bolt through the side. The bolt was on a spring that held it closed, but was easily pulled from the hole. He pushed the window upward, but could get it only about halfway open.

Squeezing his shoulders, he pushed his upper body through the space and glanced up and down the narrow alley. When he saw no one watching, he pulled himself all the way out, then stepped up on the sill and climbed onto the roof by gripping the overhang.

It pitched on a very gentle slope up toward the front of the building, saltbox style. The radio was playing loud enough for him to hear, but Nuri knew he couldn't count on it to mask too much noise. He kept his head down and slipped out two bugs, mounting them to cover the church building. Then he began moving backward, holding his breath.

He was only a few feet from the edge of the roof when the music below abruptly stopped.

Nuri froze. Someone had come into the building and was

talking very loudly—yelling about something, though the words were difficult to decipher.

THE MAN WHO HAD COME INTO THE STORE WAS UNCLE Dpap's brother, Commander John, the leader's volatile aide-de-camp. He had seen the bus out front and wanted to know who was in town. He wasn't yelling out of anger or alarm—Commander John always spoke in a very loud voice. He was a large man, so large in fact that he couldn't fit comfortably between the aisles of the store.

Commander John spoke in the tribal language, and Hera had no idea what he was saying. But when he started toward the back, she knew she had to intercept him. So she walked around the side and yelled at him, introducing herself in English and then slightly rusty Arabic as Professor Hera Scokas.

Commander John considered himself a connoisseur of women. Unlike his brother, he had three wives and more mistresses than even he could keep track of. Hera looked to him like a woman worth giving up all the others for.

Hera recognized the way his pupils dilated.

Commander John told her in slangy Arabic that he was happy to make her acquaintance and she should see more of him. Sensing she didn't understand his words, he took her hand in both of his and kissed it.

Hera gently pushed him back and began speaking loudly about the work she was doing. Commander John nodded politely, even though her accent made her words hard to decipher.

He truly had not seen such a beautiful woman in all his life. Ordinarily he didn't care for white women; most were too pale and frail in his eyes. But this one had sparkle. She would make an excellent wife.

Commander John pressed in closer. Hera edged back slightly, keeping her voice loud and willing Nuri to appear.

*   *   *

NURI WAS ALMOST DIRECTLY ABOVE HER, JUST A FEW FEET from the edge of the roof. But as he pushed his foot over to get down, two soldiers came into the alley, leaning against the building to share a cigarette.

He considered crawling to the other side of the roof but stopped when the Voice, translating what it could hear of the soldiers' conversation, told him that they were complaining about rumors they'd heard that Uncle Dpap was trying to forge an alliance with Red Henri and another rebel leader, Colonel Zsar. The alliance would never work, one of the men said, because everyone knew Red Henri was crazy and Zsar was in league with foreigners.

Nuri took the reference to the foreigners to mean the Iranians.

The man kept talking, complaining about their lack of action and their dwindling supply of ammunition. Many of the ammo boxes the soldiers carried on their neck ropes were empty, and there were no reserves at the main storeroom.

This was fresh intelligence, and Nuri was happy to sop it up. But the conversation soon changed to concerns shared by fighting men the world over: they wondered when the next chance would be for sex.

Nuri assumed there would be plenty of opportunities in a village, but he was wrong—most of the women were married, and the daughters were watched carefully by men with guns. As limited as their bullets might be, there were always enough to protect the family honor.

Finally the men were called out to the road by a friend. Nuri slipped to the back of the building, made sure no one was nearby, then dropped down and went around to the window.

Which had slid back closed and locked while he'd been on the roof.

HERA HAD DEALT WITH COMMANDER JOHN TYPES BEFORE, most often by putting her knee where it would do a world of good. But there were too many soldiers nearby for that approach, so she smiled and moved to the side as he continued to serenade her with words about how lovely she was.

His hand on her shoulder was too much, however. She pushed it off, smiled sarcastically at him, and started walking toward the front of the store.

Two of his men were standing in the aisle near the doorway. Hera lifted her head, raising her frame to its entire five feet two inches.

"Get out of my way," she said.

Her words were in English, but her tone was universal. The men glanced over her head at their boss, who smiled and signaled that they should close ranks and not let her out. But the men weren't quick enough—Hera pushed through like a halfback zipping into the gap between the nose guard and tackle.

One of the men swung around, reaching for her shoulder.

She began to duck and spin—the prelude to a rather nasty Krav Maga move that would have cost the young man his kneecap. Fortunately for the rebel, Nuri appeared in the front doorway, a big smile on his face.

"See anything you like?" he asked loudly.

"Time to go," said Hera.

Nuri was ready to agree when he saw Commander John. He'd never met the rebel officer, but the man's large frame made him easy to recognize. He stepped forward and held out his hand.

"Very pleased to meet you," Nuri said, the Arabic rolling fast and thick off his tongue. "Very pleased. Very, very pleased. I am Dr. Abaajmed. We are digging dinosaurs. Ancient history in your backyard."

Commander John shook his hand limply. He had no idea what dinosaurs were. To him, a doctor was someone who gave you pills or a shot when you were sick, and he wasn't feeling ill right now.

"We came into town for some supplies," continued Nuri. "We will be here for several weeks, maybe months. We will make you famous."

"Nice."

"That's a nice old church across the way," said Nuri. "Is the minister around?"

"What minister?" asked Commander John.

"That's not a church?"

"It is an office."

"I see. Who works there?"

The questions were starting to annoy Commander John. He shrugged.

"Does Uncle Dpap work there?" asked Nuri.

"Yes," said Commander John, suspicious that a foreigner, even one who could speak Arabic like an Egyptian, would know of Uncle Dpap.

"We have been told that Commander Dpap is a very important person here," said Nuri. "We would be honored to pay our respects."

Commander John glanced over at Hera, and decided that he could use the doctor to get a chance to spend time with the woman, who surely would fall under his charms if he had a little more time.

"Uncle Dpap is my brother," he said. "I will take you to meet him."

"Nothing would please me more," said Nuri.

15

Pentagon
Washington, D.C.

"TEN MINUTES UNTIL YOUR MEETING WITH THE ADMIRAL, Ms. Stockard."

"Thank you, Ms. Bennett."

Breanna Stockard tapped the interphone button and went

back to reviewing the Excel file on her computer. The rows of numbers——some bold, some highlighted, some in different colors—purported to show the cost effectiveness of a new shipboard cannon the Navy was angling for. But the numbers couldn't demonstrate the real need for the weapon or, even more important, whether it would truly function as designed—and how long it would take to become operational. Those were the real questions when it came to new technology. The answers were almost always guesses—sometimes very good ones, but still guesses. Breanna's office wasn't developing the gun itself—a private contractor had been working on it for several years——but she had to give a report that would either help the admiral's quest to win more funding or help kill the project. Her staff was divided, as were many of the people in the Navy.

As important as the issue was, Breanna couldn't seem to focus on it, even with the admiral on his way over. She kept thinking about Danny and Whiplash in Africa.

Danny checked in twice a day, either by secure satellite phone or text message. She could have gone over to Room 4 at Langley, plug into the MY-PID network, and find out what was going on, but she resisted. It wasn't her job to watch over every little decision Danny made, or to ride on the team's shoulder as it went in battle. That was the whole point of MY-PID—it was a tool to help the people in the field, not to shepherd them.

She didn't want to tell them how to do their job. But she was worried about them, even though she knew she shouldn't be. She found it difficult to remove her emotions from the op, separate herself from the people.

The intercom buzzed

"Ms. Stockard, the admiral has arrived early," said Ms. Bennett with the slightest hint of annoyance.

Breanna glanced quickly at the small mirror she kept under the computer monitor, checking her makeup.

"Please send him in," she said, rising to greet him.

16

Jabal Dugu, Sudan

NURI PUT HIS HAND INTO HIS POCKET, SLIPPING HIS FINGERS around one of the video bugs as he followed Commander John's men into the building. It would be risky to bug the headquarters—but well worth it.

"Come," said Commander John, looking at Hera as he spoke. "My brother is always at his desk. He will be very pleased to meet distinguished visitors."

The pews, altar, and other religious items had been removed from the church years before. A few chairs and small tables formed different islands in the interior, but for the most part the space was filled with bundles of clothes and bags of rice and other supplies, which shaped half walls and low partitions. Three overhead fans pushed warm, stagnant air around the room. Sticky no-pest fly strips, the type outlawed in the U.S. for environmental and safety reasons years before, hung from the rafters, occasionally snapping in the fans' breeze. A scent of sweat mixed with something sharp like cinnamon and dust.

Four of Uncle Dpap's aides were sitting on chairs on the right side of the building. They looked up when Nuri entered, but went back to talking among themselves when they saw Commander John.

The floor of the chancel was raised about a foot higher than the nave, and it was here that Uncle Dpap had his desk. Six young soldiers sat on the floor nearby, their rifles either in their laps or next to them.

Uncle Dpap was speaking on a satellite phone. His smooth, almost polished forehead extended into a bald scalp; his face looked babylike despite his age, which was fifty-five. No flaw or blemish marked his deep black skin. He frowned as the conversation continued, yet looked serene, a father confident of his place in the world, and of his progeny's place as well.

Nuri spotted a perfect place for the bug, on the side of a filing cabinet near a cluster of rolled-up, dusty maps. He popped a piece of gum in his mouth and began chewing furiously.

"We will wait," said Commander John. He looked at Nuri. "You have a piece for me?"

"Sure," said Nuri. He reached into his pocket for the package. It was going to taste like cardboard, but it was useless to explain that.

Commander John took the entire package, slipped a piece out, then pocketed the rest. Nuri raised his hand to ask for the gum back, but Commander John ignored him.

"Tilia, translate for me," he told a young woman at a desk behind Uncle Dpap. "We have an important visitor and must impress them."

Tilia got up slowly and walked over.

"She will help with my English," Commander John told Hera. He understood her Arabic well enough despite her accent, but having a translator brought prestige, and the whole point of the visit was to impress her. Besides, Tilia could translate from the village language, which was less arduous to speak.

"Look at this map," Commander John told Hera, taking her elbow and steering her to the far wall. "This is the area where our people live. Our ancestors toiled in this area for many years."

Tilia translated dutifully. Her English was close to flawless; she had lived in England as a child and returned there for college. She had joined Uncle Dpap, to whom she was distantly related, after her parents were killed by Sudan government troops.

"There were lions in the foothills once. My people chased them away. Ferocious lions," Commander John told Hera, emphasizing the word "ferocious" as if there might be some doubt. "There are stories—true or not, I do not know—of people facing them with just their bare hands."

"She won't believe that," said Tilia, who didn't believe it herself.

"I said, I am not sure it is true. Tell her."

Tilia knew Commander John was trying to impress the woman, and also knew that he would fail. He was constantly on the make—any female new to the village, African, European, got his attention, until he bedded her or she left the village. Tilia herself had only been spared his advances because Commander John suspected his brother was sleeping with her, an impression Tilia encouraged, though she was not.

Nuri, meanwhile, walked casually across the room and, after a quick, surreptitious glance, ducked down to tie his shoe . . . and plant the bug.

At times like this, just after placing a bug, there was often a moment of doubt, a dread certainty that he had been seen. That fear seized him as he rose, and for a second he found himself dizzy. Blood rushed from his head. His muscles tensed, ready to fight.

Nuri forced himself to breathe slowly. One breath, two . . . there were no explosions, no accusations, no one grabbing him by the neck and dragging him away.

See, he told himself. *Nothing to worry about. The only thing we have to fear is fear itself.*

Nuri turned and walked toward the center of the room. As his apprehension receded, a low-grade euphoria swept into its place, encouraging him that he could do practically anything. If his dread had been misplaced, so was this optimism, and he tried to tamp it down, folding his arms and feigning interest in the map Commander John was using for his pseudo-history lesson.

Uncle Dpap was still on the phone. He was pleading with a man in South Africa to send him ammunition—his troops had only a few hundred rounds, hardly enough to defend themselves, let alone launch an assault. The South African claimed he did not have any ammunition for sale, and refused Uncle Dpap's efforts to persuade him to find some.

The tidbit of conversation was invaluable to Nuri. For one thing, it practically eliminated the possibility that Luo had been killed by a competitor: anyone that motivated would have already made his pitch to replace him.

Confident that the bug was picking up the conversation, Nuri turned his attention to Tilia, who was frowning deeply as she translated. She'd be a perfect target to be turned as a spy, he realized: well-placed, intelligent, with a small taste for expensive things, if her rings and watch were any indication.

He smiled at her. She didn't notice.

When Uncle Dpap finally got off the phone, he called Commander John over for an explanation. The African's face lit up and his chest swelled. He put his hand around Hera and introduced her.

Nuri decided it was time to deflate some of the rebel commander's interest, if not his lust. "This is my wife," he said, putting his arm around Hera's shoulder from the other side. "We work together."

Commander John frowned. He had no qualms about cuckolding a man, especially a westerner who had strange ideas about bones. But clearly he would get no further with Hera while Nuri was around.

On the other hand, it explained her strange attitude toward him. Clearly, he thought, she would return his smiles if her husband was out of the way.

Uncle Dpap, though annoyed at the interruption and preoccupied by his supply problems, managed to feign some interest in the scientists. The discovery of large monsters on nearby land would not surprise him, he said; many tales told of fierce creatures who held sway before the land was tamed.

Then he let the conversation lag. He had many things to do.

"Well, thank you, Your Excellency, for taking the time to meet us," said Nuri. "You must come and visit sometime."

"Your camp is in Red Henri's territory," said Uncle Dpap. "I think we'll leave it to him."

"I see."

"These things are not something for you to be involved in,

or concerned about," said Commander John. "If there is a conflict, you should come to me."

"Yes," said Nuri. "But we wouldn't want to be involved. Good-bye."

ABUL HAD WAITED ON THE BUS, SURE IT WOULD BE STRIPPED clean if he left it. Nearly a dozen boy soldiers leaned against it, sheltering themselves from the sun while they chattered in high-pitched voices.

Nuri and Hera came down the steps, practically running. Hera went straight to the bus, but Nuri went back into the store—he wanted to preserve the cover story that they had come to town for supplies.

If the storekeeper was puzzled by his earlier disappearance from the bathroom, he didn't mention it. Nuri bought some canned food, overpaying just enough to make the shopkeeper look forward to his return.

"Let's go," Nuri hissed under his voice as he hustled up the steps into the bus. "Go."

Abul started the engine and leaned out the window to scoot the soldiers away. They didn't respond until he put the bus in gear. Even then they seemed barely to notice, edging off the bus as it slowly moved forward.

"Go back the way we came," Nuri told him.

"I know."

Abul turned around at the side of a wide lot beyond the center of town, giving his passengers a good view of one of the shantytowns where the bulk of Uncle Dpap's followers stayed. The street was so narrow he had to maneuver back and forth several times before finally managing to get in the proper direction.

"They're looking for ammunition," Nuri told Hera. "That's interesting."

"He told you that?"

"No, I overheard him."

"Why did you tell him I was your wife?"

"That was just to get Commander John to stop leering. I wanted us to be able to get the hell out of there."

"You're an ass." Hera put her head back against the seat. "If we had taken our rifles, no one would have messed with us."

"We're undercover. Scientists don't carry rifles."

"They've never seen scientists before. Everyone goes around with guns."

"It would have put them much more on their guard." Nuri blistered. "Listen, I've been out here a lot longer than you have."

"I've been in Sudan before, Nuri."

"Not here."

"Darfur was worse than this."

At the front of the bus, Abul did his best to pretend he wasn't hearing their argument. He stopped at the checkpoint and gave the soldier the second half of the ten dollar bill. Then he headed back toward Base Camp Alpha, happy to be out of the rebel village. Becoming a millionaire, he decided, was a dangerous business.

17

Gambella, Ethiopia

"How do you feel about evolving into the lowest form of life on earth?" Nuri asked Danny when he returned to camp.

Danny didn't know quite what to say. "If it'll help the mission," he answered finally.

"Good. We'll leave for Ethiopia with Abul before first light. The rest of the team can watch the store while we're gone."

*   *   *

TO NURI, CERTAIN CITIES VIBRATED A CERTAIN WAY, AS IF THE sounds and movement of the people within them set off a resonance in the earth beneath the streets. Some vibrated with danger, others excitement, still more with fear.

Gambella, in Ethiopia, combined all three.

Nuri had first come to Gambella barely a year earlier, but its rhythm touched something at his core, and he felt at home there, with or without the Voice's turn by turn directions to guide him through the back alleys of the old city's bazaar. The Voice's directions helped immensely, however. The jumble of streets and pathways, mostly empty a year before, were packed now, populated by a menagerie of shops and merchants, legitimate and otherwise.

There were far more of the latter than the former. Ethiopia had become a nexus for eastern Africa, a relatively stable oasis in a cauldron of trouble. Gambella, in turn, profited greatly from its neighbors' woes. Poor for years, the country's ethos held that any business was good business; Gambella's particular interpretation of that philosophy meant it was possible to buy almost anything here, including people.

"Left. The stall is in the middle of the block," said the Voice.

Nuri walked briskly, brushing past a man trying to sell watches. They were counterfeit Rolexes, of high enough quality that they would have passed muster even in Switzerland.

Shady dealers aside, the city reminded Danny of Istanbul in Turkey. It had the same otherworldly feel, and the same wide range of languages spoken in its streets. People hustled here, literally and figuratively, trying to get ahead.

"Just follow my lead," whispered Nuri, slowing his pace as he came near the shop he'd been seeking. "And don't show your gun unless absolutely necessary."

Danny glanced around. He wasn't just looking for a potential enemy, but trying to gauge how the others on the street saw them. A black man in Western clothes trailing a man of indeterminate race—Nuri would be taken for Egyptian here—they would be seen as businessmen rather than tourists. Strangers with purpose.

It occurred to Danny that the spy was adept at seeming to be whatever anyone wanted him to be. His baggy pants were similar to what the Ethiopians standing in the doorways of the shops wore. His beard, two weeks old, made him look Muslim. Nuri's skin wasn't as dark as his, but Danny had no doubt that of the two of them, he was the one more likely to be regarded with suspicion.

"Toroque!" exclaimed Nuri, spotting the owner of the stall he'd come to find. He used English, which was the language of commerce here, and second nature to most of the people on the street. "You're here. Very good."

Toroque squinted, as if trying to remember the face. He pretended to recognize it and smiled. In truth, Toroque's memory for faces was as poor as any man's on the planet. As the local saying went, he might have forgotten his own had he not seen it in a mirror every day.

"And what can I do for you today?" he asked.

"Much, I hope. My friend and I are looking for a vehicle. A special vehicle."

Toroque frowned, as was his habit when a profitable deal presented itself. "Special vehicle?" He shook his head. "No. Here there are no special vehicles. I know of a motorcycle perhaps."

"Oh." Nuri had played this game once before with Toroque. "Well, too bad then."

"But maybe if you explain to me what you need," added Toroque quickly, "then maybe I can be of aid if I hear of something."

"I need something very special to drive, for an important person. Something big. Very unique."

"No, no." Torque shook his head. "No. No."

Nuri nodded and put out his hand to shake. "Thank you," he said. "Maybe in the future . . . if you . . ."

He ended his sentence there, his voice trailing off as he turned to Danny.

"What sort of thing—my English is not very good," said Toroque, who had been awarded a medal for his English studies in elementary school. "What are you looking for? An SUV?"

"An SUV might do," said Nuri.

"Ah, too bad. I know a Land Rover."

"Too plain," said Nuri dismissively. He would settle for it if he had to.

"Yes, yes, of course." Toroque now began to worry. He had already begun counting the profit from this deal, and it was escaping him.

"The SUV is a Mercedes, maybe?" suggested Nuri. "Or for that matter, do you know of a Mercedes sedan? That would be excellent."

Toroque frowned. There were very few Mercedes in this part of Africa. Not only were they highly impractical, but the recent boom in Russia and China had encouraged the northern Africans who specialized in stealing the cars from Western Europe to ship their wares there. Few made it this far east, and the prices were necessarily exorbitant.

"I know of a sedan," said Toroque. "I can take you to see it. But it is a Toyota."

Nuri raised his hand in assent.

"Perhaps some tea first," suggested Toroque. "And a smoke."

"We have many things to do today," said Danny.

Toroque frowned. It was common here to sit with a salesman for a while. It was considered good manners, and generally improved the price. Nuri glared at Danny, but there was nothing to do about it: Toroque turned quickly and walked into his shop, practically sprinting past the two small tables of dusty knickknacks to the back room. He walked past his cluttered desk, plucking the keys to his pickup truck from the corner as he passed. He slapped the frame of the back door— it always stuck—then turned the knob and opened it. Outside, he had to shoo away some of his neighbor's chickens from the truck bed before they could proceed.

Danny realized he'd made a mistake and remained silent

as they drove down the narrow byroads of the central market area. Kids played in the dust, kicking stones around in their approximation of soccer. They were dressed in little more than rags, and all were shoeless.

The neighborhood changed quickly. On one block, small buildings leaned against each other, as if they were made of wax and had melted under the unrelenting sun. On the next, tall walls tipped with razor wire and pieces of sharpened glass rose along the pavement, protecting the homeowners from the noise and possibility of kidnapping.

And then the area changed again, the walls and houses giving way to tall chain-link fences and steel-sided warehouse buildings.

"We are almost there," said Toroque. He already knew the Toyota was not going to be acceptable—the fender was bashed and it barely ran—but he hoped an alternative would occur to him. Perhaps they would settle for one of the pickups he had.

"This vehicle, you know, is for sale," he said. "For a very good price, I could give it to you."

"It is very nice," said Nuri. "But not really what we're looking for."

"A little paint—I have a brother-in-law who could paint this very nice."

"Let's see the Toyota."

They did, and it was just as Toroque had expected—too old, too undependable, and too small besides. But inspiration struck as they walked through the gravel parking lot toward the Land Rover, which was an even older vehicle. He might not have a suitable vehicle, but a friend of his did: two in fact.

"Land Cruisers," he offered when Nuri frowned at the beat-up SUV. "Jet black. Purchased by a movie company and left here."

"Left?" asked Nuri.

"That is the story. Perhaps they did not pay the right bill. In any event, you can have them very cheap."

"Let's see them," said Danny.

Nuri suspected that the cars were stolen, though the story that Toroque told was in fact true—a movie company had shipped them into Ethiopia about a year before, planning to use them during the filming of a movie. But the movie's funding had fallen through at the last minute. Not only had the movie never been made, but the SUVs' ownership was caught up in a legal battle as the film company's creditors tried to get back some small fraction of the money they were owed.

"I hope it is settled soon," said the owner of the warehouse where they were stored. "I am owed a fortune in back rent for storage."

Despite the fact that they had been hidden under tarps for several months, the glossy black surface of the SUVs shone. Danny nodded to Nuri, who had already decided the vehicles were precisely what they wanted. Negotiating a price was difficult, since the owner of the warehouse was sure the film company would come to reclaim the SUVs at any moment.

"Then what do I do?" he asked. "Tell them they are getting a wash?"

"If that works," said Nuri.

"Perhaps we should have some tea," suggested Toroque.

They worked out a lease agreement, with Nuri having to post what amounted to a bond in case they failed to return the vehicles. The amount was high enough that Danny suspected the warehouse owner hoped they would not be returned.

Deal done, tea finished, Nuri and Danny drove the vehicles to the other side of the city, where Nuri had more shopping to do.

"Will we get that deposit back?" asked Danny as he followed in the second vehicle. They used the Voice's communications channel to talk to each other.

"Sure," said Nuri. "As long as we bring the trucks back. They'll argue us down a little, there'll be some fee no one mentioned. But in the end they're more or less honest."

"Honest? He just leased two trucks he didn't own."

"That's if the story is true."

"If it's not, they're stolen."

"They're honest enough," insisted Nuri.

"And they trust us?"

"Sure."

Toroque suspected that Nuri was CIA, and if he wasn't CIA, then surely he was an arms dealer. Either way, he could be expected to hold true to his word.

Their next stop was a veritable arms supermarket, situated at an abandoned railroad station on the north side of the city. No wares were displayed there. The dealers, about a half a dozen middle-aged men, sat at small folding tables, waiting for customers and playing dice. While a demonstration could always be arranged, no merchandise was displayed, and browsers were very much frowned on. The dealers assumed the people who came in knew what they wanted and were prepared to buy. No one would try and steal a customer from another. If a dealer a customer had worked with before was out, the others would tell him he had to return the next day. New customers were assigned according to a rotation worked out among the men themselves. If the first man in the rotation did not have what the buyer was looking for, he would be referred to the next in line, and so on until satisfied.

The last time he had been here, Nuri bought a few rifles from a man who gave his name as Amin. Amin—his true name was Mohammad al-Amin Junqai—sat in the furthest corner of the building, next to a coal stove that had probably never been used since being shipped from Italy in the late 1930s.

"I need a dozen MP5s," said Nuri when Amin looked up. He wanted top of the line submachine guns. "Ammunition for them. Not too much ammunition."

"Will you pay in euros?" asked Amin. "Or American dollars?"

"THEY DON'T SEE THEMSELVES AS EVIL," NURI TOLD DANNY as they continued outfitting themselves. "They're shopkeepers and salesmen, fulfilling a need."

"They're selling guns and stolen merchandise."

"It may have been stolen, but not by them," said Nuri. "All they know is that they got them for a good price. Wal-Mart doesn't ask you how you're going to use a rifle when you buy it."

"That's different," said Danny. "It's for hunting."

"If you're having moral qualms—"

"I'm not having moral qualms," said Danny. "I'm just trying to understand how they think. Why don't these people sell over the border?"

"You mean, why don't they sell to the rebels? They would, if the rebels would come here and pay these prices. We're paying at least triple what they would. On the bullets? Ten times as much. And they have trouble coming over the border. The IDs are checked, their vehicles searched. Going into Sudan's easy," added Nuri. "The Ethiopians wouldn't care if you brought a missile over, as long as it's leaving the country. But for the rebels, just getting into Ethiopia can be a serious problem."

"So we bring them the guns."

"No. We stop short of that. We just get in close and see what happens. If Jasmine is still around, they get back in the picture. If not, we find out who's bankrolling these guys. That leads us to the aluminum tubes."

"Getting close may mean selling guns," said Danny.

"I can play the arms dealer," said Nuri.

"Uncle Dpap has already met you."

"They probably think that story was bull." Nuri had made such switches before, but he realized that going from a milque-toast professor to an arms dealer presented a believability problem.

He could have Hera do it. She came off like a she-devil.

"I can handle it," said Danny.

"Well, put on your glasses and look threatening," said Nuri, rounding the hill. "We're just about at the meat market."

WHAT NURI CALLED A MEAT MARKET WAS ACTUALLY AN OLD convent about three miles out of town. It was now under the control of Herman Hienckel, a German expatriate. Hienckel did not own the property, which was still on the rolls of the church that once sponsored the sisters who'd lived there. But he was clearly in control of it, as he had been for the decade.

Hienckel was not a man to have moral qualms. At seventeen he had joined the East German army; by nineteen he was a sergeant, one of the youngest if not the youngest. After washing out of special operations training for a "lack of discipline"—he'd gotten into a fight with a fellow soldier—he left the army. He was lost in civilian life, living on the dole, everything complicated by the reunification of the two halves of his country. Out of desperation he took a job as a military trainer in Iraq before the first American Gulf war.

It was an extreme mistake, one that he could easily have paid for with his life, as the unit he helped train was among the first to occupy Kuwait. But in what would prove to be a career-defining stroke of luck, Hienckel managed to hook up with a British MI6 agent two days before the allied invasion began. He supplied the man with a few tidbits of intelligence and helped keep him from being detected by the Iraqis. When the invasion started, Hienckel tried to escape to the allied side. After being captured—or surrendering, depending on one's point of view—Hienckel played his intelligence connection to the hilt and was eventually released.

He ended the war by helping an American Marine unit interrogate prisoners. His language skills were not particularly good, but they were far better than the Marines', and Hienckel was easily able to gloss over anything he didn't understand. From there he became a useful facilitator for different forces in Kuwait and the wider Gulf, occasionally doing business with the CIA as well as British intelligence, until his list of enemies grew so long that he found it prudent to move on.

A brief stint in Somalia cost him the hearing in this left ear and left him with a permanent limp, but it also gave him a bankable reputation as a soldier of fortune, and a tidy sum locked in a Swiss bank account. He moved to Ethiopia and began providing services there to whatever force could afford them.

While some members of the Ethiopian government had accused him of forming a private army, his business model was much more modest. Hienckel was more like an employment counselor: He trained men interested in getting work as security guards and mercenaries—there was no meaningful difference in Ethiopia—then pocketed a portion of their salary after arranging jobs for them. Adjusted for inflation and the exchange rate, the amount he earned was barely greater than the dole wages he'd made back in Germany. In Gambella however, they made him a rich man.

Nuri's appearance troubled him. He did not know for certain that the American worked for the CIA—it was too easy for poseurs to suggest that they did—but he had all the earmarks, especially a studied disregard for the difficulties an entrepreneur like Hienckel faced, and an almost whining determination to try and talk his price down. One could not afford to refuse to do business with the Western intelligence services. Angering them would not only cut down on referrals, but could prove extremely hazardous if word got around that you were no longer one of their friends. A known CIA connection was considered safer than a bullet-proof vest.

"My friend, you are coming up in the world," Hienckel said to Nuri and Danny when his men escorted them into his office. It had been the chapel of the convent. "You are driving Land Cruisers now."

"Not as nice as your Ratel," said Nuri, referring to the South African armored personnel Hienckel had parked in the yard.

"Very poor gas mileage," said Hienckel. "And who is your friend?"

"I'd rather not say. He needs to hire some escorts for a few days, perhaps two weeks. Men who ask no questions."

Hienckel glanced at Danny. Dressed in a pair of khaki pants and a long African shirt, he exuded an air of quiet control.

His eyes held Hienckel's without emotion. He was clearly not Ethiopian, but Hienckel couldn't tell if he was American, like Nuri, or a European returning to his homeland.

Did he trust him?

Of course not. But so long as he paid, there was no need for trust.

"I specialize in men who ask no questions," he said. "Let us make the arrangements."

18

Jabal Dugu, Sudan
Two days later

THE TOYOTA LAND CRUISERS SHONE LIKE BLACK DIAMONDS in the desert sun, gleaming nuggets topped by a bar of yellow emergency lights and lined with chrome. The trucks had every conceivable option, including and most importantly a full complement of hired men, who flashed their Belgian-made MP5 submachine guns as they flew out the doors, forming a cordon for their boss as he exited the vehicle. They were dressed in identical khaki uniforms, no insignias. Their head-gear consisted of a camo-style do-rag tied around their close-cropped scalps. Each had a pair of sunglasses, and a radio with an earphone and microphone discreetly tucked up his arm. And though they were standing only a few yards from each other, the men used only the radio to communicate.

"Clear," said one of the bodyguards.

The front doors of the lead Land Cruiser popped open simultaneously. Danny Freah—known to the bodyguards as Mr. Kirk—stepped from the passenger side. His driver—Boston—came out of the other door, pistol in hand.

Way over the top, Danny thought. But the young soldiers who'd been lazing around near the front of the church had risen to their feet, staring with awe and envy.

Danny had always hated the clichés of American gangsta rap. To his mind, they glorified the worst misconceptions about black life, doing for honest African Americans what mafia stories did for Italian Americans. But the images conveyed power overseas, where they were taken as a blueprint for how outlaws should act.

And he was definitely acting the part of an outlaw—Mr. Kirk, a supposed renegade from America, or maybe Libya, or maybe parts unknown—with guns and ammunition to sell.

If the murmurs around him were any indication, his act was going over big.

"Where is Uncle Dpap?" said Danny, using an Arabic phrase he had carefully memorized. "I have a business proposition for him."

A few of the older rebels exchanged glances. One headed toward the church door, where he was met by Commander John.

The guards at the northeastern end of town had alerted Uncle Dpap to the Land Cruisers and their occupants. The vehicles alone made it clear what the man was up to, and Uncle Dpap had told the guards to let them proceed.

"Who are you?" demanded Commander John.

"You can call me Mr. Kirk. I'm here to see your brother," said Danny, still sticking to the script.

"My brother is not here."

Danny had to wait for the Voice to translate.

"This is incorrect," added the Voice, which was monitoring the bug Nuri had placed inside the headquarters two days before. "Uncle Dpap is working at his desk."

Danny folded his arms in front of his chest. Nuri had told him that Commander John was likely to run interference. He was determined to show that he wasn't intimidated by his bluster.

"What are you standing there for?" said Commander John. "Have you come here for business? If so, you will deal with me."

"Where is Uncle Dpap?" Danny repeated.

"Deal with me," said Commander John. Since being a tough guy wasn't working, he decided to try a different tact. "Let us get something to drink."

The computer translated, and when Danny didn't immediately respond, suggested what he should say.

"Thank you for your hospitality," offered MY-PID, first in English, then in Arabic.

"Where is Uncle Dpap?" insisted Danny. The computer's response seemed too polite.

Commander John frowned, then walked into the store. He came out with a pair of Cokes and the storekeeper.

"Here," he said, holding one out to Danny. "Would you like some other refreshment?"

Danny eyed the drink, then turned to Boston.

Boston took the drink, sipped, then handed it back to Danny.

"You don't trust me?" said Commander John.

"No," said Danny, in English.

The Voice gave him the word in Arabic, but Danny didn't repeat it.

"You are English?" said Commander John.

"I am not a citizen of any country," said Danny, first in English, then in the Arabic the computer offered.

"Sit, sit," said Commander John, gesturing toward a table. "Come, let us talk."

Danny shook his head.

"I speak only to Uncle Dpap," he told Commander John, first in English, then in Arabic.

Commander John was so befuddled by the stranger that he didn't even wonder why he was translating from English into Arabic if he spoke English. He noticed the earphone clipped into Danny's ear, but thought it connected him to his security team. A device like the Voice belonged to the realm of fantasy as far as he was concerned.

"My brother will speak to you. But first, some refreshment. Drink."

Commander John took a long guzzle from the bottle. Danny took a small sip. It wasn't that he thought the rebel was trying to poison him. He just didn't like cola.

"Your men should have something as well," Commander John said. He gestured to the shopkeeper.

"My men are paid not to want anything," said Danny loudly.

The members of the team—all mercenaries hired in Gambella—stiffened. A few were thirsty, but the outlaw arms dealer had already paid them the equivalent of three months' wages, with the promise of three more at the end of the week.

Uncle Dpap had listened to the conversation from the door of the church. Deciding he'd heard enough, he signaled Tilia to accompany him and went outside. Pausing on the steps, he gazed across the street at his brother and the stranger.

Was this the answer to his prayers? Or an agent of the government?

If the latter, the man would not leave the village alive.

THREE MILES AWAY, SITTING IN ABUL'S BUS, NURI WATCHED a laptop displaying the feed from one of the video bugs they'd stuck on the roof of the Land Cruisers. He was just far enough away not to be seen, but close enough to rally to Danny's aid if things went bad.

Maybe. Flash and McGowan were with him, and while he had no doubt they were good at what they did, three against thirty was still pretty poor odds.

Danny seemed to be carrying off the charade fairly well, however. He was a natural for the part—the less he spoke, the more nervous the others became. And the more nervous they were, the greater his advantage.

To a point. If Uncle Dpap became so nervous he felt he was in danger, he might order his men to open fire. The trick was not to make him quite that nervous. But Danny seemed to have it well in hand. Nuri watched as Uncle Dpap swept his hand to the side, gesturing that Danny should accompany him.

"I'd rather stay in the sun," said Danny. "I have nothing to hide."

He's good, thought Nuri. He almost has *me* believing he's a scumbag.

"WHERE IS THIS AMMUNITION? YOU HAVE IT IN YOUR trucks?" demanded Uncle Dpap.

"I'm not stupid," said Danny, in English. He let Tilia translate; the Voice indicated she was extremely accurate. "I can supply whatever needs you have."

"How can I trust you?"

"You shouldn't trust me," said Danny.

Uncle Dpap looked back at him with surprise when Tilia told him what he had said.

"You shouldn't trust anyone," explained Danny. "Just as I don't trust you. Did you kill your last supplier?"

The question angered Uncle Dpap. "I heard that he was killed by police in Europe," said the rebel. "But maybe you killed him."

"Your friend was a very small operator. The business he did was minor compared to the business I do."

"So why are you offering to sell me anything?" said Uncle Dpap. "If I am a small ant to you, I'm not worth your time."

"You're not an ant." Danny softened his expression, realizing he was pushing things a bit too hard. "You are bringing freedom to your people, and watching out for them. All of these people depend on you. You are a lion, not an ant."

Uncle Dpap knew sweet talk when he heard it, and frowned.

"My problem is my overhead, my expenses," continued Danny. "I need to deal in volume. But here is a proposition — get some of the other rebels together and I will sell to all of you. The same price, the same fair arrangements. It will be easy for you. You will all benefit."

"That is impossible," said Uncle Dpap. "We do not work together."

Danny shrugged. Then pulled open his armored vest, revealing a Beretta stuck in a holster at his belt.

Uncle Dpap's men jumped to alert. Danny bodyguards did the same.

"Here," said Danny, reaching for the gun slowly. "This is for you."

He held the gun out. Uncle Dpap looked at it suspiciously.

"It's a present," said Danny.

Uncle Dpap grabbed it and pointed it at Danny's forehead.

"If you want to shoot me . . ." Danny waited for Tilia to translate before continuing. " . . . you will need these."

He reached into his pocket for the bullets.

Arm fully extended, Uncle Dpap pulled the trigger anyway. Danny didn't flinch. Uncle Dpap took the bullets but didn't put them in the gun.

"You are a brave man," conceded the leader. "But not a foolish one."

"When you need to call me, use this phone," said Danny, pulling a small satellite phone from his breast pocket. "Use it only for that. Make one call only. Say nothing. When the call registers, I will come that night. Use it only for that purpose."

Uncle Dpap gestured for Tilia to take the phone.

"I want to deal with everyone," said Danny. "It is very expensive to bring weapons here. But I can supply whatever you want. I have no trouble getting anything. That gun is an American Army pistol. There are none better in the world."

"OK," said Uncle Dpap. "Perhaps we will have your meeting after all."

BOSTON FELT AS IF HE'D BEEN HOLDING HIS BREATH FOR THE past half hour.

"I thought that bastard was going to slap the bullets in the gun and fire," he told Danny as he maneuvered the Land

Cruiser through the crowd of people on the street. "I really did."

"He only pulled the trigger to see if I would flinch."

"Did you?"

"A little," admitted Danny.

Had Uncle Dpap put the bullets in the gun, Danny would have ordered the Voice to fire the two small guns secreted in the yellow lights on top of the Land Cruisers. The guns—basically miniturrets—had been targeted on Uncle Dpap and his closest bodyguards the whole time.

"Careful where you're driving," Danny told Boston as he came a little too close to a truck on the side of the road. "You put any scratches in this and Nuri's going to have to pay to have them fixed out of his own pocket."

Boston stopped himself from answering that the CIA was rolling in cash. The men in the back didn't speak English, but they might recognize the letters CIA and start thinking. The last thing Boston or Danny or anyone else on the team wanted was them thinking.

Nuri, of course, would have disagreed about the funds, since he was sure to be hounded about the expenditure. But leasing the trucks had been well worth it.

The handle of the gun Danny presented so casually to Uncle Dpap had been smeared with a bio marker that allowed the MY-PID system to track the rebel leader wherever he went. The phone contained a bug that uploaded audio whenever anyone nearby spoke. Any phone call would be recorded as well, though by now the NSA was listening in to practically all of his communications anyway.

Once past the guard post at the entrance to the village, Danny began to relax. They'd launched a small Owl UAV to supplement the blimps, which watched the area farther north. The Voice told him there was no traffic within the entire area.

"Pretty girl, huh?" said Boston. "That translator."

"She was."

"Like to jump her bones."

"She's too much for you to handle."

"Why do you say that?"

"She has to be tough to deal with those characters. And she looked it."

"I can charm a snake into giving milk."

Tilia reminded Danny of his ex-wife Jemma, when they'd first met. The similarity wasn't in their features—Tilia's skin was lighter, her nose a little smaller, her eyes prettier. What struck him was her expression: all business. She wasn't very old—early twenties, maybe a few years more. At that age she should be smiling more, happy. But her job weighed her down.

Jemma had been in law school, en route to becoming a professor, en route to becoming a political activist, en route to becoming an assemblywoman and state senator. She was out of politics now, out of law, out of everything—burned out before forty. The last he'd heard, she was living in Vermont, living on a farm that she'd bought with money her parents left her. A mutual friend said she was raising sheep, and selling organic wool and meat.

"I think she has a crush on you," said Boston.

"Who?"

"Tilia. She was making eyes at you. Circumstances were different," he continued, "you could have a hell of a time with her."

"You're the one that wants to sleep with her," Danny said.

"Absolutely." Boston turned to him. "You don't mind, right?"

"Hell no. As long as you don't."

"Maybe we'll have to," said Boston. "To keep our cover up."

"Dream on, Boston."

"All I'm saying is, I'm sworn to do my duty. It'll be a sacrifice, but I'm ready."

19

Jabal Dugu, Sudan

AS SOON AS THE ARMS DEALER WAS IN HIS TRUCK, UNCLE Dpap returned to his office. He told everyone but Tilia and Commander John to leave the building. Then he carefully dismantled the pistol and examined it.

"Do you think he cheats you?" asked Commander John.

"I want to make sure this is not some type of trick," said Uncle Dpap.

"What kind of trick could it be?"

"A trick. Europeans are very tricky."

"He's not European," said Tilia. "His accent is American."

"I think he's British," said Commander John.

"He was trying to disguise where he was from," said Tilia. "He is most likely CIA."

"Maybe," said Uncle Dpap, picking apart the slide group and barrel.

"Why would the CIA help us?" Commander John asked. As pretty as she was, he resented Tilia for sounding too much like a know-it-all.

Satisfied that the gun was not booby-trapped, Uncle Dpap reassembled it. He had never owned a Beretta, and knew of the weapon mostly by reputation. It was used by NATO and the Americans, a good recommendation.

Commander John reached for it. Uncle Dpap slapped his hand.

"I just want to try it," said John. "Maybe it is defective. You shouldn't be the one to test it."

Uncle Dpap loaded the magazine, slapped it into the pistol butt, then handed the weapon to his brother. "Go outside. Make sure you are not near anyone."

"You don't have to treat me like a child," said Commander John, though in fact he was gleeful at the prospect of trying the new weapon. "Should I call the others in?"

"Not yet."

Uncle Dpap reached down to the lowest drawer in his desk and took out a small pencil case filled with tools. He sorted through them and retrieved a small screwdriver, then began dismantling the phone.

"You think he was CIA?" he asked Tilia.

"Very likely."

"Why would the CIA help us?"

"I don't know. Maybe to ambush us."

"To what purpose?"

"I don't know."

"If he is CIA and not a dealer, he is trying to get us to ally together. Why would that help them?"

She thought for a few moments. There were no obvious reasons. Every American who came through the area, even the relief workers, was assumed to be working for the CIA, though Tilia knew this was rarely the case.

"We had science visitors the other day," she noted. "And now this one. The man who was our main source of ammunition dies, and now these men show up."

"I would think this Mr. Kirk killed him," said Uncle Dpap. "To get more business."

"Maybe. If he is truly dead."

Uncle Dpap did not particularly care for Luo. Except for his inability to find a new source of weapons and bullets, he would not have been disappointed in the least at his demise.

"If he is an arms dealer, why get us together?" asked Uncle Dpap. "What would be his benefit? To save a few dollars transporting the weapons?"

"He would be afraid of a price war, or of being ambushed," said Tilia. "That was Luo's concern as well. If he sold to all, yes, he could make more money."

"But Luo didn't try to gather us together."

"Luo knew Sudan. This man—he is still feeling his way."

"Yes. But he was confident."

"Or if he is CIA, he might be working with the Egyptians,"

said Tilia. "To counter the Iranians. That would not be bad for us."

Uncle Dpap took the last screw from the back of the phone and edged it up carefully. The phone circuitry was printed on a single card. There was no bomb. It was possible that the phone line was tapped, but Mr. Kirk himself had said to use it only to contact him, and not to say anything. So what would the point of tapping it be?

Uncle Dpap didn't know that much about cell phones, but unless he had been the man who designed this particular model, it was unlikely that he would have realized that the phone was actually bugged: what looked like a small magnet for the miniature speakerphone was already transmitting to the portable unit used by the other bugs in the town.

"You like this Mr. Kirk," said Uncle Dpap, starting to put the phone back together.

Tilia blushed.

"You think I'm too old to notice things like that," he continued, amused. He liked to tease the young woman, who was more like a son to him than the three he had. "His motives are not very important, except for this question—why would he want to deal with several groups together? That is our real question."

Tilia recognized from his tone that he had come up with an answer.

"The answer could be that he is impatient," continued Uncle Dpap. "As you say, he is afraid of competition, and being ambushed. But I think he has a very large amount of weapons and ammunition sitting somewhere that he must get rid of. To take the time to sell it piecemeal—you see he has us do all the work."

"It may be."

"And he is greedy. That, of course, goes without saying. Greed is impregnated in these men's souls. It is a universal disease, but the men who sell weapons have it very strongly. It is one reason they do not live very long lives. Something to consider, Tilia."

She straightened her back and lifted her shoulders, determined to remain stoic and not answer him.

"You will have to think of leaving your Uncle Dpap and the rest of your family sometime," said Dpap, suddenly wistful. He looked over at her, admired her form. She had a regal face. In another time, she could have been queen.

"We have work to do," she told him, her words and tone exactly echoing what he would have said had she suggested something silly.

Uncle Dpap chuckled and went back to the phone, screwing it together. When he was done, he handed it to her.

"There is another possibility we haven't considered," he said. "Perhaps it is the Iranians who are really behind this."

"They back Colonel Zsar."

"Yes. They give him much money. But Zsar has trouble bringing people to his side. If we joined with him, then he would have a good core force."

"And Red Henri?"

Red Henri, in Uncle Dpap's opinion, was a crazy man, not to be trusted to remain sane for more than a few minutes at a time. But his men were well-trained. They would be a valuable addition to any force.

Uncle Dpap had turned down several overtures from the Iranians. Their religion made him nervous.

But not as nervous as running out of ammunition did. The danger was not just from the government forces, but from the other rebel bands, who coveted his village and other resources.

"Red Henri would not join in an alliance with either of us," said Uncle Dpap. "He is content to herd his goats in his own way. But Zsar we could deal with. Go to him and tell him about my meeting. Tell him I do not trust this Mr. Kirk, and do not recommend a meeting yet. But maybe he will give us all a good price. Tell him I am open to buying bullets for the best price. As I have always been."

"If we tell Zsar that, he is sure to tell the Iranians."

"Exactly."

20

**Base Camp Alpha
Sudan**

BOSTON INSISTED ON COLLECTING THE SUBMACHINE GUNS from the mercenary bodyguards as soon as they got back to Base Camp Alpha. Nuri thought it was unnecessary, and maybe a little foolish, in effect telling the men that they didn't trust them. But Boston didn't care. He didn't trust them, and he saw no reason to be cute about it.

The men didn't complain. After a big lunch beneath the tent pavilion that served as their mess hall, Boston set them out in a picket watch around the perimeter, with two of his Whiplash people as supervisors. The blimps would see anyone who approached in plenty of time for them to be armed.

To a man, the mercenaries believed Danny was an arms dealer, something Nuri had been careful to hint at but not say explicitly when they were hired. They assumed that the trenches were part of whatever story Danny needed to give the authorities so he could operate here without problems. They were all illiterate, and had no idea what dinosaurs were, let alone how paleontologists worked. Their prime concern was money, and they were being paid plenty of that to keep their curiosity in check. As long as they were kept busy, they wouldn't be a problem.

The question was how to keep them busy. Boston suggested holding training sessions. Danny nixed that idea.

"That's all we need. Better trained soldiers of fortune."

"They could use the discipline."

"Come up with something else."

Boston finally decided that he would use the soldiers to dig the trenches, making them look a little more realistic. The initial response was unenthusiastic.

Then Hera came up with an idea.

"Ten dollars to the first man who finds dinosaur bones," she said.

Once she explained what dinosaur bones were, there was no trouble getting volunteers.

EVEN BEFORE DANNY AND HIS MEN ARRIVED BACK AT BASE Camp Alpha, Tilia was driving to Colonel Zsar's fortress on the other side of the hills. She'd chosen two men to go with her—one, because he was the biggest man in the troop, and the other because he was the best shot. She had no illusions, however, that they would be able to protect her if things went bad. All three of them would die, with luck quickly.

Tilia carried two pistols in bandoliers across her chest, and a sawed-off elephant gun besides. If she had to fight, she would reserve one bullet for herself.

They had to pass through a small village in the shadow of the hills to reach Colonel Zsar's stronghold. She had been there only once before, more than a year ago. The changes astounded her. The village had been a complete wreck, most of its buildings still destroyed from a raid three years before by Ethiopian forces, who at the time were angry with Colonel Zsar as well as the legitimate Sudanese government. Stones lay at the edges of the street; foundations were cluttered with weeds and windswept sand. Perhaps two dozen people lived in the surviving shanties, ramshackle structures built of cardboard and other refuse on the southern end of town.

Those were gone now. In their place was a village of prefab trailers, five dozen arranged in a tight rectangle just off the main road. On the other side of the road, where the abandoned foundations had been, sat three steel buildings, barns where cattle were kept and milk processed. Three milk trucks, with gleaming tanks, were lined up in the yard next to them. Fifty head of cattle grazed in the fields beyond.

Tilia was tempted to stop the Jeep and talk to the people. If the Iranians had brought this prosperity, there would be no question of allying with them. But it was getting late, and she wanted to be sure to conclude her business with Colonel Zsar before nightfall.

Colonel Zsar's fortress was embedded in a cliff, centered around a pair of caves dug out by successive generations of fighters and smugglers. Tilia's Jeep was observed well before she came to the checkpoint leading to the stronghold's entrance. Jeeps were not plentiful in the area, and though the colonel's forces had little interaction with Uncle Dpap's, it was quickly recognized. The colonel was alerted, and gave his permission for the vehicle to proceed.

Seeing that there were two men—as far as they were concerned, the woman didn't count—the guards at the gate decided there would have to be six escorts. Two men sat on the hood of the vehicle, two clung to the rear fender, and two others trotted behind.

Tilia drove the truck up a steep, serpentine dirt road, passing three different sandbagged machine-gun emplacements before reaching a parking area in front of one of the caves. Once again she was surprised. There were a dozen white pickup trucks in the lot, all nearly brand new. Belts of bullets crisscrossed the guards' chests, and there were extra boxes near a sandbagged gun emplacement covering the entrance to the building—if the colonel's forces were experiencing a bullet shortage, he was doing his best to hide it.

A man in a flak vest met them at the door.

"Your weapons," he demanded.

Tilia's escorts looked at her. She nodded, but did not hand hers over.

"Your gun, miss," said the man.

"My gun stays with me."

"You are just a woman," he said, with obvious disdain. "Why do you think you deserve such a privilege?"

"You are afraid of a woman?"

"Wait here."

The man turned on his heel and went back inside. Tilia realized she'd made a mistake. Uncle Dpap had told her to deliver the message no matter what. If the guard insisted on her handing over her gun, she would have to do so. It would be very bad to start the meeting with such a sign of weakness.

"Since you are a woman, we won't worry about it," said the man when he returned. He looked at the others. "This way."

The interior of the cave had been divided into a bunker with masonry and concrete walls. An external generator supplied electricity, and while the lights were relatively dim, they were still ample enough to light the long corridor back to Colonel Zsar's post. Tilia had arrived just as the colonel was waiting for dinner. Ordinarily he would have had her and the others wait—assuming he had decided to see them at all—but his men had told him about the woman soldier's beauty and he wanted to see it for himself.

It surpassed their descriptions.

"Who are you?" he asked.

"I am an aide to Uncle Dpap," she said.

"Have a seat." He snapped his fingers at the two bodyguards standing near the door, gesturing for them to bring over a camp stool. The men rushed to comply.

"I don't need to sit," Tilia told him. "Uncle Dpap wanted you to know about a visitor."

Tilia laid out what had happened, finishing before the men arrived with her stool.

Colonel Zsar had heard that Uncle Dpap had a niece working as his aide, but the stories did not adequately convey her beauty. Zsar had lost his wife two years before, but he would have lusted after Tilia in any event. He knew that she was not Muslim—none of Uncle Dpap's people followed the true religion—but her beauty was so transcendent that he didn't care about that. And besides, she was intelligent and well-spoken—he could not think of a better helpmate.

"So what does Uncle Dpap want to do?" he said when she finished speaking. "He wants us to meet with this man?"

"He wants to discuss him with you. A meeting might be too dangerous for now."

"I see."

"Uncle Dpap is considering doing business with him. Our

other friends are not always the most reliable, and sometimes their prices are not good."

The display by his men notwithstanding, Colonel Zsar was also in need of a new source for weapons and ammunition. Arash Tarid had promised that he would make new arrangements soon, when he and the other Iranian visited the other day, but an additional source might be useful. In any event, a meeting would give him an excuse to ask Uncle Dpap about this girl.

He would have to mention it first to Tarid. There was always the possibility that this was some sort of test by the Iranians.

"Maybe we can discuss it," said Colonel Zsar. "Let me consider the point."

"Thank you, then," said Tilia, starting to leave.

"Wait," said Colonel Zsar. "You're not going to go right away, are you?"

"I had only the message to deliver."

"You should join me for dinner."

Tilia thought to herself that she would rather eat dirt.

"Uncle Dpap expects me back quickly," she said curtly. "I would not be wise to disappoint him. Excuse me, please."

21

**Khatami-Isfaha airfield
Central Iran**

BANI ABERHADJI WAS IN A BAD MOOD. THE COUNCIL HAD decided to hold a special meeting, interrupting his inspection tour and forcing him home. He would not have minded so much had he not been convinced that the meeting would amount to a waste of time. But he could not afford to miss it politically. The council seemed to be softening in its stand against the government, and he needed to understand what was going on, especially if he couldn't influence it.

He was walking from the aircraft to his car when his Black-Berry signaled that he had an e-mail. Suspecting it was just a message from the ministry asking when he would return to work, he waited until he was in the backseat to check it. The message turned out to be from Arash Tarid, his agent in Sudan. There was no text; it was simply a coded request that he call.

Though his driver was also a member of the Revolutionary Guards, Aberhadji did not know him personally, and did not want to take the risk, however small, that the man might be a spy for the government. He waited until they were on the highway, then asked him to pull over.

"I will be right back," he told the man, opening the door to the Toyota Avalon.

It was nighttime, and a few feet beyond the car everything turned pitch-black. Aberhadji walked a few yards into the field, then stopped and took out his satellite phone. The signals it sent and received were scrambled, encrypted in what he was told was an unbreakable code.

"You called me," he said when Tarid answered.

"A competitor to Luo has appeared. He wants to meet with some of our friends, including the colonel."

"A competitor?"

"Perhaps now we see why Luo was killed. The Jasmine people have not been very responsive. This man alleges that he has many weapons, and that his prices are very good. I wondered if you would wish to check him out?"

The night was cool. Aberhadji fought off a shiver as he considered the matter. "Who is he?" he asked.

"He gives his name as Mr. Kirk. He gave one of the rebel leaders—not Colonel Zsar but another man, Uncle Dpap—an American pistol he claimed had been stolen from the Army."

"I will check into him. If I give the approval, you will meet him yourself. Then report to me."

"I don't know about meeting him. If—"

"Go yourself," insisted Aberhadji. "If I approve. It will take me only a few hours to check on him."

"As you wish."

"You will report to me in person. I will be in Tehran in a few days. After that, I have to travel again."

He killed the transmission without waiting for an answer.

22

Base Camp Alpha
Sudan
Two days later

FOR THE WHIPLASH TEAM, LISTENING IN ON WHAT WAS HAP-pening at Uncle Dpap's headquarters, the hours following Danny's visit passed slowly. Tilia's description of her meeting with Colonel Zsar made it clear that he had not made any decision. The colonel had sent a message to his Iranian contact, but because it was sent from a town thirty miles away, the NSA net had failed to pick it up

The evening after Danny's star turn as an arms dealer, Nuri went to bed thinking he would have to come up with a new idea. But when he woke, a new set of NSA intercepts from Sudan had been translated and forwarded to the team.

The headline on one made him forget how bad the coffee was:

COMMUNICATION INTERCEPTED
WITH IRANIAN CONNECTION

The conversation had taken place in Khartoum, the Sudanese capital. It lasted for barely a minute and was on the surface innocuous. The only reason it had been examined at all was the fact that it had been conducted in Farsi; an NSA computer had pulled it out and queued it for translation and inspection.

[call goes through; Speaker 1 answers]
Speaker 1: Hello?
Speaker 2: Kirk checks out. Proceed.
Speaker 1: Meet with him?
Speaker 2: Then report back.
[end of conversation]

Nuri ran and got Danny.

"They're talking about me?" Danny asked.

"Has to be. It's in Farsi. which means—"

"It's between two Iranians," said Danny.

"Exactly. The Republican Guard has funneled some money to Colonel Zsar. Caller one must be a contact for Zsar, or somewhere in the chain."

"Who is he?"

"I don't know. There's no ID here. The call wasn't specifically targeted. That sat phone will be now, though. Sometimes they're pretty clever about hiding identities. We may figure out who it is. We may not. He'll be at the meeting, though."

"You think this is Colonel Zsar?"

"The backgrounder says he doesn't speak Farsi." Nuri took a swig of his coffee. It was always bad, but this morning it was particularly bad. He decided that might be good luck. "Uncle Dpap will call soon. Set up the meeting as soon as you can."

"Right."

"While you're there, I'll try and get a better look at Colonel Zsar's operations," said Nuri. "I'll put some bugs in, and find out what the Iranians have spent their money on."

"Can you get into the fortress?"

"We'll have to be invited in. I'd like to post a blimp nearby, cover the approaches."

"OK."

Nuri sat in front of the laptop and began looking at satellite photos of Colonel Zsar's village. "Why do you think they have a guard on a barn?" he asked.

"Keep people from stealing the cows."

"They don't have guards on the other buildings they have in the village."

"Got me," said Danny.

"Hmmm," said Nuri. "Guess I'll take a look at that, too."

23

Near Murim Wap, Sudan

BY THE TIME UNCLE DPAP USED THE PHONE DANNY HAD given him, Nuri and Danny knew everything— that they wouldn't deal with Red Henri, and that Colonel Zsar had suggested they use the arms dealer to try and get a better price from their other dealers and contacts. They were also confident that they weren't planning an ambush, though that was one thing they couldn't take for granted.

Nuri made the call back, using an electronic voice box to disguise his voice. He told Uncle Dpap that the meeting would happen at midnight, agreeing to the place Uncle Dpap had selected, an abandoned farm building outside a hamlet that lay between Uncle Dpap and Colonel Zsar's camps.

The rebels didn't like the fact that the meeting was being held at night. And they liked it even less when, at five minutes past the appointed time, Nuri called their sat phones, dialing them all into a three-way phone conference.

"The meeting will be held at Murim Wap," said Nuri. He was sitting back at the base camp, watching the rebels on the laptop thanks to the Owl and the sensors he'd planted that afternoon. Danny and the trucks were already at Murim Wap. "The vehicles will be waiting. You have a half hour to get there."

"How do we know this isn't a trap?" said Uncle Dpap.

"Send your scouts, just as you did here," said Nuri.

"You don't dictate to us where the meeting is," protested Colonel Zsar.

But Nuri had already hung up.

The two rebel leaders brought their vehicles together to confer. Both Nuri and Danny heard the entire conversation that followed, thanks to the bugged cell phone, which Tilia had in her pocket.

"He doesn't trust you," said a voice they hadn't heard before. "Of course he's not going to meet you here. They only agreed to this place so they could watch you come."

"Is it a trap?" asked Uncle Dpap.

"Too elaborate," said the man. "It would have been easier to kill you here."

"I agree," said Tilia.

"You are sure this man is not working for the government in Sudan?" asked Uncle Dpap.

"That much I am positive of," said the man. "My spies would know."

The debate continued for a short while, but it was clear that, having gone to the trouble of arranging to meet themselves, the two rebel leaders were loath to miss the meeting with the arms dealer.

"The person who's with Colonel Zsar must be the Iranian," said Nuri. "He's the one you have to mark when you meet. Make sure you touch him on the skin."

"I'll shake his hands like a politician."

"Break the vial, daub your finger, touch him. That's all you have to do."

"Is the Owl online?" Danny asked.

"Are you asking me, or are you asking the Voice?"

"You."

"You can ask the computer. It'll tell you."

"I'm asking you," snapped Danny.

"Good snarl," said Nuri, thinking that Danny was just play-acting. In fact, he was really annoyed. "It's online. Have fun."

"I intend to."

Though they'd scouted Murim Wap and planted video and listening devices earlier in the day, they hadn't stayed there, fearing someone would tip off the rebels. Danny waited until the advance scouts Uncle Dpap had sent signaled that the place was clear, then they drove over, Boston driving as if he were racing in the Baja.

"Gotta stay in character," Boston explained. "Outlaw like you isn't going to have a wussy driver."

Murim Wap had once been an important stop on a trade route from the interior into Ethiopia and the sea. But the village's attractiveness faded when trucks and buses replaced carts and feet. A few families had remained in the area, one to run a gas and diesel station, the others to farm and catch on as best they could. Two years before, a cell tower had been built just off the highway, behind the gas station. A UN project had helped increase yields at the nearby farms, and there was a small store that sold goods to the dozen or so families that lived within walking distance. As a general rule, the village street was deserted after nightfall, with the gas station closing down a half hour after sunset.

Except tonight. The lights were still on in the station as Danny's vehicles approached.

"Think he's gonna be a problem?" Boston asked.

"I don't know." Danny considered stopping and getting gas, but that might only add to whatever suspicions the man might have. "Let's just play it," he told Boston.

They planned the meeting for a fallow field off the highway just outside of town. The area was clear of any walls or other cover. Even though they had been under constant surveillance since the early afternoon, Danny still had Boston circle around it slowly while he looked around the landscape with a set of thermal night glasses.

"We're clear," he said finally. "Let's stop and launch the Catbirds."

The Catbirds were UAVs a little bigger than the Owl. Their bodies were packed with plastic explosive, and they could be dive-bombed into targets by command. Danny launched six, enough to take out a well-positioned company of soldiers.

"Take it back by the road. Keep it running," he told Boston. He turned on the truck's dome light and switched the Voice into the radio circuit. "We leave the two trucks running, by the road, just the way we drew it out. Flash, you're with me. McGowan, you're backing up Boston."

"Right, boss," answered McGowan.

Danny got out of the truck and walked across the field to a spot about twenty feet off the road. He was wearing two sets of body armor—a very light vest under his shirt, similar to what Nuri had been wearing in Italy when he was shot, and the thicker, ceramic-insert model that the rebels expected. The combination meant that anything smaller than a howitzer shell would only give him a bruise, but it was heavy and awkward, and he spent quite a lot of time shifting it to get it to feel more comfortable.

Finally he gave up. He reached into his pants pocket and took out the vial with the biomarker, squirting it on his gloved left hand. The marker was mixed in a petroleum jelly base; in order for it to work, it had to touch skin.

Ready, he stood and waited. MY-PID was tracking the rebels, and the Voice declared that their caravan was two minutes away.

"Kill the headlights in the trucks," said Danny. "Be ready."

Behind him, Flash shifted his hands nervously on his submachine gun. In this situation, he would have preferred his SCAR-H/MK-17 or an old M-249. The latter's size alone intimidated people.

"Truck coming," said Danny.

"All right," said McGowan. "Showtime."

NURI WATCHED THE CARAVAN MOVING IN. EVERYTHING WAS in place, he thought. Danny was on his own.

"Hera, you're up," Nuri said, rising. "All right, Clar, let's get going. We only have a few hours to get everything done."

"Uh-huh," said Sugar, who'd been sitting in a chair across the room for the past half hour.

"What's wrong?" Nuri asked as she got up slowly.

"Aw, nothin'."

But her pain was obvious. She took a few short steps, breathing heavily as she went.

"Hold on, hold on. What's wrong?" Nuri asked again.

"I just—my stomach is beat up. Something I ate I guess. It's just gas—I'll get better."

"Hell no. You're staying here."

"Who's got your back?"

Hera Scokas, sitting at the console, said nothing. She and Nuri had avoided each other since the other day.

"I'll go by myself," he said.

"Oh, you can't do that."

"I'll go," said Hera, rising. "Sugar can stay on the watch."

"I can make it," said Sugar. She started to protest, then realized she had to get to the latrine. She pushed herself forward, running to the bathroom pit thirty yards from the building. She barely made it in time before her intestines exploded—figuratively, though it felt as if it were literal.

Nuri, meanwhile, cursed his crappy luck. Hera was the last person he wanted with him. Her personality had already worn thin. She always had a "better" way of doing things.

He could go to the village alone. But inflating and launching the blimp was a two-person job, and there were a large number of sensors to be planted as well.

Sugar returned from the latrine. "I can make it," she told him.

"Why don't you stay here," he told her. "Maybe you should get some sleep."

"It was just something I ate. I'll be fine."

"No."

"You're going yourself?" said Hera.

Nuri looked at them both. He did need a backup. Would Sugar be OK by herself, though?

"You have a fever?" he asked Sugar.

She shook her head.

They had defenses, the blimps, the sensors. And she could always hide.

Not that anyone was likely to bother them tonight.

"You feel all right?" Nuri asked Sugar.

"I'm great. I'm ready."

"No, you stay here on watch. All right, Hera. You come."

"Right."

She jumped up and grabbed her gear.

Nuri went down and waited for her on the motorcycle. She came down and started to get on the Whiplash bike.

"We're not taking that one," he said. "Get on with me."

"Why aren't we taking it?"

"Because we're going to have to hide it near the village, and I don't want to take the chance of losing it if someone stumbles across it. I don't want the technology compromised."

"What good is it if we don't use it?"

"When you run the outfit, you can make the call. Right now, I say we're using this one." Nuri started it up. "Hop on."

Hera cinched her rucksack tighter as she walked over to the bike. It had no sissy bar, but the seat was relatively small, and she'd have no choice but to snuggle close to Nuri and hold him tight around the chest. She tried holding her breath but it didn't help.

"Try not to fall off," said Nuri, popping it into gear.

DANNY FELT HIS HEART STARTING TO POUND AS THE FIRST set of headlights swung into view. He suddenly felt unsure of himself.

In the old days, he'd sometimes felt apprehensive just before a mission began—butterflies, some people called it, something akin to the performance anxiety actors sometimes felt before going on stage. But the feeling always disappeared when things got going.

It didn't tonight. Danny's heart continued to pound as the trucks drove up to the road. He kept his mouth shut, afraid that a stutter, a break, or something similar would give away his nervousness.

Weapons dealers weren't nervous. Whatever else they were, they didn't suffer from performance anxiety. They were calm and cool and completely in control.

So was he.

Except he wasn't.

The vehicles carrying Uncle Dpap and Colonel Zsar drove into the space in front of Danny's trucks. The other vehicles fanned out behind them, the two groups intermixed.

Colonel Zsar, anxious to show that he was the real leader here, got out of his vehicle first. He practically leapt forward, walking so quickly that his bodyguards had to run to catch up.

"Who are you?" he asked Danny in Arabic.

"My name is not important," said Danny. He had practiced the line in Arabic and could say it in his sleep, but it didn't sound smooth. He cleared his throat, trying to hide his sudden attack of nerves. "Call me Kirk. You're Colonel Zsar, I believe."

Tarid, who'd been riding with Zsar, got out of the truck slowly. He took his time joining the others, studying the arms dealer as he walked. Kirk was flashy—too flashy, Tarid thought, the sort of reckless man who makes a fortune in six months and loses his life in the seventh. His guards were well-equipped, but that wasn't much of a trick. More impressive was the fact that he had a white man as his lieutenant— they didn't come cheap here.

Uncle Dpap and Tilia got out of the Jeep together. Their soldiers, meanwhile, had fanned out from the trucks, forming a semicircle behind the rebels.

"What happened to Red Henri?" asked Danny. Once more, even though he'd practiced the phrase incessantly, it sounded stiff and misaccented in his ears.

"He is not of interest to us," said Uncle Dpap. "An alliance with him would not benefit anyone. Deal with him if you wish. I would suggest you be careful if you do."

"We'll use English," Danny told them. "There's no need for any of these to understand. There are too many spies."

Uncle Dpap glanced at Colonel Zsar, who shrugged. His English was a little better than Dpap's, but he wouldn't be able to carry out a complicated conversation, let alone negotiate.

"Is that no good?" asked Danny, in English.

"Your Arabic is fine," said Colonel Zsar in Arabic.

"I thought you both spoke English," said Danny. "Or is that your translator?" He pointed to Tarid.

"That is my lieutenant," the colonel said quickly. It was a fiction they'd worked out earlier.

"An Iranian for a lieutenant," said Danny in English. "Interesting."

Tarid swung his head toward Danny as he heard the word Iranian.

"We will speak in Arabic," said Uncle Dpap. "You speak as you wish. Use English. Why are you meeting us?"

"My aim is to sell many weapons," Danny said. "I'm not particular to whom. Or who pays. Everyone has AK-47s for sale. I can get better guns. If you can pay. MP-5s like my men have. M-16s."

"What about Galils?" asked Tarid. The Galil was an Israeli assault rifle.

"I doubt I could sell those at a price that would make you interested," said Danny. "Assuming I could get them without losing my life."

"Are the Zionists your suppliers?"

"Don't worry about where I get my weapons," said Danny. "They come from many sources."

Danny threw out an offer—a hundred AK-47s at one hundred dollars apiece. It was an extremely good deal, about a fifth of the price the Jasmine network had sold them for.

"Why so cheap?" asked Uncle Dpap.

"To get your business," said Danny. "To get you to trust me. I can see you don't. Not if you think I work with the Zionists."

He took a step closer, working out how he would get the biomarker onto Tarid. He'd shake hands to seal the deal—or to show that there were no hard feelings if a deal wasn't made. He'd clasp Tarid's left hand as he shook with his right.

Done.

Then he'd be able to relax.

Uncle Dpap wasn't interested in guns. He wanted ammunition.

Danny explained that he dealt in lots of ten thousand rounds, fifteen cents American for each round.

The price was nowhere near as good as what he had offered on the guns.

Colonel Zsar dismissed it. "You sell us the guns for nothing, and then try to make it back on the ammunition. You sell carpets, too?"

The others laughed.

"I may be able to do a little better," said Danny.

"Vehicle approaching on highway at a high rate of speed," warned the Voice. "Two vehicles—three, four. Six."

It was an ambush. A pit opened in Danny's stomach and the blood rushed from his head.

"Think it over," he said as calmly as he could. "I'll contact you about it tomorrow."

"Don't be in such a hurry," said Tarid.

"I'm not in a hurry," said Danny.

"We're not done yet," said Colonel Zsar.

"I think we are."

"No." Zsar raised his hand, and all of his soldiers shouldered their weapons. "We will settle a deal tonight, or never."

24

Blemmyes Village, Sudan

COLONEL ZSAR TYPICALLY POSTED A SINGLE GUARD ON the road at the edge of town. The man tended to fall asleep around midnight, but Nuri wasn't counting on that. He drove with his light off—he could see farther with his night visor anyway. When he was about three miles from the village, he throttled back to lessen the bike's noise.

Just over a half mile away he turned off the road, traveling due south across a fallow field until he came to an old path that wound up the nearby hill. Once used by shepherds for a pasture, the hill was now overgrown by trees eight to nine feet tall. He found a relatively clear spot just on the other side of the crest. There, he and Hera inflated the surveillance blimp, then slowly eased it skyward between the tree branches. Launching it was a calculated risk, but Nuri reasoned that no one would know precisely what it was if it came down for some reason.

With the blimp on station and its video cameras working, Nuri went back down to the field, driving across to a lane used by farm vehicles. A wall of rocks rose on each side of the lane as he drove toward the village, but they were more of an opportunity than a barrier—he planned to hide the bike behind them as he and Hera toured the village buildings.

The milk factory was his next stop. He drove until they were roughly parallel to it, then shut off the engine and coasted.

"All off," he said as the bike's momentum finally faded.

Hera said nothing. She'd resolved to say as little as possible the entire night. Clearly, the Whiplash assignment wasn't going to be big enough for both she and Nuri to work together; she'd work out some sort of transfer as soon as this operation was over.

"We'll go up this way," Nuri told her. "There's a night

watchman who patrols at the front of the barn. We'll go around the back."

He put his hand on the wall and jumped over, trotting toward a cluster of small houses scattered like fallen grapes between the lane and the road. The sides of the houses were lined with steel panels cut from a dismantled building, pieces of painted Styrofoam, and cut-up shipping crates.

Nuri slid down next to the house closest to the road. According to the Voice, which was monitoring the view from the blimp, there was no one in the front yard of the barn building.

He got up and started moving along the road. His first impulse was to go slowly, to seem natural in case anyone in the houses decided to look out. But his adrenaline got the better of him, and within a few steps he began to trot, and then run.

His speed surprised Hera, who had trouble keeping up. "You're quick for a runt," she panted, plopping down next to him at the side of the building.

"Who you calling a runt? You're a couple of inches shorter than I am."

She was too out of breath to answer.

Nuri tried pushing the window open but it wouldn't budge. "I need the tools," he whispered. "The glass cutter."

Hera turned around so he could open the rucksack on her back.

He took out the glass cutter and a small suction cup with a handle. After attaching the cup to the window, he got ready to cut a fist-sized hole around it.

"Aren't you going to check for an alarm before you cut?" she asked.

"They barely have electricity, for crap sake. There's not going to be an alarm. I've been in more buildings here than you have pocketbooks, and I've never seen an alarm."

"How many have guards?"

She was right, and Nuri knew it. He was in too much of a hurry, getting sloppy.

Even though there *never* were alarm systems in this part of Africa.

Except here: The detector found current near the sill; there was a simple contact system protecting the window.

He cursed under his breath.

"You're welcome," said Hera.

"It was a good call," he admitted.

He'd have no trouble jumping and bypassing the wire, which was part of a simple contact system. But the fact that there was an alarm told him they weren't just breaking into a barn.

Which was good, and bad—there were bound to be other alarms.

"I'd look for a motion detector in the room somewhere," suggested Hera.

"Ya think?"

Hera strained not to answer back.

"There it is," said Nuri, spotting the detector in the corner of the room.

It was about forty feet away, high in the corner, and angled slightly to the side. It might miss the window and much of the nearby wall, but there would be no getting past it to the door. While there were several ways to defeat such a sensor, the position would make it time consuming to do so.

"Let's look for a better way in," he told Hera.

25

Murim Wap, Sudan

DANNY'S BUTTERFLIES MORPHED INTO BEASTS, ROILING HIS stomach. Everyone around him tensed.

"Just so you know, Colonel, the man behind me has his rifle pointed at you," he said. "If I go down, you go down."

The Voice had been preparing Arabic translations of his English for him to use. He did so now, repeating the words so there would be no mistake.

"If you fire," said Colonel Zsar, "you'll never get out of here alive."

"There are enough explosives in the trucks to take care of all of us," answered Danny. "So let's all of us calm down. What deal is it you want?"

Tarid was angry with Colonel Zsar, who was being reckless. He suspected that he was trying to impress Uncle Dpap, who had said almost nothing the entire night.

Or maybe the girl, whom he kept stealing glances at.

"Give us a price for five hundred guns, and a hundred thousand rounds of ammunition," said Colonel Zsar. "And we will discuss it."

"Fine."

Danny told them they could have everything for sixty thousand, American.

"Half when you place the order. Another quarter paid the day before the exchange. And the rest at the exchange. It will be cash, placed where we say."

"We prefer to deal in euros," said Tarid.

"Euros are fine."

"Vehicles are within three miles," warned the Voice. "They will be within audible distance in thirty seconds."

Danny put his hand to his ear. The others thought he was talking to one of his men.

"ID?" he asked.

"The guerrilla faction aligned with Red Henri."

"I thought you told me Red Henri wasn't invited to the party," Danny said to the others.

"He's not," said Colonel Zsar.

"My lookout says he's about three miles away."

"What?" said Uncle Dpap.

"Impossible," said Colonel Zsar.

"Listen," said Tarid.

They could hear the trucks in the distance.

"Get behind the vehicles!" yelled Uncle Dpap. "Prepare your weapons!"

"It's time for you to leave, Mr. Kirk," said Colonel Zsar. "We will contact you later."

"What's happening, boss?" asked Boston over the radio.

Danny ignored him. "I have no argument with Red Henri," he told the rebels. "I'll wait and see what he wants."

"Not having an argument with you won't keep him from shooting you," said Tilia. "You had better leave, or take cover."

"Get behind the trucks with the others," Danny told his men over the radio. "Drivers, be ready to leave. Flash, you're with me."

Danny ran toward the vehicle where Tarid was crouched. But the rebel soldiers had swarmed around the Iranian and Colonel Zsar and he couldn't get close without making it obvious he was trying to squeeze next to him.

As Danny ducked down, Red Henri's ambulance siren began to wail, morphing through its different variations. The trucks carrying his troops spread out across the plain. A half-dozen flares shot into the air, shading the night red, as if it were an extension of Red Henri himself. The trucks veered around, turning in small circles about four hundred yards from Uncle Dpap's and Colonel Zsar's positions. Though they were well within range, no one on either side fired.

Red Henri, sitting in the back of his Hummer, took the microphone from his PA system.

"What happens when supposed allies are meeting behind my back?" he said. "So now I have three enemies—the government, Colonel Zsar, and Uncle Dpap. This is very disappointing. Especially from you, Uncle Dpap. Colonel Zsar believes he is holy, so we know not to fully trust him. We know this. But you, Uncle, are looked up to. I look up to you. And here—a stab in the back."

The Voice translated everything for Danny, with only a slight delay.

"Estimate Red Henri's force," Danny asked the computer.

"Ninety-eight soldiers in twenty-three vehicles. Six heavy machine guns. Two RPG-7 launchers. Sixty-eight AK-47 rifles of varying types. Six M-16s. One M-14. Additional weapons possible but not observed."

Colonel Zsar had fourteen men with him, plus Tarid; Uncle Dpap had twenty. They had nothing heavier than rifles.

Every muscle in Danny's body began to contract, tightening themselves around his nerves and squeezing hard.

He could get away by ordering the Catbirds to dive-bomb Red Henri's force. He'd plunge through the bodyguards, swat Tarid, and run off in the confusion. But his legs were stiff and heavy, and he felt as if he couldn't move.

Red Henri was genuinely upset, hurt by what he interpreted as a stab in the back.

"Uncle Dpap, are you so ashamed that you can't even speak?" he shouted.

"This man claims to have weapons for sale at a very good price," said Uncle Dpap. "We decided to check it out."

"Without me?"

"We didn't want to waste your time if he proved phony," said Uncle Dpap soothingly. "You are a very busy man."

"We are on the same side," shouted Colonel Zsar. "We should be fighting the government, not each other."

"I am not fighting you," answered Red Henri. "Why are you planning to fight me?"

Danny pushed out of his crouch. "I was hoping to meet with you personally," he shouted. His throat was so dry his voice cracked. "I did not want to insult you by having you share your time with the others."

Though he modeled himself after American rap stars, among others, Red Henri's command of English was not very good, and he didn't immediately respond.

"Translate," Danny told the Voice. He repeated the Arabic

it fed him. "You represent a large order," Danny added, first in English, then in Arabic. "And you will need special weapons, and personal care. You're a VIP."

Red Henri's ego was mollified, even though he didn't believe him.

"That's as it should be," said the rebel. "But now that I am here, what sort of deal can you arrange?"

"We should talk close together," said Danny. "I can't keep shouting."

"Come here, then."

Danny had backed himself into a corner. His whole reason for coming was to tag Tarid. But there were too many people between him and the Iranian, and going over to talk to Red Henri meant moving even farther away. Yet if he didn't go, the others would think he was a coward and never deal with him again. Which wouldn't be a problem, except that he needed to tag Tarid.

"Why don't we meet halfway, with Colonel Zsar and Uncle Dpap, and their advisors," suggested Danny. "There should be no secrets between you three. You are all allies."

"You will come to me first and talk," said Red Henri. "You will show the respect these others have not."

"All right."

Danny took a breath and started toward the rebel. The monsters in his stomach and chest had shrunk back to butterflies. Any second, he told himself, and they, too, would disappear.

"Aircraft approaching," warned the Voice.

"What aircraft?" said Danny.

"Six helicopters. Two Aerospatiziale Gazelles, equipped with rockets. Four Mil Mi-8MTV Hip-H troop carriers. Aircraft have been supplied by the Egyptian army to Sudan for use in this theater."

"ETA?"

"Two minutes at present speed."

"Why are you standing there?" demanded Red Henri. "What are you doing?"

Danny put his hand to his ear, making a show of it.

"The Sudanese army is sending helicopters to attack us," he said loudly. He turned around. "They're two minutes away!"

"This is a trap!" yelled Red Henri. "I'll kill you all before I kill them."

He threw the microphone aside and underlined his thoughts by picking up his rifle and firing through the window.

26

Blemmyes Village, Sudan

NURI WALKED AROUND THE BACK OF THE BARN. THERE WERE several windows, but all opened into small rooms protected by motion detectors.

The motion detectors worked by sensing infrared energy in front of them. He had a can of compressed air he could use to temporarily freeze the sensors, but to use it he'd have to get relatively close and move very slowly. And only one of the rooms looked vulnerable.

"What we want to do," said Hera as he stared through the window, "is go through the wall."

"We can open the windows," said Nuri, confused by what she was saying, "but once we're in the room, getting close to the sensor is tough. I need a much longer pipe, and we have to cool it down. It may be better to just bag it tonight and come back."

"We go through the wall where the detector is," she told him. "We stay behind it."

"How?"

"The detector in that room is in the corner," she said, pointing to the window at the extreme right of the building. "We get past that, and we're in."

"Assuming there's no detectors on the other side."

"Why would they bother putting one inside if they have the perimeter guarded?" said Hera.

"All right. But how do we get through the wall?"

"They're just metal panels. Screwed in. Look."

Hera leaned against the side and put her thumb into one of the small boltlike sheet metal screws that secured the panel to its post. The screw, barely three-eighths of an inch long, popped out within a few turns.

"It's junk. Some idiot tried to sell my dad a building like this when I was a kid. He laughed."

They got out their screwdrivers and went to work. The panel was roughly three feet wide by ten feet long; the last six screws were too high for either of them to reach. They tried pulling the panel up as if it were a hinge. But the metal was too stiff to bend without a great deal of pressure, and Nuri realized that if he bent it, he was unlikely to get it back properly; the penetration would be noticed.

"I'll have to boost you up," said Nuri reluctantly. "Put your foot in my hands."

"That won't work. You're too short."

"You're not exactly the Jolly Green Giant."

"I'll have to climb on your back."

Nuri couldn't think of an alternative. He leaned toward the building, bracing himself. "Take off your shoes," he told her as she lifted her foot. "I don't want them in my back."

"Oh, don't be a baby."

She planted her boot on the small of his back and lifted herself up. He was a wobbly ladder.

"Hold still, damn it. I can't get the screwdriver in."

Even standing on Nuri's shoulders, Hera could barely reach the last two screws. She raised herself as high as she could on her tiptoes, leaning awkwardly and holding onto the edge of the panel as she undid the screw. The panel slipped when she took out the next to last one and she started to lose her balance. She grabbed the panel, trying to hold on. The small screw gave way and she tumbled down, smacking Nuri in the head with the metal as she fell. He grabbed it, keeping it from crashing, but then spun and fell. Both of them tumbled to the ground in a pile, momentarily dazed.

"Ssssssh!" hissed Hera.

Nuri cursed angrily, but softly. He got up and examined his arm—bruised but not hurt too badly.

The room was to the left, separated from the panel they had removed by an interior wall, whose stud they had revealed by pulling away the metal. A hallway sat in front of them. Nuri increased the magnification on his glasses, making sure there were no sensors guarding it. There weren't.

The panels were fixed to the barn's structural posts by a network of narrow one by ones. The wood members were too close together for either of them to squeeze past. Nuri pushed against one; it gave way with a snap.

"You're going to set off the alarm," said Hera.

"There's a wall between it and us. We're good."

"Well, be quiet, then."

Nuri pushed at the next piece of wood, breaking it off, then slipped inside.

He stopped short. There was a video camera directly above his head, covering the hallway.

They must really have something to protect here, he thought. But what?

27

DANNY DOVE TO THE GROUND AS RED HENRI BEGAN FIRING. Within seconds soldiers on all three sides had begun blasting away. Both Colonel Zsar and Uncle Dpap shouted at their men to stop firing, but their voices were lost in the din.

Danny told the Voice to have two of the Catbirds strike in the space between the rebel groups, hoping to discourage Red Henri and give enough cover to Zsar and Dpap's forces so they could retreat. The explosions only added to the confusion. Worried that the others would be overrun, Danny told the Voice to launch the remaining UAVs against the spearhead of Red Henri's force as it rallied around the trucks. The four explosions crated six vehicles—but still didn't calm the fighting.

"Captain!" yelled Boston over the radio, reverting to the title he had used for so long. "Where are you?"

"I'm here," said Danny, pressing against the dirt. "The Sudanese have helicopters on the way. Somebody tipped them off. There are two gunships, four transports. You're going to have to shoot the gunships down."

"You sure you want to do that?" Boston asked.

"Do it."

The choppers were already close enough to be heard over the gun battle. Boston jumped out of his truck and ran to the rear, throwing the door open as the firing continued. He pulled out a metal box about the size of a carry-on bag and opened it on the ground.

Danny and Nuri could have purchased a dozen SA-7 shoulder-launched surface-to-air missiles in Ethiopia if they wished; they would have been more than adequate to deal with the choppers. But the Whiplash team's hip-launched Rattlesnakes had a far greater range.

"Hip-launched" was a bit of a misnomer; the missile was typically fired from a standing position with the launcher about chest high, so the operator could sight the target on the display at the top of the launching unit. The description had been coined because the missile and launcher assembly were about a third the size of the SA-7 and other traditional shoulder-fired weapons.

The name Rattlesnake—officially the weapon was known as the AIM-19x—was a tribute to the Sidewinder family of air-launched missiles. The AIM-19x was a derivative of the late model Sidewinders, with a smaller warhead propelled at extremely high speeds by a two-stage rocket motor. The first stage, which included two sets of maneuverable fins and a variable thrust mechanism, brought the missile to its target. As the projectile was about to hit, the second stage ignited, pushing the warhead through with devastating effect.

The weapon was intended to be used primarily against helicopters, though the warhead was an equal opportunity shredder of engines and other metal. Besides its terminal velocity, the secret of its success was a guidance system that could home in on heat sources, electronic signatures, or a radar reflection—or all three simultaneously. Once locked and launched, the tiny chip that constituted its brain was smart enough to see through decoys, ignoring hotter heat sources if they did not correspond to the data picked up by the other detection methods. This made defensive flares—the most common antimissile defense—useless.

A fact the Sudan gunships were about to discover.

The aircraft were flying in a staggered formation in front of the troop ships, aiming to part at the point of attack. They would sweep in opposite directions around the gathered rebels, machine-gunning their positions after launching rockets at the vehicles.

Boston zeroed in on the lead chopper and fired just before it began its attack. The Gazelle pilot's first warning that he was in trouble were the sounds of a clunk and rip above him, as if a bolt had shot down a long metal tunnel and then torn it in two. Punctured, the engine immediately stopped working, leaving the rotor to spin on sheer momentum. Fuel flooded into the turbine chamber, where it ignited from the heat of the damaged metal. The explosion blew apart the rear portion of the cockpit with so much force that the spine of the helicopter snapped in two. The chopper fell forward, bent like a paper clip. The pilot tried frantically to pull it up, not realizing what was happening. Within two seconds the Gazelle lay in a burning heap on the ground.

Defensive flares began cascading from the choppers. The second gunship unleashed its rockets, setting two of the vehicles in Red Henri's fleet on fire and cratering two others. Boston drew a bead; a moment later the helicopter went down, crumbling only a few yards from one of the trucks it had just destroyed.

Danny began crawling back toward what he thought was Colonel Zsar's position. He'd gone about five yards on his belly when he realized he was heading toward Uncle Dpap's Jeep. He started to change direction but a burst of bullets from one of Red Henri's machine guns stopped him.

Rebels were screaming and firing indiscriminately. The troopships were landing on the perimeter. The gun battle was already a chaotic swirl, and it was only just beginning.

Sensing that staying low wasn't going to protect him much longer, Danny jerked to his feet and ran, racing toward Uncle Dpap's vehicle. As he ran, a pair of bullets slapped at his ribs, twisting him around. One hit the back of his vest, the other the side. Three more bullets flew at him as he fell. One smashed straight into his chest.

The outer vest saved him, but the force still took his breath away. It took him nearly a minute before he could roll back to his stomach and began crawling again.

"Don't shoot him!" yelled Tilia.

Danny got up and ran toward her, ducking behind the Jeep as a fresh hail of bullets flew in his direction. She lay crouched behind the fender, a rifle in her hand.

By now the Sudanese troops who'd landed were firing at

the rebels. Some of Red Henri's troops swung around to meet the approaching threat. But they found themselves caught in a cross fire, as both Colonel Zsar and Uncle Dpap's soldiers fired at both them and the regulars.

"Did you do this?" Tilia demanded.

"Hell no!" said Danny.

"Who did?"

"I have no idea."

Instead of answering, Tilia raised her gun and fired a long burst at one of Red Henri's trucks, cutting down one of the machine gunners. Danny looked to her right and saw Uncle Dpap on the ground, huddled against the Jeep.

He crawled to him. Dpap's head was covered with blood, and his eyes were dazed, focused on something far beyond the battlefield.

"Are you all right?" Danny asked, but he knew he wasn't. Uncle Dpap's breath was shallow. He wasn't dead, but he had only a few minutes to live.

Danny glanced back at Tilia. Her lips were pressed tight together, her eyes half closed as she aimed her gun. There were empty magazines and bullet casings all around her.

She'd lost everything. Even if she got out of there, even if no one else in Uncle Dpap's army was hurt, Tilia's position in the troop was done. Dpap's brother, who was back in the village safe, would not give her the respect or the position Uncle Dpap had.

It was Commander John who had betrayed them. Resenting his brother's domination, he had been working with a spy from the Sudanese army for months, waiting for the right opportunity. After alerting his contact of the meeting, he had given a cell phone to one of the young soldiers who slept in his house and told him to make a call when the meeting began. Egyptian advisors to the Sudan army had been waiting; they found the nearest cell tower to the phone within seconds, and the ambush was launched.

*   *   *

TILIA LOOKED MORE BEAUTIFUL THAN EVER IN THE FIERCE red light and violent white flashes of the battle. The image burned into Danny's brain, imprinting itself in his memory.

Never had he felt so hopeless.

"You have to retreat," he yelled to her. "Get your men. Come with us."

She pretended she didn't hear him. She had already decided she would kill as many men as possible today—Red Henri's, the government's, whoever she could. And then she would take Uncle Dpap's body back to their people.

"Boss, time for us to get the hell out of here," said Boston over the radio. He'd pulled the men back to the trucks. So far no one had been injured—but that was only through sheer luck.

"Where's Flash?" Danny asked.

"He's looking for you."

"Tell him to get back to the truck," said Danny. He reached toward Tilia. "I have to go," he told her, touching her shoulder.

"Go," she said.

He took a half breath, then pushed away. His first step was toward the trucks. Then he remembered that he had not gotten the biomarker onto Tarid.

He changed direction, running in a half stoop toward Colonel Zsar's position. A knot of soldiers were crouched behind one of the trucks, firing at one of the helicopters as it backed away from the battle.

The Voice warned that there were more choppers on the way.

"Where's the colonel?" yelled Danny in English. "I have to talk to him."

No one answered.

"I need Arabic," he told the Voice. "Translate, translate."

"Translate mode operational. Phrase was already delivered."

"Again," said Danny, who hadn't heard it in the confusion. "Where is the colonel?"

The soldiers didn't respond. One of the men had retrieved a mortar from the truck and was loading it to fire.

"You have to retreat," Danny told them.

The mortar shell whipped upward, sailing far over the regular army's position. Two of the rebel soldiers began shouting corrections.

Always in the past, the rebels were the ones on the offensive. The ambushed regulars, taken by surprise, would quickly panic. They expected the same now, not realizing these were specially trained troops who'd worked for months with Egyptian advisors. They were not about to give up easily.

Danny saw a man he thought was Colonel Zsar huddled with another man behind another truck about ten yards away. As he rose to run over, the Voice warned that two more helicopter gunships were on their way.

"You have to retreat," Danny yelled as he ran, using just the Arabic words. He slid in behind the men. "Colonel Zsar, you have to retreat!"

The man turned. It wasn't Zsar, but one of his lieutenants.

"I don't have time for you, gun dealer," said the man.

"The army is sending reinforcements."

"Did you bring them?"

"I'm not a fool."

The lieutenant pulled his pistol out. He was angry about the ambush, and though he believed it was Red Henri's fault, he couldn't be sure. At the moment it didn't matter—he pointed the gun at Danny's head.

"You betrayed us," he said. "Why are we being attacked? We've never been attacked."

The Voice translated, but Danny didn't need to know the exact words— the gun was obvious enough.

"Not me." Danny pointed at his chest, where the bullet had hit his vest. "They're trying to kill me, too."

He said the words in English, ignoring the translation.

The lieutenant straightened his arm to fire. Danny felt all of the blood in his body rush away. He was paralyzed, welded to the spot. He saw the gun.

A burst of fire took the officer down.

"Let's go! Let's go!" yelled Boston, appearing at Danny's side. He grabbed his vest and jerked him backward.

"I need Tarid," said Danny.

"Screw that."

"I need to tag him," insisted Danny. But he started running with Boston toward the truck.

About five yards from the trucks he spotted a knot of men hunkered near the road. They were a good thirty yards away, kneeling and crouching. A battered pickup sat between them and most of the battle.

Tarid had to be among them, Danny thought. He wasn't anywhere else.

"This way!" he yelled to Boston.

Danny's intuition was correct. Realizing the helicopters meant they were being attacked by an elite force, Tarid had tried to escape as soon as the battle started. He'd run to the truck, but its engine compartment had been shot up by one of Red Henri's men and it wouldn't start.

He raised his rifle as the two men approached, then realized it was the arms dealer. His respect—and fear—of Bani Aberhadji was so great that it overcame his suspicions that the man had arranged the ambush. Still, he had little use for him, and debated whether to shoot him as he ran.

Danny saw the gun in his hand. He tucked his head down. He was going to complete his mission, even if it killed him, even if fear overwhelmed him.

"The army is sending reinforcements," Danny shouted. "You have to retreat."

Tarid stared at him.

"You've been shot," said Danny. He reached his left hand toward Tarid's brow, which was covered with blood. He touched it for a second.

Tarid brushed the fingers away angrily. It was someone else's blood.

"Who the hell are you?" he said. "Who are you?"

"Kirk," said Danny.

"Go," said Tarid.

"Come with us. We'll take you to safety." Danny reached for him. "Come on."

"No, you go," said Tarid, pulling back and raising his weapon.

"I'm just trying to help," said Danny, starting to back away.

"Go!" yelled Tarid.

One of Colonel Zsar's men began yelling at Tarid, pointing toward the highway. A rocket-propelled grenade streaked overhead, its whistle piercing the air before it struck the open field a hundred yards away.

"Boss!" yelled Boston.

"All right," said Danny, turning. "Time to go."

28

Blemmyes Village, Sudan

LEANING UP AGAINST THE WALL OF THE BARN BUILDING, just out of the view of the video camera he'd discovered, Nuri decided he had two options. One was to put everything back the way he'd found it, and return tomorrow with a better plan. The other was to press ahead. That made the most sense, but he wasn't sure how to defeat the camera without being detected.

He looked up at it. It was small, with a cable running from it. There was no way to tell if it was even working. The barn was very dark, but even a cheap low light camera would pick up an image. He had to assume that it did work and was being monitored.

"What if we climb up in the rafters?" he said, more to himself than Hera, who was right behind him on the other side of the wall.

"And then what?" she asked.

"I'm not sure. But this place is too well-guarded to ignore."

Nuri pulled himself up between the posts. Set about sixteen inches apart, they would have been a tighter squeeze for a taller man, but he had little trouble.

The beams running across the ceiling were just as close, but walking across felt much more dangerous—a slip was going to hurt, even if he didn't fall all the way through.

Hera started up behind him.

"Wait," he said in a stage whisper. "Put the wall back if you're coming."

"Put the wall back?"

"In case the guard comes."

"How the hell are we going to get back out?"

"Tighten two or three of the screws from the inside. We'll undo them."

"That won't work. The panels attach from the outside."

"Then you'll have to stay outside. You have to put the panel back. The guard may come around. I don't need you here. It's all right."

Hera slipped back through the posts and put the panel back in place. Meanwhile, Nuri worked himself about halfway down the room, crawling along the rafters. The factory was divided into a large work area to the right and a much smaller section of rooms to the left. The work area was open. There were machines in the large room, sinks, large drying machines, and a bagger.

There weren't, however, any more video cameras. Or any other security devices, for that matter. He looked back at the camera he'd gotten by. It was aimed directly at the hallway.

Why watch there and not the larger room? It seemed to be protecting the rooms in the back—yet they were empty.

Nuri took it for granted that Colonel Zsar knew little if anything about security systems, but whoever had installed this one had. So the camera had some reason to be there, as did the window and room alarms.

"Hera, go around the back and make sure there's nothing in any of the rooms there," he whispered over the Voice's radio circuit. "I'm confused."

"That seems to be a constant state."

Nuri worked his way over the rooms, which were covered by a Sheetrock ceiling. One had a large fan vent in the middle. Deciding it must be a restroom, he was about to move on when he noticed two different sets of wires running from the fan unit—a power wire and a smaller, stranded wire, the type typically used in an alarm unit.

"Look for a bathroom," he told Hera. "See if there's anything—I don't know. Unusual."

Hera had to bite her lip not to say something nasty in return.

"I can't find the bathroom," she told him after a moment. "It doesn't have a window."

Which explained the need for the fan, but not an alarm.

There were other things the wire might have belonged to, such as a thermostat, but Nuri was stuck on the idea of an alarm. He checked the wire, found current, then examined the fan, carefully unscrewing the upper housing. A motion detector was mounted just below the fan unit.

Why would anyone want to know if someone was taking a leak?

He decided to put his own bug into the unit. He took out a fresh stick of gum and began chewing furiously, then put a small piece on the back of the bug. As he hunted for a place to put it, the Voice told him two men were approaching the building.

"Armed, coming from the rebel camp," added the computer.

"Hera. Someone's coming." Nuri flattened himself on the ceiling. "Rebel soldiers. Be careful back there."

"Where are they?"

"On the road. Just be quiet."

"Are they going in the building?"

"I don't know. Probably not. They've never had a shift change at this time before."

But the men were guards, and were coming for a new shift. Colonel Zsar had taken his best men with him to the meeting, replacing the guards at the barn and the village. Had Tarid not been there, the colonel might not have even bothered to post another guard, but the Iranian would have had a fit if he'd found out.

To make the dull duty more palatable—and in hopes of actually keeping them awake—Colonel Zsar divided the normal shift. The two soldiers spotted by the Voice through the blimp's feed were coming to replace the men on watch.

The men went to the side door of the factory, talking and laughing loudly enough that Nuri could hear them quite clearly, even before they began shouting to wake the guard, who'd fallen fast asleep less than an hour after coming on duty. It took a few shouts before they roused him; they found that hilarious rather than troubling. When he finally woke and let them in, they claimed they had just left his wife and suggested he look for evidence in nine months.

Nuri listened to the Voice's translation, which was flat and without humor. When they were done joking, they asked if he'd seen anything, which for some reason elicited a new round of laughter. Then they told him to go home to his wife and "sloppy seconds."

The Voice confessed that it could not find the proper definition of the slang term.

As he listened, Nuri slipped across the rafters to the edge of the open area, planting a video bug in a position where it could scan nearly all of the front room. He placed another one to cover the hallway, then slipped back over the bathroom area, pressing himself down and trying to breathe as softly as he could.

29

Murim Wap, Sudan

BOSTON THREW THE LAND CRUISER INTO REVERSE EVEN AS Danny pulled himself inside. Dirt and gravel spat in every direction. Mortar shells exploded forty or fifty yards away. There were more helicopters nearby, their rotors pounding the air like the excited heartbeat of an oversized dinosaur.

They made it to the highway.

"Wait up," said Danny, struggling to get his bearings in the passenger seat. "I want to make sure they get out of here in one piece."

"We got to get the hell out, Colonel," snapped Boston. "All hell is breaking loose."

As if to underline his statement, a fresh volley of mortar shells landed nearby.

"You're going west," said Danny.

"We can't go back the way we came. We'd be running right by the Sudan troops."

"I have to make sure Tarid gets away," said Danny, still having trouble getting his bearings. "Pull off the road."

"We're sitting ducks here."

"Just pull off the goddamn road."

Boston veered off the asphalt. The other Land Cruiser stopped behind them.

Danny pulled out the control unit of the Voice. "I need the overhead images of the contact point," he told the computer.

The video from the UAV came onto the screen, streaks and flashes of gunfire, flares and explosions

"Locate marked subject."

"Located."

Two stars appeared on the screen. The Owl was supplying the image.

"One of those is Tarid," said Danny. "Who's the other?"

"Rebel identified as Tilia."

"Highlight Tarid and zoom."

The image zoomed on Tarid, but the screen was so small that Danny couldn't get a good feel for his situation. Was he trapped? He seemed to be moving, but even that wasn't clear on the small screen, which was intended primarily as a control display.

"What's Tarid doing?" Danny asked the Voice.

"Subject is moving south of the road, accompanied by seven other soldiers."

"Boss, we staying here forever?" asked Boston.

"Relax," Danny told him.

"Not understood," said the Voice.

"What is the disposition of the Sudanese army troops?" Danny asked MY-PID. "Mark the main groups on the screen."

The computer did so. All of the troops were north of the road.

"All right," Danny told Boston. "Let's get the hell out of here."

Boston got back on the road. Danny leaned his head back and closed his eyes, reliving not the firefight, but his emotions, his hesitation and the butterflies. He'd accomplished his mission, and yet he felt like a failure—a coward.

Any objective observer would have scoffed. Yet it was the fear that Danny remembered.

"Army troops approaching," warned the Voice.

"What?" said Danny, sitting up.

"Four armored personnel carriers on road ahead, traveling east at a high rate of speed."

"Will they reach the intersection before us?"

"Affirmative."

"Boss?" asked Boston.

"Keep going," Danny told him. "MY-PID, I need an alternate route back to Base Camp Alpha. Pronto."

"Working."

30

Blemmyes Village, Sudan

NURI LAY ACROSS THE RAFTERS ABOVE THE SHEETROCK, waiting as the new set of guards took their posts. One stayed in the small vestibule near the door, snuggling into the soft chair. Despite the ridicule he'd heaped on his colleague, he was dozing within a few minutes, done in by boredom, the stale air, and the late hour.

The other guard walked through the building, turned into the hallway, and headed for the restroom, his way lit by a soft red light activated from the threshold. He hummed as he walked, bouncing and full of energy.

The man had learned that his wife was pregnant with their first child earlier in the day, and the prospect of a new son — and the bonus Colonel Zsar paid to all married men when their children were born—filled him with something approaching glee. He'd taken inside guard duty before, though always when people were working; tonight the laboratory would be dark, its last batch of material processed twenty-four hours before.

Though guard duty was a boring, mindless task, he liked the chance to let his mind roam, filled with songs he was constantly inventing. He wasn't much of a soldier, as he would have been the first to admit. He'd joined the colonel's army for the pay, choosing to be a rebel because soldiers were hardly ever paid on time. Religion was also a factor in his choice; he wouldn't have joined Uncle Dpap, even though his reputation for watching over his men was better than the colonel's, because Dpap was a nonbeliever. As dim as the soldier's own concept of Islam might be, he nonetheless observed the proper forms, praying and dreaming of one day making his own hajj, the sacred pilgrimage to Mecca.

Nuri held his breath as the guard walked down the hallway nearby, then entered the restroom. The light shone through the fan covering. Nuri slipped over to the fan and peeked into the room through the open space. He couldn't see the rebel—he'd gone into the commode nearest the door—but he could see the man's rifle, an early model AK-47, complete with a battered but polished wooden stock, leaning up against the exterior of the stall almost directly below him.

The man's humming continued. Nuri wondered if it might be possible to somehow plant a bug on his gear.

He could put one of the small ones into the gun barrel. The gum would make it stick.

It was a crazy idea. The device would be found as soon as the man cleaned his rifle.

The rebels fell asleep on guard duty and laughed about it. Were they likely to clean their weapons?

And what if it was discovered? So what? By that time he would already have a decent idea of what was going on.

If he surrounded it with gum, the soldier would just think it was a stone or some sort of debris. He'd think it was a prank and never report it. It wouldn't look like much of anything.

The fan was held down by a pair of screws. Nuri undid them, then put his hand on the fan assembly and lifted it slowly. The detector of course found motion, but it would be dismissed by anyone who knew the guard was in the bathroom.

Just as Nuri got the fan off to the side, the soldier stopped singing in his commode.

Nuri started to replace it. Then the man began humming again.

The barrel of the gun was about six feet from him.

Nuri leaned over, but his small body left him a good four feet away. He slipped over some more, leaning farther, but was still at least three feet from the barrel. It was just a little too far, he decided, stretching farther.

His knee slipped against the joist, and suddenly he started

to lose his balance. He threw his hand out, grabbing on the top of the nearest stall.

"Who's there? What?" said the rebel soldier.

Nuri, leaning almost full out of the hole, reached over and took the barrel of the gun with his right hand. He pushed the bug into the barrel, then pulled himself back up. As he did, the gun slid on the floor, clattering against the wood.

The rebel hurried to finish. He couldn't see the fan from where he was, nor did he even imagine that someone had slipped inside the building. He thought his companion was playing tricks on him.

"I'll get you, I'll get you," he shouted as he pulled open the door.

He wasn't surprised that no one was there. He went and grabbed his gun, spinning all around. He checked the stalls, but didn't look at the ceiling before running out and going back to the vestibule to berate his friend.

Nuri decided it was time to leave.

"I'm coming out," he whispered to Hera. "Get the panel off. Quick! And be *quiet*."

He scrambled across the rafters. Hera pulled off the screws and took the panel away. As she did, Nuri reached the side and swung out through the opening, landing in a tumble on his feet. Hera put the wall back in place, turning the screws quickly.

"Give me some," Nuri told Hera, taking the screws.

"Sssh," said Hera.

"Yeah, yeah, yeah."

The Voice, listening through the bug Nuri had put in the gun, translated the conversation between the two guards. The guard from the vestibule said he'd been napping; the other one refused to believe him. Both then began accusing the other of trying to pull a hoax. Finally they decided to conduct a full search of the building.

They looked in the front room, then in the hallway, and finally in the empty offices at the rear.

"Maybe it was Jacob inside," said the guard from the vestibule.

"Maybe," said the other man doubtfully. He was now starting to think that he had either imagined it or that the ghosts some of his neighbors believed in were real.

"Well, go ask him, and leave me alone," said the first.

During the search, Nuri and Hera circled around to the other side of the road, back in the direction of the motorcycle in case they had to make a quick getaway.

Nuri stopped when he heard there was another man in the building.

Finally he understand what was going on there. Or at least part of it.

He reached into his pocket and took out the small iPodlike control for the Voice unit. Then he told the computer to track the bug feed on an outline of the building.

"What are we seeing?" Hera asked, looking over his shoulder at the tiny image.

"I slipped a bug into the guard's rifle."

"Where?"

"In the barrel."

"That's not an image."

"I wasn't lucky enough to get it in heads-up. Next time I'll do better."

Actually, the gum surrounding it would have made it very difficult for the camera to pick up anything. Hera wasn't sure whether slipping the bug into the gun was the ballsiest thing she'd ever heard—or the craziest. She kept silent, deciding she didn't want to compliment him. He had enough of a swelled head already.

The guard returned to the hall, and then to the area where the restroom was. And then he went behind the building—downstairs, Nuri realized, into some sort of secret basement that extended into the hill behind the building.

The earth hampered the audio transmission, but he had heard and seen enough.

"We have to plant radiation traps around the site," he told Hera. "And get some soil samples from the front yard."

"What's going on?"

"I think we just found out where those metal tubes are."

31

In the vicinity of Murim Wap, Sudan

THE VOICE TOLD DANNY THERE WAS A ROAD TO THE NORTH about a half mile away. If they took it, they could follow a series of trails north and then back east to their camp. The detour would require that they drive through two leveled fields, but seemed considerably safer than running past the approaching government forces.

Boston had trouble finding the turnoff. Then the road petered out after barely half a mile. Even with the night glasses and the GPS, it was slow going.

"Danny, you on?" said Nuri, coming over the line.

"Yeah, I'm here."

"What's your situation?"

"We're heading back to camp. Red Henri and then the Sudanese army ambushed us."

"The Sudanese ambushed you?"

"Right."

"Are they working with Red Henri?"

"No. He ended up in the cross fire. Red Henri got wind of the meeting somehow and showed up. The Sudanese army came a little while after that. With helicopters."

"There are plenty of informers in both rebel groups," said Nuri. "Colonel Zsar's especially. They may have tipped the government off."

"I guess."

"Did you tag the Iranian?"

"Yeah."

"Looks like you got someone else, too," said Nuri.

"Tilia, Uncle Dpap's aide," said Danny. "It was an accident."

"It's not important. Don't worry. Damn. The Sudanese are throwing all sorts of troops at these guys. This must be Egypt's doing, helping them. Damn."

"I don't know if our guy is going to get out," said Danny. "They have a lot of troops coming."

"That may not be critical right now," said Nuri.

"Turn into field, point-one miles," said the Voice.

Danny told Nuri to hold while he helped Boston navigate. The rutted field was filled with large rocks, but the ground was firm. They slowed to about five miles an hour, then followed a serpentine section of wall to a shallow streambed. Nearly a mile later they came to the road.

"All right," said Danny.

"I was beginning to wonder if you'd decided to drive back to the States," said Nuri when he got back to him.

"Just having trouble with the terrain. How did you do?"

"Better than expected. And worse. I think the Iranians are building a bomb."

"Here?"

"No, I don't know. We got some hits on uranium, but not weapons grade."

Actually, the detectors had found traces of material that typically accompanied uranium, signaling that some sort of storage or processing was carried out there. Finding actual weapons grade uranium required very sensitive gear placed very close to the material, and even then would have taken quite a bit of luck. Still, the finding was critical.

"I don't have it all figured out," added Nuri, "but I think they're doing this in stages. This would be an early stage. I have to talk to Reid and Stockard."

"Right."

"I'll let them know we've tagged the Iranian and we're

going to follow him. If they have other plants, he'll take us to them."

"If he makes it out of the ambush," said Danny.

"I'll be at the base in another twenty minutes," said Nuri, ignoring Danny's pessimism. "Let me know if anything comes up."

Two minutes later the Voice warned Danny that four Sudanese army trucks were traveling on the road they were headed for. Rather than engage in a firefight, Danny decided their best option would be to simply go far enough off the road so they couldn't be seen and wait for them to pass. They crossed the field until they found a cluster of low trees and waited.

MEANWHILE, THE REMAINS OF COLONEL ZSAR'S FORCES had regrouped south of the road and were sweeping east to escape the army troops. Four of Zsar's men had been killed; nearly all the rest, including himself, had suffered at least minor injuries.

Tarid was among the few who hadn't been hit. He found the colonel as he retreated, and joined him in a pickup truck. They rode together in the front of the pickup, jostling against each other and the colonel's driver as they streaked across the rutted road.

"Red Henri must have betrayed us," said Zsar. "He must have planned the entire venture."

"More likely it was one of Dpap's men," said Tarid. "Or one of yours."

Colonel Zsar bristled. "Maybe the arms dealer was the culprit."

"No."

"No rebel would do this."

"His men shot down two of the helicopters," said Tarid. "He warned us. He has very good intelligence. He's smarter than you think. Greedy, but smart."

"The helicopters may have been a show," said Colonel Zsar. He prided himself on never having retreated in the face of the Sudanese army. His ego had been stung by the reversal. "We could have taken them, all of them," he added. "If I'd brought more men."

"You can take them another time."

The more Colonel Zsar brooded about his reputation, the more he realized that he couldn't simply run. He had to do something—he had to defeat the army.

"Turn the truck around," he told the driver. He took out his satellite phone.

"What are you doing?" asked Tarid.

"We're going back."

"You can't go back—they've got you outgunned. They're bringing more reinforcements."

"So will I."

Tarid argued, but it was a waste of breath. Colonel Zsar had decided his reputation demanded that he defeat the army soldiers who had attacked. Even if the victory was symbolic—a simple return to the battlefield would do—he would be able to restore his reputation.

"You're letting your ego guide you," said Tarid. "A dangerous thing."

Zsar frowned.

"Then let me out," said Tarid.

The door was locked. As he reached to pull up the lock, Colonel Zsar pointed his pistol at him. If he let Tarid go, the others might follow.

"No cowards," he hissed.

Tarid let go of the door.

As THEY WAITED FOR THE SUDANESE TROOP TRUCKS TO pass, Danny had the Voice give him periodic updates on the Iranian's position.

He'd clearly escaped, cutting south.

Good, thought Danny.

He was stopping.

Why?

He was returning to the battlefield.

What?

"Are you sure?" Danny asked.

"Affirmative."

"What's the situation there?"

"Positioning Owl UAV," reported the Voice. A few minutes later MY-PID delivered a sitrep; situation report. "Reinforcements still en route. Sudanese army capturing wounded rebels. Helicopters approaching from the west."

Tarid was driving back into a trap. And Danny knew there was nothing he could do about it.

WHEN HE SAW THE FIRES IN THE DISTANCE, COLONEL ZSAR decided to wait on the road for his reinforcements to arrive. There was little harm in waiting, he realized; the longer he took to strike back, the more relaxed the regular soldiers would become, and the easier his victory.

He figured that it would take a little over thirty minutes for the rest of his army to arrive. Once they were there, he would sweep onto the battlefield, routing the regulars the way they had routed him.

He would pick only a small group, attack and flee. That would be enough for the symbolic victory he wanted.

The colonel was sketching his plan out in his head when he heard the helicopters approaching. He got out of the truck to look for them; when he did, he saw the dark shadows well over the horizon, heading in their direction.

"Out of the trucks!" he ordered. "Prepare for an attack."

Tarid was livid. "You idiot!" he yelled at Zsar. "We have to get out of here!"

"Shut up and prepare to fight," said Zsar, starting to turn away.

"You idiot! Where are your troops?"

The colonel stopped. "What did you call me?"

"An idiot!" said Tarid, taking two steps and screaming in Zsar's face. "You were safe. You—"

Colonel Zsar delivered a roundhouse to Tarid's head. The Iranian staggered back, then coiled his legs and arms to strike back. Before he could, Zsar's driver smashed him across the back of the head with his AK-47. Tarid fell to the ground, unconscious and oblivious to the firefight starting around him.

32

Washington, D.C.

WITHIN HOURS OF NURI'S RETURN FROM BLEMMYES Village, his discovery and theory had been disseminated to a small coterie of analysts and officials in Washington, D.C. The news focused a great deal of intelligence for the analysts, giving them a framework to arrange a veritable warehouse worth of data.

It also alarmed Breanna, Reid, and everyone else who heard about it.

The machined aluminum was now identified as part of a tool holding a centrifuge assembly. To grossly oversimplify the process, the tool could be used to separate elements of different atomics weight from each other. Such a tool was needed in one step of the process of extracting "special" uranium from "regular" uranium. The special uranium—an isotope with a different atomic number—could then be used to create an atomic bomb.

Jasmine was now viewed as part of a much larger, more important project. It could also be seen as one of several similar operations around the world, directly related or not. At least three possibilities had already been identified.

But the data raised a large number of new questions. Assuming there were other processing plants, where were they? How did material get from one location to another? Was the intention to stockpile the material, or was bomb construction contemplated—or maybe even under way? Where did this occur?

Breanna contemplated all of these questions the next morning as she waited for Jonathon Reid's car to pick her up at the Pentagon. She expected them to be raised at the hastily scheduled briefing she and Reid were going to give to the National Security Council. The council had already been scheduled to meet; they were added to the agenda when their information was added to the daily intelligence report.

The one question Breanna hadn't contemplated was the one Reid asked as soon as she slipped into the back of car: "Do you think it's time we turned this over to traditional channels?"

Surprise was obvious on her face.

"Whiplash is still experimental," explained Reid, who'd been considering the matter even before Nuri reported in. "The unit is very small. Something of this magnitude is beyond its scope."

"I wouldn't call Whiplash experimental."

"Whatever we call it, we didn't anticipate this big a situation when we sent Nuri out," said Reid. "Or Danny Freah and his people. We were looking at a bugging and surveillance operation, nothing more. The next step is more involved."

"No, the next step is to gather more information."

"We'll have to destroy the plant."

"They can do that as well. But we don't want to do that yet, do we? We need to flesh out the entire network. We don't know how big the operation is there, not to mention where else it's operating."

"A huge undertaking," said Reid. "One for a very large, and experienced, task group."

"Danny Freah can run this. He's had experience. Especially with nuclear warheads."

"I'm not questioning him or his ability," said Reid. "The scope of the project is simply greater than what we foresaw. We need more people."

Reid was also concerned about Nuri. The CIA officer had

been selected as the program's first operative primarily because of his comfort with the technology and his familiarity with Africa. He had barely three years of experience with the Agency, and before that was in college. While he'd done fine so far, at this point it made sense to bring a more experienced officer onto the scene.

"I can see more people," said Breanna. "Obviously, these other leads have to be examined. But we have people in the field. They're doing a good job. We can't pull them off."

"Who coordinates the mission? Who compiles the data?"

"We do. It moves forward exactly as it has."

"You don't understand the scope," said Reid. "Or the politics."

"What politics?"

Reid stared at the glass divider that separated the hybrid-powered Town car's passenger compartment from the driver. Many members of the Agency considered him an old school idealist, but he thought of himself as a realist. As much as he hated Agency and bureaucratic politics, as much as he isolated himself from them, he nonetheless realized they had to be taken into account at all times.

"You're DoD," he said, referring to the Department of Defense. "I'm Central Intelligence. Whiplash is split between those agencies. It starts there."

"And we can end it there."

"No. We can't."

"Do you want to be in charge?" Breanna asked. "Is that it?"

She felt her cheeks starting to flush. She was trying to control her anger, but it wasn't easy. She liked Reid, but she felt he had ambushed her in an attempt to get an advantage in a ridiculous bureaucratic game. It seemed out of character, or at least out of sync with the way he had acted until now.

"Depending on where this goes, we may have hundreds of people in the field, and thousands behind them supporting them," said Reid. "We don't have the infrastructure to pull off a large operation. It's simply a matter of size."

"You have the infrastructure, at CIA, as deputy director. Is that the point?"

"I'm not deputy director."

"He'd run it through you. So you take Whiplash out of the loop and run it on your own?"

"It's possible that would happen," admitted Reid. "But that wouldn't be my recommendation. We would turn the entire matter over to Operations, and let them handle it the way they've handled missions like this in the past. Some of the people who worked on sabotaging the original Iranian program under the previous administration—"

"There's a recommendation," said Breanna bitterly.

"They're experienced people. Some of the results were not that good. Some were. In any event, there's a structure set up, institutional memory—"

"But that's just the point, Jonathon. Everything we've done—Whiplash, MY-PID, the other gear—everything is an attempt to break out of the old mode."

"Sometimes you don't have to reinvent the wheel."

"But we did. And now that we see it working, you want to go back to the horse and buggy."

Reid put his hand on the blue briefing book on the seat next to him, sliding his fingers along the top edge. He realized she did have a point. They were pioneering new techniques for combining covert action and intelligence gathering, using high-tech tools with a streamlined command structure. They had gotten results.

"I will talk briefly about the unit, just enough to let those who aren't aware of it understand its capabilities," said Breanna, deciding to move on to what they'd planned to discuss. "You can talk about mission."

"And when they ask for recommendations?"

"I'll say we should continue. You can say whatever you want."

AS SHE STEPPED FROM THE CAR TO HEAD INTO THE WEST Wing, Breanna's personal cell phone rang. She reached into her pocketbook and took it out. Her daughter's face was on the screen—Teri was calling from school.

Breanna felt her heart stop as she hit the Talk button.

"Honey, what's up?"

"Mom—"

"She's all right, Mrs. Stockard," said a male voice in the background. "Tell her you're all right."

All Breanna could think of was that Teri had been kidnapped.

"I fell during gym, Mom."

Oh, thank God, thought Breanna. "Are you okay, honey?"

"My leg hurts."

"Is that the doctor behind you?" she asked, her relief receding. "Honey—is that the doctor?"

"Actually, Mrs. Stockard, I'm the nurse practitioner at Day School," said the man. "Your daughter is okay. I don't think she broke any bones, but with your permission I'd like to have her taken to the hospital just as a precaution. For X rays. I've seen dozens of these, ma'am. Usually this is just a little twist and bruise. They're out running by the afternoon. But I would prefer to err on the side of caution. I hope you understand."

"I appreciate that, Doctor—"

"Simon. Nurse Simon, or just Simon."

"I'm sorry, Simon. Yes, please—she should go to the hospital right away." Breanna looked up at Reid, who was staring at her with the most concerned expression she'd ever seen on his face. *It's okay,* she mouthed.

"We're going to need you or, uh, someone to meet her at the hospital," said Simon.

Today, of all days, thought Breanna.

"Someone will be there," she told him, barely remembering to ask which hospital before hanging up.

"Your daughter?" asked Reid.

"Just a silly sports injury," she said.

"Do you want me to fill in?"

Breanna was torn between the impulse to run to her daughter's side and the briefing she was supposed to give.

"Let me get Zen on the phone," she said. She forced a smile. "I think he's on hospital duty today."

ZEN WAS IN THE MIDDLE OF A COMMITTEE HEARING when his legislative aide, Steph Delanie, tapped him on the shoulder.

"It's your wife," she whispered. "Urgent."

Zen gripped his wheels— after all these years, he still preferred a nonpowered chair—and backed away from his spot at the table. He caught the eye of the committee chairman, who nodded, then turned and went out into the hall with Delanie. Another member of his staff, Jason Black, stood nearby with a cell phone.

"Probably forgot where I hid the peanut butter," said Zen, trying to joke as he reached for the phone. "Hey, babe, what's up?"

"Jeff, they're taking Teri to the hospital. She hurt her leg. She's OK, but they want X rays to make sure. Can you go over? I'm—I'm just on my way to see the President and the National Security Council. I'm right outside the door."

"Where is Teri? Is she OK?"

"Yes, she's OK. The school nurse called. They want to take her there as a precaution and I said fine. The nurse is a he, by the way."

"Which hospital, Bree? Is she all right?"

"She's *fine.*"

Zen could withstand any amount of pain without whimpering—he might complain, curse, and stomp things with his fist, but never whimper. If his daughter or wife had a cold, however, he suffered incredibly. There was simply no way he could be stoic when either of them was in pain.

"She's at Dominion," added Breanna, a little less emphatically. "In the emergency room."

"I'm on my way. I'm there."

"Jeff—"

"She'll be fine Bree. I have it under control."

Zen hung up. He told Delanie to have the rest of his day's schedule canceled, then had Jason Black accompany him to the hospital.

Black was just out of college, low enough on the totem pole that a boring job like escorting the senator seemed exciting. Ordinarily, Zen might have regaled him with stories about how boring the hearing had been, or the New York congressman who was rumored to be sleeping with his campaign coordinator, but he was too focused on Teri to think about any of that. He drove himself—he could never have been patient enough to let someone else take the wheel.

Black, sitting in the passenger seat, fidgeted silently the entire way. He longed to ask Zen some questions about his days at Dreamland, but was afraid of offending him. The senator could often be heard complaining to Delanie and others about how boring and stale those stories had become.

A security guard tried to wave them away from the staff parking area as they pulled up.

"That's for staff," shouted the man, running over as Zen backed from the wheel and pushed the wheelchair into the lift next to the door. "You have to move!"

The door opened. The forklift-like elevator pulled Zen out of the van and began lowering him to the curb. The appearance of an obviously handicapped man gave the guard pause—but only for a second.

"Sir, I'm sorry. You can't park here," said the guard, toning his voice down. "It's for doctors and nurses."

"I outrank them," Zen barked, rolling toward the door.

"Now listen," blustered the guard. "I don't care if you are handicapped. That's not where you park."

Black had to run to catch up to his boss. Zen reached into his pocket as he caught up with him and grabbed his keys.

"Move the van so Barney Fife over there doesn't have a ~~ck~~. I'd hate for Pete to lose another constituent."

~~~ doors opened and Zen glided inside the emer-

gency room. One thing about hospitals—they were generally easy to get in and out of if you were in a wheelchair.

That was about the only nice thing Zen could ever say about them.

"I'm Senator Stockard," he announced to the nurse at the desk. "You have my daughter here for X rays."

The word "senator" jarred the nurse, and for a second she wasn't sure if he was telling the truth. Before she could say anything, a doctor came out from the office area.

"Senator Stockard, I'm glad you could get here so quickly," he said as he walked over. "I'm Mike Watson. Dr. Bozzone called me and asked if I'd come down and check out your daughter personally."

"Who called Billy?"

"Might've been your wife, Senator."

"She's always a step ahead of me. Where's Teri?"

Dr. Watson—his name had been a source of jokes since med school—led Zen back through the halls to the X-ray department. Teri was sitting on an examining table, waiting as one of the techs readied the machine. A member of her school staff was sitting in the corner, a magazine on her lap.

"Daddy, what are *you* doing here?"

"Hey, angel. I was looking for someone to play golf with. The doctors mentioned you were here, so I postponed the game."

"You don't play golf." Teri gave him a mock frown, then leaned down from the table to give him a kiss. "Where's Mom?"

"With the President."

Teri frowned. She had expected her mother, not her father. She loved them both, but it was her mother who always showed up at times like this.

Plus, she had said she would.

Zen read the disappointment in her face. "Mom's working hard," he told her. "She had something very important today."

"I know."

He decided it was better to change the subject. "What, are you bucking for a chair like mine?"

"Oh get out." She hopped down from the table and began dancing around. "See? I'm fine."

"Probably, but let's let the X ray determine that," said Dr. Watson.

THE NATIONAL SECURITY COUNCIL MET IN A SECURE CON-ference room well below ground level in the White House "basement," but the room was bathed in what to the naked eye seemed like perfect daylight. The environmental controls kept the room precisely at 68 degrees, a fact that occasionally irked the President, who preferred a slightly cooler temperature, but allowed it to remain there out of deference to her aides and cabinet members' comfort.

A rectangular table sat at the center of the large room. A video screen tilted upward in front of each of the thirty-six places; the screens were tied into a conferencing system as well as the secure intelligence intranet. Each seat was equipped with a bank of secure communication lines, allowing text and e-mail as well as scrambled voice and video.

Best of all, the coffee and tea were world-class.

Breanna took her seat near the center of the far side, next to Reid and two spots from the Secretary of Defense, Charles Lovel.

Lovel nodded as she sat. He had started out as an enthusiastic supporter of the program, but lately had been rethinking its direction because of budget pressures. A relatively small part of the Pentagon's so-called "black budget," it still represented hundreds of millions of dollars, with the potential to consume much more. Lovel had bought the "multiplier effect" that Whiplash allowed—the idea that the program would pay for itself by encouraging more research and development, implementing high-tech tools faster and cheaper, and saving on manpower costs down the line. But the program was still so new that cutting it would not raise much of an outcry—far less, say, than lopping something like a destroyer out of the budget.

Lovel would have been the first to admit that counting angry heads was a terrible way to set government policy. But he called himself a "big picture" guy, and in the big picture he saw, some terrible decisions had to be made to support the overall agenda.

Breanna sat down and took a small memory card from her pocket. When she slipped it into the slot in the table before her, a keyboard appeared on the screen. She touch-typed her encryption code, enabling access to the files of her presentation, along with additional background and documentation.

She was worried about her daughter. She knew Zen could handle whatever came up—he was always taking care of them somehow. But still, she felt she should be there, reassuring Teri that everything was fine.

The attendant brought Breanna a cup of coffee. As she started to stir it, everyone in the room rose. The President had arrived.

"All right, let's get to work," said Christine Mary Todd. A tall woman, she moved with quick strides, shoulders back and head high. In a man, her quick gait might have been considered brisk, her physical style assertive. As a woman, they gave visual ammunition to critics who found her abrupt and distant.

"Ms. Stockard, Mr. Reid. Very good of you two to come on such short notice," she said as she sat. The President did not attend every National Security meeting, but had planned on coming to this one for other reasons. News of the nuclear network made her attendance even more critical today. "Who's going first?"

That was the President's style—plunge right into the situation without too much fuss. Breanna glanced around, waiting for everyone to settle into their seats before beginning.

"Some months ago, we initiated a joint program between the CIA and Defense that allows us to test and implement new technologies on an advanced basis," she said. Her voice was stiff, as was her prose. "The program is still in its very early stages, literally only a few weeks old, but we already have important results to share with you. Alarming results.

Some of you have received some information already, so I will be brief."

Breanna looked down at her presentation. She'd lost her place, but decided she didn't need to read the words. She knew what she wanted to say.

"My associate, Mr. Reid, represents the CIA. We work together. I'm going to very briefly talk about some of our technology and the unit involved, just to give you background on our capabilities. And then Jonathon—Mr. Reid—is going to talk about what we've found."

Breanna described MY-PID in simplistic terms, saying that it was a networked computer system that could be used by operatives in the field. Her description was intentionally bland; the few people in the room with a need to know the specifics already knew them. She then mentioned the Whiplash team, again in very general terms, noting that its full complement had not even been recruited yet.

She made a point of mentioning that Danny Freah was heading the team. His name was familiar to most if not all of the people in the room, adding credibility to the program.

Reid sat quietly, waiting for his turn to speak. Even now, he hadn't decided what he would recommend as the next step. His boss, mentor, and friend, CIA Director Herman Edmund, had made it clear that he wanted the entire project under CIA direction. Reid had been swayed, at least to some extent, by Breanna's arguments in the car.

"Excuse me," said Secretary of State Alistair Newhaven. "Is Whiplash intended as a strike team, or as an espionage unit?"

"A little of both," said Reid. He turned to Breanna, realizing he'd cut her off. "Sorry."

"Jonathon is right. It can be both, depending on what the situation requires. In this instance, I'd say the operation leaned toward—is leaning, I mean—toward espionage."

She paused and looked around the room. A few aides and staffers, lined up along the wall, were brimming with questions, but unless their bosses specifically asked for their input, none would dare ask them. Breanna turned and looked at Lovel, who nodded, then at Michael Bacon, the national security director. Bacon, sitting next to the President, nodded as well, indicating she should continue.

"Our first mission began with a single agent, who was attempting to gather information on an arms network, known as Jasmine, operating in the Sudan," said Breanna. "The operation—and the CIA officer, for that matter—were chosen primarily because of considerations with the systems we were testing and implementing. We wanted a real-world, real-time situation. After a few weeks we found it necessary to back him up, and so the agenda for the Whiplash team was moved ahead. And that's where things got interesting."

She turned to Reid.

"Yes, interesting. My colleague has a way with understatement," said Reid. He flashed a smile. "Let me give you the headline first: Iran, or perhaps some element of its government, is refining nuclear material in Sudan, we believe in preparation for constructing a bomb."

If the room had been silent while Breanna spoke, now it was an absolute vacuum, all potential for sound pumped out of it. Reid briefly sketched what they had found, emphasizing that though the intelligence was still very preliminary, it was nonetheless very good.

"We're not relying on spies here, agents who have an interest in leading us on. These are our own people," Reid said. "We have radiation sniffers that have data for us. We have purchases. We are still pulling everything together, and admittedly there is much that we don't know. But the basic finding is unassailable—there is an operation here to refine nuclear material that can be used in a bomb."

"But Iran has just eliminated all of its nuclear weapons," said the Secretary of State. "And dismantled its weapons program. We've inspected it. We know this is true."

"They showed us what they wanted to show us."

"They showed us what we asked for—what the CIA told us to ask for," said Newhaven pointedly.

"I would note that our estimates show there is a potential for several pounds of material to be missing from the official count," said Dr. Bacon, who'd consistently been a stickler on this point. The missing material—if it was missing—was not quite enough for a bomb, but it was close.

"We don't need to debate whether the material is there or not," said the head of the CIA. "Obviously, we need more information. And quickly. The Iranian president is due here next week."

This wasn't news to most of the people in the room, but it was to Breanna and Reid, along with some of the lower-level staff people.

"Yes, Mr. Reid, Ms. Stockard, it's true," said the President. "We've kept it a secret because he doesn't want a backlash in his country. But the Iranian president will be here one week from tomorrow."

"Maybe he plans on bringing a bomb with him," quipped Bacon as the meeting continued.

Reid pressed his lips together and wondered if that might be more than just a joke.

33

Base Camp Alpha

WHILE THE PRESIDENT WAS MEETING WITH HER ADVISORS, Danny and Nuri were trying to figure out what had happened to Tarid. The biomarker was still active and showed that he was moving, indicating he was alive. That in itself was a minor miracle—from the looks of the video shot by the Owl, the Sudanese army had overwhelmed Colonel Zsar's force near the road, killing nearly all of the men there. A much larger force of rebels, arriving after the battle was finished, had been repulsed with light losses, leaving the body of their leader behind.

Tarid and the other rebels had been rounded up and driven about a hundred miles to an outpost near the village named Al-Quazi. The camp wasn't much—a few buildings inside a minefield about a half mile from the outskirts of the village. But it was the most secure spot the army had in the area.

Shortly after dawn, an American ferret satellite picked up a Sudanese transmission indicating that the prisoners were to be taken to Khartoum for interrogation as soon as possible. The commander replied that he would set out the following day.

"Gives us a little time to rescue him," said Nuri, reading the message with Danny not ten minutes after it had been sent. Neither man had gotten much sleep.

Danny Freah furled his arms and rested his elbows on the top of the table. He leaned closer to the computer screen, staring at a satellite image of the camp area.

"Can we get them out?" asked Nuri. He unpacked a bagel from its vacuum-packed container and put the two halves on the camp stove to toast. The bagels came preslit, but tended to be a little mushy.

"I don't know," admitted Danny. He sat back. "There are a lot of troops. I'm not sure we have enough firepower."

"We can hire more mercenaries."

"That's the problem. I don't know that we can trust them if things get tough."

"I can ask Reid for more people."

"I have the military end," said Danny, only to emphasize the point; there was not enough time for reinforcements to arrive. "I'll ask."

"Fair enough."

Danny flipped through the satellite images, examining the defenses at the post. The pictures had been made over a period of several days, but the defensive posture was always the same. A pair of soldiers manned a single checkpoint on the road between the village and the camp, blocking the road with a large troop truck. They had a sandbagged position nearby where they could retreat to if necessary. Their job was to check traffic and provide a warning for the fort in the unlikely event that rebels decided to move up the road in a column.

The road swept toward the camp, veering south about a hundred yards from the gate. A Chinese-made Hummer knockoff sat blocking the turnoff. It wasn't clear from the photos how many soldiers were in the vehicle, or even if there were any inside, but Danny assumed at least two men would be posted. A simple wooden gate barred the entrance. This was flanked by a pair of sandbagged gun positions and patrolled by four or five men.

Machine guns were located at the four corners of the camp in sandbagged positions. With the exception of the machine-gun nest on the southwest corner, they were all elevated about four feet above ground level, giving the occupants a better view of the distance and excellent firing lines, but also making them easier targets. The post at the southwest was heavier than the others, angled differently, and a little farther from the base perimeter. It appeared to be a cement bunker left over from an earlier camp and incorporated into the new defenses.

The gun posts were connected to trenches that zigged backward through a minefield surrounding the perimeter, allowing the soldiers and any reinforcements to get there without going through the minefield. A single fence topped by barbed wire surrounded the perimeter of the camp. This was not guarded, the commander either short of men or trusting to the machine guns and mines to keep the base safe.

There were several sandbagged walls along the sides of the rectangular camp, which could be used for cover if the outer defenses were breached, but there were no prepositioned guns behind any of them. However, there were six pickup trucks with weapons mounted in the back bed—five of them were machine guns, the last a grenade launcher. These could easily be rallied if the camp were attacked, and Danny saw them as potentially the most difficult obstacle to an assault.

The camp itself measured hardly more than an acre and a half. There were two buildings on the north: a barracks, where the soldiers who had taken part in the raid the night before were staying, and a smaller headquarters building adjacent to it. A large pair of gasoline tanks sat in the southeast corner, not far from the entrance. Next to them was a large open pen where the prisoners were being kept. The prisoners had no shelter from the sun or elements except for a small tarp strung at one side.

"No helipad," said Danny.

"No, the choppers would have come from further west and north," said Nuri. "They're part of an Egyptian-funded initiative. They wouldn't risk them on the ground here where they'd be potential targets."

Danny stared at the screen.

"So can we do it?" Nuri asked.

"Maybe. We better ask for permission first."

"Why?"

"Because we're not at war with Sudan."

"You shot down two of their helicopters last night."

"Only because they were going to kill me if I didn't."

"I think we just do it if we can do it," said Nuri. "That's why we're here."

"We'll ask anyway," said Danny.

34

Washington, D.C.

"If Iran is trying to circumvent the agreement they just signed, we should hit them hard with everything we've got," said Secretary of Defense Charles Lovel as the debate about the uranium finding continued. "We should obliterate these weapons plants."

"We have to find them first," said Secretary of State Alistair Newhaven. "And what do we do to the ones in another country? Like here, in Sudan. Do we just attack Sudan?"

"Sudan is not one of our allies," said Lovel. "By any stretch of the imagination. And they'd be thankful we took out the rebels."

"We're not at the stage where we can plan a strike," said the President, ending the discussion. "If we attack one plant, all of the others will be hidden. Clearly, we need to flesh this out. We can discuss the ethics and practicalities at a later date."

"Preferably before the president of Iran gets here," said Dr. Bacon.

The President looked across the table at Breanna and Reid. "Good work. Keep it up, please."

"Mrs. President, I did want to point out one thing," said CIA Director Edmund. "The operation started with a very small group." Edmund chose his words carefully, trying to find a diplomatic way of suggesting that Whiplash be pushed aside. "Time being of the essence, I would suggest that we're now at a point where the operation has exceeded their ability to handle it."

"Is that so?" President Todd looked directly at Breanna.

"I think we can continue to coordinate things under the present arrangement," said Breanna. "Jonathon has a great deal of expertise. We have excellent people in the field. They should remain in the lead."

"This is going to be too big for the Whiplash unit to handle," said Edmund. He turned to Reid. "Don't you agree, Jonathon?"

The tone in Edmund's voice would have intimidated many people. But if Reid had been one of them, he never would have been invited back to the CIA in the first place.

"There is difficulty in changing horses in midstream," he said. "I would suggest that the CIA work on fleshing out the larger network, while Whiplash concentrates on the implications of what it has discovered. The situation is still developing. The team should be allowed to continue following it to its logical extreme—if only for expediency's sake."

Edmund frowned, but part of him couldn't help admiring the art of Reid's reply. "Who's in charge?" he asked.

"The President," said Reid.

It was a dodge—Edmund meant of the overall operation, and Reid knew it—but mention of the President stopped any further discussion.

"Continue as we were," she said. "Whiplash follows the trail it has discovered. Mr. Edmund—your agency will coordinate a broader search and intelligence operation. I want an update on the situation every twelve hours. Now please, Breanna, Jonathon—we have some other items on our agenda, and I'm afraid we're going to have to ask you to leave."

"THANK YOU FOR SUPPORTING ME," BREANNA SAID AS THEY walked back to his car.

"Supporting us both, I believe."

"You stood up to your boss."

"That's my job, really. He doesn't mind, too much . . . but . . ." Reid let the word hang there for a moment. " . . . if this thing does get too big, then we hand it off."

"Absolutely."

"No ego."

"None. Well, maybe a little."

Reid laughed. So did Breanna.

Their laughter was short-lived. Breanna's secure satellite phone rang as she got into the car. It was Danny, who used the Voice's communication module to call her.

"Yes?"

"We have a situation," he told her. "And an opportunity."

Danny explained where Tarid was and what they hoped to do.

"Are you sure you can get him out?" Breanna asked when he finished.

"I can't be giving out guarantees like that. I think I can, or I wouldn't have called. I may be able to do it without the Sudanese army taking any casualties, if luck runs with us. But that's a big if. I can't guarantee anything. There's a village nearby—again, I'm not guaranteeing anything. Once things start happening, a lot of their soldiers may die."

Breanna turned to Reid. "They found the subject. He's being held in camp about fifty miles from the battle site. They want to follow him."

"That's what they should be doing," said Reid.

"The Sudanese army is guarding him," Breanna said. "Do you think we could get them to release him?"

"Given the state of relations between our countries, I'd say there's no chance at all."

Breanna covered the phone. "They have a plan to get him out, but Danny's concerned that some of the Sudanese soldiers will be killed if things go wrong."

"We have to be ruthless in this game."

Breanna wondered if it was really that easy for him. There were, of course, many arguments in favor of getting Tarid out, even if it did mean casualties among the Sudanese regulars. An atomic bomb would threaten millions. But somehow she felt the calculus should take more time.

"If they think they can get him out and follow him to the other elements in this chain," Reid added, "we should urge them to do so."

Breanna put the phone back to her head.

"Do it."

*   *   *

BREANNA CHECKED WITH ZEN ON THE WAY BACK TO HER office, making sure that Teri was all right. Zen's report was filled with his usual optimism and humor; according to him, Teri had charmed the staff and would no doubt have been running the place if he'd let her. Since it was too late to return to school by the time the X rays—"very negative," said the doctor—were done and read, Zen had taken her back to his office, where Teri did a little homework and research on the Web before heading home with him.

"Research meaning sending text messages to her friends?" Breanna asked.

"We have a rule in the Senate," replied Zen. "We only text enemies."

"Har-har."

"When are you coming home?" he asked.

"I don't know."

"No sweat. Teri and I have dinner covered. I'm thinking spaghetti and meatballs."

"Again?"

"It's the chef's favorite dinner. And I don't mind it, either."

"All right." Breanna glanced to the left, suddenly conscious of Reid. "I'll probably be home around six. Maybe seven."

"Which means nine, right?"

"Close to seven."

"Love you."

"Love you, too."

Breanna clicked off the call and returned her cell phone to her pocketbook.

"Tough job with a family," said Reid.

"It can be," she admitted.

"When I was younger—it is a very difficult balance. But you seem to get a lot of support from your husband."

"He tries. He's very busy."

"You don't have a nanny?" Reid asked.

"No."

Breanna suddenly felt uncomfortable, not so much because of the content of the conversation, but because of whom she was having it with. While she and Reid had worked well together over the past few months, they'd never discussed personal matters—hers or his. She didn't even know if he had any children.

"We've had various helpers," Breanna said. "But we've always felt—we feel very strongly that, if we can, we'd prefer to raise Teri ourselves."

"Don't want her calling someone else 'Mom.' I completely agree," said Reid. "Raising them yourself—there's no substitute. As hard as it is, I'm sure she'll be better off in the long run."

"I hope so," said Breanna.

BREANNA RETURNED TO A WHIRLWIND OF TASKS AT THE Pentagon. Most of them had nothing to do directly with Whiplash, but she interrupted her schedule when her secretary, Ms. Bennett, finally managed to get hold of the man she wanted to run the group's support team: her father's former right-hand man, Terence "Ax" Gibbs.

"I'm having a fantastic time down here," Ax told her over the video phone. He looked it, too—he was on a porch on an island in the Florida Keys. "How are you all enjoying the snow?"

"It hasn't snowed all winter up here," said Breanna. "And now it's almost spring."

"Too bad." Ax winked. The former Air Force chief master sergeant had retired when Dog was assigned out of Dreamland. Up until then, Ax wasn't just the epitome of a chief master sergeant, he was a chief's chief, a candidate for sainthood or the devil incarnate, depending on your perspective.

Most people would have said he was a little of both.

"I need your help, Ax," said Breanna. "I have a new command. It's a joint operation involving intelligence and the military. I need someone who can get things done, who can work with the military side lining up support for different missions, who's not afraid of getting his hands dirty."

"Sounds like it would be right up my alley," said Ax. "If I were looking for a job."

"Now before you say no—"

"You're just like your father, you know that?"

"Ax—"

"Fortunately for you, my sources indicated that this call might be coming. And I was able to do a little research into the subject."

"How—"

"Once a chief, always a chief." Ax raised his glass of home-brewed ale as a toast. "There are some things I can't tell, even when retired. Don't worry, no state secrets have been betrayed. Who would be, well, not better than me, but nearly as good?"

"I—"

"Greasy Hands Parsons. And he has far too much time on his hands now that his grandson Robert has started school. Even better, he lives not ten miles from the Pentagon, so he wouldn't have to relocate."

"Greasy Hands? He has to be pushing eighty by now."

Ax laughed. "Everyone at Dreamland thought he was about sixty when he was there, right?"

"Seventy."

"Greasy Hands was younger than most of the sergeants he had working for him. You can't fool another chief. Especially one with access to personnel records. I think if you called him up, he'd jump at the chance to get back to doing something useful."

"Could he work at something where he wasn't going to get his hands dirty?"

"Who says that's not part of the job?"

Few nicknames had ever been as appropriate as "Greasy Hands." Parsons not only had incredible mechanical skills; he couldn't resist putting them to use. Breanne knew that his military background and association with Dreamland would be definite pluses. He got along with Ray Rubeo—not an easy task—and of course already knew Danny and would be respected by him. If she couldn't have Ax, Greasy Hands would be an excellent choice.

"Maybe I will talk to him," she said. "You wouldn't happen to know what his phone number is these days, would you?"

"As a matter of fact, I do."

FIFTEEN MINUTES LATER AL PARSONS FELT HIS CELL PHONE rattling his pocket, vibrating before it rang. He considered not answering it, since he was under his car examining a ball joint that had, in technical terms, gone all hell out of whack. But technically he wasn't actually working on the car—the mechanic at the auto shop where he'd stopped was being paid to do that. And since the young man seemed to have a rough idea of the trouble now that Greasy Hands had pointed it out, he decided he'd step outside and take the call.

"Just clunk it with the fork one time and it'll come right off," he told the mechanic. "I gotta take this call."

"Is this Al Parsons?" said a woman's voice when he hit the Call button.

"Depends on who's calling," he answered.

"Please hold the line for Ms. Stockard."

"Who?"

Breanna came on the line. "Chief Parsons?"

"Breanna, is that you? Holy God, girl—how are you?"

"I'm good, Greasy Hands, how are you?"

"Bored out of my mind. What can I do for you?"

Breanna described as much of the job as she could over the phone. Before she was done, Greasy Hands had all but volunteered to do it for free. They arranged for him to come in the following day for an interview and to meet some of the other key people in the organization, including Reid. Greasy Hands hung up practically singing—a skill Breanna hadn't known he possessed.

The mechanic working on his car might have said he didn't possess it. But he was a fairly discreet fellow and wouldn't have said anything bad about his customer, especially since his customer's good mood led to a twenty dollar tip.

BREANNA'S WORK, ALONG WITH UPDATES ON THE SUDAN and Iranian situation, kept her in her office until a few minutes after eight; in truth, she could have easily stayed several more hours and still not finished everything. By the time she finally reached home, not only was dinner done, but Teri had finished her homework and was getting ready for bed.

Breanna popped her head into the bathroom while Teri was brushing her teeth. She studied her daughter's face. It was soft and relaxed, innocent.

She'd held that face close to hers forever, it seemed; at times it was impossible to even imagine not seeing it.

Teri glanced up and caught a glimpse of her mother behind her in the mirror. Instantly, her expression changed to a scowl. She put her head down, concentrating on her brush.

"How's your leg, honey?" Breanna asked.

Teri didn't say anything.

"Teri?"

The girl leaned forward to spit out the toothpaste. She was determined not to talk to her mother. She took a paper cup from the holder and rinsed.

"The doctor told me the X rays were negative," said Breanna. "I called to check."

Mouth rinsed, Teri dropped her toothbrush on the sink and spun around to leave. Breanna put her hand out and grabbed her.

"What's wrong?" she asked, though she knew exactly why Teri was angry.

"It's time for bed."

"Teri—"

Breanna looked into her daughter's eyes. Anger, fear, and disappointment mingled in equal parts. Breanna wanted to say something, but wasn't sure what. She couldn't apologize for not going to the hospital—there was nothing to apologize for. Zen had been there, and there was no reason both of them always had to be by Teri's side. And yet she felt as if she had let her daughter down.

Teri certainly thought so, even though, if asked, she would not have been able to put her feelings precisely into words.

"I'm fine," said Teri.

Her angry tone annoyed Breanna, who snapped back. "Then put your toothbrush back where it belongs."

Teri grabbed it, practically flinging it into the holder. Breanna closed her eyes as her daughter stomped to bed—she hadn't meant to be a scold.

"Hey listen," she told her daughter when she caught up to her in the bedroom. "I'm sorry I couldn't go to the hospital for you. Dad said he could."

"You had to talk to the President."

"That's right."

Teri frowned.

Part of her thought she was making too much of this, but another part of her was just angry and didn't care. "Listen, Teri, what I do is very important for a lot of people."

"I know that."

"Well . . . good."

Breanna couldn't help thinking back to her own childhood. Her mother had been on her own, and had to work full-time. They were not poor—her mother had just become a doctor—but there were many, many nights when Breanna tucked herself into bed . . . after having come home, made dinner, studied, and cleaned up, all without having anyone home or telling her what to do.

She didn't want Teri to repeat that childhood, but at the same time, Breanna wanted her daughter to realize how good she had things.

There seemed to be no magic formula to make that happen.

"All right," said Breanna. "Good night, then."

"Good night."

Breanna leaned down and kissed her.

"Send dad in," said Teri sharply as Breanna turned off the light.

*   *   *

"OH, SHE'S FINE," ZEN TOLD BREANNA AFTER TUCKING TERI in. "Just a little spoiled."

"Are you saying I spoil her?"

"Hell, no—*I* spoil her." Zen rolled his wheelchair to the refrigerator and got out a beer. "But it's not fatal. She'll get over it."

"I don't think she's spoiled," said Breanna.

"And I don't think you have to be there for her every second of every day," said Zen.

"She does."

"She'll get over it." He wheeled over to the cabinet for a bottle opener. "Believe me. Another couple of years, she'll be saying we never leave her alone."

"I can't wait."

"Me, neither."

35

Al-Quazi

EVEN THE DIRT IN AFRICA WAS DIFFERENT THAN IN AMERICA.

It had the texture of pulverized rocks, even in a light rain. It didn't so much meld together in the rain as dissipate; the mud was more slimy than sticky. If you were crawling through it, as Danny Freah was, you noticed how it slipped into your clothes, and how it seemed to swim onto your face. You felt the rocks curl around you as you moved across the minefield, and the sting of blotches of mud as the drops splashed.

The ground had a specific smell to it, too, a scent unlike others you'd ever crawled through, either as a child or a soldier. Many times, dirt smelled like death, or the precursor to death, hot sulfur and electrified metal. Sometimes it smelled of chemicals, and other times of rot and refuse. This dirt smelled like impervious stone, absorbing nothing, and obscuring the senses, just as the rain made it difficult for the night glasses to work properly.

"Turn twenty degrees to the right and proceed forward ten yards," said the Voice.

Danny altered his course. Flash, Hera, and McGowan were behind in the minefield, moving forward slowly, not so much because they were afraid of the mines—though a healthy fear was always in order—but because they didn't want to do anything to attract the attention of the guards in the post about forty yards away. The guard was sitting in the machine-gun nest under a poncho, trying to keep dry, and not paying particular attention to the minefield alongside him. Still, the four Whiplashers were in an extremely vulnerable position, surrounded by mines on both sides, with their guns tucked up over their shoulders and secured by Velcro straps against their rucksacks. If for some reason the guard decided to get up from his post and take a walk around in the rain, he might easily see them.

The mines around the Sudanese army post where Tarid and the other prisoners were kept had been laid in a complicated pattern. They'd also been placed very close together. Most soldiers would have found it impenetrable; indeed, at least two would-be saboteurs and a smuggler had been blown up in the fields over the past twelve months.

But the Whiplash team had an advantage other infiltrators did not—the Voice had mapped the mines by looking at infrared satellite images from the past few nights. The mines were all slightly warmer than the surrounding ground when the sun went down, making them easy for the computer to spot. By watching Danny and the others move through the field with the help of an Owl, it gave him precise directions, warning him when he or one of his people was getting too close to a mine.

"Turn now," said the Voice.

Danny dug his elbow into the dirt, marking the turn so it would be easy for Flash to find. As long as they all stayed in line, they'd be fine.

"We're in position," said Nuri over the radio circuit.

"Roger that. We've still got a ways to go."

"The guard change is in ten minutes."

"Roger. Ten minutes. We'll be ready."

Danny looked up. He was a good thirty yards from the perimeter fence, and they need to be inside it when Nuri began the "attack." He started moving faster.

The prisoners were being kept in an open pen about thirty yards from the perimeter fence. Tarid was there. So was Tilia.

She'd been shot twice in the leg, but it wasn't until she ran out of ammunition and passed out from the blood loss that the soldiers had captured her. They threw her in the back of a captured rebel pickup and drove her to the compound, unconscious; her leg was bound but otherwise left untreated. In a way, she was lucky —if she hadn't been recognized as one of Uncle Dpap's lieutenants, she would have been killed on the battlefield.

After being raped. So far, she had been spared that as well.

When Danny reached the fence, he pulled himself up into a crouch and looked back. To his horror, he saw that McGowan was off course by several feet.

"McGowan, stop," he hissed, *"Stop!"*

Everyone stopped, not just McGowan.

"What's wrong?"

"You went off course. Don't move."

Danny pulled out the control unit for the Voice and told the computer to plot the mines near McGowan.

"You went right between two mines," he told him after studying the image. "You're about six inches from the next mine. And there's one right behind you."

"You sure?"

"No asshole, he's just trying to scare the crap out of you," snapped Hera.

"All right. Let's all relax. Flash, come on forward. Follow the lines I made."

"It's getting hard to see with the rain," said Flash.

"Yeah, I know. Do it, though."

Danny waited until Flash reached the fence before signaling Hera to continue. She crawled through the dirt and mud quickly, sliding her body through the markings he had left as if she were swimming an obstacle course.

"All right. You two get working on the fence," Danny told them. "We'll be right with you."

He took off his rucksack, leaving it and his rifle on the ground near the edge of the minefield. Then he dropped to his hands and knees and started back for McGowan. The rain was becoming heavier, washing away the markings he and the others had left. The water also started to soak the field, making it more slippery. Even with the Voice to guide him, he had a difficult time staying on course.

"This isn't good, huh?" asked McGowan when he finally got close.

"There's a mine right here," said Danny, pointing. "And one about six inches behind your right foot."

"Can I go right?"

"No." Danny pulled out the MY-PID head unit and stared at the screen. "Your best bet is to move to your left slightly."

"How slightly?"

"Hold on."

The cloud cover was making it harder and harder for the system to see McGowan from the Owl. Danny, on the other hand, was tracked by the satellites using his biomarker. He nudged right toward McGowan.

The Voice objected that he was going off the established trail.

"Affirmative," he told it. "Guide me toward McGowan."

"Subject cannot be definitively located."

"He hasn't moved."

"Data insufficient to confirm."

"Warn me if I'm too close to a mine," Danny told it. He

shifted right, crawled two feet to the right, then stopped at the Voice's direction. He had to zig to the right then back before drawing parallel to his trooper.

"Get on my back," Danny said.

"Huh?" said McGowan.

"The computer will tell me where to go. Rather than taking a risk and following me, I'll just carry you out. It'll be easier."

"Hey, Colonel, I can do this."

"Get on my back, soldier. That's an order."

"Yes, sir."

WHILE DANNY WAS GUIDING HIS MEN THROUGH THE MINE-field, Nuri and Boston were on the opposite side of the camp, preparing an assault. Or what would look like an assault to the men inside.

Nuri was on the north side of the road, Boston the south. They'd split the mercenaries between them. They didn't have nearly enough men to take the camp, but they had more than enough to make it look as if they wanted to.

The rain continued to fall, blocking not only the Owl's view, but making it hard to see with the night glasses as well. Nuri could barely tell where the machine-gun position was.

There were three minutes to go before the guards were due to change watch.

"Danny, you want us to delay the Catbirds?" Nuri asked. "You only have three minutes."

"Stay on schedule. We want to hit while the guards are changing."

"You sound like you're straining."

"I'll explain later."

HERA CLIPPED THROUGH THE LAST OF THE WIRE AND PUSHED it back. Then she stepped through, holding it for Flash so he could get in.

"This way," she said, pointing toward the prisoners' pen.

Aside from some smaller lights on the buildings, the only illumination in the complex came from a pair of floodlights mounted on a telephone pole at almost the exact center of the camp. Their light formed an arc that took in about two-thirds of the prisoners' area. The area between the two fences where Hera and Flash were was cast in a deep shadow.

Before the rain started, two guards had been watching the prisoners, walking back and forth in the area that was lit. The heavy rain had sent them into the trucks, though Hera and Flash couldn't see them from where they were.

"What happened to the guards?" asked Flash.

"I'm looking," said Hera.

"Maybe they're up around on the other side."

Hera saw the two trucks at the edge of the very small parade and assembly area off to her left.

"Maybe they're in the trucks," she suggested. "They can see the pen from there."

"Could be."

"You watch the truck," she told Flash. "I'll go cut the fence to the prisoners' pen."

"Go," said Flash, trotting forward through the mud.

The rain kept coming harder. Flash felt it soaking into the pores of his skin, covering his whole body with a slimy film of water and sweat.

As annoying as it was, the rain was making their job considerably easier. Visibility was cut down for the defenders, and the foul weather lessened the chance of being spotted by a random patrol or a casual cigarette smoker.

Flash slipped a grenade round into his rifle's attached launcher, ready to take out the truck quickly if necessary.

Danny had told him only to fire if the guards presented a clear danger—if they came to investigate or started shooting. This wasn't only because he wanted to keep the casualties down. They were outnumbered, and the only way to even the odds was to use trickery. When Boston and Nuri attacked, so the plan went, the defenders' attention would be drawn toward the front of the camp. Escaping out the back with the prisoners would be easy.

While Flash was watching the truck and the rest of the compound, Hera had slipped around the corner of the prisoners' area. The rain had encouraged the prisoners to clump together at the southeast side of the pen, seeking shelter under a small tarp augmented by a collection of small blankets and other rags. They were all soaked, the water leaking in a constant drip on the prisoners below.

Hera began cutting the fence. She knew Farsi, but Danny thought it might make Tarid more suspicious and told her not to use it. He wanted to make it appear that they had come to free all of the prisoners. So she used Arabic after she got into the pen and started waking the prisoners.

"Time to go," she said, first in a whisper, then more loudly. "Be quiet. The way is this way."

The first man was so battered by his wounds that he simply stared at her. The one next to him was dead.

"Come on," said Hera, shaking the third. She raised her voice. "Let's go."

The man turned his head toward her.

"What sort of devil are you?"

"Mr. Kirk sent us. Go through the fence. Stay low to the ground so they don't see you. Go!"

The man raised his head, barely able to make her out even though it was raining. As Hera grabbed him to pull him upward, the ground heaved with an explosion, the night turning white. Two of the Catbirds had just struck the minefield in front of the machine-gun posts.

DANNY AND MCGOWAN REACHED THE SAFE AREA BEHIND the minefield just as the Catbirds exploded.

"Take out the minefield," Danny told McGowan, pushing him off his back. "I'll hold the prisoners back."

McGowan pulled off his rucksack and pulled out what

looked like a misshapen football. He slid his thumb against a latch at the side, undoing the safety.

"Fire in the hole," he yelled, rearing back and throwing the football toward the end of the minefield.

As it sailed through the air, the rear of the ball burst apart and a thin Teflon net expanded from the rear. The net was studded with microexplosives. These were more like powerful firecrackers than bombs, but had the same effect on the minefield, exploding in a coordinated pattern designed to create and accentuate a pulsing shock wave. The explosives set off six mines simultaneously, in turn igniting another two dozen nearby. Dirt, water, explosives, and metal roiled into the air. McGowan pushed his head down, protecting himself as the shrapnel settled.

An illumination flare shot up from the center of the compound. Its white phosphorus gave him a good view of the minefield. The explosion had cut only about a third of the way through. He took out a second football and tossed it closer. This time he was too close for comfort; pebbles pelted him as the mines finished exploding.

Inside the fence, Danny had grabbed the first escapee, corralling him while McGowan worked on the mines. He repeated the words for "stop" and "mines" in Arabic, but the man seemed simply bewildered, still half asleep and confused by the explosions. Danny pushed him down to the ground, then signaled to the man running behind him that he should hit the deck as well.

McGowan had one more football, and roughly half of the minefield to take out. The shower from the last blast convinced him that he had to throw it from shelter, so he ducked into the trench leading to the machine-gun post. This time more than a dozen mines ignited immediately, starting a chain reaction that zigged out through the rest of the remaining field.

He started to get up out of the trench to make sure the path was clear, and to mark it for the prisoners. But as McGowan started to his feet, he heard a shout and turned to see a Sudanese soldier pointing his rifle at him.

McGowan raised his hands in surrender.

As soon as the Catbirds exploded, Nuri and Boston's teams began firing at the machine-gun posts in front of them. The guards were taken completely by surprise. The man at the northeast post, in front of Nuri, began firing wildly into the minefield, his bullets setting off several mines. The other man fired a single burst before his gun jammed. Too shaken to clear it, he hunkered down behind the sandbags and waited for the gunfire to stop.

Behind them, troops poured from the barracks. Most ran toward the front of the camp where the battle was raging, either jumping behind sandbags or into the zigging defense trench just outside the perimeter. A good dozen, however, ran to the south side of the camp where the gunfire was less intense, either unable to sort out what was going on or simply out of fear. Their retreat took them to within ten yards of the prisoner pen.

They huddled there for several minutes, unsure what to do. Then an illumination flare ignited overhead, close enough to cast shadows from the moving prisoners. It looked to the soldiers that a fresh attack was coming from that direction, and two of them began firing.

Hera had just found Tarid inside the pen when the gunfire began. She cursed—in English—pushed him to the ground, and began returning fire.

"Go!" she shouted. "Crawl out of here. Get away."

Tarid twisted back on the ground. "Who are you?" he asked.

"I'm with Kirk. *Go!* Get out!"

The gunfire intensified. Tarid began crawling toward the back of the compound. Others were gathered there, crouched down. One fell, then another. Suddenly, the rest of the crowd rose en masse and ran toward the hole at the back of the fence.

Danny grabbed one, trying to stop him, but the others

bolted past, running toward the minefield with its cleared but unmarked path.

IN THE TRENCH, McGOWAN TRIED TO THINK OF SOME WAY to escape. His rifle was at his feet, but he'd be dead by the time he got it in his hands.

"Now listen, you don't want to shoot me," he told the soldier.

The soldier heard the shriek of the men escaping and pulled the trigger. His first bullet struck McGowan at the very top of his armored vest, pushing him back.

The next bullets struck his forehead, killing him instantly.

THERE WERE TOO MANY PRISONERS FOR DANNY TO STOP, and finally he just moved aside.

"McGowan, there's a whole bunch of them coming out," he said over the radio. "Is it clear? Mac?"

Unaware that McGowan was already dead, Danny crouched down, waiting for Hera and Tarid, and yelling at the prisoners to stop when they ran by.

The first sign that something had gone wrong came a few minutes later, when one of the escaping prisoners strayed out of the path the bombs had created and stepped on a mine. Danny saw the flash—red rather than white, a blossom of color and death.

He got up and went to find out what was going on.

The man who had killed McGowan was the machine-gunner posted to the southwest pillbox. He had abandoned his post in a panic. But his confrontation with McGowan had steeled him, and now the coward was a warrior, a bold lion who threw himself against the side of the trench and began shooting at his enemies.

He killed two before he had to stop and reload. Danny, crouching by the fence line, saw the muzzle flashes and guessed what was happening.

As soon as the gun stopped flashing, he rose and ran to the trench, jumping down and racing forward.

His lungs pressed against his chest. But unlike yesterday, there was no doubt in his mind, no second-guessing. A single thought filled his mind: He had to take out the person shooting, or most of the prisoners would die.

The Sudanese soldier, meanwhile, had slapped a fresh magazine into his gun and rose to fire again. He was so intent on the shadows in the minefield that he never saw Danny coming around the tight corner a few yards away.

Danny fired a single burst from his SCAR. The bullets sliced through the soldier's neck, making neat holes on the way in and craters on the way out. The soldier died without knowing what hit him.

Worried there might be someone in the pillbox, Danny continued along the trench. He nearly tripped over McGowan's body. He sidestepped him, kept going.

When he reached the machine-gun post, he pumped a grenade through the opening and ducked.

The explosion sounded like a can of beans popping in a fire.

There was no one in the pillbox. He pulled the bullets from the gun, threw it over on its mount, and began running back.

It was only then that the fear he'd felt the night before returned. This time the emotion focused on McGowan—it was a fear, a knowledge really, that his man was dead.

Danny had lost men in combat before. Not many, but enough to know that it was both necessary and inevitably sorrowful. He dropped down near the young man, still hoping that he had survived. But the wounds were obvious, and even the downpour couldn't wash away all the blood that had spurted from the dead man's skull.

Danny felt sick to his stomach. He held his breath a moment, then stooped down and pulled McGowan up onto his back.

He seemed much lighter than he had just a few minutes earlier, when Danny had carried him through the minefield.

*   *   *

FLASH BLEW UP THE TRUCK AS SOON AS THE PASSENGER started to get out with his gun. Then he shot out the floodlights on the post above the compound and ran up along the fence to the prisoner pen, aiming to get an angle on the barracks door. By the time he reached it, however, the barracks were empty. All the soldiers had gone to the east side of the camp, where the battle seemed to be concentrated.

He crouched on one knee, hoping they wouldn't come back, ready if they did.

Flash had been in several firefights, first in Iraq, then in Afghanistan. As different as they all were, as different as each one was from this, one thing tied them all together—the sharp pain at the top of his skull, right behind his left eye. A doctor—not in the Army, he worried about being kicked out if he mentioned it—had told him that the pains were related to stress, and either to quit what he was doing or not worry about them. Flash opted for the latter.

"Whiplash team, check in," said Danny. "Boston?"

"We can keep this up all day."

"Nuri?"

"Ditto."

"Flash?"

"I blew the truck. I have the barracks covered. May be empty."

"Hera?"

"I'm taking heavy fire."

"Did Tarid get out?"

"He's a few feet away. We won't make it out unless you get this gun off of us."

"Flash, can you help her?" asked Danny.

"On my way."

"Hera, as soon as you can, get out of there."

"No kidding."

Starting along the fence, Flash realized that Danny hadn't checked in with McGowan. Not a good sign, he thought.

*   *   *

THE LAST FLARE BURNED OUT, LEAVING THE CAMP BATHED in the dull red shadow of a burning fire in the administration building.

Hera looked east, toward the gas tanks. The soldiers pinning them down were near the tanks, scattered behind the cement mounts for cover. A few fired indiscriminately, but the others were more disciplined, firing only when they had a target. The combination made it impossible to move without being shot.

Some of the prisoners were crawling slowly toward the rear of the pen, hoping to escape, but most of them were lying nearby, wounded or too paralyzed with fear to move.

The fiercest gunfire was coming from her right. A pair of soldiers were huddled below one of the gas tanks, taking turns firing into the pen. At first they'd had plenty of targets exposed and framed by the light. As the flare died, however, it became more difficult to aim. Afraid of return fire and confused by the steady rain, they resorted to holding their guns over their heads and firing short bursts, unaimed.

Hera nudged her way around two prone bodies to the corner of the pen, trying to get an angle on the men. She saw one rise at the edge of the cement pier that held the gas tank. She waited for him to straighten, then fired a single shot, hitting him in the temple.

The soldier spiraled back against his companion. Hera waited for the other man to turn and fire back, giving her a target. But his friend's death had paralyzed him, and he stayed low, out of sight.

Hera grew tired of waiting. She started for the fence, planning to cut through and then flank the whole line of them behind the piers. But before she got very far, someone began firing in her direction. She froze as bullets cascaded overhead.

The slugs chewed everything up in front of her, including the body of one of the prisoners. She started backing away. Then a tremendous explosion scooped her up and tossed her toward the rear of the pen.

Flash had blown up one of the gas tanks.

*   *   *

DANNY CARRIED MCGOWAN'S LIMP BODY TO THE RAMP AT the end of the trench. He put him down as gently as he could, tipping his shoulder forward and going to a knee to keep the dead man from flopping down. He winced as McGowan's head thumped against the dirt.

"I'll be back. I promise," Danny told him.

He turned and ran to the perimeter fence, not even ducking, though bullets were flying everywhere. Another emotion had overcome fear, or suppressed it: recklessness.

It was a strange combination, to be scared of dying yet not caring at the same time.

Danny felt the force of the exploding gas tank even from where he stood. He dropped down to his knees.

"Hera, where are we?" he barked over the radio.

There was no answer. Danny ran toward the pen. God, I've lost another, he thought.

"Hera?" he repeated. "Hera."

"I'm still in the pen. Still pinned down. One of the gas tanks just blew, but they turned the machine gun around on the southeast corner."

Danny was at the fence of the prisoner area. The machine gun was at the corner of the perimeter, ahead to his right. He'd be under direct fire if he approached.

"Boston, where are you?" he said.

"Same old, same old," said Boston. "South of the road."

"That machine gun on the southern end in front of you— can you get some grenades in it?"

"Already trying, boss."

"All right. Get their attention. I'll get them from back here."

"Working on it."

The roof of the post was thick and sharply angled, designed to deflect grenades and absorb what didn't bounce off. But its defenses were oriented outward, and Danny reasoned if he could get close enough, he could get his own grenade into it.

The problem was getting close enough to get a shot without getting killed. Having gone to the trouble of reorienting his machine gun so he could fire into the compound, the gunner wasn't skimping on bullets.

Danny pushed his shoulder against the perimeter fence as he ran forward, staying on his feet until he saw the flickering yellow of the machine-gun muzzle as it fired. He put a grenade into the launcher and crawled forward to get a better angle, almost swimming in the mud.

How long had it been since he'd done something like this? He couldn't even remember doing it in Dreamland.

After ten yards he still didn't have much of a shot. The perimeter fence was in the way—he worried that if the grenade struck it, the shell might bounce back at him.

His best alternative was to shoot through the fence. The machine gun continued to fire, blasting away at the pen. Danny raised his right knee under his chest, then levered himself into flight. The world blurred into a black swirl as he ran, flames circling in the distance.

He was almost to the fence when he saw someone on his left.

One of the Sudanese soldiers crouched on the ground, staring at him with wide eyes, the outline of his body black against the background of the flames of the gas tank near the entrance to the camp.

The eyes showed surprise, and a question: Are you going to kill me?

Danny had no choice. The barrel of the man's gun was already swiveling toward his chest.

Danny reached for his gun's trigger, pulling twice. Six bullets flew into the space between the man's eyes, permanently shutting them.

The machine gun stuttered on, the gunner oblivious to everything but the dancing shadows in the prisoner pen. From his perspective, that was where all the trouble was; he would kill them all.

The fence gave way as Danny hit it. He sprawled forward

against the chain links, abruptly stopping at a forty-degree angle. He pushed up, toes digging into the spaces in the fence. He surged forward, despite his fear. The links scraped against his knees.

His recklessness fled. But he was trapped now, unable to do anything but continue his attack.

The fence tottered forward but didn't fall. Danny reached the top and stuck his rifle through the gap under the razor wire.

He could see the machine-gunner's face, lit by the reflection of the nearby tank fire.

Not only was the launcher's trigger heavy, but the rain and exertion had stiffened Danny's muscles and dulled his sense of touch. The grenade leapt from the gun. The gunner started to duck, but it was far too late; the grenade hit the wall behind him and exploded.

"Hera! Go!" yelled Danny, pushing to slide back down the fence. "Go! Go! Go!"

HERA POKED TARID TO MAKE SURE HE WAS STILL ALIVE. HE groaned.

"Come on," she said in Arabic. She pushed herself under him, then levered him upward, half dragging and half running toward the back of the pen. The machine gun had stopped, but there was still sporadic gunfire around the compound.

"Who are you?" muttered Tarid in Farsi as they reached the fence.

Hera told him in Arabic that she was there to rescue him.

"Why?" he asked, this time in Arabic.

"I'm with Kirk."

"And who's he?"

"A bigger fool than you are," she said. "He thinks he can make money off of this."

She'd practiced the answer; they wanted Tarid to think it was being done for money, the only motive an arms dealer would embrace.

Hera pulled him from the pen, rushing toward the hole

in the perimeter fence. She saw a body at the foot of the trench as she neared the minefield, but didn't realize it was McGowan.

There was nothing she could have done if she had.

Tarid felt his strength and senses returning as they started through the minefield. Adrenaline started pumping again. A bullet had slapped against the fleshy part of his right thigh, burning and causing a great deal of pain but, as bullet wounds went, very little damage.

"Where are you taking me?" he asked Hera.

"Outta of this crap," she said.

"You're with the American CIA?"

"There's a laugh," she said. She switched to Greek, telling him he was an ignorant jerk. Then she switched over to English.

"Are you CIA?" she asked. "Is that why Kirk rescues you?"

"Me?"

"You are pretending to be Iranian. That's not true, is it?"

"I am Colonel Zsar's lieutenant," Tarid insisted, going back to Arabic.

They reached the end of the minefield. Two other prisoners were sitting nearby. Hera let Tarid slip to the ground. The field was littered with prisoners, some wounded, others too scared to move or unsure where to go.

McGowan was supposed to be out with the prisoners, directing them to run south while waiting for Tarid. They were going to help him get farther away, then play it by ear.

She couldn't see the other trooper. She'd been assigned to hold by the perimeter fence in case there was a counterattack. If she wasn't there, the others would be trapped inside.

"Mac?" she yelled, turning around. There was no answer. She yelled again and called for him in Greek.

Tarid collapsed to the ground. With his wounded leg, he wasn't going anywhere.

"Wait here, you," Hera told him in English. "I return soon."

*   *   *

DANNY MADE HIS WAY BACK ALONG THE PERIMETER FENCE.

"Where's Tarid?" he asked the Voice.

"Beyond the minefield." The computer gave him the GPS coordinates.

"Flash, Hera, we're out of here."

"I'm coming out," said Flash.

"Hera?"

"I'm at the perimeter fence. I'm holding."

"Good. Copy. Boston, get to the rendezvous point."

"On it, Chief."

"Nuri?"

"We'll keep them occupied," said Nuri. "See you soon."

"Copy that," said Danny.

Their mission was accomplished, but Danny had one more thing to do. He asked the computer to locate Tilia.

She was still inside.

"Is she alive?" he asked the computer.

"Unknown," said the Voice.

The computer could locate people, and make judgments based on their movements, but it didn't have the power to diagnose life or death. She hadn't moved in several minutes, adding to its uncertainty.

"Lead me to her," Danny told it.

BOSTON LED HIS THREE MERCENARIES BACK FROM THE rocks and trees where they'd taken shelter. Though the brush had been torn to pulp, no one was hurt. They jogged back to the truck, got in, and drove south and then back west, circling around the camp across the fallow fields before meeting Flash at the rendezvous point on the road west of the camp.

"Where's McGowan?" asked Boston. He was supposed to be there, too.

Flash shrugged. "I don't know. He should've been at the fence when we came out. I got out late and thought I'd find him back here, but I don't see him. I haven't heard him on the radio the entire operation."

Neither had Boston.

"Hey, Colonel, you know where McGowan is?" he asked over the radio.

"He's with me," said Danny.

TARID LAY ON THE GROUND, TRYING TO WILL AWAY THE PAIN of the bullet crease on his leg. He saw the vehicle down by the road, perhaps twenty yards away, and knew it must be Kirk's.

So Kirk expected to be paid for helping him escape? Was it a reward or a ransom?

Whatever it was, he wasn't getting it.

Tarid turned to the two men sitting nearby. They were staring into the distance, shell-shocked but unhurt.

"You two—come with me," he said as he struggled to his feet.

Neither man moved.

"There's a village north of here. Two kilometers," said Tarid. "Saad Reth. I have a friend there who can help us. Come with me."

One of the men blinked. That was the only acknowledgment that they had heard him.

"If you help me get to Saad Reth," said Tarid slowly, pacing his Arabic, "I will make sure you are rewarded. One hundred euros apiece."

The offer of more money than either man had handled in a lifetime stirred them to action. The man who had blinked was the first to rise. He helped his companion up, and together they started following Tarid, who was limping but moving along quickly.

"We have to stay away from the people who blew up the camp," he told them. "Go, before they pay attention to us."

"Saad Reth is a long walk from here," said one of the men, noticing his limp.

"The distance doesn't matter." Tarid pushed himself forward. "The army will be after Kirk, and we'll be long gone. Come. As fast as you can."

* * *

DANNY FOUND TILIA HUNCHED AGAINST THE FENCE. HER fists were clenched and propped against the side of her head, arms crossed at the wrists. He knelt down and touched her shoulder.

"Tilia?"

Her body heaved but she didn't raise her head or talk.

"Come on then," said Danny. He scooped her up. She was light, incredibly light.

Nuri was still firing at the machine-gun posts on the north side of the camp, but there was only sporadic return fire. The Sudanese army officers were regrouping their men, mustering for a counterattack. The battle had seemed to last for an eternity, but barely ten minutes had passed since the Catbirds initiated the onslaught.

Hera was waiting at the fence when Danny arrived.

"Did you send Tarid through?" Danny asked.

"Yes. Where's McGowan?"

"I know where he is. You think you can carry her?"

"Is she coming with us?"

"Yeah. We'll drop her off along the way."

"I don't think it's a good idea."

"I don't care what you think. Take her."

Danny deposited Tilia on Hera's shoulder. Hera didn't say anything, turning and carrying her from the compound.

Danny went to the trench. He didn't see McGowan. His heart leapt: He thought he'd been wrong about him being killed.

But the only mistake was where he had left him. A moment later Danny spotted him a little farther on in the trench.

As gently as he could, he picked up the battered body and double-timed it through the disabled portion of the mine-field.

"Skipper, we got problems here," said Boston over the radio. "Every one of these bastards wants to come with us. And I can't find Tarid."

Danny asked the Voice where Tarid was. It found him moving a quarter mile away, on the road west.

"It's OK," said Danny. "He's escaping. Better that he gets away on his own." Much better, he thought. "Hera's bringing Tilia, Uncle Dpap's translator."

"Yeah, here she comes now."

"I'm sixty seconds away."

"What do I do with these people?"

"Tell them to run."

Danny saw the small crowd ahead of him. Boston fired another burst, then pushed the prisoners away. They were angry and scared, but they were also depleted from the day spent without food. They began walking away from the camp, some north, some west.

"Jesus, is that McGowan?" said Boston as Danny put him in the SUV.

"Let's go, Boston."

"Shit."

"I said, go."

"Yeah, all right, Cap. I'm sorry."

Boston climbed in. The mercenaries squeezed into the back.

"Go south two miles and stop," Danny said. "I want to make sure Tarid's OK."

The truck's rattle settled after a minute, and they rode in relative silence across the empty land. The rain had started to let up.

"Everybody out," said Danny when they stopped. He was being crushed by two of the mercenaries, who'd crowded next to him.

He went around to the back and got a blanket from the wheel well. He wrapped McGowan's body in it and set him down in the back.

Tarid, meanwhile, had continued to the northwest. The Voice located him near a village named Saad Reth.

"Nuri, what's in Saad Reth?" Danny asked.

"Not much. Little village."

"You think Tarid can find transportation there?"

"Maybe. If he has friends there. Hard to say."

"Colonel, your lady friend wants to talk to you," said Hera.

"She's not my lady friend," said Danny, annoyed.

"Whatever. She wants to talk to you."

Hera needed a serious attitude adjustment, but now wasn't the time. Danny walked over to Tilia, who sat cross-legged on the ground.

"Am I your prisoner now?" she asked.

"You're not our prisoner. We just rescued you."

"Who are you?"

"Kirk."

"They were calling you colonel."

"I was once. I was a lot of things."

Tilia stared at him. She wanted desperately to believe in something—she wanted to believe in him. But whatever world he belonged to, it was too far removed from hers. And hers had just imploded.

"We'll get you back to your village," said Danny.

"No."

"Where do you want to go?"

"I don't want to go anywhere."

"I can't just leave you here. Come on. You can come with me."

Tilia straightened. One of the Sudanese medics had bandaged the bullet wounds in her shoulder. Her pelvis and abdomen were on fire, but the pain did not prevent her from walking.

"I have to pee," she told him defiantly.

"All right." Danny put his hand out to help her up.

"I want some privacy," she said.

"Sure."

He went back to the truck. Tilia began walking toward one of the mercenaries, who smiled when he saw her coming. Even with her wounds, even in the dark and the rain, she was a beauty.

The look in his eyes revolted her, but she continued toward him. The young man smiled nervously, unsure what she was doing. She put her hand gently on his arm, then leaned up, lips pursed as if to kiss him.

He couldn't believe his luck—he bent forward to return the kiss.

As he did, Tilia grabbed the rifle from his hand. She spun it around, put her thumb on the trigger, and blew a hole through her head.

36

North central Iran

BANI ABERHADJI COULDN'T BELIEVE WHAT HE WAS HEARing. The president of Iran, Darab Kasra, was traveling to America—*the Satan Incarnate*—in a few days' time.

Treason.

Blasphemy.

"We can't allow this," Aberhadji said. "We cannot."

General Taher Banhnnjunni stared at him. He, too, had only just heard.

"How could he make such a decision without consulting the Revolutionary Guard?" continued Aberhadji. "Did this come from the ayatollahs?"

"He must have spoken to them," said Banhnnjunni. He was stunned. The decision to destroy Iran's nuclear capability, though a terrible one, at least had some logic to it when balanced against the West's concessions. But this—this could not be explained at all.

"You are the head of the Guard, and the council," said Aberhadji. "You weren't consulted?"

"No."

"That is an insult. An insult to all of us. They feel—they think we are worms to be disregarded."

Aberhadji's anger consumed him. He stalked back and forth across the general's office, as if some of it might dissipate.

But it didn't.

"We can shoot him this morning, this afternoon. Blow up his house. Blow up his car, his plane," said Aberhadji.

Banhnnjunni took hold of himself. "You're raving," he told Aberhadji. "Calm down."

"Calm down? Our country is being led by a traitor and blasphemer. We are being led back to the days of the Shah!"

"The black robes are still in charge."

"Do you think they authorized this? *This?*"

Aberhadji could not fathom that it was possible. Banhnnjunni, on the other hand, was not so sure. He had seen the Guard decline greatly in position over the past year. His own status was also in doubt.

He struggled to think logically.

"The president will have no support when he comes back," said the general. "This will end him with the people."

Aberhadji felt as if his brain was unraveling. He had never been guided by emotion—and yet his feelings now were overwhelming. There was no way to be calm before such a gross provocation.

"He'll remain in office. And he has the army," said Aberhadji. "Better to strike then, kill him there."

"Make him a martyr?"

"It would be ironic. His death would surely serve a purpose. We could use it to rally the country. To return to purity, as we have always proposed."

Banhnnjunni hated the president as much as Aberhadji did. But murdering him was a complicated undertaking.

"The plane would be the best place to strike," said Aberhadji. "It would be easy, and it would be a symbol. Or we could arrange it so it appeared that the Americans did it. Perhaps that would be better."

"What if they retaliate?"

"They wouldn't dare. How? What would they do? Invade? Then we use the warhead."

Banhnnjunni felt a second blow, this one even harder.

"You told me the project was several months to completion, if not a year," said the general.

"It is very close. It can be pushed closer," said Aberhadji. "And—I will make contingencies."

Aberhadji had, in fact, already prepared a contingency, and had a full warhead, though as Banhnnjunni said, he had told the small group on the council who knew of the project that they were still a distance away from completing it. This was not technically a lie—they could not yet strike the massive blow they intended. But they could do great damage. And would, if necessary.

"You lied to me?" said Banhnnjunni.

"Of course not. We can strike if necessary. Just not in the exact way, in the best way, we planned. I will rush everything— we will be ready for the Americans, once we kill their bastard."

"We will not kill our president," said the general.

"We must."

"I have to think about this," said General Banhnnjunni. "I have to talk to others. To the black robes. In the meantime, you will do nothing."

"We can't let this sin stain our nation."

"Take the long view, Bani," said the general. "Compromise at the moment may be the right way."

"My long view ends in Paradise," countered Aberhadji. "Where does yours end?"

37

Base Camp Alpha

OBJECTIVELY SPEAKING, THE GOAL OF THE OPERATION against the Sudan prison camp had been a success: Tarid was free, and heading toward Khartoum. Not only was he being tracked via satellite, thanks to the biomarker Danny Freah had planted, but the CIA was scouring intercepts and digging through databases and other sources to get as much information about him as possible.

But the operation had cost considerably more lives than Danny had hoped. The Sudanese and the rebel dead weighed on him more than most people would have thought. But the real blow was McGowan.

In war, sacrifice was inevitable, and even the best leader has to make decisions that led to deaths. But Danny felt that he should have planned the attack differently, found some way to protect McGowan. He brooded about the attack, reviewing it over and over in his mind.

There were many small changes he might have made, and yet they might not have led to a different result. The ferocity of the Sudanese defenders had been surprising. In general, they were not considered either effective or fierce. They had proven to be both. With a more aggressive leader, they might have cost the Whiplash team even more casualties.

On the whole, the Americans had performed well. The small group was starting to bond; Danny found that he was coming to like Nuri as well as respect him.

There was one glaring exception: Hera. She was the sand in the Vaseline. Or as Boston put it, "The only word to describe her rhymes with *witch*. And it ain't *rich*."

Danny had worked with difficult personalities before. Special operations attracted them, and it wasn't always easy to weed them out. But peer selection and an extended training and test period helped. One fierce op generally rounded them into shape—or showed that they were never going to fit.

"I can bust on her ass," said Boston, reviewing the situation after they got back to Base Camp Alpha. "Pound a little respect into her pointy head."

"I'll handle it," said Danny.

"You going to bag her?" Boston asked.

"I can't while the mission is continuing. We're short as it is. And she speaks Farsi better than Nuri. If this guy's Iranian, that's a big plus."

"Your earphone thing doesn't translate for you?"

"It does. But it's not the same. Anyway, I can't bag her now."

"You can do anything you want, Chief. *You de boss.*"

Boston had been struggling to find a title other than colonel that fit. Boss, chief, skipper—nothing felt good on the tongue. He was just so used to calling Danny "Captain," nothing else felt right.

Nuri, meanwhile, was trying to figure out a next step.

"The good news is, Tarid's in Khartoum," he told Danny when they settled down to take stock together.

"What's the bad?" said Danny.

"Besides the coffee?"

"From now on we operate only in places with Dunkin' Donuts," said Danny. "What's the bad news?"

"The tag didn't take properly. The signal is deteriorating. The rain must have diluted the marker before you got it on him."

He'd also lost some marking Tilia. Nuri wasn't sure whether that had been an accident or not, and didn't mention it.

"Can we track him?" asked Danny.

"For a while." Nuri got up and poured himself some more coffee. "Starbucks would be acceptable, if we could get it into the budget."

"Yeah, but you can't beat the doughnuts at Dunky."

"True." Nuri took a sip. As bad as the coffee might be, he was addicted. "The signal will be gone inside a week. I want to tag him again. I'll go over to Khartoum. We're going to have pull the plug here. Our cover is toast, we have to get rid of the mercs, and I have to believe the army's going to be out for blood after this. So we're best off recycling."

"How?"

"Well, I think we have enough sensors at the milk barn down there to hold us for a bit. So we concentrate on our Mr. Tarid. Follow him. Find out where he's going. We play civilian for a while. We can base ourselves in Khartoum. There are plenty of westerners there. We go to the backup covers. Restock."

"Agreed," said Danny. "But one priority you didn't mention—we have to get McGowan's body home."

"Yeah, I know. That sucks."

Nuri had never lost a fellow officer on a mission before. He really didn't feel as if he'd lost one now, either—he still divided the team up mentally, separating himself from Danny and the Whiplash people. He felt bad about McGowan, but didn't ache the way Danny did.

"We can't take everybody into the capital anyway," said Nuri. "You oughta stay away anyway."

"Why me?"

"Because he's seen you. You and Hera. And Boston."

"And Flash."

"Right."

"I'm going with you," said Danny. "We'll take Sugar. Boston and the others can take care of getting everything out of here."

"All right." Nuri pulled over the chair and sat down. "We're going to need more people eventually."

"True. You think we would have done better last night with more people?"

"I think we did OK last night," said Nuri.

"It was a hell of a bloodbath."

"That's Sudan these days. Sucks. I'm sorry we lost McGowan," Nuri added.

"So am I."

"But we did all right. We're not—we don't have all the firepower you guys used to have at Dreamland," Nuri said, thinking Danny was comparing the two operations. "So we're never going to have overwhelming odds."

"We had some troubles in ops there, too," said Danny, thinking back. "It just gets harder."

He meant accepting the losses, but didn't explain.

"The next batch of people we get should be heavier on the Agency side," said Nuri, getting back to his point. "Your spec ops guys are OK shooters, but they're not really spies. We're going to need more spies, I think. Be useful following Tarid."

"Sure."

"I mean, we can train anybody. Not anybody— you know what I mean. I started on the paramilitary side myself, then moved over. It's not that hard."

"Yeah?" asked Danny. He got up and got himself coffee.

"I don't know," continued Nuri. "Maybe it isn't for me. It's my blood. My grandfather worked for the Agency. And my great-grandfather was with the OSS. I grew up listening to stories about it."

"Your parents were CIA, too?"

"Skipped a generation."

Nuri's father had been about as far from a CIA type as possible, at least partly in reaction to his own father, with whom his relationship had always been poor. His mom was even more opposed to the CIA and military. But in a way, both had done quite a bit to prepare him for his career. His father was an executive with an oil company, and they had lived almost exclusively in the Middle East and Northern Africa when Nuri was growing up. His mother had insisted he learn the local languages and customs wherever they lived—critical background for his job.

"I think we just take the best people we can," said Danny. "Train them the way we want. Cross-train them."

"Agreed. But for now —"

"We play it by ear," said Danny. "Just like we've been doing. Besides, just because they're from the CIA doesn't mean they're perfect."

Nuri took that, correctly, as a reference to Hera.

"What are we going to do about her?" he asked.

"Hera gave you problems too, huh?"

"I think she's jealous. She originally trained for the MY-PID program and didn't get the first selection. She can't be top dog, and her nose is out of joint."

"I'd say whoever rejected her spent some quality time with her," said Danny. "Did you know her?"

"We met a few times. We never worked together." Nuri shrugged. "She speaks Farsi. That'll be pretty useful."

"I know. We have to keep her for this mission. I'll talk to her."

"Good luck."

JUST BEFORE SHE WOKE, HERA DREAMED ABOUT MCGOWAN.

He was in the tent with her, standing across from her bed.

"What?" she asked him, sitting up.

He shook his head slowly.

"What?" she asked again. "Are you warning me about something? Did I do something wrong?"

The dream faded into daylight.

Shuddering, she got out of bed quickly. Pulling on her clothes, she went for something to eat.

Danny happened to be in the house. He was surprised when she came in—she wasn't due back on watch for another six hours—but was glad she was there. No one else was around and he could get their talk over with.

"Hera, good morning," he said. "There's coffee."

"Good."

"Bagels are good."

"They're kinda slimy. I'll stick to the powdered eggs. Thanks."

He waited until she'd had a few sips before he started talking to her.

"I want you to be more careful when you're talking to people," he told her, deciding to start out diplomatically. She had, after all, been through hell the night before.

"What do you mean?" she snapped.

"You get nasty when things get tight. With me. Yeah. With everyone else."

Hera thought of the dream. Last night, in the minefield, she'd yelled at McGowan.

"I—I yelled at McGowan. In the minefield. I called him a jerk."

"You pretty much yell at everybody," said Danny.

Hera saw McGowan's face. Her eyes began welling up. The last thing she wanted to do was cry in front of Danny Freah. She started to turn away.

Danny grabbed her arm. "Hey, I'm still talking to you," he told her. "Don't walk away."

"What? Am I your kid?" she said, struggling to hold back her tears.

Danny let go of her arm. "Look—" He stopped, wanting to soften his tone, understanding that McGowan's death hit everyone hard.

"Leave me alone," Hera said, quickly turning and walking out. She barely made it to her tent before exploding in sobs.

THE TALK HADN'T EXACTLY GONE AC HE PLANNED, AND Danny decided he'd give her a little time before trying to have a better discussion. But a few minutes later the Voice reported that Tarid left the house in Khartoum where he'd been staying. Within minutes it was obvious he was going to the city airport.

There was only one flight out for several hours, MY-PID reported: a UAE flight to Morocco.

"The question is where he's going from there," said Nuri. "The possibilities are endless."

They might have been, but MY-PID didn't have to waste its time counting them. Instead, it interfaced with a CIA database that tracked passenger manifests. Tarid had not used his real identity, but only forty people showed up for the flight. Cross-checking against earlier flights, the computer quickly identified his alias and found that he was en route to Athens.

There the trail ended.

"We just need to get to Athens before that flight," said Danny. "And we can follow him from there."

"I follow him. You can't. He's seen you already."

"We may be able to use that."

"Maybe. But not to follow him."

Tarid had a very long layover in Morocco, which gave them an opportunity, but getting to Athens wouldn't be easy; Tarid had picked the quickest route.

"He must be going to Iran," said Nuri. "Changing flights and IDs along the way. If that slows him down, maybe we can beat him there."

MY-PID had already searched flights for matches against Tarid's other aliases and possible aliases. There were only two direct flights from Athens to Tehran after Tarid arrived. The computer ruled out all but three names on those flights as possible aliases.

"How about Bahrain?" said Danny. "They fly to Tehran."

"Yeah," said Nuri.

MY-PID considered the possibilities and made a new suggestion: Arash Tarid was flying as Arash Arash, due in at Imam Khomeini Airport late that night from the Arab Emirates.

"We still can't beat him," said Nuri. "The best we can do is miss by a half hour."

"What if we flew to Kuwait," said Danny. "Or better yet, Azerbaijan?"

"From Khartoum?"

"From anywhere. If we get up to Egypt, we can get a U.S. flight. They can bring us right into Baku."

"Then what?"

"We take a boat."

38

Room 4
CIA Campus

BREANNA WAS JUST SECURING HER GEAR IN HER OFFICE ON the CIA campus when the small communications cube on the corner of her desk sounded a tone.

"Clear," she told the computer, allowing the communication. The secure nature of the building, as well as her small staff and the late hour, meant that there was no one nearby to hear what she was saying. But Room 4 wouldn't have been Room 4 without a high-tech guarantee of security protecting even the most casual conversation. Inaudible waves of energy vibrating from the walls—more nanotechnology—killed all sounds five feet from her desk, making it impossible for anyone outside of the room to hear.

"This is Danny."

"What's going on?"

"The tag marker we put on Tarid was diluted because of the rain. We want to tag him again."

"Do it. You don't need to hear from me."

"The problem is, he's on his way to Iran. We want to follow him."

Ordinarily, Breanna would have said "Go" right away, but what she heard about the visit made her pause.

For all of a half second.

"All right. How are you getting there?"

"That's why I called. We've tracked his flight schedule and have a pretty good idea of what his planes are. It's too late to get on the flight with him," Danny added. "And besides, if we take a commercial flight, there's always a chance someone will find something in our gear."

The Iranian secret police and intelligence agencies also made it a habit to follow westerners in the country. While they could get around that, Danny wanted to avoid the hassle.

"So what were you thinking?"

"We want to fly into Baku, Azerbaijan. There's a flight to Egypt from Khartoum in about an hour and a half that goes up to Cairo. If you can get a plane there and get us up to Baku, we'll make it just in time. But we need help renting some boats and getting gear together. I can't take anything on the first leg."

"Baku?"

"I was there during the Iraq War."

Zen had been there, too, flying a still classified mission he never talked about.

"All right, Danny. Tell me what you need."

"You may want to get a pen. The list is kinda long."

REID HAD ALREADY GONE TO BED WHEN BREANNA CALLED him.

"Don't you have a family to go home to?" he asked tartly, pulling on his glasses and sitting up in bed. "And don't you get any sleep?"

"Don't worry about my family," said Breanna. "Our subject is on his way to Iran."

"Yes?"

"Danny, Nuri, and two other Whiplash people are following him."

"Into Iran?"

"That's where he's going."

"Why do we need to go to Iran?" Reid asked.

"Because the marker is going to fail and we won't be able to follow him soon. I talked to Ray Rubeo. His people think we'll lose the signal in another three or four days. The computer estimates about a week. Either way, that's going to be too short."

"Maybe not."

"There's no way we can risk losing him now. They have a plan that will get them to the airport in Tehran before he lands. Tagging him there should be easy. If not, they'll follow along until they can get close."

"Losing the political agreement with Iran is a much bigger risk," said Reid. "If this blows up, the trip is sure to be scuttled."

"What good is the agreement if they're cheating?" said Breanna.

Reid reminded her that the consensus of the analysts who followed Iran was that the operation to refine the weapons grade material was being conducted by a splinter group of some sort, not the government itself. There were serious doubts about how effective or lasting such a program could be.

"You're getting pressure from Edmund," said Breanna. "Is that why you want to hang back?"

He had, in fact, been getting pressure—a phone call from the deputy director of operations as well as the big boss, both of whom implied that he was going over to the other side –that being defined as any entity not under their full control. But Reid didn't think he was responding to the pressure at all.

"I'm merely saying there's no need for haste or too much risk," he countered.

"So you don't think they should go to Iran?"

"I didn't say that."

"Good," said Breanna. "They're going to need some supplies and logistical help."

Reid put his elbows on his knees for a moment, thinking. Late night phone calls were one of the reasons he had turned down the DDO's job. Not the major reason, but still one of them.

"If things go wrong, Breanna, they're going to have our heads," he said finally.

"Isn't that always the case?"

"Yes, of course it is." Reid sighed. He knew they should go—the trail would undoubtedly lead back there at some point anyway. "Let me get dressed and make some coffee. I'll be over as soon as I can."

39

Baku, Azerbaijan
Twelve hours later

FOR NEARLY TWO THOUSAND YEARS AZERBAIJAN IN THE southern Caucasus had been little more than a vassal state, the rump end of kingdoms whose capitals lay hundreds and even thousands of miles away. The high desert and rich hills had seen more than their share of conflict, while the people who lived there had fought countless times to rewin their independence.

The land's austere beauty was part of the problem. The mountains that marked three of Azerbaijan's borders seemed to beckon adventurers, and no one who saw the calm sea at its east could withstand the temptations of the mild climate and lush vegetation nearby. At times it seemed as if everyone who came to Azerbaijan wanted to rule it.

With the collapse of the Soviet Union in the 1980s, Azerbaijan had gained independence from its most recent ruler. And with the increased demand for oil and minerals in the years that followed, the country prospered. Its deepwater oil fields offshore were the envy of the world; vast resources lay untapped, making it potentially one of the most important producers in the twenty-first century.

Baku, the capital on the Caspian Sea, had become a boomtown since independence, fueled not just by oil riches, but by the disposable income of Russian oligarchs and mafiya types, who found its mild weather, newly built nightclubs, and relaxed attitude toward wealthy foreigners extremely welcome. Baku had its old, center city, an ancient core bounded by medieval walls that seemed not to have changed in hundreds of years. But much of the city was very new, buffed by flash. There was chrome on everything, cars and buildings, even people. Money flowed freely in new Baku, attracting other money, drawing the good and ill it always draws.

Even so, the man at the marina was dubious when Nuri and Danny arrived to pick up the boat. It was 8:00 P.M., and all of his employees had gone home for the day. The only reason he had stayed was the prospect of receiving twice his normal fee for leasing the craft.

Still, the money wasn't quite enough to stop him from asking questions.

"Why so late?" he asked as Nuri began counting out the hundred euro bills.

Cash had been his first stipulation.

"It's not late," said Danny. He'd slept on the plane from Khartoum to Egypt, but those two hours represented all the rest he'd had in the past two days.

The marina owner took the hint and stopped asking questions. Holding the euros was reassuring. He fanned through them and decided it was none of his business what the two foreigners wanted to do with the boat.

As long as it was back in one piece.

"By Thursday evening, yes?" said Nuri. "To your dock."

"With a full tank of fuel."

"Yes, A full tank of fuel."

"If it fails to return—"

"It'll be back," said Danny.

"If it fails to return, you will be responsible for replacing the entire vessel. The credit cards will be charged."

"Of course."

The owner fixed Nuri with his gaze. He had pegged the black man as an American—he had the unspoken arrogance all Americans carried—but this one was harder to decipher. His English was not like the other man's, or like the American who had first contacted him about the possibility of leasing the boat. And he used euros, a European's first choice of currency. But he was too dark to be an Englishman. He certainly wasn't French or German.

"If I have to replace the fuel," said Nuri, "I want to make sure that's filled up now. To the brim."

"Of course it's filled up."

"Show me."

"There's no need." The boat was not, in fact, filled to the brim, or even three-quarters of the way up. A fact the owner was well aware of, since he had used it just that afternoon. "If there is a discrepancy, we can settle it when you get back. Don't worry. Take the boat."

"I want you to come with me and check," insisted Nuri.

"No, no, go—I'll take your word. Write it down. I have to see my wife. If I'm not home soon, she'll call her mother and they will start talking. Then I will have much trouble."

"How full you figure it is?" Danny asked as soon as he and Nuri were alone on the dock.

"I'd guess somewhere between half and three-quarters," said Nuri.

It was closer to half than three-quarters, but they had already arranged for more fuel, along with a second boat that was waiting for them about a mile down the coast. Hera and Flash were there as well.

Danny and Nuri sped southward, blowing some of the carbon out of the engines as they went. The boat was a Phantom 21, sporting a massive engine and capable of somewhere around 75 knots—expensive to lease but well worth the price. They touched fifty knots before throttling back to enter the marina at a controlled speed.

Standing on the dockside waiting as they approached, Hera did her best to keep her mouth shut, trying to block the remarks that came into her brain from traveling to her tongue. Danny and the others had been cold to her the whole trip, through Egypt and on the flight here. Even Flash, who talked to everyone and was everyone's friend, barely spoke to her.

Separation from Whiplash was inevitable. It wasn't fair, she thought—she had done her job, and done as well as anyone else. But that's the way it was going to be.

As long they didn't blame her for McGowan's death. She knew it wasn't her fault. She hadn't been anywhere near him and she'd done her job. Getting stuck in the prisoners' pen wasn't her fault.

"All right, Whiplash, let's go," shouted Danny as he nudged the boat next to the dock. "Hera, you're with me."

She tossed down their gear bags and jumped into the boat. Nuri, meanwhile, clambered out and got into the second boat, a Sunseeker with twin Mercruisers. Not quite as fast as the Phantom, but no slacker, either.

"We gonna race?" said Flash, handing down a pair of jerry cans filled with fuel.

"Let's just get across the Gulf in one piece, all right?" said Danny. "Nuri, we'll stay in touch."

"Yeah. What are we going to do if Tarid doesn't get on that plane?"

"Then we'll definitely have a race on the way back," said Danny, gunning the throttle.

40

Pentagon

BREANNA PICKLD UP THE PHONE A SPLIT SECOND AFTER IT started to ring.

"Breanna Stockard."

"Jeffrey Stockard," replied her husband.

"Oh, it's you."

Zen laughed. "Sorry to disappoint you."

"I'm waiting for a call."

"An important one, I bet. You have your serious voice on."

"All my phone calls are important," she said.

"Even the ones from me?"

"Especially yours. It's just—I've been waiting for you to call all morning."

"It's beyond morning. A half hour beyond," he added. "I thought we were having lunch."

"Oh, crap!"

Breanna looked down at her computer. The alarm noting lunch was buried under eight windows, half of which she couldn't even remember opening.

"Guess it's off, huh?"

"I forgot all about it. I lost track of the time. I'm sorry."

"You need a secretary," said Zen.

"I have a secretary."

"Where is she?"

"Lunch." Ms. Bennett had in fact reminded Breanna that she had an appointment before leaving.

"So: We having lunch, or not?"

"No. I can't. I—I have to get something cleared up."

"What you were working on last night, huh?"

"Something along those lines."

Breanna wanted to talk about the situation but couldn't— she and her husband had agreed that they wouldn't discuss anything involving national security on her side, and party politics on his. While they occasionally bent the rules, Zen would have immediately ended the conversation if she began talking about the mission.

It was too bad. There was no one whose opinion she trusted more than her husband's, especially when it came to dealing with the Washington bureaucracy.

"It's all right," said Zen. "I'm a little squeezed myself. I have an appointment with the President at one. Which means it'll be about two when I get in there."

"You're seeing a lot of her lately. Should I be jealous?"

"Ha. I'm her favorite thorn. In the side or elsewhere. You going to be home for dinner?"

"Yeah."

"Because Teri's thing is tonight."

"Which thing?"

"Concert thing. Spring concert."

"Oh right, right, right."

"I'm missing a reception at the Korean ambassador's home for it," said Zen, as if this was the greatest sacrifice in the world. Zen hated receptions, and wasn't very fond of the Korean ambassador, either. "So you better show up."

"I'm showing."

Breanna looked at the windows on the computer. She had a lot to do, but it was difficult to focus on any of it while the Whiplash mission was under way. She knew she had to separate herself—and yet she couldn't.

Maybe it would be better to go over to Langley and work from there. At least she wouldn't be checking the secure message system every few seconds, and looking at SpyNet, and checking the news . . . she could hook directly to MY-PID and get regular updates.

Her secure sat phone beeped. It was a call from Danny, asking for an update.

"Zen, I have to go," said Breanna, barely getting the words out of her mouth before hanging up.

41

Approaching the Iranian coast

IT WAS A LITTLE OVER 250 MILES FROM BAKU TO THE COAST of Iran. The speedboats made the trip in just over four hours, dodging a small patrol craft operating out of Babol.

The Voice gave them directions the entire way. Danny still felt it was intrusive but he was beginning to think of the system as a personality, rather than a computer. It definitely acted differently than any computer he'd ever dealt with before.

Technically, MY-PID was simply the sum of its various

connections and databases. The programmers had kept the interface portion extremely basic, using techniques and routines developed and tested at Dreamland. Most of these, at their very core, were barely more sophisticated than the routines that worked GPS units, or the so-called personal assistant bots that gathered Web and media feeds for smart phones. But the sheer volume of the data available to the system and the algorithms it used to sort through them shaped the MY-PID's interaction with users in the same way a human personality did.

The Voice was like a brainy, overknowledgeable kibitzer, an egghead that could be extremely valuable, but at the end of the day was still an egghead. In many ways it reminded Danny of Ray Rubeo, though the computer wasn't quite as full of himself as its real-life analogue.

They were already in Iranian waters when Breanna called, using the Voice's communications network.

"Danny, your subject is on his way to Tehran," she told him.

"Roger that. We're like zero-two minutes from shore."

"I see." Breanna paused. "I thought you were going to hold until we were positive he was in the air."

"Schedule is a little tight, Bree. We have a bus to catch."

"Acknowledged."

"You wish you were out here, huh?" said Danny. "It sucks sitting behind a desk."

"How'd you guess?"

Her voice had made it obvious. "I know exactly how you feel," he told her.

"We'll trade notes when you get back."

"Deal."

The Voice warned that a car was approaching on the road a few yards from where Danny wanted to land. He cut his speed, drifting to let the vehicle go by before moving closer to shore. As he coasted, he looked back for Nuri. Though the boat was only a mile or so behind, Danny couldn't see it; the night was too dark and it was too low to the water. The engines were plenty loud, but the hum from his own craft drowned them out.

"Trouble?" Hera asked. It was practically the first word she'd said since they left Baku.

"It's just a car. We'll let it pass," he said. "You ready to use your Farsi?"

She told him, in Farsi, that she was as ready as an old woman to bake a cake—an expression her Iranian grandfather had used to indicate that he was willing to do whatever had to be done.

The Voice translated for him.

"Simultaneous translate to Farsi," Danny told the computer. "As long as it's chocolate."

He repeated the words as the Voice reeled them off.

"Your pronunciation is off," said Hera. "And what's that supposed to mean?"

"It's a joke. I like chocolate cake."

"Oh."

"You don't have much of a sense of humor, do you?" he said.

"I laugh at things that are funny."

As Nuri's boat slipped in alongside, the Voice reported that two more cars were coming down the road.

"I don't want to wait too much longer," said Nuri. "If we miss that bus, we have no way of getting to Tehran until morning."

"Agreed," said Danny. "We'll go in after these pass. You ready, Flash?"

"Born ready, Colonel."

"Nuri let a soldier drive?" said Hera.

"Boats are easy," said Flash. "You should see me with a motorcycle."

"Maybe you'll get a chance with the bus," said Danny.

"I'm game."

Hera scoffed.

"You like driving motorcycles?" asked Danny.

"I have to be honest, Colonel," said Flash. "I've never driven one."

"No?"

"Chief Boston was going to show me in Sudan, but we didn't get a chance."

"It's practically a requirement for Whiplash. We'll have to teach you."

"I'm ready whenever you are."

"One more thing," Danny told him. "Don't call me colonel anymore. We have to stick with our covers."

"Right."

"Boss, anything like that is good."

"Right."

While they waited for the cars, Nuri sat on the deck at the rear of the cockpit, rehearsing his Farsi. He had spent much of the trip practicing with the Voice. Iran's native language had never been particularly hospitable to his tongue. While the Voice could help with vocabulary, Nuri was still having fits with the pronunciation.

"Vehicle three has passed," said the Voice.

"Let's get in while the gettin's good." Danny slid the engine up out of idle, gave it a quick jolt, then dropped the throttle back again.

The Voice steered them past a group of rocks to a shallow shelf at the sea's edge. The wind had died to almost nothing. Danny handled the boat easily, stopping just short of the shore, where the water was shallow enough that he didn't beach.

Flash had a harder time. Just as he drew his boat up to the Phantom, the bow hit a submerged tree trunk. They pitched hard to port against the other cruiser.

The impact caught Hera by surprise, sending her to the deck.

"Watch it," she said, scrambling up.

"Sorry."

"Let's go," said Danny. "Hera, grab the line."

She went to the side of the boat. Nuri, still somewhat distracted, climbed out to the bow and tossed the lead to her.

"Can't we get any closer to shore?" he asked Flash.

"Man, I'm just hoping I didn't beach us."

Nuri sat and took off his shoes and socks, then rolled up his pants. He didn't want to be too wet when he got on the bus. He had another change of clothes, but they were packed in the suitcase, which would be brought along by Danny and Hera later.

He put his foot over the side tentatively, dipping it in the water. It was colder than he expected.

"Best to just get in," he said aloud to himself, easing down. His teeth started chattering. He held his shoes above his head and walked toward dry land.

The water was nearly three feet deep and came up to his waist, soaking his pants and the bottom of his shirt.

"Damn," he muttered.

He pushed away from the boat, took a step, then slipped on the mossy bottom, dunking his entire body.

"You better grab the suitcase and get some backup clothes," said Danny.

"Have Flash get it," said Nuri, squeezing out his drenched shirt on shore.

Flash had his own solution. He stripped off his pants and held them over his head as he waded first to the other boat for the waterproof luggage, then to shore.

"Tell me next time so I can close my eyes," said Hera.

"Next time I sell tickets."

"You got the boat?" Danny asked Hera.

"Yeah, they're tied to us."

"Go ahead, get in."

"I think you ought to pull it off the tree or rocks or whatever first. Make sure they're not hung up."

"If they are hung up, we'll need their engine, too," said Danny.

"It'll float higher without me in it."

"Just do it."

Hera jumped into the other boat.

She was just one of those people who would always want

to do the opposite of what anyone else suggested, Danny thought.

He started reversing the engine on the Phantom 21. The line between the two boats grew taut—then snapped.

"How can it be so wedged in there?" Hera asked. "We're not even hitting anything."

"Get everything out and into our boat. Maybe it will float a little higher."

There wasn't much in the boat except for six jerry cans. Only four had fuel in them. Hera brought them over while Danny retied the line, doubling it this time. They got the other boat to nudge back, only to have it hang up on another submerged piece of the tree. The rope held, but the boat wouldn't budge.

"The gods are screwing with us," said Danny. "You take the helm here. I'm going across. Don't do anything until I tell you."

Because of the time constraints, the plan called for Nuri and Flash to head for the bus at the nearby stop. The bus would take them to another line that ran to the airport.

Danny and Hera would stash the boats a few miles away at a marina. Then they'd catch another bus to Tehran, arriving several hours later with the gear. Depending on where Tarid went—Nuri was betting on Tehran itself—Danny and Hera would immediately get a hotel room and start making other arrangements to support the surveillance mission.

Ashore, Nuri changed and checked his watch. They had fifteen minutes to walk the mile to the bus stop down the road.

"Flash and I have to get moving," he said as Danny settled behind the wheel for another try. "We'll take the bags with us."

"Hold on, hold on," said Danny. He revved the engine and shouted to Hera to pull backward. The boat didn't budge.

"Danny, we're going," said Nuri.

"All right," he said. "You're better off with them anyway. In case we're late."

Nuri had changed everything but his shoes, deciding that his boots would look too American. He squished with every step.

"Car approaching," warned the Voice.

"There's a car," Nuri told Flash, starting off the road.

"Maybe we should hitch."

"You have an explanation about why we're here?"

"We went for a midnight swim."

"That's not going to work in Iran. Come on—there are some bushes we can duck behind."

IT TOOK DANNY AND HERA ANOTHER HOUR TO GET THE SUN-seeker unstuck. By then they had no hope of making their bus.

"What's Plan B?" asked Hera over the radio as they finally got the two vessels pointed toward the marina. The Voice tied her team short-distance unit into its communications circuit.

"We grow wings and fly," said Danny.

"How come you can be a wiseass, and I can't?" snapped Hera.

The remark caught Danny off guard.

"I wasn't being a wiseass," he said.

"What do you call it?"

"It was kind of a joke."

"But I have no sense of humor."

"You're being awful sensitive," he said.

"If I'm going to get canned, I want to understand why."

"We're going to get a later bus," said Danny coldly. "There's one that passes four hours later."

"So we just wait? What if they need us?"

"If you have a better idea, I'm all ears."

"Why don't we see if we can rent a car?"

"There are no car rental places. Not even at the marina."

"Then let's steal one."

Danny had considered it earlier, but decided that even the slight risk wasn't worth taking if they could simply ride on the bus. Now, though, he saw the long gap as a potential problem, leaving him no way to back up Nuri and Flash for hours if something went wrong.

"All right," he said. "If you can jump a car."

"With my eyes closed."

HERA HAD LEARNED HOW TO DEFEAT ALARM SYSTEMS AND jump cars long before she joined the CIA, though the details of her training were glossed over on her résumé.

The problem was finding a vehicle to take. Danny had chosen the marina because the Voice's analysis of activity there showed that it was nearly always deserted after evening prayers, and tonight was no exception. That meant no one was there to ask questions as he and Hera lifted the suitcases from the boats and rolled them up the dock. But it also meant there were no cars in the parking lot. Nor were there vehicles near the houses or on the road leading up to the small village nearby. The houses were small and battered, and didn't even look occupied.

The village was centered around a very small mosque. Structures leaned up against it on all sides; these were more stalls than buildings, painted and repainted, covered with tarpaper, and lean-to roofs. Half of them had not been used for years. The others were small stores and stands where a variety of goods were sold when the owners took the time to open them.

Beyond them sat the bus stop, a post on the main road. There were more houses on the other side of the highway. These were modern structures, far larger than the ones in the village. The owners were more prosperous than the people who lived in the village, though none were considered rich, even for Iran. The real money and power—as in most places, they tended to go hand in hand—lived in the hills overlooking the seaside.

"There's something over there," said Hera, pointing to a battered pickup truck. It was a late nineties Toyota, easy for her to jump.

"Looks like it's their only vehicle," said Danny, examining the property. "I'd hate to take somebody's only car."

"You can't have a conscience in this game, Colonel. It'll eat up your gut."

"Go."

Danny took the bags and walked with them over to the bus stop. A few minutes later Hera drove up at the wheel of a late model Hyundai Genesis.

"I saw a house with two cars in the driveway. This was the fancy one," she said, rolling down the window.

Danny brought the bags around the back.

"I have to change," said Hera, running over to the bag. She pulled out the long dress and scarf, covering her black jeans and shirt. The outfit was somewhere between conservative and fashionable, typical of younger women who lived in Tehran, but had strong ties to tradition.

"You better drive," she told Danny. "Women usually don't when they're with a man."

"I intend on it," he told her, adjusting the seat so he could fit his knees under the dashboard. He made a three-point turn and headed down the highway, in the direction of Tehran.

"How far we going?" Hera asked.

"That bus stop at Karaj, I guess. It'll only be a half hour or so from there."

"Why don't we just drive it all the way to the city?" she asked. "We can get there before Nuri and Flash."

"Let's not push it."

"There's no traffic. Which means no police," she insisted.

"The briefing I heard said there was the possibility of roadblocks."

"Not at night. That stuff happens down in the south, near Iraq and Afghanistan. Here the police all sleep. Even during the day."

"You seem pretty sure of yourself."

"I've been in Iran a lot, Colonel," said Hera. "I know the country pretty well. It's not as bad as you think. There aren't police on every corner, or checkpoints everywhere."

"All we need is one."

He leaned back in the seat, trying to relax a little. His neck muscles had seized up on him, and his knees felt as if they were stiff wooden hinges—old injuries reminding him of the past.

"I didn't cause McGowan's death," Hera blurted.

"I know that," said Danny. The comment seemed to come out of left field; no one had accused her of that.

"You think I don't fit in."

"You don't."

"Why not?"

"You're pissing everyone off."

Hera pressed her lips together, trying to think of what to say.

"I'm not a screwup," she tried finally.

"I didn't say you were . . . but you do have to get along with the people on the team."

"If I point stuff out—"

"There's a way to do it, and a way not to do it."

"And I don't do it right?"

"No," said Danny bluntly. "You come off—you're being a bitch, basically. You second-guess everyone."

"I'm just giving my opinion."

"Maybe you should hold onto it a little tighter."

"I'm trying," she said.

Hera could feel the tears coming again, hot at the corner of her eyes. She hated that—hated the cliché of the weak woman.

"Just do your job," said Danny. "We'll discuss this all later."

"I am. I didn't have anything to do with McGowan dying. Nothing."

Danny reached his hand across and patted her shoulder. "Every one of us—we all were affected by it."

"Not you."

"Yeah, me too," he said.

"You don't have to worry. No one thinks you're a screw-up."

"I don't think you're a screw-up, Hera."

She choked back her tears, feeling like a fool. Danny sat

silently, thinking of his own doubts, his own fear, and the terrible knowledge of the price that had already been paid on the mission, not just by McGowan, but by everyone who'd died.

"I'm sorry Carl died," Hera said again. "I never had someone—another officer—someone on the team—die on me. Not during the op."

"It sucks," said Danny, leaning back in the seat. "It affects us all. More than we know. Or want to admit."

42

Base Camp Alpha

DANNY HAD LEFT BOSTON AND SUGAR TO PAY OFF THE mercenaries, close the camp, and get McGowan's body and the rest of the gear back home.

The mercenaries were now a liability. Boston couldn't just dismiss them—they'd sell him out in a heartbeat. But they were clearly on edge, and just from the expressions of the men on watch, he guessed he had a fifty fifty chance of making it through the day without trouble. Boston told the bus driver, Abul, to find out what the men were thinking. Abul told him he didn't have to ask.

"They're anxious about getting paid. They're wondering what happened to Kirk And they're worried about the government making trouble for them."

"They'll get everything they've been promised," Boston said. "Unless I'm shot."

Abul smiled nervously.

Danny and Nuri had driven the Land Cruisers to Khartoum, leaving them at the airport, where they could be picked up by a CIA contact and driven back to Ethiopia. Boston and Sugar had the bus, and two options for evac.

He could have Abul drive them over the Ethiopian border and then to the airport at Bole, just south of the capital of Addis Ababa. Crossing the border with a dead body was a problem, however. Without proper papers, it wouldn't be allowed. Hiding him would be hard—the Ethiopian border guards thoroughly searched incoming traffic, and by reputation were difficult to bribe.

Driving north to Port Sudan would take longer and probably bring them into contact with regular army patrols— including the one that tried to hold Danny up on the way down. If anyone remembered the bus, they were unlikely to get by without a bribe large enough to buy Manhattan.

Boston opted for Ethiopia, and had asked Breanna to see if something could be arranged with the Ethiopian government to allow the body through without any questions. They were still working on it as night fell. He decided they were bugging out no matter what; it didn't make sense to give the Sudanese army another day to recover from the drubbing it had taken.

Which brought him back to the question of what to do with the mercenaries.

They'd come from Ethiopia, and so taking them back there seemed like the logical thing to do. But they were frowning when he had Abul tell them at dinner they would go the next day.

"What's wrong?" he asked Abul.

"They don't have the right papers. They want to go to Port Sudan."

"They're welcome to do that."

"They say Kirk promised them extra money. And they want more on top of that—twice what they were hired for. The fight with the Sudanese was not what they had planned."

"I'll pay them what Nuri left," said Boston, who knew nothing about any extra bonuses. "It's not worth debating— I'll give them everything I have."

"They think you are cheating them."

"I'm not."

"I think they have friends in Port Sudan," said Abul. "Or maybe nearby. You should give them something, just to appease them."

Boston looked around the two tables where the men were sitting. Not one of them was smiling.

"I'll give them the money right now," he said. "I don't have a problem with it."

He went and got the strongbox Nuri had left with the euros. Maybe, he thought, they'd take the hint and leave that night.

But he wasn't counting on it.

IT WAS JUST ABOUT MIDNIGHT WHEN SUGAR WENT TO THE northwestern observation post with some water for the guard there. A minute after she arrived, a shell streaked overhead. She and the guard on watch stared at it wide-eyed, not quite comprehending what was going on.

There was a flash, then a rumble.

"Incoming!" yelled Sugar, throwing herself to the ground next to the sandbags.

The guard followed as several more shells streaked through the air.

Sugar reached for her radio. "Boston! We're being shelled. Mortars!"

Her words were drowned out by machine-gun fire near the road. Sugar grabbed her gun and started returning fire.

"Go get help!" she yelled to the mercenary. "Go!"

The man didn't speak English. More important, he didn't think leaving the safety of the sandbags was a particularly good idea.

"We need help," she told him. "Bring men and ammunition."

The machine-gun fire from the other side of the perimeter ratcheted up another notch. Bullets flew nearby, smashing into the rocks behind the post. Shards of stone flew against the sandbags at the side of the post.

"That way, that way," said Sugar, pointing to the north and then making a loop with her finger. "They're attacking from this side here. If you go down the hill, they won't be able to hit you. *Go!* Get more people!"

She grabbed the radio to call Boston again. The other lookout post had started to return fire, but Sugar couldn't see anything to aim at. Another shell came overhead. It had been launched from a mortar near the road.

Still not sure what to do, the mercenary took a few tentative steps toward the opening in the sandbag wall at the rear of the position. Another shell landed, this one closer than all of the others. The explosion showered him with dirt and pebbles. That was the last straw—he threw himself into motion, running with his all his might to the main area of the base.

"God, I thought he'd never leave," said Sugar.

"Careful," said Boston over the radio. "Some of those guys speak a little English."

"Yeah." She pulled her rifle up and fired a few rounds toward the road.

Abul was sleeping in his bus when the gunfire started. He woke with the first explosion. As he scrambled to get his shoes on, two of the mercenaries knocked on the door.

"Driver, come. We're getting out," shouted one of the men.

"What's going on?" answered Abul.

"The army has come. This isn't our fight. Let us in."

"My bus will be a target."

"Let us in!" shouted the man. He smashed the door with the butt end of his rifle.

"No, no, no!" yelled Abul. "Not my bus. Wait! Wait!"

He scrambled forward to the driver's seat and opened the door. The two mercenaries ran up the steps.

"Where is Commander Boston?" Abul asked.

"Go, just go," said the man who had pounded on the door. He pointed his rifle at Abul.

"What about the others?"

"Go! Go!"

Abul's hands began to shake as he struggled to get the key

into the ignition. He turned the motor over. It caught but then stalled.

"Out of the seat, you worthless scum," said the mercenary. He grabbed Abul and threw him down. As Abul struggled to get up, the man's companion pushed him into the aisle, first with his hand and then with his foot. Abul flew to the floor, tripping over his bedroll and tumbling against the body bag.

The soldier got the bus started and put it into gear. The entire compound was under fire now, from both mortars and machine guns. He pulled the bus out into the open area near the building. Three of his companions were crouched at the edge of the flat, firing toward the blinking guns down the hill.

He threw open the door.

"Get in! Get in!"

As the men jumped onto the bus, Abul got up and yelled at them. "We're easy targets! Don't go that way!"

"Shut up, bus driver," said the mercenary who'd taken the wheel. "We don't need you."

The bus jerked into motion. Abul interpreted the soldier's last sentence as a warning that he could easily be killed. Rather than tempting that fate, he made his way to the back of the bus, sidestepping the dead American's body with a short prayer asking for forgiveness. He leapt to the door, pushed up the lever, and dove out the back, unsure whether the mercenaries would object to his leaving.

A hundred yards away, Boston zeroed the focus on his night glasses and watched Abul hit the dirt. Things were moving faster than he had planned.

He pulled up the remote detonator and pressed a three-number sequence, detonating a charge on the road about thirty yards in front of the bus. The explosion sent a flash of flames shooting upward—gasoline bombs were always spectacular that way. But the bus driver continued straight along the road, passing through the smoke and staying on the road.

"You better stop that bus, Chief," said Sugar. "Or we're gonna be walking outta here."

"Keep your shirt on," said Boston.

He lit another explosive, this one in the minefield near the road. More dirt, more flash and smoke. The bus drove on.

Boston had one more charge down the road, but it was obvious that the driver wasn't stopping for anything that didn't obliterate the bus. He shoved the detonator into his pocket and picked up his rifle, aiming at the front left tire.

Hitting a tire on a moving bus at 150 yards in the dark is not easy, even with an infrared scope. Which explained why it took him two shots for the first tire and three for the second.

The bus was shaking so much that the driver didn't realize at first that the tires had been blown. The first hint came when he tried to round the curve. The bus wobbled, then refused to turn. He jerked the wheel hard and the vehicle lurched to its left, the rear wheels skidding forward. He jammed the brakes, which in effect pirouetted the back end of the bus toward the front. It flew over on its side, sliding off the road.

Abul, watching from the roadway, covered his eyes.

Dazed, one of the mercenaries punched out a window and raised himself out of the bus. He emptied his magazine box at some imagined enemy soldiers behind them, then began running down the road.

One by one the others joined him. They ran toward the road for all they were worth, disappearing into the darkness.

Sugar yelled at them from the observation post. "Don't run away, you bastards! Come back! Come on! Don't give up!"

They couldn't hear her over the din, and wouldn't have stopped if they did.

The gunfire kept up for another ten minutes, mortars lobbing shells and machine guns firing. All were radio-controlled remote units, originally part of the Whiplash defense perimeter. The entire battle had been directed by Boston's blunt index finger smacking against the buttons of the remote control unit.

"I think you can stop," said Sugar, watching the mercenaries run off over the hill. "They're out of sight."

"Look at my bus!" cried Abul as Boston came down from his lookout post. "Destroyed!"

"It ain't destroyed," said Boston. "Why the hell did you jump out?"

"They were going to kill me."

He pronounced "kill" like "kheel," dragging out the vowel.

"I hope this don't mean we're walkin'," said Sugar.

"We'll have to pull it over with the motorcycles," said Boston.

Sugar was doubtful. The bus lay at the side of a ditch; they would have to fight gravity as well as the bus's weight.

But gravity turned out to be their friend, indirectly at least.

They had trouble finding a place to attach the ropes, until Boston realized he could simply tie them through open windows. Then he and Sugar—Abul was too depressed—got on the motorcycles and revved them together, starting up the hill. The older bike was too small and weak to do very much; it strained at the rope, but no matter how much gas Sugar gave it, couldn't budge the bus.

Boston, sitting on the Whiplash bike, had better luck. The big bore V engine had good torque in the lowest gears, a function of a design requirement that called for it to be able to tow a small trailer. But even the Whiplash motorcycle was still just a motorcycle, not a wrecker or a crane. It pulled the bus up about six feet, then refused to go any further.

Boston leaned forward, trying to sweet-talk the bike as if it were a mule.

"Come on now, Bess," he said, inventing a name. "Just a little more. Almost there, babe. Come on. Come on."

The bike grunted and groaned. Together they managed to lift the bus another foot and a half. But the strain was too much— the bike's engine stalled. The bus's weight pulled it backward. Boston and then Sugar threw themselves to the ground as their motorcycles flew down the hill. The bus slammed down—

then, with gravity's help, rolled over onto its roof, flipped onto its side again, and jerked upward on one set of wheels. It teetered there for a second, its momentum in balance.

Then gravity asserted itself, and it fell forward, landing on its tires.

Abul was practically in tears when he reached it.

"My bus, my beautiful bus," he said in Arabic. "What have they done to you? What have they done?"

"Suck it up, big boy," said Sugar, walking down the hill. "Get inside and see if you can start it up."

The engine had flooded when it turned on its side. Abul tried the key, pumped the gas, then got out and went to the hood. The front end of the bus was so banged up he had to bend the hood to the right to get it open. He fiddled with the air filter and carburetor, then went back into the cab. It started on the second turn.

The next problem were the flat tires. Abul drove it a few yards to a flat spot straddling the roadway and a sharper drop to the left. Then he and Boston went to the back of the bus and wrestled the spares out from their carriage underneath the chassis.

The first was fine. The second was a bit soft.

"Not a problem," said Abul, pulling it toward the front. "Come on."

Sugar called Boston over as he pulled down the jack.

"There's somebody near that ridge," she told him, pointing with her rifle. "I think our friends decided to come back."

Boston picked up the gun and peered through the scope. He couldn't see anything.

"Hey, Abul, how long will it take you to change that tire?"

"Ten minutes. You help me with the jack."

They had just pulled the last nut off when the gunfire started.

"The tire is stuck!" yelped Abul, ducking and pulling at the same time.

Boston threw himself around the tire, put his right boot on

the wheel well and pushed. He fell back with the tire, sliding down the embankment.

"Go, get the damn thing on!" he yelled.

Sugar started returning fire. The mercenaries, realizing they had been duped, were determined to get revenge—and the millions of euros they were sure Kirk would pay in ransom for his people. They spread out in a line, slowly climbing the hill. They were every bit as careful as they'd been at the two earlier battles, but now much better motivated.

Abul's fingers felt as if they were frozen. He threaded the nuts onto their lugs, turning each slowly.

"Faster, faster, damn it," said Boston, running up the hill. "Go, get in the bus. Get it going—let's go."

He jerked on the last nut himself, then screwed them with his fingers, tightening them as best he could.

"Let's get out of here!" he yelled to Sugar.

"The bikes!"

"I got them. You get in the bus. Go! Get down the road. I'll catch up."

Boston ran to the bikes. He fired a few rounds through the gas tank of the smaller dirt bike, then into the tire. He grabbed the Whiplash cycle and started to jump on when something punched him off and threw him to the ground.

A pair of bullets from one of the mercenaries' guns had struck his bulletproof vest. He looked around and realized that the man was less than thirty feet away.

And still firing.

Boston ducked down, trying to pull his body around so the vest would absorb the bullets.

The slugs from the MP-5 felt like hammer heads striking his body. He'd lost his rifle as he fell, and for a moment couldn't locate it. When he finally saw it out of the corner of his eye, it was too late—a boot kicked him in the jaw, sending him over.

The man began cursing him, angrily denouncing him for trying to cheat them. Now he and his employer were going to pay.

Boston drew a quick breath, then exploded upward as the soldier tried to kick him again. His elbow went deep into the man's solar plexus, knocking the wind from him. A hard chop across his windpipe threw him to the ground.

There were shouts nearby. Boston grabbed the motorcycle, kick-started and gunned it to life as bullets began to fly. Hunkering over the handlebars, he revved toward the bus, now lumbering down the road.

One of the bullets caught his rear tire. The bike began skidding hard to the right. Boston let off on the throttle, then dropped the motorcycle. But he couldn't quite get off clean and his foot knocked against the gas tank, sending him over to the ground.

He rolled back up and started to run.

Sugar was at the back door of the bus, watching. When she saw Boston fall, she yelled to Abul to stop. Then she started firing at the mercenaries who were following.

"Stop the bus, stop the bus!" she yelled.

Abul had heard only the gunfire. Frightened, he stepped on the gas. Sugar turned and screamed at him.

"Slow down, damn it!"

Abul slapped on the brakes. Sugar flew forward, tumbling all the way to the front.

Boston got to the bus a few seconds later, grabbing the rear door and throwing himself inside.

"Go! Go! Go!" he yelled.

Abul stomped on the gas and the bus jerked forward.

"Get a grenade!" yelled Boston.

"What?" said Sugar.

"Grenade!"

Sugar grabbed her ruck, fished out the launcher, and snapped it to the bottom of her gun.

"Take out the bike," Boston told her. "Abul, stop so she can aim."

"That's a word he doesn't understand."

Sugar opened the door as the bus stopped, a little more gently this time. The mercenaries had stopped firing, and she couldn't see where Boston had left the motorcycle. She pumped a shell across the hill in the general direction.

"I don't know if I got it," she told him.

"All right. Let's just get the hell out of here," said Boston. "We have to get some distance between us and them."

"They're pretty pissed," said Sugar. "You think they'll follow?"

"Maybe. More likely they'll try to turn us in somehow. Hopefully we'll be in Ethiopia by then." Boston went up to the front. "Let's go, Abul. Let's go."

"My bus," said Abul. "It's ruined."

"It's still running, right?"

"Yes, but—"

"We'll buy you ten when we get home. I promise."

Encouraged again, Abul put it back in gear.

43

Imam Khomeini International Airport

WHILE THE VEHICLES THEMSELVES WERE MOSTLY A DECADE or two old, the Iranian bus system would put those in many Western countries to shame. Bus lines crisscrossed the nation, and even in the worst traffic were within five minutes of the schedule nearly ninety-five percent of the time. The drivers were friendly, and helpful, even toward foreigners.

The bus Nuri and Flash took was nearly empty, its passengers mainly Tehran residents who worked in one of the large villas near the seashore. They were men mostly, and sat near the front of the bus; even on long distance routes the seats were segregated by gender, with women sitting at the back.

Nuri had the Voice play Farsi voice tapes over and over, until the sentences merged into a singsong that put him to sleep. The next thing he knew, Flash was shaking his shoulder.

"Hey," whispered Flash in English. "You said we had to get off around here somewhere for the airport."

Nuri jerked awake, angry at himself. He pulled up out of the seat and ran to the front, flustered.

He couldn't remember anything in Farsi.

The driver looked at him as if he were a madman.

The word "airport" finally drifted from his mouth. In English.

"Imam Khomeini International Airport," Nuri said.

The driver put on the brakes. "You missed," the driver told Nuri, using English himself. "Oh, I am so very sorry. You need the other bus. You go back. Take bus."

"How far?"

"One kilometer. You go back. I let you off. You fell asleep? Bad. Very sorry."

Flash followed him off the bus with his bags.

"I'm sorry," Nuri told him. "I didn't realize I was so tired. I didn't sleep in Sudan."

"No sweat," said Flash, who'd nodded off for a while on the bus himself. "It's like a klick this way?"

"The bus we need is, yes."

"Hey don't feel so bad," said Flash, pushing to keep up. Even though Nuri was short, he walked very fast. "One time I was in Afghanistan, right? We were doing this thing—we were flying into this valley where these guys had gotten themselves stuck between two different groups of Taliban assholes. We're in this big Chinook, right? Anyway, the point of the story is—my lieutenant, he fell asleep and we had to wake him like sixty seconds from the landing zone."

It was a slight exaggeration, but Flash figured the changes were worth it if they cheered Nuri up.

"That guy, man, he could sleep through anything. He was very cool," said Flash. "Didn't help him in the end, though. He got blasted the next time out."

"That's a real heartwarming story, Flash."

"Hey, just trying to cheer you up."

They made it to the bus stop a few minutes before the bus. The ride to the airport was only a few minutes, but Nuri took no chances of falling asleep this time, sitting forward in the seat and tapping his feet. He felt the energy starting to rev inside.

Imam Khomeini Airport, named after the Revolution's great leader, was centered around a large, glass-faced terminal building. It was still relatively new, and an easy airport to navigate. What it wasn't was a good place to wait inconspicuously for someone. There were only a half-dozen vendors in the large hall, and even at the busiest times there were no real crowds to get lost in.

Their bags presented a problem. No one coming to meet someone would bring luggage. Nuri didn't want to risk leaving it outside, so he decided to go in through the departure area. From there the Voice could help them slip across to arrivals by looking at a schematic of the airport.

They walked in the front door and made a show of looking around to get their bearings. Security had two lines set up to check everyone entering the terminal, one for women, one for men. A handful of men stood on line, waiting for their turn to prove they had no weapons. Nuri had hoped to avoid the security check—generally the checks were farther on, just before the gates—but he had taken the precaution of printing tickets in Baku just in case.

"What do you think?" Flash asked, sidling up to him.

"I think we have to get through the security line. It won't be hard. Keep your mouth shut as much as possible. Fracture your English. You're Italian, don't forget."

"*Si.*"

"You had a great time, for an engineer. You like pipelines."

"*Si, si. Grazie.*"

"You have your passport?"

"*Si. Fa bene.*"

Flash had exhausted his knowledge of Italian, but it was unlikely the Iranians manning the security check would speak even that.

Both Nuri and Flash had EU passports that said they were from Italy, which was enjoying a spate of good relations with Iran due to a series of oil deals. Those deals were part of their cover; both men carried credentials identifying them as employees of a legitimate company that made and leased derrick and pipeline equipment. The company had recently sent over a thousand people into Iran, and the Iranian media had done several stories on them.

Nuri took the Voice's command unit out of his pocket and double-clicked the center button, putting it into iPod mode just in case the security people became overly curious. Then he pulled the handle on his suitcase all the way up and wheeled it over to the line.

The guards who worked the terminal could be easygoing to the point of being neglectful. Or they could be excruciatingly thorough. Tonight they were being thorough, forcing each man to open his suitcase and rifle through the contents for them. The man in front of Nuri, an Iranian, had two suitcases with him. He objected to opening either, agreeing to do so only when one of the guards started to do it for him. Even so, he continued haranguing the guard as he undid the locks, growing more and more heated as he went.

Even the Voice had trouble deciphering all of the tirade, translating obscure curse after obscure curse. He was going to be late for his plane. The men had the brains of retarded goats. Holes drilled in their putrid skulls would improve their IQs one hundred percent. And on and on and on.

The guards were not deterred. If anything, the protest made them move more slowly. Each item of clothing was examined. The man's Koran was opened—by him—and inspected. Even his toothpaste was squirted to make sure it was real.

We're going to be here all night, thought Flash.

The guard began looking through the man's second suitcase. He found a bag of mint candies and opened it to try one. This was too much for the passenger, who began stomping his feet up and down.

The guard flipped the candy back into the suitcase and closed it up. Then he grabbed the man's arm, his companion grabbed the other arm, and together they dragged him, screaming and shouting, toward the security office on the other side of the hall.

Nuri looked at Flash, then behind him at the other passengers. He waited a few moments, then wheeled on past the now empty checkpoint. Flash followed. The rest of the passengers stared at them. Then, one by one, they went through the checkpoint as well.

"You think this is a good idea?" asked Flash.

"Tarid's plane is landing in two minutes," said Nuri.

Nuri walked past the check-in counters, again acting as if he were a slightly harried traveler trying to make sure he was in the right place. Then he walked through the corridor behind the counters, sidestepped a rope, and entered a corridor formed by a temporary wall. The path was a shortcut used by employees that would take him to the baggage claim area.

"Where we going?" said Flash, following.

"Just walk like you belong here," said Nuri.

It was a good, time-tested strategy, but it wasn't foolproof. Not ten feet from the baggage area a soldier suddenly stepped into the space. He looked quizzically at Nuri and Flash. He wavered for a moment, unsure whether he should say something. Nuri smiled, but before he could get past, the soldier put out his hand.

"W.C.," said Nuri in English. "Restroom? We need."

The soldier demanded, in Farsi, to know what he was doing in the corridor.

"W.C., W.C.," said Nuri. "Restroom."

The soldier didn't understand. Nuri pointed downward, gesturing that he was desperate for some relief.

"W.C.?"

The soldier shrugged. Nuri switched to Italian.

"The man said it was there but I can't find it. I must go. Is it back there?" Nuri turned and pointed in the direction he had come. "Or this way?"

The soldier finally understood.

"You want the restroom?" he asked in Farsi.

"W.C., W.C.," repeated Nuri, deciding to stick with the ignorant tourist routine.

"Passport," demanded the soldier, using the only English word he knew.

Nuri reached into his pocket and took it out. The soldier held his hand out to Flash, who gave him his as well.

Nuri did everything but cross his legs, trying to convey a sense of urgency and even desperation. The soldier looked at the passports closely. He had seen only a few from the European Union, as his job ordinarily did not involve inspecting documents. The ink on the Iranian visas was a bit blurry, making it difficult to see which dates they were for—they might have been stamped for entry today, or three days before, a strategic error Nuri had arranged to cover any contingency. The soldier tried to decipher the date, then gave up.

"W.C.?" asked Nuri as the passport was handed back.

The soldier pointed across the hall.

"Grazie, grazie," said Nuri.

Nuri walked so quickly across the hall that Flash had trouble keeping up.

"What was he all bugged up about?" Flash asked in the restroom.

Nuri pointed upward and shook his head. A year before, a CIA agent had discovered that one of the restrooms at Mehrabad Airport was bugged; he didn't want to take any chances here.

Flash waited while Nuri used the commode—all that acting had actually encouraged his bladder.

"I'm thirsty," he said when Nuri emerged.

"Don't drink this water," said Nuri. "Buy some outside."

He took a medicine bottle from his pocket—it was the vial for the biomarker, disguised as eyedrops—and applied a healthy bit to his left hand. Outside, he slipped Flash a pair of video bugs.

"Put them on the wall opposite the ramp up to the customs station, in case we have to move," he told him. He pulled out a stick of gum. "Put a little gum on as adhesive."

"These are tiny."

"If they were big, they'd be easy to spot," said Nuri. "Is your sat phone on?"

"Yeah."

"In case we get split up, I'll call you. We can always meet outside, near the bus stop."

Nuri took the bag and walked toward the conveyor belt. Half a dozen passengers from the plane had come off and were looking for their bags. They eyed Nuri's jealously, wondering how he had managed to secure his when the belt wasn't even working.

The door from the gate opened and another group of passengers came out, walking quickly toward customs. Tarid was with them, looking straight ahead.

He had a carry-on, no other luggage.

Nuri swung into action immediately, turning abruptly and walking toward the ramp. He kept his pace slow, wanting the others to scoot around him. As Tarid passed, he would reach out and touch him.

But the man behind him slowed down, and the crowd clogged behind Nuri. Realizing Tarid would never catch up now, Nuri angled toward the side wall.

I'll tie my shoe, he thought, and wait for him to come.

Just as he stepped over, the soldier who had accosted him earlier walked up the wide gangway toward him. Nuri decided his shoe could wait and picked up his pace, nodding as he passed him.

Once again the soldier stopped him, holding out his hand.

"Sir?" asked Nuri.

"W.C.," said the soldier.

"Yes, I found it."

"Why are you coming to Iran?" asked the soldier in Farsi.

"Io, no capisco." Nuri knew he couldn't just start speaking Farsi, when he'd been pretending earlier not to understand a word. "I don't understand. Where is customs? Passport area?"

"Go down that way," said the soldier, quite a bit of disdain in his voice. He couldn't understand why visitors didn't take the trouble to learn the language.

"Grazie," said Nuri. He could see Tarid passing at the other side of the wide ramp.

"Stop!" said the soldier.

Nuri turned around.

"Where is your friend?"

Nuri gestured that he didn't understand. The soldier held up two fingers.

"He's coming, he's coming," said Nuri in Italian, pointing. "He needs his bag."

"You should be together. It's easier for the official."

It was all Nuri could do to stop himself from throttling him. He made a sign that he didn't understand, and turned around. But it was too late—a flood of other passengers had come up, and now Tarid was far ahead. Nuri scrambled, but before he could close the gap, Tarid had gone off to the lane with Iranian passport holders.

There were two lines for foreigners. Both were moving quickly, which gave Nuri some hope. He got on the one at the left, then turned around to look for Flash. He saw him—with the soldier who had just accosted him.

Flash didn't have to pretend he didn't understand what the Iranian was saying; he didn't speak any Farsi, nor could he figure out what the soldier was complaining about. He simply shrugged and pointed toward the exit. The soldier told him that his friend was a jerk, and that he should find better people to travel with.

Flash nodded, because it seemed like the right thing to do.

"Go," said the soldier. "Go."

Flash saw Nuri near the front of the line on the left. He

steered to the right, figuring that if there was a jam-up for some reason, at least one of them would get through quickly. Nuri spotted him and nodded.

The customs officers were in their sixties, men who had first gone to work for the government when the Shah was still in power. They were honest, not especially officious, and above all deliberate. Each had a list of people who were not to be allowed in the country on his desk. The list was 375 pages long, with the names from each country listed separately. When they received a visitor's passport, they dutifully checked it against the list. They did this because it was their job, and also because the government had recently established a bonus system for customs officials who identified anyone on the list. Especially prized were men—all but two of the names were male—who had received judgments in suits against Iran over the years. In those cases, the men were allowed into the country—then detained and, essentially, blackmailed into paying some or all of the money before being put back on a plane and sent home.

These names were identified by small daggers. While most of the names were American, there were quite a few Italians as well.

"Why are you coming to Iran?" asked the customs officer in English as Nuri stepped up.

"I have business," said Nuri, answering in Farsi because he hoped it would get him through the line quicker. "I am involved in the pipeline construction for the government's new wells in the south."

The customs officer was impressed. He took Nuri's passport and cracked it open.

"So you are working here? This is a business trip?"

"There are some matters that have to be attended to," said Nuri.

"You are fixing the pipeline?"

"Actually, the derricks," said Nuri. "The pipelines are another department."

"Hmmm."

The Customs official looked at the visa. "You know that this visa is only good for seven days," he said.

"Oh?"

"They should not have given you this one. In your case, because it is an important government assignment, you should have been given a six-month pass."

"It should only take a day or two."

"But that is the way it should be done." The customs official reached under his desk and took out a pad. "Take this to the window over there," he said, starting to write a note. "She will give you the proper documentation."

"This matter came up in Dubai," said Nuri. He spoke slowly, struggling with the words. "There was a debate. My boss went to the top official. They asked the ambassador himself. He said, this he said—give him the short visa only."

"Well, if the ambassador said that. I could not overrule an ambassador."

"Of course not."

"He is wrong, though."

"It wouldn't be my place to say."

The customs inspector shook his head, then crumpled the note up and put it in his pocket. He started to wave Nuri through, then realized he hadn't checked his name against the list.

Slowly, he began leafing through the pages.

Nuri caught sight of Tarid walking out the main entrance.

"I'm sorry. We have procedures," said the inspector as he found the Italian section.

"Take your time," said Nuri, turning his eyes toward the ceiling.

44

Tehran

Tehran had always felt like a foreign place to Arash Tarid. He'd been born in the southeastern corner of the country, about as far away from the capital as one could get and still stay in Iran. His first trip to the city had been when he was a teenager on some family errand, now long lost to memory. But he vividly remembered the city, all lit up. Cars whizzed everywhere—there was much less traffic, but just as much pollution. His eyes had stung the whole time he was there, and for three days afterward.

Tonight the traffic was worse, and the pollution just as bad. The taxi driver had asked 80,000 rials for the thirty-five-kilometer ride to the city; the fee hadn't changed since the airport had opened.

"Returning home from business?" asked the driver, slowing with the traffic as they approached the city.

"Yes."

"It must be exciting to go abroad."

"It can be."

Tarid shifted in the seat. While his leg injury hadn't been serious, his body still ached from the firefight and the escape from the Sudan holding pen. He decided he would make a detour to Istanbul when his meeting with Bani Aberhadji was done. He would spend several days there, soaking in a bath in the old part of the city. A friend of his swore by the waters and the old man who ran the place, claiming they had curative powers.

And the apartments above were a good place to have drinks, if you knew the owner. He would not drink alcohol in Iran—the possibility of Aberhadji finding out was too great—but in Istanbul a man could relax, and even pose as a westerner if the mood struck him. No one would care.

"So, you were in Dubai?" asked the driver.

The question caught Tarid by surprise. He gripped the back of the driver's seat and pulled himself close to the man.

"Who are you?" he demanded. "Why are you asking me these questions?"

"I—uh—I just, I thought you were on the plane from Dubai. It was the one that just landed."

"How do you know that?"

"The plane—the same plane every night. I take people into the city."

The driver was trembling. He was in his mid-twenties, already losing his hair.

Tarid sat back.

"Just drive," he told the man.

TARID COULD HAVE STAYED IN ONE OF THE HOTELS IN THE CITY owned by the Revolutionary Guard; Bani Aberhadji would have seen that his bill was settled for him. But he found their atmosphere stifling, and chose a smaller guest house on the outskirts of the old city instead. The owner recognized him when he came through the door, and came out from behind the counter to personally take his bags and welcome him to Tehran.

"We will get you a very nice room," said the owner, whose name Tarid tried to recall but could not remember. "But first—a little tea? You look tired from your journey."

"Tea would be nice."

"Very good, Arash," said the owner, turning toward the office behind the desk. He clapped his hands together. "Simin, get our friend some tea. A few cookies, too."

The hotelier practically pushed Tarid to an overstuffed chair at the side of the lobby, then sat down across from him.

"There are many rumors around the city," he told Tarid as they waited for the tea. "The president has made peace with the U.S.A."

"Yes, I've heard."

"The rumor is that he's going there soon."

"I wouldn't trust the devils," said Tarid. "They're not truthful."

"Maybe you're right. Still, it is an incredible thought."

"A bad one."

The host, who had relatives in America, stopped talking, afraid he might insult his guest.

His daughter Simin appeared a few moments later, carrying a tray with tea and cookies. Tarid hadn't seen the girl in just over a year. She'd grown considerably in that time, blossoming into a beautiful woman. She wasn't there yet—he was looking at a piece of fruit that had just begun to shade from green, its blush hinting at the sweetness still a week or two away. But the potential was obvious.

Her scarf slipped to one side as she poured the tea, exposing the curl of hair at the back of her neck. As someone who freely traveled the world, Tarid had numerous opportunities to see much more than that on women, yet the modest exposure made his heart surge.

"I've forgotten your name," he said, reaching out to stop her hand as she poured.

"Simin."

"A wonderful name. *Silver*. A precious piece of metal."

Her eyes held his for a moment. Simin felt a confused mixture of emotions—excitement, dread, attraction. She knew from her father that Tarid was an important man, somehow connected with the Republican Guard. That he felt attracted to her—his eyes made that clear—was the most momentous thing that had happened to her since her birth.

Or so she believed. She flushed, and finished pouring the tea.

"Could I have some sugar?" asked Tarid. "Just one spoon."

She put the teapot down, then bent to one knee to put it into his cup. Tarid admired the curve of her breast against her dress. To his mind, the suggestion was infinitely more seductive than the actual flesh.

The innkeeper saw the glances with alarm. His daughter was still young, not ready for marriage. If she left him, he would have no one to do the work here.

"Simin, off to your chores," he said sharply. "I will see to our guest."

"She is a very beautiful girl," said Tarid when she was gone.

"Yes."

The innkeeper's nervousness amused Tarid. He said nothing else as he drank his tea, taking it in minuscule sips to savor the sweetness. Every so often he glanced at the doorway behind the desk, catching a glimpse of Simin as she went about her duties.

Finally, the cup was empty.

"Well, perhaps I will go up to my room now," said Tarid. "I've had a long day and need to rest."

"Yes, a good idea," said the innkeeper with great relief. "Let me show you the way."

NURI HAD THE CAB DRIVER DROP THEM OFF TWO BLOCKS from the hotel where Tarid had stopped.

"You want here, mister?" asked the driver. He spoke slowly in Farsi, forming each word carefully, convinced that it was the only way his foreign fare would understand. "I take you to a good hotel. Better for tourists."

"This will do," said Tarid in Farsi.

"But—"

"We're meeting some friends. This is good."

"If you wish."

The driver pulled in the general direction of the curb, though not so far off the main lane of traffic that anyone could have squeezed around him. Nuri and Flash got out. After collecting their bags, Nuri gave the driver a 100,000 rial note and told him to keep the change.

"Thank you, sir. Thank you." The driver opened his door. "Are you sure that you don't want a ride to a proper hotel? I know of many."

"That's OK."

The driver shrugged, then left.

"Probably going to take us to his brother-in-law's, right?" said Flash.

"No, he's probably pretty honest. Most of the Iranians are kind to tourists. A few you have to watch out for, but most would give you the shirt off their back. Of course, everyone thinks you're rich."

Nuri glanced around the street. The area was shabby, not quite poor but far from prosperous. The same could be said for much of Tehran, and the entire country for that matter. Except for oil, there was not much going on in the economy, one reason the government had agreed to get rid of its nuclear weapons.

Or at least pretended to, he thought.

"High crime area?" Flash asked.

"Crime's not too much of a problem in Tehran," said Nuri, though he realized that the area was not the best. "We have a lot more to worry about from the police."

He began walking down the block. The Voice had identified the building where Tarid was staying as a small, private hotel. It had been unable to get more information about it, however— an indication to Nuri that it catered exclusively to Iranians. It was possible it was connected to the government in some way, or the Iranian secret service, if Tarid was employed by it.

They stopped at the corner, still a half block from the hotel There was a small painted sign in Farsi.

"What do you think?" asked Flash. "We going to check in?"

"I'm not sure."

Checking into a hotel controlled by the intelligence services would be needlessly dangerous under the circumstances. Nuri decided to take a look at the place and see how difficult it would be to wait for Tarid outside. Bumping into him in the street in the morning might be the easiest way to accomplish their mission.

On the other hand, the Voice said that Tarid was in the lobby. Perhaps he could go in and ask for directions—tag him as he stood nearby. Then he'd be able to get some real sleep.

"Wait here," Nuri told Flash. "I'm going to check the place out."

"What do I do with the bags?"

"Sit on them."

"Thanks."

The hotel was a narrow four-story building squeezed between two apartment houses. The entrance to the lobby was up a flight of steps from the street, situated just high enough to make it impossible to see inside without going up the steps, though Nuri tried as he walked by. He continued down the end of the block, crossed, and passed again on the other side. There were two restaurants and a café almost directly across from the place; it was likely Tarid would go there in the morning. Even if he didn't, it would be easy to wait for him there.

"Locate the subject in the building," said Nuri. "What floor is he on?"

"His elevation indicates floor three."

"He's not in the lobby?"

"Elevation indicates floor three."

"Front or back?"

"Back."

"When was the last time he moved?"

"Subject is moving."

"Still in that apartment?"

"Within the previous parameters."

The Voice couldn't tell whether he was in a specific room; all it could do was compare how far he had gone to where he had gone earlier.

Nuri turned around at the corner, looking back down the street. He'd plant some video bugs to make surveillance easier, then come back in the morning.

But what he really wanted to do was plant one on Tarid.

Maybe he should wait until Tarid fell asleep, Nuri thought, then break into his hotel room.

A car sped down the street, passing so close that the wind nearly knocked him over. A loud, Western-style beat pounded from its speakers, the bass vibrating throughout the narrow street. He watched it for a moment, then crossed over, deciding he would go into the lobby and plant a bug.

Though the lights were on in the lobby, the hotel owner had locked the front door for the night. Nuri banged the door against the dead-bolt lock, not realizing it was closed.

Disappointed, he turned and looked for a spot where he could slip the bug.

He had just set one of the larger bugs beneath the rail when the door opened behind him, catching him by surprise.

"What do you want?" asked the hotel owner. His earlier good humor, when he first welcomed Tarid, had drained away.

"Oh, I—a wrong address," said Nuri.

"You are looking for a room?"

"No, no, it's OK," he said

Nuri's accent made it plain that he was a foreigner. The hotel owner's bad mood—provoked by Tarid's attention toward his daughter—were moderated by the prospect of unexpected business.

"I can find you a very suitable room," he told Nuri. "At a reasonable rate. Come."

Nuri hesitated, then decided he might just as well go inside.

"Where is your bag?" asked the owner.

"I don't have one. The airline—" He shook his head.

"Did you give them this address to deliver it?" the hotelier asked.

"No. I'm supposed to go out and pick it up," said Nuri.

"Probably better for you. Sometimes they get lost on the way." The hotel owner shook his head. "You have had a terrible time. I'm very sorry for you. Perhaps a bath will cheer you up. How did you find us?"

"I was looking for a hotel a friend told me of," said Nuri. "I don't know that it was yours, though. It was in this block—the Blossom?"

"I've never heard of it. Who was your friend?"

"Riccardo Melfi, of Milano," said Nuri, offering the first name that flew into his head. It belonged to a friend of his whom he hadn't seen since grade school.

The hotel owner, naturally, didn't recognize it. But he said that he'd had an Italian recently, just to be polite.

"This may be the place he mentioned, then," said Nuri. "He said it was a very nice place. With a professional staff."

"Of course. And good rates. I do need to see your passport."

"Certainly."

Nuri handed it over to be copied.

"I'll give it back in the morning," said the hotel owner. "Collect it at the desk. Your room—"

"Would it be possible to make the copy this evening?" asked Nuri. "This way I won't forget in the morning. And I can go out early."

"You're going out early?"

"I have business at the oil ministry very early. I was told to meet the minister immediately after morning prayers. If I am late, it is possible that I would not see him. Then I will lose my job."

Ordinarily the owner would have made some excuse about the machine not working and put the guest off, but the casual mention of the minister had impressed him. He took the passport and went into the back room, where his daughter was still cleaning the bowls he had put her to work on hours before. He berated her, telling her it was well past time for her to finish and get to bed—and reminding her that she was not to go near any of the guests.

"Any guest," he repeated.

"Yes, Papa."

Out in the lobby, Nuri slipped a bug under the ledge of the desk, then tried to look at the ledger for the number to Tarid's room. But the owner hadn't bothered to record it.

"Your passport," said the owner, returning. "And here is

the key. There are only four rooms on each hall. Should I show you?"

"I can find it."

Nuri walked to the end of the lobby and started up the stairs.

"The elevator is right there," said the owner.

"Yes, yes, thank you," said Nuri. He stepped over and pressed the button, getting in as soon as the doors were open.

He got off at the fourth floor, guessing that the hotel owner might be watching. His room faced the street. It was small, barely big enough to hold a bed, lamp, and table. A picture of Imam Khomeini looked down on him from above the bed.

Nuri examined the lock on the door. It was a simple latch, easily opened with a plastic card. Instead of a chain, there was a bar about neck high above the doorknob. This could be defeated by holding the door only partly ajar and pushing it in with a pen or something else long and slender. It took a little practice, since the bar had to be pushed just right, but he'd had plenty of practice.

Still worried that the hotel might be owned by the intelligence service, Nuri scanned the room for bugs, then checked for a live circuit at the door, just in case there was a device to indicate whether he was in the room. He found none.

"Locate Tarid," he told the Voice.

"Subject's location is unchanged."

"When was the last time he moved?"

"Fifteen minutes ago."

There were no TVs in the rooms. He had to be in bed, sleeping.

Nuri decided he would break into his room, mark him, and be done with it. If he could, he'd plant a bug on his bag as well. He made sure the vial of marker was ready in his pocket, then slipped out into the hallway.

THE SECOND TIME THE CAR WITH THE LOUD MUSIC PASSED, Flash became apprehensive. He had no weapon and didn't understand any Farsi at all. There were no lights on in the windows on this part of the block. As far as he was concerned, he was an inviting target, obviously a lone foreigner, probably a hick one at that, in a place where he didn't belong. He'd have been worried even if he were back home.

He started walking down the street, hoping he'd come to a place where there were more people.

He could feel the pulse of the bass as the car approached a third time. Flash's muscles tensed.

The car jerked to a stop. Three young men got out, leaving the driver and another in the front. They swaggered over to the side of the street as Flash continued to walk. Despite the general prohibition on alcohol, all three were drunk; the smell of stale scotch wafted toward Flash as he walked.

"Hey, hey, look at this fag," said one of the men. "Carrying two suitcases. He is such a little girl."

"I bet he is a rich one."

"One of the cases has makeup and his veil," said the third.

Flash couldn't understand the words but the gist of what they were about was obvious. He got ready for an attack.

"I think he is a tourist," said one of the men in English. "Are you tourist? *Tour-ist?* Maybe you have euros, yes? Money for us."

I have something for you, thought Flash. But he knew his best course was to be quiet and maybe slip away. That was the irony of being on a covert mission: You had to act like a coward.

He quickened his pace, walking so fast that they had to trot to keep up.

The man who had been speaking ran up behind him, trying to tap him on the shoulder as a tease. Flash saw his shadow growing on the pavement in front of him. Just as he got close, Flash spun and caught his arm, pulling it past him and throwing the man forward. He crashed head first against a car.

"Hey, hey, hey," said a second man. He ran up and took

a swing at Flash. This was easily ducked—and when Flash came up, he threw two rights and a left into the man's mid-section, bowling him over.

The third young man, some years younger than the others at eighteen, began backing away. But it was too late for him—Flash stomped his right leg down, using it as a spring to leap forward. He hit the young man squarely in the chest, throwing him backward to the ground. The kid's head hit the pavement. The rush of pain was so intense he blacked out.

The man he'd thrown against the car rebounded and tried to swing a roundhouse at Flash's side, thinking he could catch him unawares. But Flash knew he was close and partly deflected the blow with his left arm. That left the Iranian open for a counterpunch, which Flash quickly scored to his face. The man staggered upright, shocked at the force of the blow. Foreigners were supposed to be weak; this man hit harder than anyone he'd ever fought.

Two more punches and he fell back, staggered and dizzy. He spun off to the ground and began throwing up the booze he'd drank earlier. Flash put his boot heel in the man's side, knocking him to the ground in a swirl of vomit.

The attacker he'd punched in the stomach got up, took a step toward him, then realized he didn't have a chance. He turned and ran up the block.

Before the fight began, the driver and his front seat passenger had been jeering and egging the younger men on. With their comrades faring poorly, they decided the time had come for them to get in on the action.

The driver pulled the latch on the trunk release, then jumped from the vehicle and ran to the back, grabbing a tire iron and tossing it to the other man. Then he pulled a crowbar out, and together they advanced on Flash.

Flash was deciding which one of the men to hit first, and how, when a gunshot broke the silence. He ducked, but the shot had not been aimed at him—it broke the back window of the car, blasting the glass.

"Get the hell out of here before you are next!" growled a

woman in gutter Farsi. She stood in the middle of the street, the wind whipping at her long skirt. Her face was covered by her scarf. She had a pistol in her hand; a man dressed entirely in black stood behind her with a rifle.

Hera and Danny had arrived.

"Now!" Hera yelled, pointing the gun.

The two men looked at each other, then at her.

"My car," said the driver.

Danny raised the rifle, pointing it at his chest.

"You're next," he said in Farsi, parroting the words the Voice gave him.

The two men ran for the car.

NURI WAS JUST REACHING A THIN PLASTIC CARD INTO THE latch slot of Tarid's door when the gunshot sounded a block behind the hotel. He froze, unsure if the sound was loud enough to wake Tarid.

It was. He heard him stir and backed away from the room quietly.

TARID BOLTED UP IN BED, ROLLING ON THE FLOOR. HIS FIRST thought was that he was back in Sudan and under attack. Then he realized the sound had come from outside.

He ran to the door, pushed the latch closed and made sure the knob was locked.

It wasn't going to hold anyone. He told himself to relax— the shot had been fired outside the hotel, surely not at him.

But if not at him, who could have been targeted? Shootings were very rare in the city, and this hadn't been a celebratory outburst.

He thought of the hotel owner—and his daughter. He started putting on his pants and shoes, to make sure they were all right.

NURI WAITED DOWN THE HALL, HOPING TARID WOULD COME out. Two other guests came out and began asking what was going on.

"A gunshot," said Nuri.

"Where, where?"

The elevator door opened and the hotel owner came out. He looked up and saw Nuri. He was surprised to find him on the third floor.

"There's been a shooting," said Nuri quickly.

"It's under control," said the man, who'd come to get Tarid in hopes that Tarid could help him figure out what was going on. "Go back to bed."

"What's going on?"

"Go, it's under control."

Nuri decided to retreat. By the time Tarid opened the door, he was back upstairs.

"Nuri, what's going on?" Danny asked over the Voice's communications channel.

"I could ask you the same thing."

"Flash almost got mugged. Where the hell are you?"

"In the hotel. Trying to tag Tarid."

"You got him?"

"No, there's too many people. We'll have to try in the morning," said Nuri reluctantly. "I'll meet you at the hotel in an hour."

45

Eastern Sudan

"AT LEAST FORTY MEN THERE, CHIEF." SUGAR HANDED BACK the long distance night vision binoculars. "Two platoons, spread out in the positions. Then whatever they have behind them at the barracks."

Boston refocused the glasses. Not only were there plenty of

soldiers, but the Ethiopian army had brought up two armored cars to cover the road and surrounding area. A troop truck blocked the road near the gate. Nearby, a group of forty or fifty Sudanese were squatting on the ground near the border fence, denied permission to go over the line.

"The border is often closed at night," said Abul. "Maybe in the morning."

"There'll be more troops there in the morning," said Boston, raising the glasses to view the barracks area beyond the checkpoint.

There were two dozen troop trucks parked near the dormitory-style buildings used as quarters for the border guards. The trucks had arrived late that afternoon, sent as soon as word reached army headquarters that there had been a massive raid on rebel units nearby. Such raids always increased the number of refugees trying to cross the border. As it had periodically in the past, the government decided not just to shut the border, but to be serious about it. The soldiers had been authorized to shoot to kill rather than allow the refugees to cross.

Boston wasn't worried about getting shot, but he had yet to hear from Washington about the arrangements for diplomatic passage. He couldn't see anyone near the checkpoint who looked as if they might be from the embassy, sent to help them across. Being interred in an Ethiopian prison camp—or kept among the refugees—was hardly how he wanted to spend the next few days. Or years.

"There is another passage one hundred kilometers south," said Abul. "We can be there shortly after daybreak."

"That one will have troops, too," said Boston.

"Why don't we just go south until we find a spot, and cut through the fence," said Sugar. "Pick a spot, then drive across."

"It's not just the fence," said Boston. "Satellite photo shows the ditch extends the entire way."

The ditch was an antitank obstacle, designed to prevent exactly what Sugar was suggesting. It would probably only slow a determined tank attack an hour or two at most, but the steep sides made it impossible for the bus to scale.

Boston considered splitting up—he could go across with the body of their dead comrade, then wait for the others to pick him up after crossing legitimately. But that would be inviting even more complications, completely unnecessary if Washington could just make the arrangements.

"Let me talk to Mrs. Stockard," he said, handing the glasses back to Sugar. "Maybe they've made the arrangements. Otherwise our best bet right now is just to sit and wait."

"You hear that?" asked Sugar, turning quickly.

"What?"

"I'm hearing a motorcycle over the hill."

She'd heard it several times earlier as well. They'd checked once, Boston dropping off as the bus went ahead, but hadn't seen anything.

He didn't hear anything now. He shook his head.

"Maybe I'm just being paranoid," she said.

"Hopefully," said Boston.

46

Room 4
CIA Campus

HALFWAY ACROSS THE WORLD IN ROOM 4 ON THE CIA's Langley campus, Breanna Stockard was sitting at her desk, keeping tabs on Danny and the others in Iran. She'd left a message for Ms. Bennett, telling her how to reach her, then brought her work here.

Being tied into the MY-PID system made her feel a little better. But not much.

As originally conceived, MY-PID took over many of the support functions spies and special operations units needed, and in theory there was no need for her to watch them from afar. But theory and reality were still struggling to fit together.

Breanna found it almost impossible not to check on their progress every so often, monitoring their communications and watching their locations. She hadn't done this when Nuri started out the Jasmine mission alone, but now the stakes were considerably higher. And she knew more of the people involved.

Maybe the missions should always be directly monitored by someone, she thought, even if that was a deviation from the original plan and philosophy. She'd have to discuss it with Reid.

But if they were, she wouldn't be the one doing it. And then she'd feel left out.

The communications system buzzed with an incoming call from Boston. The wall screen opened a window at the lower right-hand corner, mapping where the call was coming from. Had the area been under real-time visual surveillance, an image would have been supplied.

"Go ahead," she said, allowing the transmission to connect. Technical data on the encryption method and communication rates were added to the screen.

"Mrs. Stockard?"

"Hello, Boston. I see you're at the border. I'm still waiting for the embassy. They need to get permission from the Ethiopian government. They don't think there'll be a problem, but they have to make contact with the right officials. The situation remains the same—they've closed all the crossings."

"Do you have an ETA on that permission, ma'am?"

"I wouldn't expect it before morning. It may not come until the afternoon. They are working on it."

"Yeah . . ." Boston's voice trailed off.

"Is there a problem, Chief?"

"As I told you before, we left the base camp in kind of a

hurry. I'm not sure that the people we left behind are, uh—
well, they may be a little pissed at us, if you know what I
mean."

"You can present yourselves at the border and go into Ethiopian custody if things get crazy," said Breanna.

"That's not my first preference."

"It's not mine, either. We should have an answer in the
morning," she told him. "I don't think there's going to be any
problem in the end. It's just the paperwork on their side. And
getting to the right person."

"All right," said Boston.

The resignation in his voice was so obvious that Breanna
told him not to worry again; she'd get him out under any cir-
cumstance.

"I'm not worried. I know you will," said Boston.

"I'll talk to you at nine A.M. your time," Breanna told him.
"Can you hold out until then?"

"That won't be a problem," he said.

As soon as Boston hung up, Breanna called back over to
State to check on the request. But instead of the undersec-
retary who had been acting as a liaison, she got a bubbly
assistant—the first bad sign.

The second bad sign came a moment later, when the assistant told her that all border crossing into Ethiopia had been
closed "for the near future."

Her voice made it sound like she had just scored tickets for
the Super Bowl.

"I know that already," said Breanna. "The ambassador is
supposed to be explaining that we have a special situation."

"Oh. Please hold."

Breanna tried not to explode. The assistant was part of the
night staff, and clearly not the best informed.

"We're still working on it," said the assistant, coming back
on the line.

"And how long is that going to take?"

"Well, it's nighttime over there now. Very late. You realize
they're several hours ahead of us. Six, actually."

"Thank you," said Breanna, confident the sarcasm in her voice would go right over the woman's head.

It did.

"I think we have to make other arrangements," she told Reid a short time later. "If we can't count on help from the Ethiopian government."

"They'll help us, I'm sure."

"But in how long? Two weeks? I don't want to leave my people in an Ethiopian jail for two weeks. They'll put them in a detention center until this gets straightened. And God knows what will happen there."

"If we have the ambassador send someone to the border with passports," said Reid, "we can get them over on diplomatic cover."

"I already suggested that. They claimed the border shutdown applies to everyone, even diplomats."

"That's nonsense."

"I've been pointing that out for hours now, Jonathon. Why don't you give it a try?"

"I will," said Reid. "But maybe the easiest thing would be to have them sneak across the border."

"And leave McGowan's body behind?"

"If they must."

Breanna wasn't willing to do that. "I'll work something out," she told him. "Even if I have to get them myself."

"Now listen—"

The screen flashed, indicating she had another call, this one from the Air Force Airlift Command.

"Let me call you back," she told Reid. "I'm getting a call from the people who are supposed to meet them in Ethiopia. I'm guessing there's a problem there, too."

Her intuition was correct. The major on the line was calling to tell her that the plane originally scheduled to fly to Ethiopia had suffered a mechanical breakdown in Germany. The next flight from Europe wouldn't be available until the following afternoon.

"We do have a possible solution," added the major, "but it would take some string pulling."

"No one likes pulling strings more than I do," lied Breanna.

"There's an MC-17 Stretch due in at Andrews Air Force Base in about two hours. It's en route to Turkey, but could be diverted if the right person were to make the request, if you catch my drift."

"Your drift is just perfect," said Breanna. "Who would the right person make the request to?"

The aircraft happened to be en route from, of all places, Dreamland, where it had picked up a pair of MV-22-G Osprey gunships. The Ospreys were to be delivered to a Ranger unit temporarily based at Incirlik. A detour to Ethiopia would put the delivery off schedule by about half a day; the Whiplash people could catch another flight home from there.

The general who was expecting the Ospreys took Breanna's call. He'd served with her father, and it took only a few seconds of explanation before he agreed that the Ospreys could arrive a day late. But Breanna met a more serious roadblock when she called the wing commander responsible for the aircraft. The pilot had gotten sick on the flight east and was due to be relieved as soon as he landed.

"It's not a big deal, really, but I can't get a full crew until tomorrow," said the colonel.

"You don't have anyone tonight?"

"You know how tight these staffing cuts have us. We're low priority on head count. This is a reserve unit and—"

"I know where you can find a pilot," she interrupted. "And she works cheap, too."

47

Tehran

AS SOON AS THEY HEARD THE SIREN, THE MEN WHO HAD attacked Flash rallied from their injuries. Despite six broken bones between them, they managed to get into their vehicle and flee before the first police car arrived.

Two people had seen the youths and offered a good description of the vehicle. One of the policemen dutifully wrote down the details, though he knew nothing would come of it. The car described was well-known to him and the other officers who had responded; it belonged to a member of the Iranian parliament, though it was customarily driven by his youngest son. The son and his companions were the subject of several reports, mostly from tourists, who reported being beaten and robbed during late night strolls under circumstances remarkably similar to those Flash had found himself in. The only difference in this case was the outcome. The witnesses' descriptions made it clear that the attackers had gotten the worse end of the deal, something that cheered the policeman, though of course he didn't let on.

Tarid and the hotel owner stayed back with the rest of the crowd, watching more out of curiosity than purpose. The city had its share of thugs operating under the guise of religious police; a number were known to assault people for offenses, real and imagined, for a price. To Tarid, this looked like just such a case.

"I think I'll go back to the hotel," he said when it became obvious there would be no resolution that night.

"Yes," said his host.

Together they walked back around the corner. Tarid could not stop himself from thinking about the man's daughter. He considered asking if she had many suitors, or if a marriage was being arranged. But he didn't want to make his lust too obvious.

She was the sort of beauty that would make even a man like him change his thinking about the entanglements of a family. Logically, he remained steadfast; he had no desire to give up the freedom and luxuries he currently enjoyed, which would be greatly diminished if he were to marry. And he knew his own temperament would stifle any sort of commitment or relationship. He could not be happy staying in one place, yet he could not imagine there was a woman on earth who would be glad to move around as he did. Women were creatures of the hearth, he believed, destined to tend to domestic needs. If he were to wed the hotel owner's daughter, he would see her only two or three times a year, and even then inevitably grow bored.

Not that his desire implied marriage. But it couldn't be talked about with the girl's father, even obliquely, without implying that it did.

"A cup of tea?" asked the hotel owner as they reached the building's threshold.

"No thank you," said Tarid, calculating that it was unlikely the girl would be woken to prepare it. "I will see you in the morning."

"Good night, then."

Tarid's satellite phone rang as he walked to the elevator. Taking it from his pocket, he saw that it was Bani Aberhadji, his boss and patron. With no one nearby, he clicked the button to let the call through.

"This is Tarid."

"Why have you not checked in? You arrived in Tehran several hours ago," said Aberhadji.

"I did not believe I was to call until I was ready for the meeting," he said. "And, given the hour of my arrival—"

"I will meet you at one P.M. tomorrow, at the building in Karaj," said Aberhadji.

"Yes, sir."

The line went dead.

While the curtness was characteristic, Bani Aberhadji was normally a very even-tempered man, not one to casually display annoyance. The emotion in his voice filled Tarid not just with apprehension but dread, as if he had done something wrong and was about to be brought to justice for it.

He had, as a matter of fact, occasionally skimmed a few million rials off the payments forwarded to the groups he watched over in Africa. There were also some inflated fees for weapons, along with an occasional unreported kickback. Bani Aberhadji would not have approved, but compared to the men he usually dealt with, Tarid knew he was hardly avaricious. And, he thought, it would certainly be difficult for Aberhadji to prove that this had taken place without some direct complaint against him.

Most likely, he thought, Aberhadji's displeasure had nothing to do with him. But it made him nervous anyway, and he knew, even as he stepped into the elevator, that he would get little sleep the rest of the night.

IN A WESTERN HOTEL NEARLY A MILE AWAY, NURI TOLD THE Voice to replay a snippet of video and audio he and the Whiplash team had just seen. It showed Tarid looking longingly at the room where the hotel owner had just disappeared, then walking slowly toward the elevator. Three steps from it his satellite phone rang. He took it out, looked at the caller ID, then turned around and made sure no one was nearby before answering.

The conversation was extremely brief. All they had was Tarid's side, but his responses were so close together that Nuri knew whoever he was speaking with couldn't have said more than a sentence or two himself.

"This is Tarid . . . I—I did not believe I was to call until I was ready for the meeting. And, given the hour of my arrival . . . Yes, sir."

"So he has a meeting," said Hera, watching the video. "That was already obvious."

"He's scared of whoever he's talking to," said Flash. "Look at his face. He's worried he's going to be shot or something."

Danny Freah dropped down to one knee, studying the image.

"Flash is right. Remember how defiant he looked when we rescued him? Whoever he's meeting is a hell of a lot scarier than bullets."

"So how does it help us?" said Hera.

"Man, you are Ms. Contrary tonight," said Flash. He laughed.

Hera reddened, and swore to herself that she wouldn't say anything else.

Nuri replayed the conversation again. Aside from the fact that the meeting must be imminent, there was no other useful information in the words. Meanwhile, the signal from the biomarker was deteriorating rapidly. They had to get him first thing in the morning.

"We're going to have to line up some vehicles," he told Danny. "Two at least."

"You think we're going to be able to follow him in cars?"

"If he's in a vehicle, we need to be in a vehicle. We need to rent them."

The problem with renting a car was timing; the agencies wouldn't open until nine-thirty, which in practice would mean close to ten. By then Tarid could be well on his way to the meeting, or perhaps even done with it.

"We won't need to be that close as long as we tag him in the morning," said Danny. "Let's concentrate on doing that well so we don't have to worry."

"Yeah, but if we're close, we may be able to bug the meeting place," said Nuri. "We really want to be inside there. Look at how valuable this was, and it's only a little snippet from the distance."

Hera didn't think it was all that valuable. But she remembered her resolve and said nothing.

"We may not be able to get that close," said Danny "I'd suspect we won't."

"Why don't we just bug him?" asked Flash.

"How?" asked Danny.

"Paste something onto his shoe?"

The others laughed, but the suggestion gave Nuri an idea. He went over to the closet where he'd put his jacket. He took it out, then unscrewed the top button, revealing the bug hidden there.

"This would work," he said.

"You going to make him wear your coat?" said Danny.

Nuri went back to the laptop they were using as a video screen and called up an image showing Tarid's clothes. He wore a jacket that featured large buttons. Nuri zeroed in on one and magnified it.

"You see anything unusual about these buttons?" he asked Hera.

"No. They're black. They have four holes."

"Right. Do we have anything like them?"

Though the button was a simple, basic design, it didn't match anything anyone was wearing.

Hera waited until no one else said anything.

"We can get one from the bazaar in the morning," she suggested. "The stalls for women, the practical ones, will be open very early, right after morning prayers."

"How do you get the bug into the button?" asked Danny.

"Look how thin this is," said Nuri, showing it to him. "It sits on the other side, like a holder—you see? The computer figures out how to focus through the holes in the material and the plastic."

"I think it could work," said Hera. "But how do we get his jacket?"

"That's easy," said Nuri. "The problem is getting the button on real fast. How well do you sew?"

"Terribly."

"I can sew," said Danny. "What did you have in mind?"

48

Washington suburbs

GREASY HANDS PARSONS WAS ABOUT TO GRAB HIMSELF A beer when the phone rang. He debated whether to answer it. Generally, the only people who called at this hour were trying to sell something he didn't want. But he was one of those people who could never stand to let a phone go unanswered, and so he detoured from the refrigerator to the phone.

"Parsons," he said, his answer conditioned by years in the military.

"Greasy Hands—I wonder if you'd like to start work a few days early," said Breanna Stockard.

"Hey, boss. Sure. When?"

"Tonight. We have a C-17 coming into Andrews that has to go right out. I was wondering if you could take a look at it."

"I'm sure those boys will do a fine job for you, Bree." The Air Force base's many assignments including caring for Air Force One, and the crews there were second to none, including Dreamland. "But I'd be happy to shoot over for you—"

"Good," said Breanna. "And just out of curiosity . . . what are you doing for the next few days? Anything pressing?"

"Pressing?"

"Could you take a trip?"

Greasy Hands mentally reviewed his commitments over the next few days: He had to do laundry, he ought to overhaul the lawn mower, and sooner or later he was going to have to get his car inspected.

And then there was the dentist and the dreaded biannual teeth cleaning.

"Slate is totally free," he said. "Where are we going?"

"Let's just say you won't need your thermal underwear."

"I'll be there inside an hour."

*   *   *

Breanna was confused when she pulled into the driveway and saw that none of the lights were on inside her house. Then she remembered Teri's recital.

She buried her face in her hands.

"Oh God," she said, slamming the wheel. Her hand hit the horn by mistake. The sharp blast echoed around the quiet suburban street, jolting a pair of robins that were nesting in the tree in the front yard, as well as the neighbor's cat.

She leapt out of the car, jogging inside to get her things. Maybe, she thought, there would be time to stop by the school and hear her daughter play for a few minutes. But a glance at the clock in the kitchen told her that was a pipe dream; she was already running late.

There was a note for her on the kitchen table. *Hey?* was all it said.

"I know, I know," she muttered, running to the bedroom. She grabbed her overnight bag from the closet, threw a change of clothes inside, then stepped into the bathroom for her toothbrush. She caught a glimpse of her face in the mirror—it was the face of a woman she only vaguely recognized: a harried, overtired soccer mom.

Not a combat pilot.

Breanna slid some toothpaste, an extra bar of soap, and some toilet paper—you could never be too sure—into her bag. Then she went down the hall to Zen's office, grabbed a pad from his desk, and went into Teri's room to write her daughter a note.

"'Honey,'" she started, speaking aloud as she wrote, "'something came up—'"

Oh crap, that sounds terrible, Breanna thought, wadding the paper up.

Ter—I'm sorry I couldn't make it tonight. I'm flying to Africa. Someone died and I'm responsible—

Garbage. And she shouldn't write *Africa*. It would sound too dangerous.

She ripped that note up, too.

Honey, I love you, and I'm sorry I couldn't be there tonight. I'll explain when I get home in a few days.

That wasn't much better than the others, but she decided it would have to do. She left it on Teri's bed and ran back outside, nearly forgetting her keys in the house.

She was about ten minutes from the airport when Zen called her on the cell phone.

"Hey, there, Mrs. Stockard, should we save this front row seat for you or what?"

"Zen—God. I can't—I'm flying to Ethiopia."

"What?"

"It's a long story. I can't explain right now—it's classified."

"Bree, you better explain a little."

"We have a problem in Sudan. It's under control, but one of our people died. I have to make sure his body gets back. And I have to get the people he was with out."

"But why are *you* going?"

"Because if I don't, they won't be picked up for another day. And they have to get out now."

Zen said nothing for a moment.

Breanna knew she hadn't really answered the question: Why was *she* going?

For a moment she felt foolish, realizing she had acted impulsively. Her job wasn't to fly airplanes, and she wasn't the twenty-something woman with something to prove.

But she *had* to go.

"You still there?" asked Zen.

"Yes, Senator."

"Hey, listen, we'll cope. I know you gotta do what you gotta do," he added. "I just want to be able to tell Teri something."

There was a sound in the background: muffled music.

"They're starting up inside. I oughta get going," Zen said.

"Bring me in with you," said Breanna.

"Huh?"

"Bring the cell phone in and let me listen."

"Good idea."

By any objective standard, the music was absolutely . . . trying.

Naturally, the parents who filled the auditorium thought it was incredibly wonderful. So did Breanna, who took her hands off the wheel and applauded when it was done.

"Thank you," she told Zen. "Tell her I thought she did great, and I'll call as soon as I can."

"All right, Bree. Listen, babe—you take damn good care of yourself, all right? I don't want to be chairing a Senate inquiry over this."

"Don't worry, Senator. I intend to."

BREANNA WANTED GREASY HANDS ALONG ON THE FLIGHT because there would be no air force crew in Ethiopia; in case something went wrong, she needed someone who could get the plane back together in one piece.

"You have an awful lot of faith in me," said Greasy Hands, looking over the MC-17. As he had suspected, the maintainers at Andrews needed absolutely no encouragement from him, let alone help. But then again, the chief master sergeant they reported to had trained under him a few years back. "I haven't worked on an MC-17 since Dreamland."

"Have they changed since then?"

Greasy Hands laughed. "Not all that much."

"Can you do it?"

"With my eyes closed," said Greasy Hands.

After walking around the aircraft with Breanna and the pilot, Greasy Hands went inside and looked over the Ospreys. Ostensibly, he was making sure they were secured properly. In reality, he was indulging himself in a little bit of Dreamland nostalgia.

The MV-22/G Ospreys were upgraded versions of the tilt-rotor aircraft used for heavy transport by the Marines and some Air Force units. The M designation alluded to the fact that these Ospreys were designed for special operations and, among other things, included gear for night missions, extra fuel tanks, and armor plating. The aircraft were also outfitted with cannon; missiles and a chain gun could also be mounted on the undercarriage or the forward winglets, which were specific to the G version. Besides these goodies, the G Block models included uprated engines and provisions for autonomous piloting, another Dreamland innovation that allowed them to be flown by only one pilot or, if the situation warranted, completely by remote control. Finally, they were designed specifically for easy transport in the MC-17/DS "Stretch."

The transport's nickname alluded to the most obvious of its improvements over the standard airframe—namely, its fuselage had been lengthened to nearly double the cargo bay, bringing it to 140 feet. Its portly belly was also another two feet wider. The changes had been designed specifically to allow the transport to carry two Ospreys or an Osprey and two Werewolf II UAV gunships, along with crew and a combat team. With everyone aboard, the fit could be a bit cozy, but the configuration allowed the U.S. to project considerable power into hot spots with very little notice.

Greasy Hands had worked on the Osprey project for several years, before the arrival of Colonel Bastian and Dreamland's renaissance. The aircraft and its tilt wings were the bastard children at the facility then, a project no one wanted. Everyone agreed the Osprey had incredible potential; they could land where standard helicopters could, but fly twice as fast and several times as far. Reaching that potential, though, seemed impossible. The planes were expensive, difficult to fly, and an adventure to maintain.

When several were detailed to Dreamland as part of a Defense Department program to help the Osprey "reach its full potential," Greasy Hands was assigned to the team. He'd tried to duck it at first but within a few weeks was the aircraft's biggest fanboy. He was responsible for suggesting that weapons be added, and even worked with the engineers on some of the mechanical systems. Then he'd helped Jennifer

Gleason refine the computer routines that allowed the complicated aircraft to fly itself, an accomplishment that cinched his promotion to chief.

He thought about Jennifer as he looked at the aircraft. He hadn't been as close to her as some of the people at Dreamland, but the memory of her still choked him up. He finished looking at the Ospreys, then went back upstairs to the flight deck.

Breanna and the pilot, Captain Luther Underhill, had just finished the preflight checklist.

"Have a seat, Chief," said Breanna. "We're about to take off."

As he walked toward the seat behind the pilot, Greasy Hands's attention was caught by the zero-gravity coffeemaker in the small galley. It looked suspiciously like the design they had pioneered at Dreamland some twenty years before.

"Mind if I grab a cup of joe?" he asked the crew chief, Gordon Heinz.

"It's there for the taking."

Greasy Hands found a cup in the cabinet next to the machine and poured himself a dose.

"Just like old times again, huh, Bree?" he said as he slid into the seat. "Even the coffee's the same."

49

Tehran

AS TARID HAD FEARED, HE DID NOT SLEEP AT ALL AFTER THE call from Aberhadji. He tossed and turned, then finally gave up all pretense of resting several hours before morning prayer.

With the meeting set for 1:00 P.M., he knew he had a long,

torturous wait. Karaj was located a little over a half hour outside of Tehran, and it would be senseless to get there too early. He needed something to do.

Had it not been for Aberhadji's tone, he might have spent the time in the lobby, where the wait would have been quite enjoyable. Simin was working in the office, but her father, not used to the late night, had slept in. Aberhadji's stern voice lingered in his ears. Clearly, his boss had spies in the capital. Perhaps the hotel owner was one of them—it would not have surprised Tarid at this point—and so he had to be on his best behavior.

"I am going across for some breakfast," he told the girl. "If anyone is looking for me."

"Are you expecting someone?"

"No one in particular."

DANNY LINGERED IN THE AISLE OF THE BAZAAR, WATCHING as Hera looked through the basket of buttons in the nearby stall. The bazaar was the Middle Eastern equivalent of an American shopping mall, covered and divided into dozens of alleys, each lined with shops. Most weren't open yet, but as Hera had predicted, a good number that catered to household necessities were.

She looked at the black buttons, turning each over before tossing it back into the basket. *Just pick one*, he wanted to shout, *we're running out of time*. But Hera kept looking, trying for a perfect match to Tarid's jacket.

She selected a half dozen, all very similar, all subtly different. She turned and looked at the material, ignoring Danny's exasperated glances, before showing the buttons to the woman who ran the stall.

"Is that your husband?" asked the woman.

"No," said Hera. "Just a friend."

"Hmmmph," said the woman.

Hera wasn't sure whether she disapproved because they weren't married or whether the fact that he was black bothered her. There weren't many black faces in Tehran.

The woman told her the price. Hera opened her mouth to object—generally, it would be considered odd for a native not to at least attempt to haggle—but the woman told her there would be no negotiating. She frowned, then took out a note large enough to pay for half the entire basket.

The vendor rolled her eyes.

"I can't change this," she said. "Something smaller."

Hera turned to Danny and told him, in Farsi, that she needed change.

The Voice translated. Danny dug into his pocket and handed over a few coins. The woman who owned the booth gave him a smirk. Hera counted out the money, then waited while the woman found a small paper bag for the buttons.

"Come on, come on," hissed Danny under his breath. He started walking for the exit.

"We're supposed to be shopping," said Hera, catching up. "Relax."

"The hell with that. Tarid just went to breakfast."

"Why didn't you tell me?"

"What was I supposed to do, use ESP?"

"Everyone on the team should be hooked into the Voice," said Hera. "It would make things much more coordinated."

"They don't have enough units."

Hera thought that was bull—in her opinion, Reid and Stockard simply didn't trust everyone—but kept her mouth shut.

As they neared the exit, Danny spotted a stall selling tools. Among the items on display was an engraving tool. He veered toward it, looked at the box, then discovered a small Roto-Zip knockoff nearby that came with some grinding tips. He took it and a clamp he could use as a small vise, gave them to the merchant, then reached for his wallet and the two million rial the tags indicated.

"Hold on," said Hera in Farsi just as the shop owner was about to grab for the money. "How much are you paying?"

"Uh—"

"A hundred thousand rial," Hera told the owner.

It was a ridiculously low price, and the man made a face.

He looked at Danny, wondering who wore the pants in the family. Then he started to put the items back where Danny had gotten them.

Danny gestured at Hera.

"Two hundred thousand," she said.

The man ignored her.

"Two fifty," she said.

Again the shopkeeper ignored her, contenting himself with straightening the display. She could have offered a billion rial and he would not have accepted the deal.

Danny didn't want to arouse any more suspicions by speaking English. Angry at Hera, he turned and started away.

"A million and a half rial. It is a very fair price," said the shop owner behind him.

Danny turned around and took out his wallet, glaring at Hera to keep her quiet. As far as the shop owner was concerned, the price was more than fair, given the merchandise. He felt the discount was well worth it to teach the overbearing wife a lesson. It was no surprise that she was wearing a colorful scarf, and a shirt that seemed far too modern.

"Let that be a lesson," the man told Danny. "You don't need a shrew to run your life."

"Thank you," managed Danny.

"Screw him," said Hera as they walked outside.

"Why did you do that?" he said, "We have a time limit here."

"I had to stay in cover."

"Get some common sense, damn it. We're running late."

"What if someone gets suspicious and follows us?"

"Just use common sense."

Danny pushed one of the earphones into his ear and heard Nuri say that Tarid was now taking a table.

"We're on our way," Danny told him, starting to run.

NURI ORIGINALLY WANTED TO STEAL A WAITER'S UNIFORM for Flash, but the waiters at the small restaurants worked in regular street clothes. And then Tarid made the job even harder by wearing his jacket to the table rather than hanging it up near the door.

"Wait outside," Nuri told Flash. "When Danny comes, go and rent the car."

"And back you up if something goes wrong, right?"

"Nothing's going to go wrong."

Flash shrugged. In his experience, Murphy's Law accompanied every operation. He walked down to the end of the block, looking for Danny and Hera.

Nuri, meanwhile, went inside, hoping for a table next to Tarid—right behind him would be perfect—but they were all taken. He allowed himself to be steered to a place near the window, biding his time until Danny and Hera were ready.

"We're in the alley," said Danny breathlessly a minute later.

Nuri asked for some eggs and tea. The waiter disappeared into the back.

The waiter working the other side of the room approached Tarid's table with a platter of food. Nuri rose quickly and went over, intending to knock something onto the coat. But Tarid chose that moment to get up, and before Nuri could provoke a spill, Tarid headed for the restroom.

Frustrated, Nuri followed. A dozen possibilities occurred to him, but the presence of an attendant in the restroom ruled all of them out. Nuri smiled at the man, then went to the far stall, hoping some opportunity would present itself.

It didn't.

Tarid hated public restrooms. He held on tight to his jacket, finished quickly and left, not even bothering to tip the attendant.

"This isn't going to be easy," Nuri told Danny over the Voice communications channel.

"We have all day," said Danny.

"What are you drilling?"

"I'm fixing the buttons. Relax."

"Buttons? More than one?"

"We have a couple just in case. We'll match it exactly. If you can get us more time, we'll use the original."

Nuri looked up and saw Tarid leaving.

"Tarid's coming out," he told Danny.

"What?"

"Yeah."

Unsure whether he had been spotted or if someone was working with Tarid to check for a trail, Nuri went back to his table. His tea and eggs had just arrived.

The Voice gave him a running commentary on what Tarid was doing.

Not much: He simply walked back across the street to the hotel.

"Meet me around front in five minutes," he told Danny. "I have another idea."

TARID HAD DECIDED THAT HE WOULD COLLECT HIS THINGS, take a drive and look up an old friend before meeting with Aberhadji. It was something to do; he hoped the trip would divert his mind from the horrors it kept suggesting Aberhadji would inflict on him for skimming money from the Guard. He thought of calling his friend, but decided not to bother. The diversion was what was important.

"I'm going out for a while," he said loudly. "Do you want the key?"

His heart fluttered when she came out. Her eyes met his for a brief moment. His resolution began to melt; the temptation to linger was too great.

"Will you be gone long?" asked Simin.

"I'm not sure."

Their fingers grazed as he handed over the key. Simin flushed. She took the key, slid it into the box behind the desk, then rushed back into the office.

"Simin, wait—" Tarid took a step to follow her.

She slammed the door. For a moment he hung suspended between his desire and his fear of being punished. Aberhadji would be even more angry if he found out that he had seduced the girl.

On the other hand, Aberhadji might be planning to kill him anyway, Tarid reasoned. And in that case. . .

Tarid started around the desk. But as he turned the corner, he walked into another woman, a little older, and if not quite as pretty, certainly beautiful in her own way:

Hera.

Who slipped a small razor blade out from between her fingers and snapped it through the middle button on his jacket as she fell backward against a plant next to the wall, then stumbled to the ground.

"Where did you come from?" said Tarid, momentarily confused.

"I'm looking for a friend," she said.

"I meant, how did you get in my way?" said Tarid.

"Oh, your button." Hera picked it off the floor. "I'm sorry," she said, holding it up.

Puzzled, Tarid looked down for the spot where it had been.

"I'll fix it for you," Hera said, getting up. "Give me your coat."

"I'm fine," said Tarid, on his guard.

"No, no, I insist."

Hera held out her left hand, keeping her right, which still had the razor, behind her back.

"Who are you?"

"Maral Milian."

She bowed her head slightly, as if too timid to look him in the eye, but then reached up and put her fingers on the inside collar of his coat, gently starting to tug it off.

Tarid resisted for only a moment more; the desire that Simin had provoked saw a potential outlet.

"Maybe we can go up to my room," he told her, forgetting he had dropped off the key.

"I can fix it here." Hera folded the jacket over her arm. "I'll just get a needle and thread."

"No, no," he said. "Just give me my coat back. Never mind."

"I insist," she said. "Let me fix it for you."

"I have an appointment."

OUTSIDE, DANNY FREAH AND NURI WERE LOOKING AT EACH other, realizing that they were going to lose another chance, probably the last, to bug Tarid. Hera had marked him when he bumped into her, so there was no question that they could continue to follow him. But having gotten this close to him, it seemed a shame to give up the opportunity.

"I'm going in," said Danny.

"He'll recognize you."

"I'm counting on it."

Danny rounded the corner quickly, practically leaping up the block to the steps and the entrance to the small hotel. He bounded up to the door, then forced himself to take a breath as he opened it.

He came in just as Tarid was taking the coat from Hera's hand. The Iranian stopped, stunned, staring at Danny as if he were looking at a ghost.

"Well, isn't this a surprise," said Danny in English. "What are *you* doing in Tehran?"

"You?"

"Yeah, it's me," said Danny. "You didn't think I was dead, I hope."

"Why are you here?" said Tarid in Arabic.

Danny glanced at Hera.

"Use English," he said. "We don't need women with big mouths listening to what we say."

Tarid wasn't sure what to make of this at all. He was worried about Kirk's English and loud voice. If the hotel keeper was informing on him, this would be something more to add, another nail in the coffin.

"I can fix your coat," said Hera, her hand touching his.

"What's wrong with the coat?" asked Danny.

Tarid frowned. "Nothing," he said, in English.

"Have her fix it while you and I talk. Let's have some coffee. There are restaurants across the street."

"Fix the coat right away," said Tarid, handing it to Hera as if she were his employee. "I'll be across the street."

50

North central Iran

BANI ABERHADJI HAD SCHEDULED HIS MEETING WITH TARID for the afternoon because he had more important things to do in the morning, the primary one being to arrange for the assassination of the country's president.

He had pondered General Taher Banhnnjunni's reaction for many hours, praying until he reached what should have been an obvious conclusion: Banhnnjunni was as guilty as the president. The fact that his fellow council member did not return his call in the morning made the conclusion even more obvious. Aberhadji decided, therefore, to act without him—and then move against the general to oust him from the council.

The task itself was simple. The president was flying to America in three days. A small bomb, located strategically in the aircraft, would accomplish the task very easily. Aberhadji would have no difficulty getting the bomb made or placed. Two members of the Khatam-ol-Anbia, the engineering division of the Guard, who worked with him on the nuclear project, had already volunteered to fashion it in secret. The men, brothers, were highly competent weapons engineers; they had helped fashion much of the warhead's metal structure, working under the direction of the Koreans. They were also old friends, having served with him on the battlefield.

Security at the airport was shared by a Republican Guard unit, and the Guard staffed most of the departments there, including the maintenance facilities. There were at least two men Aberhadji believed had access to the plane and would gladly plant the weapon.

More difficult was what to do about General Banhnnjunni. While the general did not control the council, he certainly controlled enough Guard units to make things difficult after the president was assassinated. He could even conceivably take over. Aberhadji did not want that. So he decided to enlist another old friend and general, Muhammad Jaliff, who commanded the Guard units based in Tehran. His support would neutralize Banhnnjunni. In fact, Jaliff would make an excellent president after the revolt.

The men had known each other since boyhood. While their duties now meant that they had little contact with each other socially, they still spoke at least once or twice a month. They were committed Islamists, fervent both in faith and in their support of the Revolution. Aberhadji considered Jaliff among his closest friends.

Which made Jaliff's reaction to his plan all the more shocking.

"It is an imbecilic idea," said his friend, rising from his office couch. "It is treason. I should have you arrested right now."

Aberhadji stared at his friend in disbelief. Jaliff walked to the door. For a moment it looked as if he was going to carry out his threat—Aberhadji imagined him opening it and calling in the two guards from the hall. But he was merely making sure it was locked. He checked it, then went back to his desk.

"You don't understand the world, brother," said Jaliff. "You believe you are above the rest of us because you are pure."

"I don't," said Aberhadji.

"We've known each other a long time." Jaliff shook his head. "You don't have to lie to me."

"I'm not."

Slightly exasperated, Jaliff leaned back in his seat. A reaction like this was to be expected from Aberhadji, he realized, even though he was the most rational of men.

"It was good that you came to me first," he said. "Very good. This is a thing you must not act on. You must not do anything."

"I don't understand how you can sit and watch the greatest enemy of our country, of our religion, win this victory."

"It is not a victory for the Americans," said Jaliff. "In the long run, it will be a victory for us. And for now, it is necessary."

"How?"

Jaliff slammed his hand on the desk. "Look around you, Bani. Don't you see the poverty? The country is in shambles. People aren't eating. They're not eating."

"There's rice."

"Rice!"

"It's because of the American boycott."

Jaliff rose. In his mind, the greater culprit was a corrupt system that for years had rewarded connections, not competence. While he did not like the new president for many reasons, he was at least taking the necessary steps—even when it came to dealing with the Satan Incarnate. In time he would be left by the wayside, as all Iranian presidents were. But first Iran's economy would be restored.

Aberhadji's nuclear program—which Jaliff had only superficial knowledge of—would be of critical importance in a year or two. That, as much as their friendship, persuaded Jaliff to rein in his anger. He had to persuade his friend to be reasonable.

"Do you really think the president would have proceeded without assurances that he was on the right track?" asked Jaliff. "Do you think none of the religious leaders have pondered the question of how one speaks with his enemy? Who should do it?"

Aberhadji felt as if the ground beneath his feet had started to tilt. He wasn't sure how to answer the question, though his old friend waited for an answer.

"It has been discussed," said Jaliff finally. "I have discussed it. Why do you think you are proceeding with your program? Do you think it's an accident? Do you know its great cost?"

"I know its cost." Aberhadji's gaze fell to his shoes. But then he raised his eyes and looked in Jaliff's.

He should not be ashamed. He was not the one making the deal with the devil.

"Promise me that this is the end of this idea," said Jaliff. "Promise me, Bani, that you will have nothing more to do with it."

Aberhadji drew a slow breath, letting the air fill his lungs.

"Have faith in the Revolution, and in the Prophet's words, blessed be his name."

"It is not my role to kill the president," said Aberhadji finally. "I am a faithful son of the Revolution."

"And you will remain faithful," said Jaliff.

"I will remain faithful."

Jaliff had trusted his life to Aberhadji on the battlefield several times. He remembered one of them now, when his weapon had jammed and only Aberhadji's steadfast shooting had prevented the Iraqis from picking him off as they retreated from a hilltop.

"I'm glad, old friend," Jaliff said kindly. "Let us get something to eat."

51

Tehran

DANNY'S INTERVENTION AS KIRK MEANT HE WASN'T AVAILable to fix the jacket.

"You have to figure it out," Nuri told Hera when they met around the corner from the hotel. "I'm not mechanical."

"What does that have to do with anything?" asked Hera. But she took the sewing kit from him.

The first task was to match the button. Even with a dozen choices, there was no perfect match; the closest in size was a little off in color, and vice versa.

"Take the right size. He'll feel it as he closes his jacket," said Nuri. "But he won't look at it."

"So you want me to do it but you're the expert?"

"It's just how I button my buttons." He demonstrated, miming the action on his sweater.

Danny had hollowed out the back of all the buttons while they were waiting, and lining up the bug was not difficult at all. Pushing the thread through wasn't easy at first—she didn't have a thimble. Nor was she sure exactly how she was going to tie it off at the end. She guessed that she was supposed to use a special knot, but looking at the other buttons gave no clue as to how it might be tied.

"You better hurry," said Nuri. "I don't think we should leave Danny in there with Tarid too long."

"He can take care of himself," said Hera. "I'm going as fast as I can."

"How did you find me?" demanded Tarid as they sat down in the restaurant.

"It wasn't an accident," said Danny. He leaned closer as the waiter approached. "I am a Libyan businessman. I buy and sell apricots. And I don't speak Farsi."

Tarid frowned. There'd be no need to use the cover story here; no one cared. The waiter asked what they would have. Tarid said he would have some tea. Danny ordered a coffee, using perfect Farsi.

He was a difficult one to figure out, thought Tarid. Clearly, the research Aberhadji had done did not go far enough. The man must have connections, probably to the Russians, though nothing could be ruled out, even the CIA.

But the CIA connection was unlikely. This man was too good to be an American spy.

"What is it you really want?" Tarid asked.

Danny shook his head. "English. No accidents. There are gossips and spies everywhere. Especially in Tehran."

"English will make us more suspicious," said Tarid, still in Farsi.

"They'll see I'm black and know I'm a foreigner."

Tarid conceded the point, switching to English. "Were you the one who told the Sudanese army we were meeting?"

"Don't be ridiculous. I'm wondering who tipped them off myself. When I find out, he is a dead man."

"It wasn't me."

"Of course not."

Danny spotted the waiter and stopped talking. The man put their food down on the table, then retreated.

"I want to supply arms to the people in Africa who need them," said Danny. "I want to start in the Sudan and branch out. You have connections with people who pay. We can work together. There are people with good connections who help me. No one would do poorly, yourself included."

The suggestion pushed Tarid back in his seat. Was that what this was all about? Had Aberhadji arranged to test him?

Of course. How else would he have been able to follow him to Iran?

Everything had been a test—Aberhadji must have heard something on his visit, and decided to send Kirk. No wonder he vouched for him—Kirk was his agent.

"Out," said Tarid, his voice soft but harsh. "Out."

"What?"

"Out. I'm not taking any bribe. Out. Out!"

Hera appeared at the door, the repaired—and bugged—jacket in her hand. Danny saw her out of the corner of his eye.

"I am not going to be bribed," said Tarid. "Go quietly, or I will have you arrested."

"I think you have the wrong idea."

Tarid reached to his pocket for his phone. "Should I call the police?"

Danny rose. "Call this number if you change your mind," he said, writing down a safe satellite phone number that would be forwarded to his own. "Say nothing. I'll contact you."

"Out," insisted Tarid.

"I'm gone. I'm gone."

Danny tossed a bill on the table, then left. He passed Hera at the door but ignored her.

Tarid took the card with the phone number and started to rip it up, then stopped halfway, realizing it might be of use. He paid the bill without using Danny's rials. He stalked from the table, heading for the door. Hera held the coat up.

"Are you part of this?" Tarid asked.

"Of what?" she said.

He grabbed the coat, started to put it on, then stopped and examined it carefully, half suspecting there would be a bomb or perhaps a needle stuck with poison. When he didn't find any, he jammed his right hand through the arm, pulling it on.

"I have no time for you," he told Hera. Then he strode out of the restaurant.

"And I don't have time for you, either, asshole," she muttered under her breath.

52

Over the Atlantic Ocean

BREANNA HAD FLOWN C-17s OFF AND ON FOR YEARS AS part of her Reserve Air Force commitment, but there was something different about this flight. In a good way.

Part of it was the plane: She had never flown the longer Stretch version before. More powerful engines and improvements in the wing design not only minimized the impact of the aircraft's larger payload capability, but subtly improved its handling characteristics when compared to the stock model. The avionics were also cutting edge, a considerable improvement over the 1990s era technology in the C-17s she was used to.

But the largest difference, Breanna realized, was in her own attitude. She felt content in the seat, happy even. She was far more relaxed than she'd been at any time since taking the Offfice of Technology position. There was something about being in the air, and being on a mission, that felt *right*. Unlike at work, where even at the most intense times her thoughts often strayed in a dozen different directions, here her focus stayed on her instruments and responsibilities.

Her "office" was an all-configurable glass control panel not unlike those she had helped perfect in the EB-52 Megafortress. While a basic configuration was preset to show the instruments and gauges a copilot would typically need in flight, Breanna was free to reconfigure the board just about any way she could imagine. A small world map at the lower left side showed their progress; above that, the Sky News International worldwide cable feed played.

"Mind watching the store while I take a little break, Colonel?" said the pilot, Captain Pete Dominick. Breanna had told everyone to use her Reserve designation; it seemed more professional than "Ms. Stockard."

"Go right ahead," she said.

"Just thought I'd take a constitutional," joked the pilot. "And check to see if Greasy Hands's coffee has eaten through the pot yet."

"He does like it strong, doesn't he?" said Breanna.

"I think when a guy becomes chief, they replace his stomach with a cast-iron wood stove. Nothing harms it."

Parsons was oblivious, sleeping in his seat directly behind the pilot.

Breanna checked the instruments. They were on course, slightly ahead of schedule.

A few minutes later her satellite phone buzzed in her pocket. Thinking it was the embassy in Ethiopia—they still hadn't received an approval from the government—she pulled it from her pocket without looking at the screen and flipped it on.

"Stockard."

"I'll see your Stockard and raise you a pair."

"Zen!"

"Hey, babe. What's up?"

"Oh, same-old, same-old," said Breanna. "Is something wrong?"

"No—but I do have someone here who wants to talk to you."

Breanna's heart jumped. She'd meant to call Teri earlier. It was way past her bedtime—she must not have been able to sleep.

"Mom?"

"Hey, baby, how are you?"

"Dad said you listened to the concert by phone."

"That's right. It was wonderful. Now you really should be in—"

"How come you didn't come?"

"Well, I didn't—I'm on a mission, actually."

"Like, a military mission?"

"Something like that."

"Why couldn't it just have waited until after my concert?"

"Teri—honey—unfortunately, it doesn't quite work that way."

"When are—"

Teri stopped, though the rest of the question was clear: When are you coming home?

Breanna thought of all the times when Zen had to work late. Teri had never objected, not once, that her father wasn't around.

But the person she was really angry with was Zen, who in her mind had put Teri up to calling and embarrassing her.

Even if it wasn't his idea, she thought, he should have know what would happen and not let her call.

Or maybe, she thought, he resented her working as well.

Not working, just having something important to do.

"Teri, are you there?" Breanna asked.

"She's a little overwrought right now," said Zen, who'd taken the phone from their daughter.

"Well of course she is—why did you put her up to this?"

"I didn't. She told me she wanted a good-night kiss."

"God, I can't believe this. I would never do this to you."

"Listen—"

"Where is she now?"

"Sounds like her bedroom."

"Zen."

"Relax, Bree. She'll get over it. I apologize. I'm sorry. I shouldn't have called. It won't happen again."

"Good," she said angrily, before clicking off.

53

Tehran

FLASH PICKED UP THE OTHERS IN THE VAN HE'D RENTED AT the Tehran equivalent of Hertz. The man at the desk had never rented to a foreigner before, but he was in Rome a few years back and happily engaged in small talk as he handled the arrangements on the computer. Flash had only been to Italy as a passenger on military flights stopping to refuel. He'd memorized a great deal of information about pipelines and related tools, but knew very little about the country he was supposedly from. He didn't let that stop him, however—he told the man several stories of the incredible things going on in the country, including a plan to extend Venice's canals to Rome.

"Roma? Really?" asked the man.

"*Si, si,*" said Flash. The conversation was in English—fortunately for him—but Nuri had advised him to throw in an Italian phrase every so often. *Si, si*—yes, yes—and *dove il bano* were about all he knew.

"Canals up the mountains?"

"Under," said Flash. "Tunnels. *Si?*"

"Ah, yes."

Flash's congeniality got a hundred thousand rials knocked off the rental price as a special perk. But while he thought the van would be perfect because of its size, it turned to be less handy that he'd hoped. It barely fit down some of the streets in the old part of the city, and kept threatening to stall when he stepped too hard on the gas.

By the time he got over to the hotel, Tarid had already gotten into a taxi. Nuri and Hera flagged down their own, leaving Danny to wait for Flash.

The Voice steered them away from the knotted traffic in the center of the city, following as Tarid had the taxi take him southeast. They were still about five miles away from him when he stopped in Kahrizak, a small village in an agricultural area south of the city. They continued until they got to within a half mile, and then the Voice started picking up Tarid's conversation. Flash pulled off to the side of the road while Danny listened.

Everything was a confused jumble for the first minute or so. Gradually, Danny realized this wasn't the meeting they'd hoped to be led to. Tarid was looking up an old friend who apparently had died a year before. The woman who owned the house now had no idea where the family had moved.

Nuri called in from the taxi, which had been stuck in traffic and was still several miles away.

"Sounds like he's looking up an old friend," said Nuri. "What do you think?"

"Has to be."

"We're going up to Qemez Tappeh," Nuri told Danny. "We'll see what happens from there."

Qemez Tappeh was a slightly larger village a little north of Kahrizak.

Within minutes, Tarid had gone back to his cab and was heading for the highway.

"They're on their way to Tehran," Danny told Flash. "We'll have to turn around."

"Just a wild goose chase?"

"So far."

TARID DECIDED HE COULDN'T FACE THE TEMPTATION OF THE hotel keeper's daughter for even a few minutes. He had the driver take him to a café he was once a regular at in Punak, on the northwest side of the city. It would be as good as anywhere to kill time.

Once a hangout for young men and university types, it now catered to a much older, quieter crowd. In truth, many of the people Tarid remembered still came here; they had simply grown older. But his mind couldn't quite adjust, and while some of the faces seemed familiar, he couldn't attach a name to any.

He took a seat by himself in the corner, then brooded over a tea, trying to convince himself that Aberhadji wasn't going to have him arrested, or simply executed.

Finally it was time to leave. He paid his bill and went outside, walking down the block to a gas station that he knew rented cars. He didn't see anyone in the office as he walked up, and for a moment a fresh dose of panic upturned the melancholy stoicism that had settled over him: Aberhadji would not like him to take a cab to the meeting, though he had cut things so close now he might not have an alternative. But the man who ran the station had merely gone to the restroom; he yelled from the back as soon as Tarid rang the bell at the front desk.

The rental was quickly arranged, and within a half hour Tarid was wending his way through the mountains north of the city.

The bright sun glinted off the metal roofs of the large

warehouse buildings north of Darreh Bagh as he hunted for the turn he had to take off the main road. The terraced hills above still showed traces of snow, and he worried about the shape of the roads. He'd come here once during the dead of winter—one of the worst ever on record in Iran—and nearly got stuck before reaching the farm.

Aberhadji called it a farm, though the buildings hadn't been used for agriculture in more than two decades. They'd been falling down when Aberhadji found them, neglected and forgotten in a dead-end valley in the hills. Their obscurity was exactly what Aberhadji wanted. It was doubtful that anyone except those who'd had business here even knew that they existed.

The narrow road was muddy but passable. Tarid drove carefully, avoiding the largest of the ruts as he negotiated the hairpin turn that marked the midway point from the main road to the actual driveway. Within a few hundred feet of the turn, he came under surveillance from a sentry. He didn't know exactly where this point was, nor did it matter to him— he had felt he was being watched from the very moment he left Tehran, and acted accordingly. If he was not resigned to his fate, he was at least under the impression that he was trapped, with no way out. Running would only prolong his agony and deprive him of any slim chance he had of talking Aberhadji into sparing his life.

Tarid's fears had doubled each hour over the past twenty-four, pushing not just logic but every other thought from his mind. He drove up to the large yard in front of the ruined main house a condemned man, as if arms and legs were bound in chains to his waist. There were no guards near the car parked there before him, and he saw no one at the front of the large building slightly downhill on the left, which was used as the compound's headquarters.

Had Tarid been thinking clearly, he would have interpreted this as a positive sign. But he was no longer thinking, clearly or otherwise. He closed the car door and walked slowly down the path, each step measured, each length the same.

He knocked. There was no answer. He knocked again. Once more there was no answer. He pulled open the door.

Aberhadji was standing over a table at the far end of the room, distracted, studying a schematic.

"You are ten minutes late," he said.

"I—"

"It's all right." Aberhadji waved his hand. "I was delayed myself."

Tarid stayed near the door, frozen by his fear.

"I'd call for tea, but there's no one to make it," said Aberhadji. "The crew has been dismissed until June."

"Is the operation—are we shutting down?"

Aberhadji looked up, startled by the question. "No, no. Just the normal lull in gathering materials. So—your report?"

"My report." Tarid's throat narrowed to the size of a straw. He could barely breathe.

"What happened in Sudan?" asked Aberhadji.

"Sudan . . ."

"What is wrong with you, Tarid?" Aberhadji came out from around the table for a better look at his lieutenant. Even in the dim light near the door, Tarid seemed paler than normal. "Have you been drinking?"

"No. Drinking? Of course not."

"Don't pretend to be what you are not," said Aberhadji sharply. "What does this arms dealer want? What does he know about us?"

"I don't know. They—"

Tarid stopped speaking. Blood was rushing from his head. He had been wrong—Aberhadji wasn't going to confront him about his skimming, and hadn't sent Kirk to catch him.

"Are you all right? Have a seat. Here."

Aberhadji took Tarid's arm and gently led him to the side. Tarid didn't smell as if he'd been drinking, though that might not prove anything. Still, it seemed more likely he had caught the flu.

"I—Kirk is in Tehran," said Tarid.

"Tehran?"

"He wants—he wants to strike a deal. There was an attack in Sudan. I was captured. I was shot."

"Shot?"

"Yes. In the leg. Nothing. It's nothing. He freed me."

"He freed you?"

While Aberhadji had made inquiries about Kirk, the information the intelligence service had turned up—that he had been active in Somalia and had contacts in South Africa and Germany—did not completely rule out the possibility that he was working for a foreign spy service, such as the CIA, or even the Israelis. The story that now unfolded from Tarid worried him further. This Kirk clearly had impressive resources—perhaps too impressive.

On the other hand, would someone who worked for the CIA or the Zionists dare come to Iran?

"Were you followed here?" Aberhadji demanded when Tarid finished telling him about his misadventures.

"No, absolutely not."

"You're a fool, Tarid. How many people followed you here?"

"I wasn't—No one."

"How did Kirk know you were in Tehran?"

"I'm not sure."

"Did he follow you from the airport?"

"Impossible."

"So he guessed?"

"I thought he was working for you."

Another possibility presented itself to Aberhadji—Kirk was working for the government. Yes, the Iranian spy service could easily arrange all of this.

But to what end?

The past two days had been a terrible upheaval for Aberhadji. He wasn't sure which way to turn. The CIA, the Zionists, his own traitorous government—everyone had fallen under Satan's spell.

He could trust no one.

"This Kirk wants a really big arrangement," said Tarid.

"He's greedy. He thinks he can supply weapons to all of Africa, through us. I'll bet he killed Luo to get in position. But it might be something we should consider. He does have—"

"Stop," said Aberhadji. "How are you to contact him?"

"I have a phone number."

"Give me what you have."

Tarid reached into his pocket and took out the half-torn card Kirk had given him in the restaurant. His hand trembled as he turned it over, realizing that Aberhadji thought it was an elaborate trap.

"You checked his background," said Tarid. "You know as much about him as I."

The glare in Aberhadji's eyes told him immediately that saying that was a mistake.

"I want you to go back to Tehran," said Aberhadji. "I will contact you in a day or two. You'll call Kirk and set up a meeting."

"He can't be Mossad. He's black."

Aberhadji exploded. "You fool! You think the Zionists aren't smart enough to hide behind a black man? And so what? You said yourself from his accent he's American. He is probably CIA."

"No. He risked his life—"

"Out! Before I lose my temper."

DANNY, NURI, AND THE OTHERS WERE PARKED IN THE VAN about a half mile below the farm. They'd heard the entire exchange.

"Let's get back to the highway," Nuri told Danny. "Before he reaches the car."

"He's right," Danny told Flash. "Let's get out of here."

"Are you guys going to tell us what's going on, or are we just along for the ride?" asked Hera.

"Tarid just met with the person in charge of the program," said Danny. "He wants to set up a meeting with me. They think I'm CIA."

"Or Mossad," Nuri said. "Or maybe just a greedy arms dealer."

"So they know we're on to them," said Hera.

"They suspect it," said Nuri. "They don't actually know it. If we can get the ringleader to that meeting, we can tag him. Maybe even bug him. We have a couple of days—we can get some special bugs made up."

"You're not going to go ahead with a meeting," Hera told Danny. "That would be suicide."

"I don't know," he said.

"No, no. We'll set something up." Nuri studied the map on the Voice command unit, looking for a place they might stop to eat before Tehran.

"Set something up? You're nuts," said Hera. She leaned forward from the backseat. "You can't go to the meeting, Colonel. There's just no way."

"If we arrange it right—"

"We have to get close to him," said Nuri. "We have to follow him."

"Then you should take the meeting if you're so gung-ho," said Hera.

"Maybe I will," he told her.

"You don't have to actually meet him," said Flash. "Just have him walk through a populated area, brush by him and mark him."

"It'll need to be more elaborate to get a bug on him," said Nuri.

"It's not for another couple of days," said Danny. "We have plenty to do in the meantime. I want to get inside the compound and take a look at it."

Danny's heart pounded at the idea of meeting with Tarid's boss. Hera was right—it would be a setup, one almost impossible to escape from. And yet, part of him believed he had to agree to it, had to go, just to prove he was brave.

Why should he have to prove that now? Hadn't he been brave in Sudan? He'd frozen for a moment, the briefest moment. No one else had seen, or known. How much courage was enough?

He'd acted bravely, yet he felt like a coward.

Because McGowan had died. That was part of it. His man had died. The cost, the terrible cost.

He was measuring himself against an impossible standard, yet he couldn't help it.

"That farm isn't on any CIA surveillance list," said Nuri. "It's most likely just an arbitrary meeting place. There probably won't be anything there."

"Then it'll be easy to check out," said Danny. "We weren't doing anything interesting tonight anyway."

AS SOON AS TARID LEFT THE BUILDING, ABERHADJI SLIPPED out the small two-way radio he kept his pocket.

"Have someone take the car and follow him," he told the head of the resident security team. "Make sure he goes to Tehran. I want to know everything he does, everyone he meets. Go yourself."

"That will leave you with only one guard to watch the building. And yourself."

"I can count."

"Yes, Imam."

The security team had assured Aberhadji when Tarid arrived that he wasn't followed, but Aberhadji no longer knew what or who to trust. For this reason alone, prudence suggested he shut down the operation, keep it completely inactive for six months, a year, then arrange for a new incarnation. There was already the one warhead, after all, with material hidden for two more; he could wait.

Especially given that the council had decided to back the president and his treacherous acts.

They were the more serious problem. He would have to increase his influence before the president could be dealt with.

Aberhadji felt a headache coming on. It had been months since he'd had one.

He bent to pray, asking forgiveness for his sins, and requesting that the pain be lightened.

Allah was merciful. The metal prongs that had begun to tighten around his skull receded.

So he would lay low. That was the best direction now. He would dismantle everything, starting here. The tools would be moved to the mines. The material and the warhead would be relocated.

He'd need a crew here immediately. And more security as well. Even if it attracted attention.

He picked up his sat phone and started to dial, then stopped. The Americans were very good at stealing transmissions and breaking encryptions. He would have to assume, for the time being, that they would be able to listen into any conversation he had.

It meant inevitable delay, but it couldn't be helped.

He took the radio out again.

"I am going into town," he told the lone watchman. "We will need reinforcements. I will arrange for them to arrive as soon as possible. In the meantime, shoot anyone you find on the property."

"It will be done, Imam."

54

Eastern Sudan, near the border with Ethiopia

BOSTON, SUGAR, AND ABUL SPENT A DIFFICULT NIGHT SLEEP-ing in the bus, taking turns on watch. It wasn't just the threat of the mercenaries' revenge that kept them awake; their dead colleague's body affected each to some degree. None would have admitted it to the others, but each kept his or her own distance from the body bag at the back aisle of the bus.

Abul remembered a childhood story involving a lion that preyed not on the dead, but the mourners who watched over the bodies. The story haunted him so badly that every shadow outside the bus took a lion's shape, until he could neither look at the windows nor close his eyes, certain that they were about to be attacked. He sweated profusely as he lay across the seats, the moisture creeping like acidic slime across his body, eating away at his skin. His breathing became shallower, and quicker, until he gulped the air without absorbing the oxygen. Not even the idea of the money he would get from enduring this horror calmed him. Instead, he thought only of the many ways it could be wrested away.

Sugar had not heard any similar stories, but she felt uneasy nonetheless. She hadn't known McGowan very well, but working with someone during an operation compressed time greatly. And it was impossible not to wonder why he had died, and not her.

For Boston, McGowan was a reminder of his responsibility to the others, and the fact that even the best commander might lose people, no matter how hard he fought or tried to protect them.

The dawn offered little solace. The battery in the UAV they'd launched during the night ran down shortly before sunup, and Boston launched a replacement. But its battery failed prematurely less than a half hour later, and it took nearly twenty minutes to get another aircraft ready to fly. Sugar and Abul hunkered over their rifles as Boston prepared the tiny plane, his fingers turning klutzy just when he needed them calm and precise. By the time he had the plane up, the sky was bright blue and the temperature was rising quite high.

The mercenaries were not within the five-mile radius the Owl patrolled. On the Ethiopian side of the border, however, a hundred more troops had just arrived. Boston stared at the screen, mentally counting the force and trying to guess its intentions.

"Maybe they're coming to party," said Sugar, joining him.

When Boston didn't laugh, she asked what he thought they were going to do.

"That many troops, without a threat—I'd say they were going to push the refugees away from the border," said Boston. "It'll be a massacre if they do."

"Maybe they won't use force," said Sugar.

On screen, the men were jumping from their trucks, rifles in hand.

"I don't think you can count on them not using force," said Boston. "Those aren't aid workers."

Abul, his eyes burning with fatigue, came over and squinted at the screen.

"There are no UN people there?" he asked, looking around the screen.

"No," said Boston. "Why?"

"The agency that deals with refugees. They're not there."

"Why's that important?" asked Sugar.

Abul shook his head. "There are many different attitudes here. Mostly, the Ethiopians are a good people. But sometimes . . . it is possible that they would see the refugees as members of a different tribe."

"They're going to just shoot them?" asked Sugar.

"No, no. Not at first. But, if they didn't move or, worse, if they resisted."

Abul made a face.

"What will they do?" asked Sugar.

"Tear down their tents. Push them to disperse," Abul said. "Get them away from the border. The camps—they consider them a breeding ground for political dissension. And they are not related to the people."

"They push those people away, they're just going to die," said Sugar.

"Maybe your boss on the phone can help," said Abul. "Washington."

Washington hadn't even been able to get permission to let them cross, but Boston decided it was worth a try.

"WE'RE ANOTHER HOUR FROM TOUCHDOWN AT THE CAPI-tal," Breanna told Boston when he called on the sat phone. The MC-17 was over Egypt, legging south toward Addis Ababa. "The ambassador is going to meet me at the airport, and we're going to go over to the prime minister's residence and have him work out something. The bureaucracy has just been throwing up roadblocks."

"There's another problem."

Boston explained the situation. Breanna punched up a detailed map of the area, then opened a window to connect with the Air Force's frontline intelligence network. Ethiopia was not an area of prime concern, and all of the bulletins were generic, warning of tensions along the border with Sudan, but containing no current information about troop movements or the like. The number of soldiers involved were simply too small and the area too isolated to generate an alarm.

"Boston, what's your situation now?" said Breanna.

"We're about half a mile from the refugees, up on the side of a small hill. We can see what's going on down there," he added. "There ain't much."

"How many civilians?"

"A hundred, around there."

"I'll get back to you."

Breanna used the aircraft's satellite communications system to call the embassy in Addis Ababa. By now she was on first-name basis not only with the operator, but with the ambassador's personal assistant, Adam Clapsuch, who took most of his calls.

"Adam, it's Breanna again. Any word from the Ethiopian government?"

"No, ma'am. Ambassador's right here."

He handed over the phone.

"This is John, Breanna. I'm sorry. I have nothing new. They're stalling for some reason that's unclear."

"A few hundred more troops just arrived at the border near where our people are," said Breanna. "There's a small refugee group there. The troops may be thinking about attacking the refugees."

"Which side of the border are they on?"

"The Sudan side. But they want to get over."

"The Ethiopians have had a lot of trouble with refugees. It wouldn't surprise if they wanted them to disperse. But I don't think they would attack."

"Is there some sort of protest, or anything we can do to stop them from hurting these people?"

"If they're not willing to speak to us about moving our own people across, Breanna, I'm not sure what we can do."

"Has Washington spoken to their ambassador?"

"He's been called to the State Department for an urgent message this morning. That's all I know."

With Washington several hours behind Africa, the meeting would be several hours away. Even if it went well, the civilians—and the Whiplash team members—might be overrun by then.

"I'll keep trying the president. And I'll talk to Washington immediately," said the ambassador. "I'll update them with this. In the meantime, if I hear anything, obviously, I'll let you know. Otherwise I'll see you when you land."

"All right," said Breanna, though she had already decided she wasn't waiting for the Ethiopians anymore. As soon as she ended the communication, she punched the information display to double-check the map.

"Pete, we're going to land at Dire Dawa," she told the pilot, Captain Dominick. "It has an 8,800-foot runway. Can you get us in and out?"

"Not a problem. We can land and take off on three."

"Good. We'll have to declare some sort of emergency going in."

"What'd you have in mind?"

"Engine out or something like that. OK?"

"As long as I don't really have to screw up my engines,

that's fine." The pilot laughed. The long flight had twisted his sense of humor.

Breanna pulled off her headset and got out of her seat. Greasy Hands was snoring behind the pilot, his head folded down to his chest.

"Greasy Hands, wake up," said Breanna, shaking him. "Wake up."

"Huh? We're here?"

"We have a ways to go. About an hour."

"Oh, OK."

"Do you think you and the loadmaster could get the Ospreys out of the cargo bay?"

Greasy Hands rubbed some of the sleep from his eyes, then shot a glance across the aisle at the seat where the loadmaster was sleeping.

"Probably," he said. "I mean, sure. Of course. Why?"

"How long will it take to get them ready to fly?"

"Jeez, I don't know, Bree. They should be ready to go right out of the box."

"What if they're not?"

"I don't know. Depends." Greasy Hands pulled himself upright in his seat, trying to think. "It's all automated. I mean— with this system, it's going to work or it's not. Nothing in between."

"They have to be fueled?"

"If you want to go anywhere."

The aircraft carried a minimal amount of fuel in their tanks, but not enough for a mission.

"How long will that take?" Breanna asked. "An hour?"

"Depends. Could be a lot longer. Might be less. Though that I wouldn't count on," he added. Greasy Hands unbuckled his seat belt. "I'll go down there and take a look at 'em. Let me know what I'm up against."

55

CIA headquarters

JONATHON REID HAD JUST BEGUN TO PORE OVER THE LATEST situation report out of Sudan when Breanna's call came through. He immediately punched it into his handset, resting his chin in his hand.

"Reid."

"Jonathon, the Ethiopians are being unresponsive. They've sent troops to the border—we think they're planning on pushing the refugees there back. Or maybe just killing them. Our people are right nearby."

"We're just getting information from the embassy to the same effect," said Reid.

He'd also seen an opinion from one of the analysts within the past fifteen minutes speculating that the Ethiopians, under pressure from the Egyptians, would not only refuse to open their borders to refugees, but would seek to actively dissuade anyone from crossing over into the country. They needed little encouragement: Sudanese refugee camps were a notorious breeding ground for terrorists and other "disruptive influences," as the report put it.

"I'm going to land in Dire Dawa and get our people out," said Breanna. "We can't wait for the Ethiopians."

"I think you're taking—" Reid stopped short. "I don't want you risking your own life, Breanna. It's not your job."

"Jonathon, I'm here. I have the tools. I'm going to get it done."

Reid had made similar decisions himself, many times. He knew from experience that the lines looked very clear and bright when your people were in danger and you were nearby.

From the distance, though, they were hazy and complicated. She was suggesting interfering in another country's affairs, a country with whom they had decent relations, because of a corpse.

And a few hundred refugees. Some of whom might or might not be terrorists, and none of whom were likely to be grateful.

"We're going to have to tell the White House what's going on," said Reid.

"Go ahead."

"State may object. Among others."

"I'm not leaving our people."

"I wouldn't, either."

As soon as Reid hung up, he checked Breanna's position on the map. She was forty-five minutes from Dire Dawa. If he waited until dawn to call the White House, the operation would be over before anyone objected.

That was the coward's way.

Let them object. If they gave an order directing her not to proceed, he would simply neglect to call her back. He'd take full responsibility—as soon as the operation was over.

He picked up the phone and called the White House operator.

56

White House

CHRISTINE MARY TODD HAD BEEN A NIGHT OWL FOR MUCH of her adult life. In college, she used the early morning hours to hit the books; when her children were born, she found rising for their nightly feedings somewhat less onerous. As a governor, she'd loved to use the early morning hours to catch up on her reading—not of the newspapers and political blogs, but old-fashioned cozy mysteries, which she was famously addicted to.

But in those days, she'd always been able to grab a nap during the day. Now naps were out of the question.

Still, she stayed up late. Sometimes she had work to do, and other times she simply couldn't sleep. Her mind refused to shut off. She would lie in bed next to her husband for an hour and sometimes more, occasionally falling asleep, but more often getting up and going down the hall to the room she'd converted into her private study. Her staff knew her habits, and when there was an important call, would try her there before deciding whether to try the bedroom.

Tonight she answered the phone on the first ring.

"This is the President."

"Mrs. President, I'm sorry to wake you," said Jonathon Reid. "I expected I would be connected to one of your staff people."

"You didn't wake me, Mr. Reid. Please explain why you called."

"There is a situation in Ethiopia . . ."

The President listened as he laid it out.

"I will call the Ethiopian prime minister myself," said Todd before he finished. "That should solve the problem, don't you agree?"

"Absolutely."

"Very well. Let's see what we can do. Please stay on the line in case they need some background. I trust you can speak to them without giving away any critical secrets."

57

Eastern Sudan, near the border with Ethiopia

"THEY'RE GETTING READY FOR SOMETHING," SAID SUGAR, standing on top of the bus and pointing down toward the Ethiopian troops. "They're mustering behind the trucks."

Boston reached up and took the binoculars. He wasn't quite high enough to see over all of the buildings, but what he did see made it obvious the Ethiopians were planning on moving out. Boston saw several of the soldiers checking their rifles as they formed up.

The civilians were in their makeshift camp, milling around aimlessly. They didn't have any lookouts posted. Children played near the fence and road.

Boston pulled out his sat phone and called Breanna back.

"Things look like they're about to get pretty desperate over here," he told her. "What's going on with the government?"

"We're going to pick you up," she told him. "But it's going to take us another hour and a half to get there. We're about five minutes from touching down. We're sending an Osprey."

"Can you get here sooner? They look like they're ready to move."

"Boston, we're doing everything we can. Are the Ethiopians threatening you?"

"It's not us I'm worried about. Whiplash out."

Boston looked up at Sugar.

"Hey," he shouted, "remember that idea you had for a diversion that I said we weren't desperate enough for?"

"Yeah?"

"Well, we're desperate enough now."

SUGAR'S IDEA WAS TO START A FAKE FIREFIGHT, DRAWING the Ethiopian army away. She'd wanted to move south about a mile to do it, but there wasn't time for that; they'd have to launch it much closer to their own position, here on the north side of the crossing.

Boston had another idea to make sure they got the Ethiopians' attention.

"You're going to set my bus on fire!?!" exclaimed Abul as Boston opened one of the spare gas cans and prepared to douse the interior. They'd already off-loaded their supplies and McGowan's body.

"We'll pay double for it," said Boston.

"Already you are paying ten times what I was promised," said Abul. "Double is less."

"Ten times, whatever." Boston began spilling the liquid liberally down the aisle. "Look at it—it's all battered anyway. Bashed and whatnot. This will save you the trouble of having to fix it up. You want to be the one to light the match?"

Abul would sooner have thrown himself into the flames. He sat on the steps in the open doorway, dejected, mournful, his head buried in his arms as Boston got it ready. After making sure the interior was as flammable as possible, he rigged three Molotov cocktails next to the driver's seat— bottles half filled with gasoline that he could ignite to turn the bus into an inferno. With everything set, he leaned over Abul and shouted up to Sugar, who was still watching the border from the roof.

"Sugar, what's the story?"

"Troops are in formation," she yelled from above. "The drivers are getting in the trucks."

"All right, get off!" shouted Boston. "I'll be back!"

"You better be."

Boston turned the key. The engine cranked but didn't catch.

Damn!

He tried again. Nothing.

"Abul! How the hell do you start this crate?"

Abul looked up from the steps. "Pump gas pedal twice," he told Boston. "Praise Allah, then pump while you turn the engine."

Boston followed the directions, pumping, cranking, and praying. The engine caught.

"Get off the steps. Stay here with Sugar!" he yelled.

Abul hesitated, then did a half roll forward, staggering off the vehicle.

The fumes made Boston feel a little high as the bus rumbled out of the little crevice where they'd parked. He headed for the road, at first aiming directly for the refugee camp and the fenced border crossing beyond.

Boston took a deep breath as the crossing came into view. He could see the refugee camp to his right. Beyond it to his left were the trucks and the Ethiopian soldiers. They were starting to move.

He began beeping the horn, then turned the bus off the road. The ground was soft, and the battered vehicle wobbled but stayed upright, picking up speed as it started toward the fence.

Boston reached down and slipped a big rock he had taken with him onto the gas pedal, keeping his speed up. Then he took a smoke grenade from his vest pocket, pulled the pin, and dropped it into the makeshift sling he'd set on the mirror. A plume of smoke began trailing from the bus, whipped around by the wind so the bus almost completely disappeared.

The last thing he needed was his lighter, which he'd slipped into his upper vest pocket. But as he fished for it, the bus jerked sharply, and he nearly lost control before he could get both hands back on the wheel. He was moving faster than he'd planned—nearly eighty kilometers, according to the speedometer. The terrain, though it had looked fairly smooth from the distance, was pockmarked with holes and studded with rocks. Dirt and pebbles flew everywhere, a minitornado consuming the vehicle as it sprinted toward the fence.

He'd planned on jumping about fifty yards from the fence, as soon as he was sure he had enough momentum for the bus to get through the fence and maybe jump the ditch. But the swirling dust and the smoke from the grenade, as well as the bus's speed, made it difficult for him to judge his distance.

By the time he grabbed the lighter, he was only thirty yards from the fence. He let go of the wheel, and the bus careened to the right. He pulled back, then flicked his lighter. The jerking bus made it difficult to ignite the wadded fabric in the bottles. He cursed, pulled his hand down—then felt the crush of glass and metal spraying on his back as the bus hit the outer fence.

By now it was going over a hundred kilometers an hour. It sailed right over the tank ditch and pummeled over a second, shorter fence partly hidden in the dirt. Boston flew against the metal rail, then back against the dashboard, as the bus plunged onward. He looked at his hand and realized he'd lost the lighter.

Then he looked up and saw that the rag in one of the bottles was burning.

With a shout, he threw himself down the steps and out of the bus as it careened through the second fence. He landed in a tumble, arms crossed in front of his face, temporarily blinded by the smoke and dust.

The Molotov cocktail exploded, setting off not just the other two, but the fumes that had gathered in the rear of the vehicle. The bus turned into a flaming mass of red, an arrow shooting across the empty plain.

Boston pushed himself on all fours for five or six yards, swimming more than crawling, flailing forward through a tangle of smoke and dust. Finally he hit a clear patch and realized he was going the wrong way. He jerked himself to his feet and began running as quickly as he could back toward the others.

The Ethiopian soldiers had watched the spectacle with disbelief. As the bus finally ground to a halt and began exploding, one of the officers directed a squad to investigate. A fireball shot up; he sent a full company, then ordered the rest of the troops to take up a defensive position as he consulted headquarters.

Up on the hill, Sugar held her breath until she saw a second spray of smoke erupting near the damaged border fence. She realized that had to be Boston, letting off another smoke grenade; he was OK. Sure enough, he emerged a few moments later, sprinting in a wide arc back toward their position.

She went back over to the laptop, which was displaying the image from their last airborne UAV. The Ethiopian soldiers were responding to the bus exactly as they had hoped, moving away from the refugees.

She also saw something they hadn't counted on—a motorcycle followed by four pickup trucks filled with men, coming toward them from Sudan.

The mercenaries had followed them from a distance the whole way, and hadn't given up hope for revenge.

58

Dire Dawa, Ethiopia

LANDING THE MC-17 AT DIRE DAWA WAS EASY ENOUGH. The airport was used primarily as a military base, but Ye Ityopya Ayer Hayl—the Ethiopian Air Force—had only a token presence, with most of its very small force of combat aircraft stationed at the capital. The local squadron consisted of four MiG-23 fighter-bombers dating from the 1960s. None of the planes had been flown in the past six months, due to a shortage of pilots and spare parts. Aside from the MiGs, there were two Hueys in good condition, along with an Antov AN-12 transport.

The controller directed Captain Frederick to park near the MiGs. This was at the far end of the complex, isolated from the main buildings; it suited them just fine.

Greasy Hands was waiting with the loadmaster as the pilot brought the aircraft to a halt. The Ospreys were loaded onto a skidlike trolley, which could be operated by a single man. It took less than three minutes for the first aircraft to be pushed out of the bay onto the tarmac.

Setting up the Ospreys took a little more time. Much of the process was automated on the newest attack version of the aircraft—including the unfolding of the wings—but Greasy Hands still had to personally oversee the computer running through the checklists. This meant sitting in the cockpit while the computer went through the processes at its own speed. While streamlined for battle, the procedure still took twenty minutes before the first aircraft was ready to fly.

While he was working on the tarmac, Breanna was talking to Reid, who'd just got off the phone with the President and the Ethiopian prime minister.

"Very interesting conversation," said Reid. "The prime minister grants us his permission to cross the border without problems. And then he says he's not sure the army will honor that permission."

"What?"

"One of their periodic political breakdowns," Reid told her. "I've got two generals trying to get ahold of their generals to get the order carried out. Meanwhile, their army's mobilizing against Sudan. They're sick of the rebels, and the government. Not that I can blame them."

The pilot tapped Breanna on the shoulder and pointed out the windscreen. A trio of Ethiopian officials were just stepping out of a car.

"Looks like the air force wants an explanation of what's going on," Breanna told Reid. "I'll get back to you."

"Very good."

Breanna met the head of the delegation—a lieutenant—on the runway.

"You have an emergency?" he asked.

"Oh yes." She launched into a cock and bull story about an onboard fire in one of the Ospreys, which required them to be off-loaded and checked. Her story was so convincing that the lieutenant had the base fire truck come over on standby. While he went to alert his superiors, the loadmaster got two fuel trucks to fill up the Ospreys before starting to top off the C-17.

"Number one is ready to fly," Greasy Hands told Breanna. "But it'll take another half hour to get the missiles on the launching rails and all the weapons systems checked out."

"We can't wait that long. We'll launch One now," she told him. "I'll fly it. Put the missiles on Two. You can follow."

"Me?"

"The computer flies it. You just have to tell it what to do."

"I don't know, Bree. I don't know."

"Are you telling me you *can't* fly it, Chief?"

Greasy Hands frowned. It was true that the automated systems flew the aircraft—the ones that patrolled Dreamland did so with no crew aboard, responding to verbal instructions from the Whiplash security team's base station. Still, there was something about sitting in the pilot's seat that made the old crew chief hesitate.

"Frederick has to stay here with the C-17," said Breanna. "So it's either you or the loadmaster. You have a hell of a lot more experience with the aircraft and its systems. What do you say?"

"I can do it," he grumbled.

"Good." She started off the flight deck, then turned at the door. "And don't break my aircraft."

It was a line Greasy Hands had used countless times when turning an aircraft over to Breanna, and hundreds of other pilots. Now he didn't think it was funny at all.

WHEN HE WAS COMMANDER OF DREAMLAND, BREANNA'S father had insisted that every pilot on the base familiarize him- or herself with all of their aircraft types. Breanna had flown an Osprey a few times, but only as the second officer or copilot. She would not have been able to handle the tricky tasks of taking off vertically and converting to level flight without the help of the computer.

Breanna manually entered her service ID into the control panel, then identified herself to the computer over the interphone system. It was like old times—even her verbal password was unchanged.

"Acknowledged," said the flight computer. "Welcome, Breanna Stockard."

"Assume autonomous pilot mode," she told it. "Begin preflight checklist."

The aircraft went through its checklist faster than a human pilot could have, giving itself a pat on the back as each system was reviewed and found in the green. The autopilot section in the center portion of the control panel flashed, declaring itself ready to go.

"Take off," she told it.

A message flashed in the screen:

UNABLE TO COMPLY WITH COMMAND.

"Why not?" she asked.

The computer didn't reply. Breanna rephrased the question, but again got no response. The computer's verbal command section was more limited than in the late model Megafortresses, and would not attempt to interpret commands it couldn't understand. This was by design—the environment Ospreys operated in made it possible that an unauthorized person might attempt to take command, so the system had been purposely limited to help ensure that only trained and therefore authorized personnel could control it.

Breanna stared at the control screen, knowing something was wrong but unsure what it could be.

"Prepare for takeoff," she told the computer.

The message changed.

PREPARED FOR TAKEOFF. ALL SYSTEMS GREEN.

"Take off."

UNABLE TO COMPLY WITH COMMAND.

She saw a vehicle approaching from the terminal area. Was the computer worried about running into it?

"Prepare for vertical takeoff."

PREPARED FOR VERTICAL TAKEOFF. ALL SYSTEMS GREEN.

"Take off."

UNABLE TO COMPLY WITH COMMAND.

"Damn it."

UNABLE TO COMPLY WITH COMMAND.

"I'll bet," she said. She slammed her hand on the side of the console.

Relax, she told herself. Think back to Dreamland. What did we do?

It was too many years.

She remembered one flight vaguely. She'd been working with one of the civilian test pilots. Johnny Rocket was his nickname, his real name was buried somewhere in her unconscious.

Johnny Rocket—frizzy red hair, goofy smile. He was a stickler for very precise preflights. "Plan the flight, fly the plan," he used to say.

Over and over again. It was annoying.

The flight plan! The computer needed to know where it was going before it would take off.

Breanna opened up the window for the course plan and fed in the proper coordinates, directing the aircraft to fly at top speed in a straight line.

This time it accepted the command to take off. In seconds they were airborne and hustling toward the border with Sudan.

*   *   *

AFTER CONSULTING WITH HIS COMMANDING GENERAL, THE Ethiopian air force lieutenant was ordered to ground the American cargo aircraft until further notice. The Americans had not asked for permission to land, and therefore would have to wait until the proper protocol was worked out.

"And what proper protocol would you like us to follow?" asked Captain Fredrick when the lieutenant explained, with much apology, what his orders were.

"I just need permission," he said. "These things are decided far over my head."

Frederick didn't like the order, but at the moment he had no intention of taking off without Breanna and the Whiplash people. Rather than arguing, he told the lieutenant that he would consult with his superiors.

"Yes, yes, an excellent idea." The lieutenant turned and waved at the fuel crew, telling them to stop fueling the plane.

"Why are you stopping them?" said Frederick.

"Just until I have permission."

The C-17 already had plenty of fuel, but Frederick protested for a while longer, somewhat in the manner of a basketball coach working the refs from courtside, figuring to gain an advantage in the future.

And in the meantime, the trucks continued to pour fuel into the jet. By the time Frederick gave in, the tanks were about three pounds from capacity.

"Where did the first aircraft go?" the Ethiopian lieutenant asked.

"The Osprey?"

"Yes."

"Just testing the systems. It'll be back in a little while."

"I don't know if I can allow that."

"Maybe you should check with your commander," said Frederick.

"Yes, yes, good idea."

As soon as he was gone, Frederick trotted to Osprey Two.

"Better get in the air ASAP," he told Greasy Hands. "Before Mickey Mouse comes back and tells you that you can't take off."

59

Eastern Sudan

SUGAR TRACKED THE PICKUP TRUCKS AS THEY CROSSED off the road and headed toward the bus. She could see Boston running well off to her right, camouflaged by the smoke. With luck, she thought, he would escape to the hills without her having to fire.

No such luck. Someone in the rear of the lead truck noticed him just as he reached the road. They banged on the roof of the cab, and within seconds the truck and then the motorcycle veered in Boston's direction.

Sugar started firing as soon as it turned. Her first shots missed low, the slugs burying themselves in the sand about thirty yards in front of the truck. She pushed down on the handle of the gun, bringing the machine-gun barrel up slowly until the stream of bullets sliced into the Toyota's radiator. The men in the back of the vehicle threw themselves off as the .50 caliber slugs smashed the engine compartment and windshield to pieces, chewing through the vehicle like a pack of crocodiles going after an antelope at the edge of the river.

Sugar swung the gun left, taking out the motorcycle. Then she turned to aim at a second truck that had started to follow the first. But the driver had seen what was happening and jammed on the brakes. As he nose-dived to a stop, he jumped from the cab and got behind the truck for cover. The men in the back did as well—except for the machine-gun operator and his assistant, who began firing in earnest at Sugar.

The ground shook with the thick stutter of their Russian-made heavy machine gun. It was ancient but dependable; its ancestors had backed swarms of troops in suicide attacks against the Germans north of Moscow in the dead of winter. Sugar put a dozen rounds into the truck's side and the sandbags protecting the gunners, then had to duck as the enemy weapon found its range, splintering the rocks she was hiding behind. Before she could get back up, one of the mercenaries manned the machine gun in the back of the first truck and began firing as well. All Sugar could do was hunker down and wait for the firestorm to let up.

Boston managed to reach an outcropping of rocks at the base of the hill before anyone remembered him. He ducked behind them to catch his breath and plot his next move. Daily PT may have kept him in decent shape, but it was no substitute for the decade or so that had passed since he'd last done something like this.

His rifle was with Sugar and Abul up in the rocks; the only gun he had with him was his Beretta sidearm. He'd never been a particularly good shot with a pistol, and at this range the weapon was practically useless. His only option was to circle back to Sugar and Abul around the sheltered side of the hill. The only way to get there, however, was to leave the outcropping and run across an exposed rise for about thirty yards.

The distance didn't seem like all that much until one of the machine gunners spotted him and bullets began cascading around the rocks. By that time Boston was about halfway to cover and committed to moving forward. He pushed up like a sprinter, head low, legs pumping. As he reached the rocks again, he threw his arms out, diving head first into the small depression, curling his body into a ball as the fusillade intensified.

He didn't just taste dirt in his mouth. He tasted the metal

scent of the air, roiled by the passing bullets, the fury of the battle permeating everything.

On the other side of the fence, the Ethiopians crouched in a holding pattern, baffled and confused by what was going on. From their point of view, it seemed as if the bus and the trucks were part of the same unit, probably a rebel group trying to crash the border as they fled Sudanese army regulars. They concluded that the force in the hills was an advance group of regulars, assigned to ambush the rebels and hold them back until the main unit arrived.

While they were under orders not to let anyone cross, they were more than happy to let the Sudanese battle among themselves; they liked neither side. The Ethiopian commander formed a defensive cordon in front of the bus, then moved the bulk of his army behind it. The equivalent of a platoon was left to watch the refugees back near the gate; they could be dealt with later.

The mercenaries had been reinforced by another troop trained by Hienckel, which had come down from Port Sudan. Shortchanged by their employer—a trucking company hired and protected by the Sudanese—they saw their brothers' cause of revenge as holy, and had vowed to assist them before the entire group moved on to Khartoum and a job waiting there. Their courage—as well as their anger—had been enhanced by a homemade alcoholic berry drink that was nearly 180 proof. Though terrible tasting, the liquid was said to convey nearly magical powers on anyone who drank it, making them impervious to bullets. Most of the mercenaries didn't believe this, but after a few drinks it didn't really matter.

With her machine gun position caught in two fields of interlocking fire, Sugar slid down the hill a few feet to her rifle and grenade launcher. Picking it up, she packed a grenade in the launcher, then rolled onto her back and lobbed the fat pellet toward the second truck. Unaimed, the grenade flew too far right, exploding harmlessly thirty yards away from it. But the explosion drew the mercenaries' attention; the ones who had been firing at Boston changed their aim, thinking the grenade had come from the fence area. While Boston scrambled up the hill, they concentrated their anger on the smoldering bus. Their bullets whizzed toward the Ethiopians, several of whom began returning fire, despite orders not to.

Boston scrambled up the rocky side of the hill. Abul crouched behind their gear, cradling a rifle against his chest and mumbling a prayer nonstop. His exhaustion paralyzed him; he looked wide-eyed at Boston as the American took the rifle from him.

"You all right?" Boston asked.

Abul didn't answer.

"We'll get outta here," Boston told him. "Don't worry about it."

An explosion against the side of the hill seemed to put the lie to Boston's promise, shaking the ground so severely he lost his balance. The mortar shell didn't hurt anyone, but it put a good dent in the rocks, pummeling them all with dirt and rock splinters.

Sugar loaded the grenade launcher again. This time she rose over the crest of the hill just far enough to get her bearings and fired point-blank at the nearest machine gun.

It was a hell of a shot: The grenade hit the gunner square in the chest. The explosion diced him into so many parts that only his Maker could have put him back together again.

But the gunfire hardly slowed down.

"Put a grenade into the trucks," yelled Boston as he scrambled up to her. "Blow them up so they can't use them for cover."

"You don't think I'm trying to do that?" Sugar yelled back.

"Just making sure we're on the same page."

She fired another round. This one went short, exploding harmlessly in the dirt forty yards from their nearest enemy.

Boston circled back to a cluster of rocks on the left, peeking out from behind them to try and sort the battle out. The mercenaries had concentrated into two groups, one clustered near the four trucks by the road, the other to the right around the battered vehicles, spread out between them and a dried gulley that ran down from the hill.

Meanwhile, the Ethiopians had increased their fire. If they kept it up, the mercenaries would have to retreat pell-mell, or try to take the hill so they had some sort of cover.

The north side of the hill wasn't the easiest to defend, but Boston believed they could hold the mercs off as long as they had ammunition. The western side gave no cover, but to get there the mercenaries would have to backtrack quite a bit.

Unless the ball of dust appearing on the horizon was being raised by their reinforcements.

Cursing, Boston scrambled back to the gear, grabbing a set of binoculars. He took a few grenades as well and ran back to the outcropping. The dust had grown somewhat. He focused the glasses and saw that there were a half-dozen pickups in front of it.

Boston thought the trucks held more mercenaries. In fact they were a Sudanese militia responding to monitored radio reports. The commander who paid them promised a two dollar bonus per rebel killed, but generally didn't ask for much proof of allegiance once the dead man's ear was presented.

Women's ears were worth only a dollar. Since there was generally no way to tell what their owner's gender had been, the ears presented were almost always male.

"More company on the way," Boston told Sugar.

"We're going to run out of ammo soon."

"Yeah. We need the Ethiopians to fight harder."

"We don't want them too aggressive," she said. "They may just come for us, too."

"I'll take some grenades and hit the reinforcements from the west," said Boston. "I'll take them out before they can get close."

"I don't think we should split up. When's that Osprey coming?"

"Soon," said Boston. Optimistically, he thought it was at least twenty minutes away—and more realistically maybe an hour. "But we can't afford to wait for it."

"All right," said Sugar. They didn't really have much choice.

"Put the radio on. Stay in touch," said Boston, grabbing some grenades.

THE SMOKE FROM THE BUS LINGERED ON THE HORIZON, A black snake curled around a pulverized victim. Breanna told the computer to head directly for the smoke. Then she dialed Boston's sat phone.

Boston didn't answer. The phone had fallen from his pocket when he jumped from the bus. He hadn't even realized yet that he'd lost it.

HEAVY GROUND FIRE AHEAD, warned the computer.

"Circle east," said Breanna. "Bring altitude to two thousand feet."

ALTITUDE NO LOWER THAN 15,000 FEET RECOMMENDED.

At 5,000 feet, the Osprey was an easy target for a shoulder-launched missile. It had several defensive systems—flares and a laser detonator, as well as a design that minimized the heat signature of the engines. Still, like all aircraft, it was vulnerable, a fact the computer had been programmed to dislike.

"I realize that," Breanna said, though she knew the computer wouldn't respond. She wanted to grab the yoke and take direct control, but knew the computer could do a much better job than she could, especially at low altitude.

There was a column of trucks on the road to her right as she approached, and two knots of soldiers firing guns in the direction of the border and the hill. Then there were the troops on the Ethiopian side. But where was Boston?

BOSTON HEARD THE OSPREY APPROACHING IN THE DISTANCE as he ran to take his position on the road. He reached for his phone, then realized he didn't have it.

His only alternative was to use his radio to broadcast a message on the international rescue frequency. The problem was, anyone with a radio could hear him, including both the mercenaries and the Ethiopians.

"Whiplash ground unit to approaching Osprey. Can you hear me?" he asked.

The Osprey didn't respond.

"Osprey, this is Boston. You there?"

"Roger, Whiplash, we're reading you," answered Breanna. "Where's your sat phone?"

"Lost it. We're under fire. Can you take out those trucks?"

"Negative. Set a rendezvous point."

"South of the hill," said Boston. "Just in its shadow. We can get there in zero-three."

"Osprey One is inbound," said Breanna.

"Sugar, the Osprey is three minutes away," Boston said, switching over to the team channel. "We're going to meet them down at the base of the hill. Can you get there?"

"I thought you'd never ask."

"Don't forget Abul."

"I won't forget, don't worry."

"Leave anything you can't carry easily."

Sugar rolled up out of her hiding spot and fired one last grenade at the mercenaries. Then she scooted toward the pile of their boxes and rucksacks. Hidden among the gear were explosive charges she'd set earlier; she'd blow them by remote control.

Abul was crouching where Boston had left him earlier, rifle in hand.

"Help me with McGowan," Sugar told him. "The Osprey's going to pick us up."

"The helicopter?"

"It's like a helicopter."

"Where?"

"At the base of the hill."

The words were no sooner out of her mouth than Abul

charged down the hill like a madman. Sugar yelled after him, but it was no use; he didn't hear her and wouldn't have stopped if he did.

McGowan was heavy, his body stiff and bloating. Bent low under its weight, Sugar began treading her way down the hill, sliding as she went. She was only halfway down when the Osprey appeared above her, its tilt rotors full overhead, helicopter style. The wash threw dust and grit in her face. She lost her balance and fell on her back, McGowan's body bag on top of her. They rolled together down the hill, dirt swirling around them.

Sugar's nose and throat clogged with the sand as she slid into a crevice between two rocks. McGowan fell on top of her. The world closed in. She coughed, having trouble breathing. Two mortar shells shook the hill, crashing more rocks around her.

Forty yards away, Abul froze, watching as the black Osprey settled down. It looked more like a dragon than a helicopter, an angry beast with two hammerlike arms ready to smash any creature in its way.

The rear hatch slapped to the ground. Breanna ran from the back of the aircraft, sprinting toward him.

"Get aboard!" she shouted. "Get in there. Where are the others?"

Abul looked at her as if she were an alien.

"The others?" she demanded.

He held out his hands and said in Arabic that he didn't understand what she was saying.

"Get in the aircraft," she told him.

Something moved in the rocks about forty feet from the Osprey. Breanna began running to it. There was a large gray-green bag there—a body bag.

It was moving.

God, she thought, did they put McGowan inside when he was still alive?

She ran faster. The bag slumped. Breanna reached it and started to pull upward. She heard a moan.

"I'll get you out," she said, but something wasn't right. The body was stiff and heavy, not moving. She pulled it up, dragged it to the side, then saw Sugar beneath it.

"Come on, come on!" Breanna yelled.

She reached down, grabbed Sugar's shirt and pulled. But Sugar was too heavy and her grip too loose; she slipped and fell back.

Sugar's right leg had wedged into the rocks. She pounded with her hands and elbow and pushed, but that only moved the rocks tighter around her.

Another mortar shell hit the hill behind them, shaking the ground with a ferocious jolt.

"We have to get the rocks first," yelled Breanna. She grabbed the biggest she thought she could handle and found it was too much. She took a smaller one and barely got it out of the way.

"My leg," cried Sugar, suddenly feeling the pain.

"Push, push!" yelled Boston, huffing and out of breath as he ran over. He grabbed two rocks and threw them away.

"Help me with this big one," said Breanna.

Together they rolled it to the side. Boston leaned down, wrapped his upper body around Sugar and hauled her up.

"Out, let's go, let's go!" he yelled.

Breanna turned, then remembered the body bag. She grabbed it but couldn't lift it over her head. She had to drag it toward the Osprey.

"Blow our gear," Sugar told Boston. She thought she was shouting, but the dust had strangled her voice, and Boston didn't understand what she was saying. He got her into the Osprey, then went back and helped Breanna with McGowan. They had to drag it the last ten feet, both of them spent.

Realizing the position was no longer being held, the mercenaries charged up the hill, firing as they went. Two more mortar shells hit near the peak. For a few seconds the ground felt as if it were made of water.

Breanna punched the door panel to close the ramp, then scrambled forward.

"Emergency takeoff," she yelled to the Osprey's computer as she reached the flight deck. "Authorization Stockard. Go! *Go!*"

The aircraft launched. As it rose, a hail of bullets began spraying from the hill. The aircraft stayed on course, ignoring bullets and everything else once placed in emergency takeoff mode.

They were flying through a hail of tracers.

Breanna scrambled into the pilot's seat. She grabbed the controls.

"Emergency override. Authorization Stockard!"

The aircraft bucked sharply to the side as she ducked away from the gunfire. She held it in the air, mostly by instinct, climbing away over the Ethiopian lines.

BREANNA'S HEART POUNDED IN HER THROAT.

"Computer control. Authorization Stockard. Orbit here at three thousand feet. No, five thousand feet. Climb to five thousand feet and orbit."

The computer flashed the command in the center display. Breanna got up and went into the back.

Boston was cleaning Sugar's leg, which had bruised and been cut by the rocks. One of her ribs felt broken. Her right elbow and wrist were sprained.

"You're the bus driver?" Breanna asked Abul.

He stared at her, then nodded.

"I'm sorry I yelled at you. My name is Breanna Stockard."

It took him a second to respond. "Amin Abul."

"We didn't blow up the gear," mumbled Sugar.

"What are you saying?" Breanna asked, dropping to her knee next to Sugar.

"The gear," said Boston. "She didn't get a chance to blow it."

"The detonator is in my pocket," managed Sugar.

Boston slipped his hand in—delicately—and retrieved it. The device was essentially a short-range radio. Once the proper code was punched in, it would blow the charges. But they had to be within a half mile for it work: Nothing happened when Boston pushed it.

"We'll go back," said Breanna.

60

North of Tehran

THE PERIMETER OF THE FIELDS BEHIND THE BUILDING WHERE Tarid and Aberhadji had met was surrounded by what appeared at first glance to be a dilapidated wire fence. With posts poked down in places, and strands bent and twisted in others, it looked like the forgotten remnants of the farm's old boundaries, a doomed attempt to keep out ruin as much as animals and other trespassers.

But looks were not everything. Examining the series of satellite images taken of the area, Danny realized the wire was part of a perimeter surveillance system. Video cameras were placed near or on a dozen posts. Small transformers indicated the wire was powered. He suspected that it was a tripwire as well, rigged to sound an alarm if it was moved more than a very minimal amount. Motion sensors, with floodlights and video cameras, were stationed close to the building. More subtly, there were several spots on the property that looked as if they could be used as defensive positions in case of an attack.

MY-PID analyzed the security system and showed several vulnerabilities, giving Danny a crooked but easy-to-follow path to the rear of the building. The only difficulty would be getting over the fence without touching it—a problem solved by stopping at a Tehran hardware store just before it closed.

The only stepladder the store had was an eight-foot aluminum model. Sturdy enough inside a building for light maintaining or maintenance, the legs were somewhat rickety on the uneven terrain where Danny wanted to cross the fence.

"Don't hit the wire," he hissed at Hera as she helped him get it into position. "We don't know how sensitive it is."

"I'm not doing it on purpose. The damn thing keeps shifting."

The ground where she was standing was wet, and the leg kept sagging. She pulled it to one side, finally finding a sturdy spot.

Danny jiggled the ladder back and forth, testing how wobbly it was.

Very. No way it was going to hold him.

"Get some rocks and slip them under the right leg," he told Hera. "I'll hold it."

The rocks made it a little sturdier, but not much.

"Are there any ground units in the rear of the building?" Danny asked the Voice. They had launched an Owl UAV before approaching the fence.

"Negative. Path remains clear."

As far as they could tell, there was only one security person on duty, and he was down in a command post near the main building. Aberhadji had left the building some hours before nightfall.

"You climb over the ladder while I hold it," Danny told Hera. "Then you hold it while I come over behind you."

Hera grabbed her rucksack and rifle, cinched them against her chest, and squeezed past Danny and up the rungs. The sun had just set, and the field where they were was cast in deep shadow. This made it hard to judge where the ground was as she descended, and when she stepped off the last rail, she slipped and fell, pushing her weight against the ladder.

Taken by surprise, Danny barely kept it from hitting the fence.

"God, be careful," he barked.

"I'm sorry. The damn ground is pure mud."

"Ready?" Danny asked.

"Ready."

Danny tested his weight on the first step, then the second. The ladder jiggled to the left but remained upright. He climbed up two more steps, then swung his leg around, barely avoiding the wire below.

"That was harder than it should have been," he said as he reached the ground. "Help me get the ladder up."

Hera moved to the side. They lifted it up carefully, Danny taking it up gingerly to clear the wire. He folded it and set it down near the fence.

Then he grabbed Hera as she started across the field.

"I didn't think you had anything to do with McGowan's death," he told her. "Your attitude has been bad. You've been riding everyone."

"I'm sorry," she said, her tone anything but.

"All right."

"I feel like you're watching every step I make, every move. Like I have to prove myself."

"We all have to prove ourselves, every single day," said Danny. He reached into his ruck for the night goggles, not wanting to stop for them later.

"You don't. Your medal says it all."

"That medal doesn't mean crap here," he told her. "Come on. It ought be easier from here, at least until we get to the wall."

61

Eastern Sudan, near the border with Ethiopia

BREANNA HADN'T FORGOTTEN ABOUT THE REFUGEES, BUT they were pushed far to the periphery of her consciousness as she concentrated on rescuing her people. As she headed back toward the hill to blow up their gear, she saw them in their makeshift camp, nearly all of them standing and straining to get a view of the black aircraft hurtling through the nearby sky.

The firing had died down. The mercenaries were now on the hill, caught between the Ethiopians and the Sudanese regulars in the pickups, who'd stopped near the road.

The ready light lit on the detonator. Breanna was in range to blow up their gear.

She was about to push the button when she spotted a black speck in the sky to the north. It was the other Osprey, belatedly coming to back her up.

Breanna clicked on the radio. "Osprey Two, this is Osprey One. Can you read me?"

"Hey, roger that, Colonel Stockard," replied Greasy Hands. His voice shook with adrenaline and nerves. "I'm here."

"Good. Take the aircraft over the hill and orbit around the refugee camp."

"I don't have it in view yet."

"You will. It's south of us. You have weapons?"

"Oh, roger that. We are loaded for bear."

"Copy. Hang tight."

"Osprey Two."

Breanna directed the computer to fly the aircraft near the camp and land. Then she got up and went into the rear of the aircraft.

"Boston, Sugar, Abul—we're going to land by the refugee camp."

"We're landing?" said Sugar.

"We'll evac the refugees to a UN camp. There are a dozen in northern Sudan." Breanna looked at Abul. "Right, Mr. Abul?"

Abul felt as if he were walking down a long tunnel, coming back from a dream, approaching reality.

"There are refugee camps in the north run by the UN," Breanna said to him. "We can take these people there."

"Yes," said Abul.

"Will you help me? I don't speak Arabic."

"Yes," said Abul, still distant. "Yes, I will," he added more forcefully. "Yes."

"Good. Get ready."

ABOARD OSPREY TWO, GREASY HANDS WAS HAVING THE time of his life.

Not that he wanted to do the pilot thing full-time. But sitting back and giving the computer orders, that he could live with.

As long as he didn't have to use the weapons. Not that he couldn't figure them out—he'd tested them many times— but the idea of using them against real people was a whole different kettle of fish, or ball of wax, or waxed kettle of fishballs, as his grandpa used to joke.

But hell, if he *had* to . . .

BREANNA ESTIMATED THAT THERE WERE JUST OVER SEVenty refugees: very close to the payload capacity of the Ospreys with their uprated engines. But even if it took two trips, getting them away from the border to a safe place would be worth it.

She stood at the back of the aircraft, holding the handle at the ramp as it settled onto the desert floor. She punched the ramp button and looked back at Boston. He nodded, though in truth he had started to doubt this was a good idea.

"Come on, Mr. Abul," Breanna said, tugging at the bus driver's shirt. "Come on."

They walked down the ramp together. The sun had just set; it would be dark inside a half hour.

A small knot of refugees stared at the front of the aircraft as they came around. One or two thought they were about to be shot. The others were simply in awe at the strange looking plane that was able to land vertically.

"We're here to take you to a camp," Breanna said. "We're going to help you."

The Osprey's engines were still rotating, and it was hard for Abul to hear her, let alone for any of the crowd. Breanna pulled Abul with her away from the aircraft. More refugees were coming forward. Boston had his rifle with him, pointing it at the ground, trying not to spook them.

More intimidating was the other Osprey circling above, its cannon hanging down from its chin.

"We're here to take you to camp," said Breanna again. "Tell them, Abul."

Abul hesitated. These were not his people. None of them were Muslim, and he didn't recognize their accent when a few asked him what he was doing. But the Americans had galvanized him. He was amazed that they would come back, that they would want to come back, after having so narrowly escaped death. They were risking their lives to save people they didn't know. And Allah clearly approved, because he had rescued them and stopped the shooting nearby.

He was part of a noble project. Goodwill flooded into him. He felt stronger than he had ever felt. The things he had lost—his bus mostly—were no longer important.

And so when the elders of the group turned their backs when he told them they could go to the camp, he felt crushed.

"What's the matter?" asked Breanna as they started moving away.

"They don't want to go."

"Why? Are they afraid of the aircraft?"

"No. They think the borders are artificial. And the camps, they say, are hell."

"That fence is real," said Boston. "Tell them that."

"I've tried explaining," said Abul. "They don't want to go to the UN camp."

"They'll be safe there," said Breanna.

"They could have gone there in the first place," said Abul. "They didn't. They want to cross over the border, but if they can't, they would rather stay here. This is tribal land. Here, there, on both sides of the fence. They say it goes back many hundreds of years. They'll stay right on this spot if necessary."

"How long?"

"Until the dead walk. That's how they put it."

Abul shook his head. He thought they were crazy, but he understood their doubts about the refugee camp. As well-intentioned as the camps might be, none had good reputations.

"Look, it's getting dark," said Boston. "We can't stay here too much longer. And the Ethiopians over there are eventually going to move. Or the mercenaries. Tell these people this is their last chance."

"Try again, Mr. Abul," said Breanna. "Make them see logic."

"It's not a matter of logic," said Abul, but he tried again. This time the elders spoke directly to Breanna. Their words were in Arabic, but the gist of what they were saying was clear enough. They didn't and wouldn't go.

"If you stay here," said Breanna, "you may be killed. On purpose or by accident. You can't get any water or shelter—what will you do in the rainy season?"

They were unmoved. She grabbed Abul's arm.

"Make them understand," she pleaded. "They can't stay."

"Tell them they were going to be killed by the Ethiopian army," said Boston.

"I did."

Abul tried once more, but by now no one was listening to his hoarse voice.

"But we want to help them," said Breanna. "We want to help."

"We can't do any more, Ms. Stockard," said Boston. "We better get out of here."

An alert tone sounded on Breanna's radio, a sharp whistle followed by Greasy Hands's gravelly voice.

"Bree, there's something serious going on with the radar. What's your status?"

"How serious, Chief?"

"It's picking up a lot of aircraft at low level. Several warnings. Something big is happening. They're coming almost right at us."

Breanna stared at the refugees, trying to think of something to say to them. But there was nothing that she hadn't already said. Reluctantly, she went back to the Osprey.

62

North of Tehran

IT WAS COMPLETELY DARK BY THE TIME DANNY AND HERA reached the stone wall twenty yards behind the building. They stopped there, making sure they understood the security system before continuing.

Whoever designed the system had counted on an intruder not being able to get past the substantial network of detectors that ran up the driveway. But that also left a hole they could exploit.

The rear of the building was protected by motion detectors, as well as video cameras posted on the back wall. There was no motion detector on the side or the front of the building, however, and the only video camera on that side of the property covered the front door.

The video from the bug on Tarid's coat showed that the windows were protected by a simple contact alarm system similar to those used in many homes and businesses in the States. Even Danny could defeat it.

"We have to make a zigzag across the courtyard to the

window," Danny told Hera, drawing it on his palm with his finger. "Just follow me."

"Go."

He started toward the stone wall. The Voice told him when to jump it.

Hera followed through the field as Danny crisscrossed toward the side of the building, trying to go step by step in his path. She was resigned to the fact that this was going to be her last mission with Whiplash, that Danny would dump her when it was over. She'd have to rebuild her career.

She was glad he'd taken her along tonight. It wasn't so she could redeem herself—she knew it was because she spoke Farsi. But going gave her something to concentrate on. It was better than sitting with Flash or Nuri, who were watching Tarid at the hotel. There would have been too much time to brood, about McGowan, about everything.

Maybe she had been a bitch. It seemed like such a sexist label, something a man would put on a woman for things a guy would never be called on. But maybe, she conceded, maybe there was a tiny bit of truth in it.

Maybe it would have been more accurate to say she was conceited and thought she had a better way to do things.

The focus now was on the mission, not her. She continued through the field, moving with Danny to the building.

Danny had the current scanner out. "Only the wires," he said, easing to the side.

Hera slipped a suction cup on the glass, focusing on the task. She cut around it quickly, concentrating on making the perfect scribe on the first pass with the cutter. Then she focused on pulling it away, then on jumping the wires.

"We're good," she said, pushing up the window.

They took a good look around the inside before going in, making sure there were no motion detectors or other devices nearby.

Danny climbed in first, entering a large storeroom, behind the one where the meeting had taken place. Most of the room was empty; there were large crates at the far wall. Danny turned around slowly, examining the walls. They were painted and smooth, making it more difficult to find a place to put the bugs where they wouldn't be seen.

Taking out a stick of gum, he wadded it into his mouth as he looked for a hiding place. He settled on the molding beneath the window. Once it was in place, he pulled off his rucksack and removed the pane of glass he'd brought to replace the small panel they'd cut through.

Hera walked over to the boxes and took out a radiation detector—a miniaturized Geiger counter sensitive enough to pick up a shielded weapon at a meter's range. The screen lit before she could even get it calibrated.

"Bingo," she said.

Danny came over and looked.

"This is it," she said. "There's uranium in those boxes. They may be all bombs."

He looked at the readings, then the crates.

"I don't know if any of these are warheads," he told her. "There's definitely material here, but it may be the residue from refining."

"Let's take them apart and find out."

Danny bent down and examined them. They varied in size from about six by three feet to ten by eight.

"We don't know how long Aberhadji's going to be gone," he said. "Let's tag them, get out the chemical sniffer, check for chemicals—I'll get the window ready in case we have to leave. Then we'll see if we can get these open without being detected."

"Can't we just blow them up?"

Danny thought they might be able to rig something, but the explosion would only damage the warhead mechanism; the bomb itself could be salvaged. They'd have to take the warhead—or warheads—to permanently end the threat.

"Let's take this one step at a time," he told her. "Tag them while I get the window ready."

There were two dozen crates; Hera only had enough tracking bugs for six. She bugged the box that had the strongest radiation signal, sticking the tiny device between the slats at the very bottom. Then she tagged two boxes next to it, unsure whether she was picking up radiation from them or the larger crate. She placed the other three tags arbitrarily on more boxes, each a different size and shape.

When she was done, she took out the chemical sniffer and began examining the area around the crates.

The device was called a sniffer because it took air samples and then analyzed the contents. The sensitivity varied according to chemical, but certain substances—such as anthrax—could be detected in extremely minute amounts. About the size of a palm-corder, the device required a bit of patience and a steady hand, but its small size and power were light-years ahead of the devices used at airports and ports to detect bomb materials and other dangers.

There were traces of explosives. No biological agents. No chemicals used in warfare.

On the other side of the room, Danny chipped out the last of the glass and carefully put the new pane in place so no one would suspect they had broken in.

Or rather, he tried to —it didn't fit exactly. The window was slightly smaller than the standard size, and he had to cut the pane they'd brought with them to fit. He got down on his hands and knees and etched the edge of the panel freehand, sliding the glass cutter gingerly so he didn't break the glass. Twice he thought he was done, only to find he was still off by a few fractions of an inch. Finally he got the glass into place, rolling putty around it to keep it there.

Now came the hardest part— matching the color of the old putty. It had started out pure white, then faded with age. Danny worked with two jars of stain to get the right shade. He took off his goggles and used a flashlight, experimenting with the shade. It took several minutes before he found a reasonably close shade.

"What'd you find?" he asked Hera.

"Just explosives." She explained how she had arranged the bugs. "Which crate do we start with?"

"I don't know. Go fix the window with the jumper so we can get out easily while I take a look."

"Are we going to glow when we leave?" she asked, only half joking.

"Yeah. We won't need our night goggles." Danny smiled. "No, it's not really that much. Fix the window."

The amount of radiation emitted by a bomb before it exploded was minute; it posed no danger to the people handling the weapon. The amount they detected here was extremely small—the Iranians had every incentive to be very careful handling and preserving the material.

Danny spotted a nail in the wall and decided to plant a bug there before trying to open the crates. He climbed up on one of the boxes and stuck a bug just above it. He was just getting down when the Voice sounded an alert in his ear.

"Vehicle approaching. Similar in size and shape to vehicle observed on property earlier in the day."

Aberhadji had returned.

63

Eastern Sudan

BY THE TIME BREANNA GOT BACK TO THE OSPREY, THE radar had identified twenty-four individual planes, all flying on a path a few miles north of them. Most had already passed; the radar showed them gaining altitude quickly.

She took one look at their flight patterns and the plane types and knew two things instantly: They were on a bombing mission, aiming at a target in Sudan. And they were Israeli.

She took out the secure sat phone and called Reid immediately.

"Jonathon, I think the Israelis know about the Iranian plant in Sudan," she told him. "They're on their way to blow it up."

"What?" said Reid.

"They're at low altitude, flying at high speed not too far from here. The radar in one of the Ospreys picked them up."

"Stand by."

He came back a few moments later to tell her that the bugs Nuri had placed in the complex had just gone off line due to explosions.

"I'm going to have to get back to you," said Reid. "This hasn't hit the network yet."

"Go," said Breanna. "I have everyone. We're en route back to Dire Dawa."

There was one more thing they had to do before leaving—blow up their gear.

Breanna had the Osprey circle over the hill. The mercenaries were in the rocks, sitting uneasily between the Ethiopians and the Sudanese.

"I want you to tell them to get away from the boxes," she told Abul, going into the rear of the aircraft. "I want you to warn them that they're going to be blown up."

"We're going to land again?" said Boston.

"No. We're equipped with a PA system for crowd situations. We'll use the loudspeaker."

Abul followed her into the cockpit. He was shocked when he saw the empty seats.

"Who's flying the plane?" he asked.

"It flies itself. Tell them."

Breanna sat in the pilot's seat and handed him a headset, channeling the mike into the PA. Abul handled it awkwardly, then began ordering the mercenaries to leave the hill.

They made no sign of complying.

"The hill is about to be exploded," he said. "You must leave for your own safety."

They responded by firing into the air at the Osprey.

"Evasive maneuvers!" Breanna told the computer.

The Osprey swung hard to the right, then rose quickly. Out the side window she saw the tracers flying toward them.

"Screw this," she said, and detonated the gear.

The gunfire stopped.

"Computer, begin return flight to Dire Dawa as programmed," she said. "Let's get the hell out of here."

64

North of Tehran

"WE HAVE TO GET OUT *NOW*," DANNY TOLD HERA, MOVING quickly to the door separating the warehouse from the office where Tarid and Aberhadji had met. He wanted to bug it.

"The crates."

"Never mind them. Aberhadji's car is coming up the road."

Danny stopped short. The door was protected by a contact alarm system. He dropped to his stomach. He wanted to slip one of the bugs underneath the door, but the space was blocked by rubber weather-stripping that brushed along the metal threshold. Instead, he took a jumper and defeated the contact alarm, easing the door open just wide enough to put the bug on the edge of the kick plate.

The bug slipped as he started to close the door. He pushed it higher and squeezed the tiny, round, plastic disc hard against the aluminum.

Meanwhile, the Voice was giving him a running commentary on Aberhadji's progress, narrating practically every step: The car rounded the hairpin, the car pulled past the video checkpoint, the car approached the front of the building. A figure got out. MY-PID analyzed the figure's gait as it walked, and found a correlation with Aberhadji, concluding with "eighty percent probability" that it was him.

By the time Aberhadji unlocked the front door of the building, Danny was stepping through the window. Hera pulled the window down behind him, then tugged the jumper wire out, resetting the alarm.

ONCE INSIDE, ABERHADJI TOOK A MOMENT TO LET HIS EYES adjust to the light. Everything was slightly blurry; years of staring at motor vehicle forms had ruined his eyesight.

The stockpiled materials and the tools would be dispersed and hidden in several places around the country. For the most part, the hiding places were in buildings and mines well off the beaten track, obscure places where no one would think of looking, least of all a foreign intelligence service.

Aberhadji had decided, however, that the warhead would have to be taken someplace where it could be guarded—and where he could get to it easily if necessary. He had arranged for it to be kept at a small base about thirty miles away, controlled by the Guard and commanded by a man who had been a friend since his youth. The base was hardly secret, and Aberhadji worried that the government or regular army would sooner or later find out about the weapon. But it could be protected there from outside agents. And it was two miles from the airstrip at Tajevil, where the No-Dong A and its launching systems were stored.

The nuclear warhead was useless without a way to deliver it. For all the speculation in the West about how a cargo container or some other seemingly innocuous transport might be used, in the end the most reliable and practical way of launching a nuclear strike was by missile. Aberhadji had acquired the No-Dong A very early in his project. It was one of several delivered by North Korea during the late 1990s as part of the deal that helped Iran develop its nuclear capabilities. The No-Dong As had been studied and used as the basis for Iran's own family of rockets.

This missile had malfunctioned on the test bed, then

stored and forgotten—by all except one of the engineers Aberhadji recruited for his program when the disarmament talks began. It was refurbished and, while its range was limited compared to the weapons Iran subsequently developed, it was still quite adequate to deliver the warhead up to two thousand miles away—more than enough to hit Israel, for example.

Which, Aberhadji thought, he might someday decide to do.

First he had to make sure his project survived. Dispersing the material was only the first step; he would have to reevaluate everything he had done, examine where things had gone wrong. There was also the council to deal with—clearly his position within it needed to be considered. But he could only deal with one part of the crisis at a time.

Eyes focused, Aberhadji reached into his pocket for his phone. Before he could dial, however, it began to ring.

Aberhadji did not recognize the number, but the exchange indicated the call was coming from a government building. He answered immediately.

"Two dozen Israeli aircraft are reported to have flown into eastern Sudan," said the caller in a low voice. He was an intelligence analyst, a friend to Aberhadji, though not on his payroll. "Some sort of bombing raid. They flew over Egypt and Ethiopia."

"What was their target?"

"The service is still working on it."

"Call me when you know more," said Aberhadji, though he'd already guessed where the bombers were going.

HERA FOLLOWED DANNY TO THE STONE WALL BEHIND THE building, jumping over and hitting the dirt.

Danny waited for her to catch her breath, then began retracing their steps back through the field to the edge of the woods, not stopping until they reached the stepladder.

"Let me get my bearings," he told her. "Hold on just a minute."

*   *   *

ABERHADJI FELT THE PICKAX STAB HIS TEMPLES AGAIN, cleaving his head in two. The pain had never been this intense—it dropped him to the floor. There was complete agony for a minute, for two full minutes; everything was pain as all other sensations bleached away from him. He couldn't see; he didn't know how to see. He struggled to breathe.

Gradually he became aware of the room. The migraine lessened somewhat, the blades retracting a few inches. The room, invisible to him at the height of the attack, shaded from black to a dark brown, then lightened slowly to sepia.

The pain strangled the back of his neck, paralyzed his shoulders. He tried pushing himself to get up but could not.

Aberhadji had never believed the headaches were a sign or a curse from Allah; he had always accepted them as part of his self, a flaw in his biology, not his spirit. His view did not change now. His faith was unshaken, not just in God, but in his view of the universe, of the way things worked, and must work.

But the headache nonetheless revealed one great truth to him: He would never survive another attack. Even if the next was merely as bad as this one —if they continued to increase exponentially, as they had over these past weeks, he simply could not survive.

Logically, then, it was time to initiate the plan. Israel had just bombed his plant—there could be no other place where their jets would go in Sudan.

Very possibly more fighters were on their way here.

The Zionists must be destroyed, and the traitor president killed.

This was not so much a decision as a realization, and it eased Aberhadji's pain substantially. Though his head continued to pound, he was able to stand up. Only then did he see that two men were standing at the door.

One was a truck driver, the other a Revolutionary Guard officer he had called to help supervise the truck loading.

"I slipped, but I am all right," he told them.

They would proceed as planned, except that he would go with the warhead, and divert it at the last minute.

The brothers would be needed to mount it onto the missile and prepare the rocket, and he would have to stay with them to supervise, as well as code the warhead at the final preparation. This meant neither they nor he could bring the bomb to the man who would plant it aboard the plane.

Who did he trust to do that job?

No one.

Tarid?

But perhaps Tarid had been the one to give away the Sudan location to the Israelis.

No, if he had done that, he never would have come back to Iran.

Not purposely. Perhaps he had made a slip.

If he had done so inadvertently, while still a sin, it was at least less mortal. And he could make up for it by placing the bomb in the plane.

"Are you all right, Imam?" asked the Guard member.

"I needed a moment to gather my thoughts. The articles must be transported. Load them into the separate trucks. I will give each driver specific instructions once you are ready to leave. In the meantime, I must make a phone call in private." He reached into his pocket and took out the key to the large warehouse-style door. "Go to the side and begin your work."

"THEY'RE TRANSPORTING THE CRATES," DANNY TOLD HERA as the Voice translated what Aberhadji told the men inside. "He got a phone call. They must realize we're on to them."

Danny looked at the MY-PID screen. There were a dozen trucks gathered in the front lot. Each crate had to be going to a different location. They'd lose track of half of them.

He debated whether to try attacking. Besides the drivers, there were another twenty men, all with visible weapons, according to the Voice.

There was no way.

And even if the odds were better, what would the next step be? Blow up whatever was in the crates? If it was nuclear material, it would be spread all over.

Then what? Gather it and smuggle it out of Iran.

But if they failed, everything would be lost—the Iranians would find the bugs, realize they were being watched. The material—and the bombs, if there were any—would be lost again.

"How many soldiers are there?" asked Hera.

"Too many," said Danny, rising. "Come on. Let's get back to the van. We'll pick one of the trucks and follow it."

65

Washington, D.C.

PRESIDENT TODD HAD JUST FINISHED SHAKING HANDS WITH the National Chamber of Commerce delegation when David Greenwich, her chief of staff, strode into the Oval Office. His lips were pursed, a signal that a serious problem was at hand.

Still, she kept her expression neutral. Her guests had come to press her on changes in the proposed universal health care bill. Not yet approved by Congress, it was the subject of intense lobbying. Everyone, it seemed, was for it—as long as it could be changed.

"The Israelis have just struck one of the sites Whiplash was looking at," whispered Greenwich in her ear. "In the Sudan."

"Thank you, David. You're right. I guess I will have to take that call." The President rose. "I will just be a few minutes," she announced. "Relax for a moment—Peg will see to some coffee or tea."

Todd smiled at them, nodded as they rose, then went with the chief of staff to the cloak room next to the Oval Office.

Though called a cloakroom, as in many previous administrations it was used as a small getaway office by the President.

"What's going on?" she asked as soon as the door was closed.

"There's been an attack within the past fifteen minutes," said Greenwich. "About a dozen Israeli jets came over the border into Sudan. They attacked two places, one of which we were watching. We're still trying to round up information on the other."

"How do we know this?"

"Our people were coming over the border when the planes passed. In addition, we'd put bugs in and around one of the targets. The raid was extremely well-planned—the Israeli planes weren't detected at all. They must have flown right over Egypt, otherwise we could have picked them up. I'd guess they've been planning this for quite a while."

"They must have been the ones who assassinated the Jasmine agent. This is part of the same operation."

The chief of staff hadn't made the connection yet. "Yes," he said, nodding. As always, Greenwich was impressed not so much by his boss's intelligence as by her ability to dive so deeply into the issue quickly.

"They should have told us," he said. "If we're allies."

"That's not the issue at the moment, David." Most likely, the Israelis had learned their lesson during the previous administration, when the U.S. had all but vetoed an operation against Iran—and then blabbed about it a few months later. "Find out where Dr. Bacon is. I want to talk with him in twenty minutes. In person would be better than over the phone. Have Herman available as well. And Mr. Reid. I assume our friend Ms. Stockard is still away."

"She's the one who spotted the planes," said Greenwich.

66

Tehran

TARID SPENT A MISERABLE AFTERNOON AND EVENING IN Tehran. While initially relieved that Bani Aberhadji did not suspect him of skimming, the fact that his leader felt the operation had been compromised was nearly as bad. While Tarid didn't want to believe it could be true, the more he thought about it, the more he realized that everything that had happened since he met the arms dealer named Kirk could have been arranged to increase his confidence in him.

Bani Aberhadji had checked the man out himself, and directed him to meet him personally. But that fact was unlikely to persuade Aberhadji toward any sort of leniency if it turned out that Tarid had brought the CIA to Aberhadji's doorstep.

The hotel seemed particularly drab when he returned. Simin was out. The hotel owner was in a quiet, almost hostile mood. Tarid passed dinnertime in his room, lying on his bed, considering what he would do next. It occurred to him that he could run—flee not just Iran, but Africa as well. But there were few places he could go where Bani Aberhadji and the Guard could not reach if they wanted. No place was safe, short of Israel, and the idea of spending the rest of his life amidst Zionists seemed worse than death. He kept telling himself that he could persevere, that he had been in worse spots. His morale would hold for a few minutes, then fade.

For a while he dozed. When he woke, it was dark and his stomach growled. He decided to go out and find some food.

Tarid had just pulled on his shoes when his sat phone rang.

His fingers froze in a cramp as he grabbed it, paralyzed by fear when he saw the number on the screen. It was Bani Aberhadji. The only reason he could be calling, Tarid thought, was to tell him to initiate the meeting with Kirk.

He was standing at the edge of a precipice he had to jump from, yet he was too scared to edge forward.

Finally, he hit the Receive button.

"This is Tarid."

"I need you to meet someone and make a delivery."

"I—" Tarid was so taken by surprise that he didn't know what to say. But there was no refusing Bani Aberhadji. "Yes," he managed finally. "Tell me where and when."

AFTER RENTING TWO CARS SO THEY WOULD HAVE TRANS-portation and a backup, Nuri and Flash spent the evening going from one restaurant to another, lingering as they watched the hotel where Tarid was sleeping. Nuri drank so much tea that his whole body vibrated with caffeine. It had no noticeable effect on Flash.

"It doesn't affect you at all?" asked Nuri.

"Not a bit. Coffee's the same way."

"You should leave your body to science."

Nuri had decided he would bug the hotel room the next time Tarid went out. While Bani Aberhadji was now a more interesting target, Tarid might yet reveal a few more useful tidbits, especially if he returned to Sudan. So Nuri had prepared another bug to attach to his suitcase.

They were sitting in the restaurant directly across the street from the restaurant when MY-PID flashed the news of the Israeli attack on the Sudan facility. Nuri was still digesting the implications when the bug picked up Bani Aberhadji's phone call to Tarid.

He put his hand to his ear, ducking his head to the table as he listened. From Tarid's side of the conversation, it sounded as if Aberhadji was telling him to arrange for the meeting with Danny, aka Kirk. But within moments the text of the entire conversation was available via an elint satellite that had been scanning for the signal from Tarid's satellite phone.

Something else was up. Though what it might be wasn't clear.

"We need our car," Nuri told Flash, rising and leaving some change for a tip.

They left the restaurant and walked down the block.

Tarid was going to be assassinated, Nuri thought.

If that was the case, it was a fantastic opportunity—if Tarid could be rescued just in the nick of time, Nuri reasoned, he would be grateful to his rescuers and have nothing to lose by cooperating with them. If he played the situation right, they would not only have a wealth of information about the Iranian weapons program, but statements and a witness who, in some form, could be used to implicate the Iranians in the wider world.

But arranging for Tarid's rescue was a difficult task, especially for two people working on the fly.

"We'll ride together," Nuri told Flash. "You drive. I need to figure something out. All right?"

"I'll try."

Nuri checked in with Danny as soon as they got into the vehicle. Danny and Hera were on their way to the van, planning to follow one of the trucks.

"Stay with Bani Aberhadji," Nuri told Danny. "He's the main target right now. They're scrambling because of the attack on the weapons plant. He may lead you to other parts of the network."

"If they uncrate what they've got, we'll never be able to find them," said Danny. "And we only marked half of the boxes. We don't even know what's in them. At least one was big enough for a warhead—"

"Don't worry about all that right now," said Nuri. "Just trust that we can find them again. Stick with Aberhadji."

Nuri suspected that Danny was thinking about striking the trucks. He was a military man, and thought like one. But it was too impractical; if they failed, they'd lose everything.

"Subject Tarid is exiting the hotel," said the Voice.

"Danny, I'll check back with you in a few minutes," Nuri said. "We're going to follow Tarid. We may end up picking him up if it looks like they're going to kill him."

"How?"

"That's a problem for the future."

67

Over northern Ethiopia

BREANNA REALIZED THE ISRAELI ATTACK ON THE SUDAN weapons material factory would complicate the operation in Iran. Even if the government wasn't responsible for the program there, the high-ranking people who were might make things difficult for foreigners, either as a smoke screen or simply for revenge. Iran had an ugly history on that score.

She immediately began working out the details for an evac mission. Fortunately, she had some of the key ingredients close at hand—a pair of Ospreys, and the rest of the Whiplash crew.

"The closer you can get us to the border, the easier it'll be," said Boston when she reviewed the situation with him using a map display on her console. "Easiest thing to do is let them come out the way they planned: They get into their speedboats and go out to sea. Then we have the Ospreys meet them and pick them up."

"But what if they can't get to the speedboats?" asked Breanna. "That's what I'm worried about. They can't get the speedboats and they can't get out through the airports, because they're shut down or being watched."

"Then you either send a new set of speedboats to make a pickup, or we have the Ospreys grab them. Another thing," Boston added, "would be to have them sneak over the border into northern Iraq. Trouble is, the Iraqis are kinda on guard there. The smuggling's not as bad as it is down south, but you'd still have patrols to dodge."

"We could work something out there with the government," said Breanna. "It'd be just a question of going through channels."

"I'll tell you right now, you want to avoid as many channels as possible where the Iraqis are concerned. The command structure's a sieve. Anything they know in Baghdad is known in Tehran inside an hour, as a general rule."

He was exaggerating, though not by much.

"We're going to land in Turkey and refuel in a few minutes," Breanna told him. "Tell me what sort of reinforcements you'd need for a rescue operation. I'll get them lined up."

"Hell, I'd take whatever we can get. Battalion of soldiers. Company of Rangers." Boston smiled. "Or a squad of Marines. Same difference."

68

Northern Iran

DANNY WATCHED THE SMALL SCREEN AS THREE MEN LEFT the warehouse. It was impossible to tell who was who on the small screen, but the Voice had no trouble identifying one of the men as Bani Aberhadji.

He got into the cab of one of the trucks with the two men. The truck did not contain one of the marked crates. In fact, the box it carried was rather small. The truck took up its spot at the rear of the convoy, following the other trucks as they headed down the narrow farm lane with its tight cutback to the dirt road and then south toward the village.

There was no way of knowing where the trucks were going in advance, but Danny guessed that they would pick one of the bases in the Great Salt Desert. Most of Iraq's special weapons programs had been located there before the treaty agreement, and a network of underground bunkers and other facilities remained where the material could be protected. While inspections of the known and announced sites were conducted on a random basis, there were still plenty of places where the material might be hidden.

So he wasn't surprised when the first vehicle, which had one of the marked crates, turned toward the southeast. He directed the Voice to keep the Owl over it. Then he started the van and did a U-turn in the deserted roadway. The convoy was roughly two miles away; he figured that was a good distance.

Once it reached good roads, the convoy began stretching out. The lead driver had something of a lead foot, and in less than a minute the Owl could no longer catch the train of trucks in one image.

"Circle back so you can see the entire convoy on a regular basis," said Danny. "Fly in a surveillance pattern above them."

"Confirmed."

"Are all the trucks together?"

"Truck One, Truck Two, Truck Three, Truck Five, Truck Six, and Truck Seven are on local route 31."

"Where are the rest?"

"Truck Four and Truck Eight are on local route 2. Truck Nine is on local route 25. Truck Ten is on an unmarked road heading west. About to exit range of Owl."

Truck Ten was the vehicle with Bani Aberhadji.

"Display a map," he told the Voice. "And locate the trucks."

The map popped into the screen. Truck Ten was nearly parallel to them, on a small road to the north that snaked through the mountain. Danny stared at the screen, trying to guess where Aberhadji was headed.

"Danny!" said Hera.

He looked up, then turned the wheel sharply, veering the van back onto the highway. He'd drifted all the way to the opposite shoulder.

"Sorry."

"Why don't you let me look at that?" she asked.

"It won't interact with you."

"I can lean over and look at the goddamn map," she told him.

She unsnapped her seat belt and moved closer. Danny held it out to her.

"That's the truck with Aberhadji," he told her. "Where do you think he's going?"

"The computer didn't tell you?"

"It's not omniscient."

"It must be to another hiding place. Why disperse the crates?"

"It would help if we knew what was in them," said Danny.

"You were right to check the place out and have it ready for us to leave first," said Hera. "They would have caught us in the middle."

"I know. I'm going to turn around and follow Aberhadji," he said, slowing and looking for a place to do just that.

BANI ABERHADJI RAN HIS FINGERS DOWN BOTH SIDES OF his Adam's apple as they drove, contemplating what would happen after he unleashed the weapon on Israel.

The Israelis would attack Iran. Of that there could be no doubt. The suffering would be great. But in the aftermath, the Guard could reassert itself. Following a period of great hardship, Islam would begin to rebuild itself. Purity of belief, and as always Allah's help, would provide the victory.

The most critical period would come in the weeks following the retaliation. Muslims would rally to Iran's side, but what would the rest of the world do? The Americans were particularly unpredictable. It was very likely they would try and seek him out, make him and other brothers in the Guard scapegoats for the attacks.

He would stand defiantly. He would pray for a trial where his views could be heard.

Or he could drive to Tehran after the missile was launched and wait for the expected counterblow. Becoming a martyr was a welcome prospect. He felt tired, and daunted by the enormity of the next steps he would have to take.

"No, not here," he told the driver as the man prepared to pull into the Guard base. "Keep going straight."

"I'm sorry, Imam. I thought—"

"It's not your fault. We are going to a base at Tajevil that I use," explained Aberhadji. "It is only a little way further. Be careful in your driving. Our cargo is precious."

THE ROADS WERE SPARSE IN THIS CORNER OF IRAN, AND Danny had to drive nearly five miles north before finding one that would take him back toward the area where Aberhadji had headed. By that time, the truck had stopped at a small air base in the mountains near Tajevil. According to the Voice, the strip was long but only made of packed dirt.

"There are no aircraft on the ground," said the Voice. "Database indicates strip has not been used within past decade. Runway length estimated at 3,310.7 meters, not counting apron area and—"

"Get me Breanna Stockard," said Danny.

Breanna, en route to Turkey, answered from the C-17.

"Someone must be on their way to meet him at this airstrip," he told her. "We have to track the aircraft."

"I'll get back to you," she said.

"Computer, examine the defenses around the airstrip," said Danny.

"Facility is surrounded on three sides by barbed-wire fence. There are two guard posts at the entrance, and one lookout. There are two barracks buildings. One building is not presently heated. Conclusion: building is unoccupied."

"Are there flak guns?"

"Antiaircraft weaponry not detected."

"How many people are at the base?"

"Impossible to determine."

"Estimate."

"One to two dozen, based on typical security measures for Iranian air force facilities."

The computer was scaling down its estimate from actual bases, which might or might not be a good method.

"Ask it what's in the building on the north side," said Hera, examining the image. "There are a couple of trailers and a long, narrow building beyond the runway area, set off behind another set of fences."

"Are any of them airplane hangars?" Danny asked.

"They're too small. There are some antennas nearby."

MY-PID IDed the facility as part of a Russian-made SA-6 antiaircraft installation, though it was missing several key parts, most significantly the missiles. The long, narrow building was IDed as a storage facility for backup missiles, which, at an operating base, would be moved onto nearby erectors after the first set were fired.

A search of Agency records revealed that the site had been prepared for American Hawk missiles during the Shah's time. These had never been installed. Though conversion had been started for Russian weapons, they too had never arrived, and it had been delisted as a possible antiaircraft installation a few years before.

Breanna broke into the Voice's briefing.

"Danny, we have an AWACS in Iraq that we're going to get up to track the plane," she said. "Can you get close enough to get a visual ID of whatever it is in the meantime? Is that doable?"

"We'll try."

ABERHADJI PRACTICALLY LEAPT OUT OF THE CAB, STRIDING quickly toward the missile storage building. He was met halfway by Abas Jafari, the son of a man whom he'd served with during the war with Iraq. Tall and gaunt, Abas had his father's eyes and voice, and in the darkness Aberhadji could easily have confused the two.

"Imam, we are ready to store the weapon as you directed," Abas said.

"There has been a change of plans," said Aberhadji. "Move the missile from the storage area and prepare it. Give me some men to take the warhead from the truck. The Israelis have already struck," he added. "You must move as quickly as you can."

Abas blinked in disbelief.

"We will be ready within the hour," he said.

69

South of Tehran

THE CAB DRIVER WAS A TALKATIVE SORT, BABBLING ON TO Tarid about his horrible in-laws. The father was a swine and the mother ten times worse. The man had loaned the driver money twice during the early days of his marriage, and though the loans had been repaid long ago, he still acted as if his son-in-law was a money-grubbing leech. His mother-in-law never washed, and filled every place she went with an unbearable stench.

Tarid was too concerned with his own worries to pay more than passing attention. Aberhadji wanted him to go to an industrial park several miles south of the city. He couldn't imagine what sort of package would be there, especially at this hour of night.

Half of him was sure it was some sort of trap. The other half argued that if Aberhadji had wanted to kill him, he'd have done it that afternoon, when it would have been easier. He thought of telling the driver to take him to the airport instead. But instead he leaned forward from the backseat, head against the neck rest.

"I brought a fare here two years ago," said the driver as they neared the turn off the highway. "He was a very respectable man from Egypt. Ordinarily, I do not like Egyptians. But this man was an exception."

"Mmmmm," muttered Tarid.

"He used a very nice soap. A very nice scent."

Tarid wondered what he himself smelled like. Fear, most likely. And resignation.

The cab driver continued down a long block, flanked on both sides by large apartment complexes. The lights on the poles cast the buildings a dim yellow, and turned the dull gray bricks brown. They came to an intersection and turned right, passing a pair of service stations before the land on both sides of the road cleared entirely. As the light faded behind them, Tarid felt as if they had entered the desert, though in fact they were many miles from it.

"Which building were we going to?" asked the cab driver. It was only luck that he knew of the complex, due to the fare he had told Tarid about. While the names of the roads within it were predictable—there would always be a Victory Drive, an Imam Khomeini Boulevard, and a Triumph Way—the layout was a pretzel. He would have to hunt around for his passenger's destination.

Past experience told the driver that the best tips came if he pretended to know precisely the place, however, so he tried not to reveal his ignorance.

"The building is number ten," said Tarid.

"The one on Victory Drive?" asked the driver.

"I don't know the street. Just that the building is number ten. I assume it is the only number ten in the complex."

Tarid's admission made things easier, since the driver could now pretend to have been confused by vague directions. He saw the sign for the complex and turned, feeling triumphant that the place was exactly as he remembered it. Then, too, he had come in the dark, though not this late.

There were no numbers on the first two buildings he saw. A plaque on the sand in front of the third declared it was 209.

"It will be in the back," said Tarid, guessing.

"Toward the back, yes," said the driver. "I thought so."

NURI AND FLASH KNEW EXACTLY WHERE THE BUILDING WAS, thanks to the Voice. But Nuri had not been able to get a lead on the taxi driver, and decided he'd have to hang back as the cab drove into the complex. He passed by the entrance as the taxi turned in, then he drove down the block looking for an easy place to turn around. There were none, and so he pulled all the way over to the shoulder, made a U-turn and went back.

Nuri turned into the complex, then took an immediate right—a shortcut suggested by the Voice.

Number ten was at the very end of the street.

"Where is subject?" he asked the Voice.

"Two hundred meters to the west."

"He's behind me? South?"

"Affirmative. Subject is heading north."

The cab driver was lost. Or Tarid knew he was bugged and had slipped him written instructions.

"Let's see if we can get to that building before he does," Nuri told Flash. "His driver is wandering around on the other side of the complex."

"Go for it."

Nuri continued down the street. The complex was used mostly by small manufacturers, companies that made items from iron and wood. The larger buildings at the front were all warehouses, and most were empty. A row of empty lots separated number ten from the rest of the buildings on the block.

Nuri slowed down, looking at the building carefully as he approached. It was a large two-story structure, with a well-lit lobby. There wouldn't be much opportunity to interfere if they decided to kill Tarid inside somewhere.

"Somebody in that SUV," warned Flash, pointing to a black Mercedes M-class at the side of the road ahead.

The door to the SUV opened. Out of the corner of his eye Nuri saw someone stepping from the shadows on his left. He had a rifle in his hand.

"Shit," muttered Flash.

"Relax," said Nuri. "Just play cool."

The man with the rifle stepped in front of the car, waving at him to stop. Flash had his pistol ready, under his jacket.

"We're just lost," Nuri whispered to Flash. "Keep quiet. Keep the gun out of sight. Ignore theirs. We'll just smooth-talk this. They'll want to get rid of us quick."

Flash's inclination was to step on the gas, but he wasn't in the driver's seat.

The man who'd gotten out of the SUV shone a flashlight at them as they stopped. Nuri rolled down the window.

"Who are you?" demanded the man with the rifle.

"Please, we are looking for number three-one-two," said Nuri in Arabic. "Do you know it?"

"Who are you looking for?" said the man, still using Farsi.

"Three-one-two."

The man with the flashlight came around to Nuri's side. The two Iranians debated whether they should help him or not.

"Do you know where three-one-two is?" repeated Nuri. "I have an appointment. We were late coming from Mehrabad Airport but I hoped—"

"Three twelve is back the other way," said the man with the flashlight. His Arabic had an Egyptian accent, similar to Nuri's. "Turn your car around, take a right, then a left at the far end and circle back down. You will find it."

"Thank you, thank you," said Nuri.

Tarid's cab drove toward him as he finished the three-point turn.

Nuri cursed.

The men had stepped back into the shadows but were still nearby; there was no way to warn him.

"You think they're going to shoot him?" asked Flash as they passed.

"Fifty-fifty," said Nuri, watching from the rearview mirror.

TARID FELT HIS THROAT CONSTRICT AS THE MAN WITH THE rifle stepped out from the side of the street. He'd focused all of his attention on the passing car and was caught completely off-guard.

The taxi driver jammed the brakes. As the man raised the rifle, the drive turned and started to throw the car into reverse. But a man with a flashlight ran out from behind an SUV on the other side and shone it in the back. The driver froze, unsure what to do.

"We're not going to harm you!" yelled the man with the rifle. "Stop the car. Tarid?"

"Tarid!" yelled the man with the flashlight. "You're here for a package."

Tarid leaned toward the door and rolled down the window.

"I am Arash Tarid. Aberhadji sent me."

"Come with us," said the man with the flashlight. He shone the light toward the driver. "You stay here. He'll be right back. Don't worry. He'll pay you."

Tarid's fingers slipped on the handle. Still, he thought it was a good sign that the man with the flashlight had said he'd be back.

But what else would he have said?

Tarid's legs became less steady as he walked. He tried remembering a prayer—any prayer—but couldn't. He couldn't think at all.

The man with the flashlight stopped near the bushes. He reached down and pulled up a large duffel bag.

"You're to give this to the man with the red jacket at Imam Khomeini Airport," he told Tarid. "Go to Hangar Five. The man will ask you what time it is. You reply that it is a nice day. Do you understand? You don't give him the time. You say it is a nice day."

"OK."

"Go," said the man with the gun, pushing him toward the taxi.

Tarid felt a surge of shame. He'd been in life and death situations before. Never had he acted like this—never had he felt such fear. Even just the other day, when the camp was under assault in the Sudan, when he was hurt, he had acted calmly.

Here in Iran he'd been reduced to a coward. Why?

Because of Aberhadji. He was deathly afraid of him. He'd always been afraid of him.

You couldn't give one man that much power over your life. To be afraid of a single man like that—however righteous or powerful—if you lived like that, you were nothing but a dog, a cur begging in the street.

Tarid grabbed the handle of the taxi and angrily pulled it open.

"We need to go to the international airport," he told the driver. "Take me to Hangar Five. And no more complaints about your in-laws. I have more important things to worry about."

"Identify and locate Hangar Five," Nuri told the Voice as he pulled onto the highway.

The Voice identified the hangar as a civilian facility at the center of the airport's service area. It was used by foreign airlines, primarily Turkish Airlines.

"What's he doing?" Flash asked.

"Delivering a package to somebody at the airport," said Nuri. "It's too big."

"Bomb?"

"Probably papers," said Nuri. He guessed it had to do with the network, documents or plans of some type. "It's way too small for a nuke."

"Could it be bomb material, though?"

"It could be." Nuri thought about a bomb. The actual amount of pure uranium or plutonium needed was relatively small, though very heavy. The package might contain enough for a third or even half a bomb, depending on how sophisticated the design was.

Actually, he realized, it could contain the entire bomb—but only if the design was very advanced.

"You know, we don't really have to rescue Tarid," said Flash. "We can just make it look like we did."

"There's only two of us, Flash. We can't set up a whole operation like that. Especially at an airport."

"Why not?"

"How do we get away?"

"We'll be at an airport, right?"

"We have to take Tarid with us."

"We knock him out."

It wasn't a horrible idea, just totally impractical. Nuri let Flash talk about it as he drove. He thought about what else the box might contain.

Traffic was light, but not so light that they could count on not being seen if they ran the taxi off the road. Still, that might work: push him off the road, rob him, grab the bag.

The Iranians would realize they knew. But they were already shutting down the operation, so what did it matter?

"How would we grab the bag?" Nuri asked Flash finally. "How can we take it?"

"The bag? Not him?"

"What if we just got the bag?"

"We just point our guns at him and grab it. Shoot him if he won't hand it over. Straight robbery, dude."

Somehow, Nuri didn't think it would be that easy.

70

Northern Iran

THE VOICE DIRECTED DANNY AND HERA TO AN ABANDONED farm about a mile from the air base. Danny parked just off the road, then led Hera as the Voice guided them down an old creek to a farm lane where they climbed up a hill about a half mile from the rear of the complex. Until they crested the hill, they saw nothing. Hera kept wanting to complain that they were going in the wrong direction, and struggled to keep her mouth shut.

And then, suddenly, they saw floodlights in the distance. They didn't even need their night glasses to see what was going on.

"It's a missile," said Hera. "Oh my God."

ABERHADJI WATCHED AS THE WARHEAD WAS BOLTED INTO place. The process was delicate—not because of the warhead, which would remain inert until after it was launched, but because of the rocket fuel and oxidizer being pumped into the tanks.

Fueling the missile was not quite as easy as loading a truck with gasoline. The liquids had to be carefully monitored; their temperature and pressures were critical, and a spark in the wrong place would ignite a fireball. While Aberhadji's team had perfected quick fueling methods, his short notice added another level of difficulty. Still, he knew it should take only a little more than an hour before they were ready to launch—a prep time that would be the envy of the best-trained crew in the West.

"Imam, the warhead is ready to be coded," said Abas, the head technician.

The code was part of the fail-safe lock that prevented unauthorized use of the warhead. It allowed the bomb to arm itself following launch. Without it, the warhead was simply a very heavy piece of complicated metal.

Aberhadji moved quickly to the panel at the side of the warhead. The code was entered on a very small number pad. The display screen was a small panel sixteen boxes long. It displayed an X as each number was pressed in. When the boxes were finally filled, Aberhadji had to press the unmarked bar at the bottom to enter them. He had only two tries. If the number was entered incorrectly a third time, the fusing circuit was designed to overload, rendering the weapon useless.

He pressed the bottom bar. The display flashed. The X's turned to stars.

They were ready to go.

"How much longer?" he asked Abas.

"An hour and ten minutes, if nothing goes wrong."

Aberhadji nodded. He could barely stand the suspense.

71

Imam Khomeini International Airport

FROM THE LAYOUT OF THE AIRPORT GROUNDS, NURI THOUGHT it might be possible to set up an ambush on the utility road at the eastern side; it was long and, according to the satellite photos and schematic MY-PID reviewed, generally deserted. But as soon as they neared the airport, he saw his plan would never work. There were police cars and Iranian army vehicles all around the grounds. Lights flashed; cars were being stopped at the entrance.

"What the hell's going on?" asked Flash.

"Yeah, good question." Nuri continued past the access road. They had weapons and surveillance gear; there'd be no chance of sneaking past a search. He drove two miles until he saw a small grocery store off the main road. He pulled off and drove around the back to the Dumpster.

A man was sitting in front of it, smoking a cigarette.

"I thought if you were Muslim you weren't allowed to smoke," said Flash.

The man threw away the cigarette and scurried inside. But Nuri didn't want to take a chance, so he drove through the lot and back onto the highway, continuing until he found another store. This time there was no one in back. They stashed the weapons midway down in the Dumpster, then went back to the airport.

A pair of policemen stopped them at the gate and asked for ID. As soon as he saw Nuri's Italian passport, he had them both get out and open the trunk. His partner went through the interior, tugging at the seat cushions and rifling through the glove compartment.

"What are these?" asked the policeman, pulling one of the transponders from Nuri's overnight bag. It was a booster unit for the bugs.

"We use them to receive signals from the pipeline, when it is examined," Nuri handed the man a business card "You would be interested in hearing about this. It is very high technology. Holes in the pipe cannot be detected by the human eye. But even a small leak could cost very much money. Imagine if the faucet in your house were to drip all day. What a—"

"Your Farsi is very good," said the man, handing him back the passport. "Have a nice trip back to Italy."

"What is going on?" asked Nuri. "Was there a robbery?"

"No, no. The president is taking off in a few hours. The airport must be kept secure."

Nuri and Flash got back in the car. About halfway down the main entrance road, Nuri took a right onto a utility road that would swing him back around to the hangar area. They got only fifty yards before they found the way blocked by an army truck.

"I have to go to Terminal Five," Nuri told the soldier.

The man waved him away, directing him to turn around. Nuri tried arguing, but the man wouldn't even listen.

"Now what?" asked Flash as they turned back.

"There's another access road on the other side of the airport," said Nuri. "We'll try that."

WHEN THE POLICEMAN WALKED OVER TO THE TAXI, TARID leaned forward from the back and showed the man his ID. The notation in the corner made it clear he was with the Revolutionary Guard. The officer frowned, then waved the cab through.

The soldier blocking the route to the hangars was not so accommodating. He glanced at the ID, then told the driver he couldn't pass.

Finally Tarid got out and demanded that the soldier call his superior officer. The man asked to see the ID again. He pretended to study the photo and the official designation, which showed that Tarid was the equivalent of a colonel in the regular army. While he did this, he contemplated the consequences of displeasing a high-ranking Guard official. If Tarid made life miserable for his captain, things would become very uncomfortable. The Guard was notorious for that.

"Well?" said Tarid.

The soldier handed back the ID, then went and pulled the truck out of the way.

It was only as he walked back to the cab that Tarid realized he was being followed; a dark-colored SUV was sitting about fifty yards up the road. It was too far away for him to make out who was in the front seat, but he was convinced that the men who had given him the package had followed him here.

In fact, he was half right; the man with the flashlight had followed him by himself, ordered by Aberhadji to make sure he completed the mission.

Killing him so he wouldn't be a witness was his own idea. His companion would take care of the man in the red jacket later on.

The sight of the truck rekindled Tarid's paranoia. Once more he was convinced he was about to be killed. But rather than being filled with fear or paralyzed by his doubts, as he had been earlier, he began getting angry. The emotion grew steadily, and by the time the cab reached Hangar Five, he was livid. A dam had broken, and as it rushed out, his fear had drowned itself, leaving only the raw emotion.

"Wait for me," he barked at the cab driver, slamming the door behind him. The bag's strap caught against the door. He pulled it sharply, spinning it hard against the fender as he freed it.

A man with a red jacket ran toward him.

"Careful," he said.

"Careful yourself," said Tarid. He threw the bag to him.

The man caught it, cringing. "You idiot," he said. "Get the hell out of here."

"The hell with you, too."

Tarid whirled and went back to the cab.

"Is that the president's plane?" asked the cab driver timidly after he got in.

Tarid hadn't even realized what was going on. Suddenly the fear returned.

"I have no idea," he muttered.

NURI AND FLASH FOUND THE OTHER ACCESS ROAD CUT OFF as well. The closest they could get was a small building used by a food services company as a short-term warehouse. They parked the car and went around to the side, looking at Hangar Five with a set of binoculars. Nuri saw the cab drive up, and saw Tarid get out of the car, but his view was blocked and he couldn't see what Tarid was doing.

The Voice, however, picked up their conversation. The exchange left Nuri baffled. The man in the red coat was afraid as well as angry, but of what?

Careful.

What would Tarid have to be careful of? Certainly not of papers or computer records.

If he'd had nuclear material in the bag—a distant possibility, Nuri thought—there'd be no danger of it going off. Though perhaps the other man wouldn't know.

A conventional bomb?

With the president's plane nearby. . .

"You drive," Nuri told Flash. "We want to follow the cab, but not too close."

"Sure. But what are you doing?"

"I'm going to dig out our backup chemical sniffer and calibrate it. Then we have to figure out some way of getting into that cab right after Nuri gets out."

72

Washington, D.C.

PRESIDENT TODD STUDIED THE VIDEO IMAGE ON THE SCREEN at the front of the White House Situation Room. It was remarkably clear, considering the vast distance it was being transmitted from, let alone the conditions.

There was no doubt. The image was of a medium-range intercontinental missile, topped with a heavy warhead.

"We have to guess at what's in the warhead," said Jonathon Reid, narrating the impromptu slide show from Room 4 at the CIA campus in Virginia. "But given everything else we've found, I really don't think there's much doubt."

The image was coming from the Owl that Danny and Hera had launched. The weapons analysts at the CIA had identified the missile in the video as a member of the No-Dong A family, a North Korean weapon capable of carrying a nuclear warhead 2,000 to 2,900 miles.

"A small number were supposedly lost during testing and destroyed, according to the official antiproliferation documents," said Reid dryly. "I would suggest that the documents are not entirely correct."

"Do we have any indication of a target?" asked Todd.

"None," said Reid. "But I think we can assume it's Israel. It would be in retaliation for the strike on the plant in the Sudan."

"I don't think we have the whole picture here," said Secretary of State Alistair Newhaven. "I agree that Israel is the logical target if this is being loaded with a nuclear warhead. But I think we're leaping to conclusions."

"They're not going to spell out their intentions," said Herman Edmund, the CIA director. "Clearly, the missile is going to be launched. And only a fool would think the warhead won't be nuclear."

"They're trying to disrupt the Iranian president's rapprochement with the U.S.," said Secretary of Defense Lovel. "I've warned about this for months."

Lovel had taken a hard line against Iran since the beginning of the administration.

"If that's the case," said Newhaven, who agreed with the theory, "then it argues that the missile isn't nuclear. It's a demonstration of their ability, but not a suicidal attack. Any nuclear attack would be suicidal, and the Iranians are not suicidal."

"Not all Iranians," said Lovel. "But maybe just these ones."

"Mr. Reid, when will the missile launch?" asked President Todd.

"Again, we have no direct intelligence on their intentions. Typically, it can take anywhere from a few hours to a dozen to prepare for a launch, depending on the personnel and conditions."

"Most likely it will be at the far end of the spectrum," said Michael Bacon, the National Security Advisor. "At least twelve hours, if not longer. The Iranians in the past have taken upward of a day to prep their launches once they've reached the ready stage, and I doubt we're dealing with a crack crew here."

"I'm not sure about that," said Reid. "In theory, the missile could be fueled very quickly, especially if the safety protocols were disregarded."

"This isn't the main government force here," said Bacon. The information gathered by Whiplash and NSA intercepts seemed to indicate that the missile had been developed by a small group within the Iranian Revolutionary Guard, possibly one at odds with the organization's legitimate leadership. "If they're a splinter group, they're not going to have the same level of expertise."

"On the contrary," said Reid. "They'll be highly motivated and competently trained. They may be the elite of the elite."

"I still believe there's time to demand that the Iranian government take action," said the Secretary of State. "That's a better solution in the long run."

"Nonsense," said Bacon.

"We cannot let them point a missile at Israel—at anyone," insisted Lovel. "Especially after they've declared that they don't have any."

"But this isn't the government," said Newhaven. "It should be handled in a completely different way. If their government stops it—"

"Would they? And in the meantime, we're risking a nuclear catastrophe," said Lovel. "Millions of people will be killed."

"That's not my point. I'm not in favor of *not* acting. I'm just saying that we should first encourage the Iranians to move, then act if they don't. If we have twelve hours—"

"Gentlemen, let's not get sidetracked here," said the President. "We are going to remove this threat. We are going to assume it is real. And we are not going to rely on the Iranians. That would be too risky. All that will do is make our mission harder." She looked to the right, at the screen showing the Pentagon ready room. "How long before the bombers are ready?"

"We can have planes in the air within the hour," said the Defense secretary. "A pair of F-15Es are being loaded with weapons in Saudi Arabia as we speak. They'll have four F-15Cs as escorts, along with two F-16s for antiair suppression as necessary. Additional Navy flights will be available from the Gulf. We're still working on some of the support details."

"How long before they reach Iran?" asked the President.

"Roughly an hour after they take off," added Lovel. "With the Iranian air defense system not on high alert, their task is . . . robust, but not impossible."

"What if they're on alert?" asked Reid.

"Then things become trickier. Their aircraft and surface-to-air missiles will be ready to launch. We'll have a second package of attack and fighter aircraft ready to go as a backup. But our people have trained for this. We *will* accomplish the mission, Mrs. President. I'm confident."

"What happens when we bomb the warhead?" asked the President.

Lovel turned to an Air Force general who was an expert on nuclear accidents. The general began by citing a study that had been done in 1975. To everyone's relief, Todd cut him short.

"General, the executive summary," she said.

"Yes, ma'am. Sorry. Predicting with one hundred percent certainty is impossible. But—if the warhead is constructed properly, there will be little harm to it. The rocket fuel and the oxidizer explode, of course. You have a fire, etcetera." The general waved his hand, dismissing the cataclysm.

"What about the explosive lens around the bomb?" asked the Secretary of State.

The general gave him a condescending smile. "We don't really know what sort of design they've used, Mr. Secretary. Now I agree with you that it's very likely that they've followed the North Korean mode. However—"

"Short answer, please," said the President impatiently.

"All nuclear weapon designs do contain explosives. However, as a general rule, they can't just explode. But if that were to happen, almost surely the warhead won't be ignited."

Reid noted the disclaimer—almost surely—but said nothing to the others. The CIA had concluded that the explosives would survive a bomb strike without igniting, citing accidents in the 1950s.

"The worst case scenario—short of something we don't know about with the material," said the general, referring to the uranium, "would be the explosives in the design getting on fire. But even if that happened—and I have to say it's highly unlikely—even if that happened, the weapon would not go critical."

"We have to recover the material once the missile is destroyed," said Todd. "How do we go about that?"

"I don't know that that's feasible," said Lovel.

"Will the material be scattered?" Todd asked.

"No ma'am," said the weapons expert. "I mean, again to give you a definitive answer would require quite a lot of study, but the nature of—"

"Thank you. You've told me enough," said Todd. She looked around the table, then back at the screen. "Charles, how do we get the remains of the warhead? What's our plan for that?"

"We have a Delta Force unit in the region," said Lovel. "They can recover it."

"The material is not necessarily dangerous," added Reid. Contrary to popular belief, an unexploded bomb presented no health hazard. "And as it happens, there is one person in the region who not only has been trained to deal with warheads, but has had considerable experience doing so."

"Who?" said Todd.

"Danny Freah. The colonel disarmed a live nuclear warhead a few seconds before it exploded in South America during his Dreamland days," said Reid. "And before that, he was tasked to a team that secured weapons following the fall of the Soviet Union."

"Before he went on to bigger and better things," said Lovel admiringly.

"Then the colonel is the person we want handling it," said President Todd. "Fortune has put him in exactly the right spot."

"There is one consideration," said Reid. "He'll have to be close to the bomb site when it is bombed. The rocket fuel can be quite unpredictable when it explodes. And it does explode with quite a lot of force."

"Then he'll have to keep his distance," said Todd dryly. "I would assume he knows that better than we do."

The President turned back to the Pentagon feed.

"Charles, work with Mr. Reid and Ms. Stockard to get a plan together. And get those bombers airborne as quickly as possible. I don't care what it takes. We're stopping that missile."

73

Tehran

TARID'S HEAD CLEARED AS THE CAB TOOK HIM BACK TO Tehran. He had to leave Iran; even if Aberhadji wasn't out to kill him, not even the Guard would be able to protect him from the army's wrath when the president's plane blew up. Whatever life remained to him, it was as a permanent exile.

The Sudan was the first place they would look; then they would get to Somalia, Egypt, and Kenya, hunting him down at the other parts of the network he had tended. Turkey wouldn't be safe, either.

His best bet at the moment was Europe, though the thick Iranian spy networks would make staying for a long term problematic.

The one thing he had was money, squirreled away in Swiss and German bank accounts. The first step would be to rearrange those accounts, in case Aberhadji had been on to the skimming. And then he would decide where to go and what to do.

Leaving by plane was out of the question. He'd have to sneak over a border on foot, or take a boat.

Calm settled over him as they drove to the city. It was only a veneer, a brittle shell that could be broken by even a light shock, but he was functioning again. Even if he was only a shadow of the man he'd been—or thought he'd been—in the Sudan, he was still a capable and formidable opponent, a man who had lived by his wits for many years in the most hostile environments.

He had told the cab driver to take him to the hotel, but that was only to give him a destination to head toward while he figured out where he really should go. He finally decided that his best plan would be to take a bus westward, to the coast. But realizing the stations in the city could easily be watched, he had the driver turn around and head west, to a small suburban station he knew.

By now the cabbie was scared of his passenger and complied without protest. He'd stop talking since the man with the gun had flagged him down. His only thoughts were of his two children. He wanted desperately to remain alive; if he died, there was every chance his wife would take them to live with his in-laws.

"WHERE'S HE GOING?" FLASH ASKED NURI AS THEY LEFT the highway.

"No idea. Maybe he has to report back in. Maybe he's running away."

"Why didn't he just get on a plane at the airport, then?"

"Don't know."

Flash checked his pistol, double-checking that no one had

messed with it in the brief time it had been out of his possession. They'd swung back to grab their gear; he'd hoped to get something to eat as well, but the shop had closed.

Nuri leaned over and glanced at the fuel gauge. They were starting to run low.

Especially in the dark, the towns around Tehran looked similar to the close-in towns around capitals in the West, with clusters of apartment blocks punctuated by small lots of single-family houses. Except for the spirals of the mosques lit by spotlights in the distance, they could have been practically anywhere in the developed world, at the edge of Brooklyn or Naples or Moscow, Istanbul, Berlin.

"Maybe he's looking for a McDonald's," joked Flash. "I could use one of them myself."

"You're not full from dinner?"

"There's always room for a Big Mac."

"There's no McDonald's in Iran."

"Shame."

The Voice told Nuri that Tarid's cab was stopping three blocks ahead. Flash closed the distance just in time to see Tarid leaning in to pay off the driver. He was in front of a bus station.

"Get out and get the cab," Nuri told Flash. "Have him stop two blocks down."

"Tarid's going to see me."

"Don't worry about it. We have to scan the interior. We don't need him anymore."

Flash opened the door and got out, walking briskly toward the cab. Tarid turned, saw him, then darted in front of the cab, running across the street to the bus station.

"I need a ride," said Flash in English.

The taxi driver pretended he didn't understand. Before he could start away, Flash grabbed and opened the rear door.

Sure he was about to be killed, the driver stepped on the gas. Flash threw himself into the taxi, diving into the backseat and pulling himself up. The driver swerved down a side street, then back up another.

The tourist gig wasn't working. Flash decided to take a different approach.

He pulled out his pistol and placed it at the man's neck.

"Stop," he told him.

The driver started to shake his head.

"Stop."

Flash pressed the barrel harder against the driver's flesh. He reached into his pocket and tossed the bills he had on the front seat. It was a considerable sum, more than the driver ordinarily made in a month.

"Stop," said Flash, poking the gun hard into his neck.

The bills allayed just enough of the driver's fear to make him stop.

Nuri pulled up behind him and sprang from the car. He carried the sniffer in both hands, holding it in front of him as if it were a divining rod.

"Do not worry," he told the man in Farsi as he pushed the detector toward the open window. "This will not harm you or your car. We will leave you alone in just a minute."

He didn't get a read. He opened the door to the back, bending in as Flash slid to the side, still holding the gun at the man's neck.

The detector was set to pick up traces of chemicals used in Semtex and other plastic explosives. It was negative; there were no traces in the cab.

Though extremely sensitive, the sniffer could be defeated. A very careful bomb maker working in a clean room could, for example, wrap the explosive very securely and make sure that there were no stray traces on the bag. But in Nuri's experience, that simply didn't happen; bombs were almost never constructed that carefully.

"Nothing?" asked Flash.

Nuri started to back out of the vehicle. The president's plane would be inspected before it took off. The Iranians undoubtedly had equipment similar to his, though not as powerful nor as portable.

So a plastic explosive would be discovered.

Fuel, though . . .

"Wait here," Nuri told Flash. He stepped to the side of the road, closer to the street lamp, and recalibrated the device. Then he took a second sample from the back, pushing the sniffer right against the floor.

There was a very slight hit of an ammonia compound.

"You use rocket fuel to power your taxi?" Nuri asked the man.

The cab driver was baffled. Nuri reached into his pocket for some bills.

"I already paid him a fortune," said Flash, getting out the other side.

Nuri tossed the money on the man's lap anyway. "Forget tonight," he told him. "It will be the best for you. Go home to your family and forget everything else."

TARID RAN INSIDE THE BUS STATION. THERE WERE ONLY TWO buses at the queues, and neither was ready to leave. He glanced at the empty driver's seat of the one at the head of the line, thinking he might steal it. But a bus would be too easy to follow, and besides, he wasn't sure if he could even drive it. He trotted in front of it, crossing to the other side of the platform.

As he reached the other side, he saw a man walking briskly into the station across from him, his hand in his pocket. Tarid ducked behind a closed newsstand, moving to the opposite end. He started to look around the corner, but stopped as he heard the footsteps; the man was running toward him.

Tarid turned. The station had a low cement wall on the other side of the bus queue, with several openings to a nearby parking lot. He sprang toward it.

As he did, a shot rang out.

"THEY'VE PUT A BOMB ON THE IRANIAN PRESIDENT'S PLANE," Nuri told Reid as he got back into the car. "It has some sort of fuel in it—they're probably going to set it into one of the fuel tanks or the wing area."

"You're sure?" asked Reid.

"There was some sort of fuel in whatever Tarid carried to the airport," said Nuri. He was using the Voice to connect to Reid's CIA phone, and there was a slight but noticeable delay as the transmissions synced. "I'm guessing at everything else."

Flash backed the car up into a nearby driveway, then drove back toward the bus station.

"Where is your subject now?" asked Reid.

"He looks like he's going on a bus ride. I'm going to follow. We may have a chance to grab him."

"That may not be wise."

"He'd be a great source."

"You'll have trouble getting him out. We may not even be able to get you out."

"We'll see what happens," said Nuri. "I'll be back."

"Hey—that SUV is up on the curb," said Flash. "And it wasn't there before."

Nuri realized it was similar to the truck that the man with the flashlight had been sitting in at the complex. He didn't even need the Voice to make a comparison.

"Stop the car," said Nuri. He grabbed the door handle. "Come on. Quick."

TARID FELT THE BULLET HIT HIM IN THE LEG. THE PAIN FELT absurdly minimal, barely a sting from a bee. He was even able to stay on his feet, running behind a car and throwing himself down as two more shots sailed over his head.

It was only when he hit the ground that the real pain began. His leg felt as if it had been twisted below his knee. It was on fire. Then it seemed that something had grabbed his calf. It was a lobster claw, gripping and twisting.

He started to get up but his leg betrayed him. He no longer had control over it.

He was going to die here, in a parking lot outside of Tehran.

What a shame that he hadn't made love to Simin.

Tarid began pushing himself forward, crawling away.

He heard the footsteps again, louder, coming for him. Desperate, he rolled himself under a nearby car, trying to quiet his breath.

For a few seconds it seemed as if he had escaped. The footsteps grew faint. The lot was silent. Tarid's head began to float, his body entering protective shock.

Then something grabbed his good leg. He was dragged out from under the car.

The man who'd held the flashlight when he picked up the bomb was standing over him, grinning. He had a pistol in his hand.

Smiling, the man raised the gun to fire.

THE IRANIAN ASSASSIN WAS SO CONSUMED WITH HIS PREY that he didn't hear Flash and Nuri running into the lot behind him. Nuri went to the left, Flash to the right.

Flash saw him down the aisle, raising his gun to fire.

Flash clamped his left hand to his right, leaning forward slightly—there was no time to think, or even consciously aim; he pointed the gun and fired.

The bullet hit square in the back of the assassin's head.

Flash ran forward. He gave a double tap of the trigger into the already dead man's skull, taking no chances.

Nuri raced from the other side of the lot. He slid on one knee next to Tarid.

"They're going to kill you," he told him in Farsi. "We will help you escape. Come with us."

Tarid was in no position to argue. "Allah be praised," he said, half delirious from the pain and shock.

74

Approaching Saudi Arabia

BREANNA LEANED BACK IN THE COPILOT'S SEAT AND PULLED off her headset. Then she pressed the Receive button on the satellite phone and held it to her ear.

"Stockard."

"The President wants to recover the warhead after the bombers hit," said Jonathon Reid. "She wants Danny to help recover it."

"How?"

"The bomb material should be intact. The rest of the warhead will be mangled, of course. They're pulling together a team of Delta people and a few other experts. I know Danny has done this sort of thing before."

"Jonathon, I don't know—"

"This is exactly the sort of mission Whiplash was conceived for," said Reid. "Adjusting on the fly."

There were adjustments, and then there were adjustments. Physically picking up a warhead wasn't the problem. The mission would require them not only to stay in Iran after the bombing, but to stay near the site.

She worried about losing them. She worried about them dying. Whatever danger they were in now would be multiplied tenfold.

Her father had told her about the fear he felt over losing people before he left Dreamland. Ordering an op might be the right thing to do, but that didn't salve his conscience. He was always haunted by the cost.

"The Delta people are about two hours away from Baghdad," Reid said. "They'll hook up with some Agency people in Azerbaijan who just finished helping some of the inspection teams in Iran. They want to use your Ospreys to get in and out. Do you want to talk to the commanders?"

*   *   *

THE HEAD OF THE TASK FORCE IN AZERBAIJAN WAS A former Delta Force colonel named Tom Dolan. He was under contract to the U.S. government as a "consultant"—a nifty way of denying direct responsibility for him if things went south on an operation. Dolan told Breanna that his team would be ready to go in roughly two hours.

She sketched a plan to pick up the Delta combat team in Baghdad at the airport, then fly the MC-17 up to Azerbaijan. There, the two Ospreys she was carrying would be off-loaded and used by the task force and Delta to get to the Iraq site. Boston and Sugar would go as well.

Danny was silent as Breanna explained the plan.

"Something wrong?" she asked.

"We're talking forty troops?" he asked.

"I didn't ask the actual count. Not enough?"

"Depends on what happens."

"There's a Marine combat team."

"Get them."

"Are you sure you're okay?"

Danny hesitated. "Yeah, it'll be enough," he said finally. "Don't worry. Once the bombers hit, there won't be anyone left here. And we're pretty far from their forces."

"If you need something, tell me."

"I'm fine, Bree. I've done this before, remember?"

"So have I," she said.

"Auld acquaintance be forgot . . ."

75

Northern Iran

"SO WE'RE SUPPOSED TO SIT HERE AND WATCH THEM launch the missile?" asked Hera after Danny told her what was going on. "What if the bombers don't get here in time?"

Danny ignored her, examining the missile site. There were a dozen men working on the weapon, pumping fuel from underground tanks and making adjustments to the warhead and engine mechanisms. They clearly didn't think they were in any danger: There were no guards on the runway, and the only sentries the Voice had seen were near the rocket, alternately helping and standing guard.

"So what if the bombers don't get here?" Hera asked again. "Then what?"

"They'll get here. The question is where we want to be when they do."

"And?"

"The other side of this ridge. The hill will absorb or deflect most of the blast."

"It's not going to explode?"

"You mean, go nuclear?"

"Hell yeah."

"No. The warhead may even end up intact. If not, it won't be a big deal."

"We won't get fried?"

"Nah."

"You've done this before, right?" Hera's voice betrayed more concern than she would have liked.

"Don't worry," said Danny. "I've done it before."

In fact he had done it before; once, when he'd disarmed a warhead a few seconds before it went off. The scientists analyzing the bomb later confided they'd guessed about which of the wires he should cut as time ran down.

Then they'd tried reassuring him that the weapon hadn't been made particularly well, and rather than yielding the twelve megatons it was designed for, would probably only have delivered six or seven.

"Which means it would have only blown up everything within six miles, right?" he had answered. "Rather then twenty."

They didn't get the joke.

He'd never been around when a nuke had been bombed. Nor had he pulled one out of a fire. And even if he had—those things were past.

If he had to defuse the bomb now, could he? He remembered getting the instructions over the radio. It had been nerve-wracking.

It would be worse now, ten times worse. A hundred times worse. He'd lost something. He wasn't a hero—wasn't *the* hero he'd been.

He was thinking too much. He used to hear people say that about other commanders, about guys who, to him, seemed to have lost a step, gotten older and more cautious. It wasn't age maybe, not directly—just experience.

Thinking too much. About what? *The cost.*

"Looks like they're finished with the fuel," said Hera.

Danny looked up, surprised. "Already?"

"Look."

"No, it's the oxidizer," he said. "Shit."

The fuel and oxidizer were loaded separately, but it took roughly the same amount of time to load each one. They must be nearly done, Danny realized. The missile crew was moving quickly, much more quickly than he would have thought possible.

The men swarmed over the erector, getting ready to raise the missile.

"The bombers aren't going to make it," said Danny, jumping up.

"What do you mean?"

"I mean, they're going to launch that sucker any minute. Come on."

76

Washington, D.C.

THE PRESIDENT HAD JUST REACHED THE OVAL OFFICE WHEN her assistant chief of staff told her Jonathon Reid needed to talk to her immediately. She picked up the phone as she sat down, tapping her finger hard on the button to connect.

"This is the President."

"Mrs. Todd, we've just learned that plotters in Iran are targeting their president. We believe it's the same group responsible for the missile. They've put a bomb on his plane at the Tehran International Airport."

"We're certain of this?"

"Reasonably certain. The plane is due to take off for the States inside an hour. It's on the ground at Imam Khomeini International Airport, near Hangar Five. The bomb was just delivered to the airport."

"Thank you, Mr. Reid." The President pushed back her chair. "Do we have new information on the warhead?"

"No ma'am. The Air Force F-15Es should be ready to take off in just a few minutes. The task force in charge of securing and removing the weapon is being gathered. We've added a Marine combat team, and will get additional forces if possible."

Todd put down the phone and bent her head down, resting her forehead on her fingertips.

It made sense now—a faction of the Revolutionary Guard would attempt to assassinate the country's president, while launching a suicide attack against Israel. There would be chaos in the country. They would take over.

Except there'd be nothing left to take over. Israel would turn the country into a nuclear wasteland, desolate for the next two hundred years.

No. They would stop it all in time. She had the right people in place, thank God.

If she warned the Iranian president, would it inadvertently hamper the mission to stop the missile and retrieve the warhead? If the army and air force in Iran went on alert, how much harder would it be for the Air Force to find its target?

But she had to warn him. Just as she had to warn the Israelis.

Todd picked up the phone. There was a good chance the Iranian president wouldn't believe her, but she would try anyway.

77

Over Saudi Arabia

BREANNA AND THE C-17 PILOT, CAPTAIN FREDERICK, HAD just settled on the course into Baghdad when Danny Freah called her from Iran. The MY-PID routed the call from its network to her sat phone; the connection was slightly delayed but so clear she could hear him gulping for air as he ran and talked to her at the same time.

"They're getting ready to launch," said Danny. "They have the oxidizer in and they're almost done with the fuel. They're putting the nose to the warhead on. They're going to launch, Bree."

"Now?"

"Any second. Ten minutes at most. I'm going to stop them."

"Danny—"

"Hera's with me. We'll blow up the missile."

"But—"

"I'm on it. Don't worry."

There was a strain in his voice she'd never heard before. For the first time since the mission began, Breanna felt truly scared.

"Godspeed" was all she could say.

78

Northern Iran

DANNY PUSHED DOWN THE RAVINE, CUTTING TOWARD THE rear of the complex in a wide arc. He came up a short hill, then plunged into a thicket of prickle bushes. The stickers clawed at him and the brush was so thick that he realized after a dozen yards that he had lost his way. He stopped to get his bearings and gather his breath.

"What are we doing?" said Hera.

"Tell me how to get down to the rear of the missile storage building," Danny told the Voice. "I want to get down there without being seen. But I want to get down as quickly as possible."

"Computing," said the machine. "Go thirty meters to the east, then make a fifty degree turn."

For the next sixty or seventy yards, the Voice seemed omniscient. First it took them out of brush, guiding them to a copse and an easily climbed set of rocks. But then the computer started them to the north, working through an open field that Danny thought they could easily have cut through.

Did he trust MY-PID or not? It couldn't explain itself when he asked why it was leading them that way, saying only that it had calculated the route according to his specifications.

"We're going to end up back at the sea the way we're going," groused Hera.

Finally they took a turn to the east. But the going became much tougher—they were walking through thick sticker bushes, which pulled at their clothes and smacked at their faces.

The Voice told Danny they would have to crawl for twenty meters. He got down on his hands and knees. Feeling a little like he was the butt of a joke, he crawled until he came to a barbed-wire fence. He held up the fence and waited for Hera. Once she was through, he slipped under himself.

"Target shed is three hundred meters ahead. Follow the unused roadbed."

The computer had used old satellite images, as well as its view from the Owl, to find the roadway, which after the turn under the fence was hidden from the launch area by the buildings. Danny slipped his night goggles down around his neck; there was more than enough light to see. He checked his grenade launcher and rifle.

"Be ready to fire," he told Hera. Then he rose and began running toward the missile building.

BANI ABERHADJI WATCHED AS THE WORKERS BALANCED ON the ladder, performing the last checks while the fuel was topped off. The elation he'd felt earlier had dissipated. He was back to being the man he'd been throughout his life—the quiet problem solver, the thinker always several steps ahead.

After the missile was launched, he would go north to a safe house in the hills overlooking the Caspian Sea. There, he would begin reaching out to his Guard contacts, getting things in line to take control of the council.

If he had to, he could evacuate temporarily to Baku. It was not his preferred course, but it might be necessary, depending on the West's reaction.

"Imam, we are ready to begin the countdown," said Abas. "You need to unlock the code on the primary pump."

It was an extra safeguard the brothers had worked out, making it impossible for anyone but him to fire the weapon.

Aberhadji nodded, and began walking toward the base of the erector.

THE BUZZ OF THE MACHINERY WAS SO LOUD THAT DANNY had trouble hearing the Voice.

"Repeat."

"Battery in Owl UAV is drained to within five minutes."

"Copy," he said. There was nothing he could do about it.

As he neared the back of the missile building, he angled toward the launching area, trotting, trying to conserve his energy for the final charge, trying to keep his adrenaline and emotions under control.

Just then two men came out of the front of the building, turning the corner toward him.

The fear that he had struggled alternately to contain and to ignore broke its bounds, exploding inside him. It was a dragon inside his chest, its hot breath immolating every inch of his flesh, every bone, every organ.

Kill, or be killed.

Danny fired a burst into their midsections. They crumpled, almost disintegrating in front of him.

Everything blurred. He bent forward, running faster, his head pounding. His chest felt as if it would explode. The blood vessels in his neck bulged, the blood threatening to spurt through their walls.

The missile was forty yards away. He dropped to a knee and fired a grenade. The projectile rose in a high arc toward the body of the missile, sailing directly toward the thick midsection. At the last moment it veered to the left, skimming against the side and falling beyond.

Danny pumped in another round. Someone began firing at him. The grenade exploded in the distance.

"Get down!" yelled Hera, throwing herself on top of him as he fired his second round.

He fell forward under her weight. His grenade sailed across the pressed dirt apron area, bouncing off the small hand truck of equipment and rebounding directly against the base of the rocket.

Where it exploded, igniting the fuel in the long hose nearby.

BANI ABERHADJI HEARD THE SOUND OF AN EAGLE PASSING nearby, its spread wings pushing the air away in a rush. He hadn't heard that sound since he was a boy, hunting in the mountains with his father. Those had been glorious days, days he hadn't treasured until his father died, stolen from him by the Shah in one of his sweeps against dissidents.

There were no eagles here. The sound was the noise a weapon made, a shell or a grenade or a rocket, passing nearby.

Bani Aberhadji looked up. As he did, everything around him turned red and hot.

It was an eagle, he thought. And then he thought no more.

HERA EMPTIED HER RIFLE, FIRING BLINDLY INTO THE FIREBALL and the billowing black smoke. Flames surrounded the missile, leaping up its sides.

"The tank underground," she said.

Danny realized the danger at nearly the same moment. He pushed himself up, grabbed her shirt and began pulling her back the way they'd come.

"No, across the field," she said. "The tank will be under the shed."

They started to run. Thick smoke choked Danny's lungs. His eyes began to burn.

"Run!" yelled Hera.

The ground rumbled, then ripped apart, throwing them forward. Danny smashed against the hard ground with a groan, barely getting his hand out to help break his fall.

He lay on the ground for an eternity. His lungs no longer worked. His diaphragm, his stomach muscles—everything felt paralyzed. Even his heart seemed to have stopped beating.

But they weren't going to launch that missile. He'd done it.

Five minutes passed. Another eternity.

Hera lay on her side. Her knee had banged so hard against the ground it felt numb.

"Danny?" she said.

"I'm here."

"I screwed up my knee, I think."

Slowly, Danny got his feet. He went over and helped her up. As she put weight on her foot, pain flashed through her eyes.

"You all right?" he asked, recognizing her fear.

"Yeah, I'm okay. It just got whacked."

"Let me see."

"No, I'm okay," she insisted. She took a few steps. Hobbling, then gradually willing the pain away. "Just twisted it."

Danny picked up his rifle. He slipped his finger gently against the trigger and started back toward the missile.

The shock wave from the last explosion had blown most of the fire out. The missile had toppled, breaking into three different parts. The warhead was black and bent, but still intact.

Eight bodies lay scattered around it, all burned so badly it was difficult to tell that they were human. Two other men were lying at the edge of the runway about thirty yards away. One was severely burned, dying even as Danny reached him. The other was unconscious, knocked out by the explosion but otherwise not wounded.

Hera cut his shirt off and used it to tie his hands and feet. Danny, meanwhile, went back to the warhead section. It was still hot from the fire.

They could move it. It wasn't very big, two hundred pounds at most.

Less, maybe. Easy to move.

Too easy, Danny thought.

He and Hera were almost out of ammunition. If the Iranians got here before Delta and the task force did, the nuke would be theirs practically for the taking.

79

North of Tehran

SOME SIXTY MILES TO THE SOUTHWEST, NURI AND FLASH had gassed up the car and were heading for the sea, traveling as fast as Nuri dared. They were a bit over three hours from the resort town where Danny had stashed the boats.

Tarid lay passed out in the back. Flash had stopped the bleeding and cleaned the wound in his leg. He'd lost a good amount of blood, but the injury didn't look life-threatening. Flash had given him three hits of morphine from their first aid kit, enough to keep him slumbering for at least a few hours.

They hadn't bothered to tie his hands. Nuri figured it was worth the risk; it would be hard to explain if they were stopped.

Tarid's Guard ID was in Nuri's pocket. It would be useful, if they were stopped.

Not that he intended to stop.

Flash reached over to the radio and turned it on. Europop music blared from the speaker. Flash jiggled the volume down, then began scanning the dial for a station that played something a little more friendly to his ears. The radio stopped for a few moments as it scanned to a station, then continued on. It hit a classic station, then a news channel. A sonorous voice said the word "emergency" before the radio continued on.

Nuri slammed his hand to stop it, but it moved on.

"Get that back," he told Flash.

Flash hit the button. The radio went forward, but the same program was playing on several stations at once.

"What's he saying?" asked Flash.

"The president is announcing there's been an attempt at a coup," said Nuri. "Shit. They're closing the airports, mobilizing troops. It sounds like they're going after the Revolutionary Guard, too."

"Not good."

"Not for us, no."

The Voice told Nuri that Danny had succeeded in blowing up the missile. Nuri turned down the radio and told the Voice to connect him to Danny.

"Danny, are you all right?" he asked.

There was no response.

"We're going to the rendezvous point. We'll meet you there," he said. "You hearing me?"

Still no answer.

"Problem?" asked Flash.

"I don't know. He may just be too busy to open the communications channel."

"Think they need help?"

Nuri glanced back at Tarid. His lips were moving but he made no sound.

"We're not in much of a position to help them if they do," Nuri told Flash. "Hopefully they don't."

80

Northern Iran

DANNY DIDN'T REALIZE THE WIRES TO THE MY-PID CONTROL unit had been severed until he tried to use it to contact Breanna. Somewhere during the battle, the earphones had fallen, then snagged on something when he moved. They'd been torn off, disappearing on the ground. The control unit had been smashed up pretty badly as well.

He had to use Hera's satellite phone to tell Breanna the missile was destroyed.

"The warhead is still intact," he told her. "Should be easy

to move—the assembly is scorched, but in one piece. I tore off some of the circuitry, just in case."

"I just spoke to Nuri," Breanna told him. "He has Tarid and is on his way to the boat."

"Yeah, copy that."

"Do you want him to meet you?"

"He's probably better off getting out as soon as he can," said Danny. "We're going to be here awhile, right?"

"Danny, are you sure you can hold out there?" asked Breanna.

"I'm fine, Bree. See you in a few hours."

He ended the transmission.

MEANWHILE, HERA HAD GONE BACK TO BRING THE CAR TO the field. At first she walked slowly, flexing her knee. Then, feeling cold, she started to trot and finally to run. Her knee was a little shaky, but okay. The exercise calmed her body, the slow trickle of sweat a balm for the tension that had seized her.

The confrontation at the missile had happened incredibly fast. It belonged to the moment between the flashes of a very fast camera, lost in a sequence that began with her firing the gun and ended with her looking up into Danny Freah's confident but grim face. She knew what had happened between those moments, but couldn't picture them.

They'd left the van about a half mile up from the entrance road. She trotted past the chained fence, still holding a good pace, and started along the shoulder of the road. After thirty yards she heard a car coming.

Hera leapt off the road and ducked into the ditch. She crawled to the side, watching in the direction of the entrance to the airfield.

She had no way to warn Danny; he had her phone.

She'd ambush whoever it was when they stopped to open the gate.

Hera began moving in that direction, then froze as the headlights came into view.

It was an Iranian army command Jeep. It passed right by the entrance, continuing up the road, passing Hera. As soon as it was gone, Hera began running along the ditch. Her wind started to fail after a hundred yards; she slowed, but kept moving, worried that whoever had passed would find the van even though they'd left it off the road.

THE TWO SOLDIERS IN THE JEEP WOULD HAVE DRIVEN RIGHT by it, had the headlights of the Jeep not reflected off a bottle on the shoulder of the road about twenty yards away from the turnoff for the farm.

The lieutenant in the passenger seat couldn't tell what it was at first, and told his companion to back up. It was only as they started in reverse that they saw the van in the field up at the right.

The two men got out cautiously, pistols drawn.

Though the missile launcher had exploded only a half hour before, neither man had seen or heard the explosion. The base was so isolated that, while it was spectacular, no one had been close enough to witness what was happening. A few night owls in the distance had seen flares, but they dismissed them when they died down, too far away to realize what was going on. The soldiers in the Jeep had been playing cards with the rest of their unit at a small post about fifteen miles away. A phone call had woken them, alerting them to the attempted coup and placing the unit on high alert.

Told that the Revolutionary Guard might have weapons caches in the hills, the unit immediately organized scouting parties. Literally hundreds of other small units were conducting similar surveys all across the country, while much larger units were rushing to keep the Guard in its barracks.

The van was the most interesting thing they had spotted since setting out. The locks were only a nuisance—the lieutenant fired through the keyhole on the driver's side door. When that failed to release it—the bullet severed the connection to the rod, leaving it closed—he fired three more shots through the window, then broke it with the butt of his gun.

Hera heard the shots, and knew that the men had found the van. She slipped into the woods and climbed the slight rise to the woods behind the old farm field. She came out to the right of the van, parallel to the rear fender.

The soldiers, meanwhile, had pulled out the suitcases with the Whiplash gear. They hauled the cases next to the van, opening the passenger side door for light. The light framed them perfectly.

Six bullets later, both men were dead.

As soon as Danny heard the gunshots, he began running down the road, sure Hera was in trouble. By the time he reached the access road, he was out of breath—spent not just by running, but by the past two weeks. His legs felt as if they'd been pummeled, and his arms hung almost limp from his body. His fingers barely gripped his rifle.

He stopped and crouched by the side of the road. It was hard to accept, but this was the best he could do.

A few minutes later he heard something coming. He went to one knee, steadying himself to fire.

He nearly pressed the trigger when the vehicle came into view. At the last moment he realized it was their van; a second later he saw Hera at the wheel.

He rose. She jerked on the brakes. Worried that someone was holding her hostage, he pointed his gun at her.

"Hey, don't shoot!" she yelled, leaning over to the passenger side. "It's just me."

"What happened?"

"Two army guys saw the van. They're dead."

"Where's their truck?"

"Back at the road. We should get it."

"Yeah," said Danny.

"What's the matter?"

"What do you figure they were doing up here?"

"I don't know."

"Somebody probably heard the explosion," he said. "I don't know how long we've got."

The sat phone rang. It was Nuri.

"Freah."

"Glad to hear you're OK," said Nuri, who'd just been talking to Breanna. "Listen, the Iranians have mobilized. Their president thinks the Guard is revolting against him. Which is a pretty good assumption."

"That's an understatement."

"They've started blocking off the roads. We just barely turned away from one before we would have been caught. I don't think I can get to the boat, so I'm going to come up to the field."

"All right."

"We're forty-five minutes away. Maybe less, if Flash keeps us on the roadway."

"Be careful. Hera just picked off two soldiers on patrol. What kind of shape are you guys in?"

"Shape? You mean wounded? Both of us are OK. I have Tarid with me. His leg is shot up. Why?"

"You have experience moving nuclear weapons?"

"You mean the warhead?"

"Yeah."

"No experience. I've seen pictures of them exploding. That was back in high school."

"All right. Get here as soon as you can."

"We're on our way."

"What are you thinking?" Hera asked when he put down the phone.

"I think if we wait for Delta, we'll be dead when they get here." He punched Breanna's number into the sat phone.

81

Over Iraq

THE ABORTED ATTEMPT ON THE PRESIDENT OF IRAN HAD sent the country into high alert. Army troops were moving on Revolutionary Guard installations around the country; half a dozen were already fighting pitched battles. Two Iranian warships were having a gun battle with Guard raiders—essentially speedboats with guns—in the Persian Gulf, and the air force had scrambled all of its aircraft.

The U.S. Air Force strike package tasked to hit the missile base was being held on the ground; the plan now was for the group to follow up and hit the base once the warhead had been removed.

A second group of fighters, along with AWACS, a tanker, and other support units was being readied to act as escorts for the Ospreys. Rather than accompanying the transports, the flight group would operate over the Iraqi border, just close enough to come to the rescue if something happened. The idea was that any activity would alert the Iranians that something was going on. If they didn't know something was up, the Ospreys would be able to scoot over and back without being detected.

That was the theory anyway.

"Danny, everything's moving on schedule," Breanna told him as soon as he called. "We'll have you out in a few hours."

"I'm not sure that's going to be quick enough." He explained what had happened.

"Get out of there and find a quiet place to hide," Breanna told him. "Change the rendezvous with Nuri."

"If we do that, they'll end up with the warhead," Danny said. "I have a better idea. You're in an MC-17, right?"

"Yeah?"

"I think you can land on the strip here. It's hard-packed."

Breanna brought it up on the screen and looked at the specs. It was just long enough for the C-17.

And it was less than an hour away. They could land and be back over the Iraq border as the sun was rising.

She turned to the pilot. "Do you think we could get in and out of Iraq in one piece?"

"Colonel, I thought you'd never ask."

"Danny," said Breanna, "We'll be there in forty-five minutes."

82

Iran

SEVERAL ARMY VEHICLES PASSED NURI AND FLASH AS THEY made their way to the field. Nuri ducked a little lower in the seat each time. A fatalism had settled over him; he was sure they were going to die now, apprehended probably by chance. He'd run his streak of luck too far into the ground for the result to be anything else.

Flash was too busy paying attention to the road to feel optimistic or pessimistic about anything.

"There," said Nuri, pointing to the turnoff. "Stop in front of the gate. I'll put some video bugs to cover the road before we go up."

Danny and Hera had left the gate open when they retrieved the Iranian army vehicle. Nuri and Flash found them next to the van at the end of the airstrip.

"Put the car back on the other side, opposite the missile storage building," Danny told him. "The army Jeep is there, along with a couple of others that were here."

"What building?" asked Flash.

Danny pointed to the wreckage. "Leave the lights off."

"Help me with Tarid," Nuri told him. "He's a bit heavy."

"How'd you knock him out?"

"Morphine, and lots of it. He's probably due for another hit. He took a bullet in his leg, but I don't think it's too bad."

They carried him to the van, where the Iranian they'd helped earlier was still clinging to life.

"How long before the C-17 gets here?" Nuri asked.

"Ten minutes now," said Danny. "A little more."

"You sure they can land here?"

"I've seen them land on smaller strips."

"You've seen everything, huh?"

"Not everything." Danny stared at Nuri. "I'm just as scared as you are," he told him. "But we'll get out of here."

Neither one of them spoke for a moment.

"Where's the warhead?" asked Nuri finally.

"It's up by the wreckage."

"How do we get it into the plane?"

"We'll have to rig something to carry it," said Danny. "They usually have a come-along and some other loading tools in the back."

"Why don't we use the van to pull it in?" said Nuri. "If we can get it into the back."

"Actually, we could just drag it," said Danny. "If we had a chain."

"The one on the fence at the gate."

"Good idea."

They took Tarid and the wounded Iranian out, then drove down and got the chain. As the van backed up near the warhead, Danny realized they could tip it into the back if they could lift it just a little. The gear the Iranians had used to move it around had been destroyed by the fire, but Flash figured out how to use the van's jack to push the nose of the warhead cone up just enough to get it onto the bed of the van. Pushing back slowly, they levered it far enough inside to get it in.

"Sucker is heavy," said Flash.

"Not as heavy as you'd think," said Danny. "Look at it. It fits in the back of the van."

"Considering what it can do, it ought to weigh a million pounds," said Nuri.

"Exactly."

"You sure it ain't going to blow us up?" said Flash.

Before Danny could answer, the high-pitched whine of the approaching MC-17's engines broke over the hillside.

IT WAS NO HYPERBOLE TO SAY THAT THE MC-17 HAD NO peer among jet transports when it came to flying behind enemy lines. The stock version of the aircraft had been designed to operate under battlefield conditions, landing and taking off from short, barely improved airfields, and it did that job superbly. The MC-17/M shared those qualities, and added a few of its own. It could fly in the nap of the earth, hugging the ground to avoid enemy radar. It could maintain its course to within a half meter over a 3,000-mile, turn-filled route—no easy task, even for a GPS-aided computer. And it could land in a dust bowl without damaging its engines.

Actually, the latter was not part of the design specs. While the engines were designed and situated to minimize the potential for damage, especially from bird strikes, there was only so much the engineers could do. Their debates about where to draw the line had filled several long and surprisingly heated meetings at Dreamland, not to mention countless sessions after hours in the all-ranks "lounge," aka bar.

Those discussions came back to Breanna as the wheels of the C-17 hit the ground. Dust flew everywhere. The dirt was packed down and hard, but it wasn't asphalt, let alone cement. The plane shook violently, drifting to the right but finally holding to the runway area and slowing to a crawl well short of the cratered apron where the van and warhead were waiting.

"Let's turn it around," said Captain Dominick. "The tail will be right next to them."

It was a narrow squeeze, but they managed to make it, pulling around in a three-point turn that even a driving instructor would have been proud of.

Boston, Sugar, and the loadmaster sprinted down the ramp. Nuri was already at the wheel of the van.

"You sure we ain't gonna glow sittin' next to this sucka?" asked Sugar.

"You glow already," said Boston.

There wasn't enough room for the van with the Ospreys in the rear. But the loadmaster improvised a chain and tackle and a pair of impromptu ramps, allowing them to bring the warhead into the bay and place it, without too much groaning, onto a pair of dollies. They wheeled the weapon alongside the Ospreys, chaining it to the side.

By that time, Greasy Hands had helped Hera bring Tarid and the wounded missile technician inside. They lay them on temporary stretchers behind the Ospreys in the seating area. The accommodations weren't exactly first class, but neither was in a position to complain.

"Greasy Hands? What are you doing here?" asked Danny when he saw Parsons.

"Enjoying retirement," said the chief, clapping him on the back.

"Social Security doesn't stretch as far as it used to," said Boston. "So he decided to moonlight. We pay him under the table."

"Well I'm glad as hell to see you," said Danny.

"Same here," said Greasy Hands. "Next time you guys kidnap somebody, though, pick someone about fifty pounds lighter."

THEY GOT OFF THE GROUND A FEW MINUTES LATER, THE aircraft shuddering as the wind kicked up, but lifting them up with plenty of room to spare.

Plenty of room being defined, in this case, as three and a half meters.

Breanna worked out a course that would bring them back

to Baghdad International Airport, where they could refuel before continuing on. They would also be able to get a doctor for Tarid, who'd woken but remained dazed on a makeshift stretcher below. The other Iranian didn't look as if he'd make it, though he was still alive.

"Twenty minutes to Iraqi territory," Breanna announced. "We'll be in Baghdad inside the hour."

The MC-17 had come east without a direct escort, operating on the theory that they were safer if the Iranians had no idea they were there. The fighters tasked to protect it remained over southern and northern Iraq, ready to scramble if necessary, but otherwise attempting to look as if they were interested in something else.

The theory had proven correct on the flight in, but now reality injected complications. Because of the coup, the Iranian air force had scrambled several flights of MiGs. While they were slow to get in the air—the C-17 had already landed at the missile site before the first one took off—there were now a full dozen over the western half of the country, with more on the runways.

The AWACS detected one of the patrols flying up from the south on a rough intercept with the MC-17 shortly after it took off. Though it didn't seem likely that the Iranians had spotted the cargo aircraft, the fighter group commander decided to take no chances. The group of F-15s to the south were told to intercept.

The fighters were picked up immediately by Iranian air defenses. Radars and missile sites began tracking them along the border area, trying to lock on and launch missiles. One of the antiaircraft sites was almost directly in the MC-17's path. The northern group of interceptors, which included an F-16 Wild Weasel SAM suppressor, was ordered to take out the defenses. More MiGs came out for them as they started toward the site.

In the space of ninety seconds the sky became intensely crowded and angry.

The cargo aircraft, however, remained at very low altitude, undetected by either the SAMs or the Iranian interceptors.

"I think we can sneak by all this," Dominick told Breanna. "We just stay on course."

"Exactly."

The word was no sooner out of her mouth than the AWACS announced a new warning: A pair of Iranian fighters had taken off from Tabriz and were heading south, in their direction. Two more aircraft were coming off the runway right behind them.

Breanna looked at the IDs, which were flashed over via a messaging system from the AWACS. The planes were Su-27s, older Russian aircraft recently sold to Iran. They were long in the tooth—but would have no trouble shooting down an unarmed cargo aircraft. Both were equipped with improved versions of Slotback radar; the "look-down, shoot-down" radar system made it easy for them to locate and destroy aircraft at low altitudes.

The MC-17 was a sitting duck. Even a Megafortress would have had trouble against them, if it didn't have its Flight-hawks.

"They'll see us as soon as they come further south," Breanna warned Frederick. "We need to get as close to that border as we can. I'm going to call the F-15s south. Maybe they can help."

As soon as the Eagle pilots hit their afterburners, the Iranians changed course and headed for them.

So far no one had fired at each other. The Iranians protested that the Americans were trespassing and would be shot down; the Americans replied that they were covering an operation on the Iraqi side of the border and would return as soon as they were confident that the Iranians would not interfere. The white lie led to considerable huffing and puffing, but no gunplay.

Not yet, anyway.

"We're clear," said Breanna, following what was going on via the AWACS link.

But they didn't stay clear. The second flight of Sukhois continued south, directly toward their path.

"We have thirteen minutes to the border," Breanna told Frederick. "Just keep on keepin' on."

But the Iranians had finally spotted them. The lead Sukhoi asked the MC-17 to identify itself.

"What should I say?" Frederick asked Breanna.

"Tell them we're on a mercy mission," she said. She remembered the list of injuries, all minor except for Tarid's bullet wound, that her people had suffered. "We have a patient who requires burn treatment."

"Maybe you ought to talk to them," said the pilot, doubtfully. "Maybe they'll believe a woman."

They didn't.

"Unidentified aircraft. We see that you are a U.S. warplane," answered the Iranian. "You are ordered to turn to the north and fly to Tabriz airport."

"Negative," said Breanna. "We have a very sick patient we've evacked from one of your facilities. You better check in with your superiors. Your English, by the way, is very good. Where did you learn it?"

Flattery got her nowhere. The pilot increased his speed. The two Sukhois were now less than thirty miles away, closing the distance between the two aircraft at a little over four miles a minute.

The border was just over twelve minutes away. More importantly, the closest American fighters, off to the south with the MiGs, were nearly fifteen minutes from firing range.

Depending on what missiles the Iranian interceptors were carrying, they might already be in range to fire. Even if they were under orders to obtain a visual identification before making an attack, they would get to the MC-17 well before the Eagles did.

Frederick tried to get more thrust from the engines, even though they were already at max.

"Maybe we should do what they want," he suggested as the Sukhois continued to gain.

"I don't see that as an option," said Breanna coldly.

"What I mean is, we make it look like we are," explained the pilot. "We turn and head north very, very slowly. We give the F-15s a chance to catch up. When they're here, no more problems. We turn around and go home."

Draw the encounter out and stall for time, then run away. There didn't seem to be another choice.

"Maybe you're right," said Breanna. "Let's play it by ear."

"Iranian flight, please state your intentions," she said as the Sukhois closed in.

"We are going to shoot you down if you do not comply with our directions."

"Have you checked with your commander? We are on a mission authorized by your president." Breanna could almost feel her nose growing.

"You will change your heading immediately," replied the pilot.

Nine minutes to the border. Eleven to the Eagles.

"They're going to shoot us down," said Frederick. His voice cracked, betraying the pressure he felt welling inside his chest. He'd never been in combat before. He was starting to gulp air, hyperventilating despite his efforts to stay calm.

"It's all right," said Breanna. "They're under orders to see what they're firing at first. We have more time. Just play it out slow."

The Iranian jets lined themselves up on a course that would take them over the MC-17's wings. They didn't slow down as they approached, deciding that a close buzz of the aircraft might intimidate the pilot into doing what they wanted.

Or crashing. Which would be just as good.

Breanna saw it as one more minute in her favor. That gave her seven to the Eagles.

Who now checked in with a warning of their own.

"Iranian aircraft approaching the Iraqi border, identify yourselves," said the lead Eagle pilot.

The Iranians declined. Instead they circled back behind the MC-17 and fired a pair of warning shots over its wing.

"What do you want to do?" asked Frederick.

"I want to shoot the bastards down," said Breanna.

"That's not an option."

"I know. But it's what I want to do."

If she'd been flying a Megafortress, even without missiles or Flighthawks, it would be an option. She'd sucker them in close, then open up with the Stinger air-mine cannon in the tail.

The MC-17 didn't have that capability. But it did have the Ospreys.

"Greasy Hands, when you load the Ospreys into the bay, do they go in head first or tail first?" she asked, turning around to the chief.

"Tail first. Want to be able to take off right away. Truth of it, though, I don't think it matters."

"Do you think you could fire the cannon from inside the cargo hold?"

"Shit, I don't know."

"It's either that or get used to Iranian food for quite a while."

Greasy Hands unbuckled his seat belt. So did the loadmaster across from him.

Captain Frederick was breathing hard. His hand trembled on the yoke.

"Don't take this the wrong way," Breanna told him. "But maybe I should fly the plane through this. OK?"

"Colonel, that's fine," said Frederick.

"You're doing all right. Just hang with me."

One of the Iranian jets came up close to the side. The other remained behind them.

"You will comply or be shot down," said the lead Iranian.

Breanna flipped on the cockpit lights, making sure he could see. Then she gave the Iranian a thumbs-up.

"I need to know the heading and the airport data," she told

the Iranian. "And how long is the runway? Will I be able to land? How strong is the wind?"

"You will turn to ten degrees, northeast."

"Which airport am I going to?"

"You will turn to ten degrees, northeast."

"I have to tell my superiors where I am going," she said. "I don't want to get in trouble."

The plane behind her fired a short burst. One of the bullets grazed the bottom of the fuselage.

"All right, I'm turning," said Breanna, slowing down.

GREASY HANDS WAS ALREADY OUT OF BREATH AS HE reached the bottom of the ladder from the flight deck. He pushed himself toward the Ospreys, which were secured close to the ramp.

Danny Freah jumped up from his seat.

"Gotta get to the Osprey," Greasy Hands told him, huffing toward the aircraft.

"What's going on?" asked Danny, following.

"Iranians. Bree's got something up her sleeve. Help me."

Parsons slipped as the C-17 dipped. Danny caught him, holding him upright against the second Osprey.

"We need to get into number two," said Greasy Hands. He pushed upright and ran to the aircraft nearest the tail. The chief twisted past the retaining strap and squeezed into the cockpit, pushing down into the pilot's seat.

There were two problems with Breanna's idea. The Ospreys were transported with their wings folded up over the body, extending toward and over the front of the aircraft. That made it difficult to see through the windscreen. But they wouldn't have much room to aim anyway; the best strategy would be to fire straight back, hoping to catch the Iranian plane by surprise.

The second problem was more formidable. The computer initiated a systems lockdown when the aircraft was in transport mode. There was a software override, but Greasy Hands had no time to initiate it. Instead, he ducked under the panel and pulled out the master power feed, killing the computer entirely.

"I gotta get power into this panel to get the gun working," he told Danny. It was a shortcut they'd often used while checking the mechanical systems, but it would still take time to implement. "Tell Bree it's gonna be a few minutes. She's gonna have to move in front of the Sukhoi when she wants to fire. She's aiming. And tell the loadmaster not to open the ramp until I say so."

"You're opening the ramp?" said Danny.

"Well I sure as hell ain't gonna fire through the door," said Greasy Hands, trying to picture the wiring diagram in his head.

BREANNA TOOK THE TURN AS SLOWLY AS SHE COULD, LETting the MC-17 drift downward and to the west, edging closer to the border. The F-15s tried another hail but weren't answered.

The Iranian on her right wing pulled a little closer. She used that as an excuse to duck off to the left.

"Whoa, don't get so close!" she shouted over the open microphone. "You're going to hit us!"

"Get back on course," said the pilot behind her.

"Get that guy off my wing. I can't fly! I can't fly!" She put as much panic into her voice as possible.

"Calm down, Yankee."

"Get him to move off. Please. *Please!*"

The Sukhoi started away. Breanna checked her watch. The Eagles were about five minutes away. She was a little more than three from the border.

She cut her power again.

"No games!" said the Iranian behind her. He punctuated his message with a few rounds from his cannon. They passed overhead and to her right.

"We're ready!" said Danny over the interphone. He'd grabbed a headset downstairs.

"Open the hatch, and hang on. I have to dip low—you'll have about two seconds to nail the son of a bitch."

"Go for it!"

"Crew, hang on," said Breanna.

A light on her panel came on, indicating the rear ramp was opening.

"One thousand one, one thousand two—now!" said Breanna. She shoved the aircraft downward, its tail directly in the nose of the Sukhoi.

"FIRE! FIRE! FIRE!" YELLED DANNY, WHO WAS STANDING ON the skid on the right side of the Osprey, his arms clamped around the spar. He could see the nose of an Iranian plane less than fifty feet away.

Greasy Hands pressed the trigger.

Nothing happened.

"Fire!"

Greasy Hands cursed, then slammed his hand on the yoke button. Bullets sputtered from the chin of Osprey, streaming from the belly of the big cargo plane.

The pilot in the Sukhoi couldn't understand what was happening as the plane swooped and its tail opened. He thought the American might be bailing out. As he started to correct to get back on the MC-17's wing, tracers flew through the air at him. He pushed hard to his right, tumbling away.

"Flares!" yelled Breanna, slamming the throttle to military power. "Button up down there and hang on!"

She pushed the MC-17 hard left, sliding into a turn toward the Iraqi border. The aircraft fell through the sky, skidding in the air. It wasn't designed for high g evasive maneuvers like a fighter was; it shuddered and creaked and complained, whining about the forces trying to tear its wings apart.

But it held together nonetheless.

The Iranian pilots circled around to follow. But the surprise gunfire from the rear of their aircraft had thrown them off, and they hesitated before pressing an attack.

Just for a few seconds.

"Missiles in the air!" yelled Frederick, his voice drowning

out the alarm from the launch warning indicator. "Heat seekers! Two! Three!"

"More flares," said Breanna calmly.

The decoy flares shot out around the plane, sucking away the missiles as Breanna pitched the MC-17 into a half turn, feinting north again but pulling back toward Iraq.

"More missiles!"

"Flares."

The big plane shook and started to drop as Breanna tried a hard jink to the right. The plane began to stall—it simply couldn't do what she wanted and stay in the air.

Breanna eased back on the controls, dipping the nose slightly to gain a little more speed. The first missile sniffed the decoys and exploded behind them.

The second hit the outboard right engine.

The plane quaked. Breanna felt the shake run up through her hand and into her spine.

She knew exactly how this felt. She'd felt it before, over India, flying an EB-52.

That time, there had been multiple hits. She'd wrestled the plane out over the ocean where they could be rescued.

She'd also been in an EB-52, built to deal with serious abuse. Not a C-17, which generally didn't encounter anything nastier than a bird strike.

"Going through two thousand feet!" said Frederick.

They were falling.

"Fifteen hundred feet!"

"Help me with the engines," Breanna told him.

They shut down engine four, trying to compensate by trimming their controls and adjusting the other engines.

"We need more altitude," warned Frederick.

The F-15s, meanwhile, were coming in range of their AMRAAMs. The Iranians changed course north, trying to get away.

"Globemaster, do you require assistance?" asked the lead F-15 pilot.

"Chase them away. We'll take care of the rest," said Breanna.

"Coming through fourteen hundred feet," said Fredericks, "going to—going to fifteen hundred feet."

They were climbing. They had it under control.

"Let's bring it up to three thousand and hold it there," said Breanna. "Until we catch our breath."

83

Washington, D.C.
Three days later

SENATOR JEFFREY "ZEN" STOCKARD ROLLED HIS WHEEL-chair forward as the C-20 taxied up the ramp, lights twinkling in the dim evening haze. The aircraft stopped less than ten yards away; a moment later the forward doorway opened and the stairs popped down.

"Mama, Mama!" cried Teri Stockard, running from her father's side as Breanna appeared in the doorway.

Teri caught her at the foot of the steps, wrapping her in a bear hug.

"Hey, love, I'm so glad to see you," Breanna said, returning the hug. "I missed you so much."

"I'm sorry," said Teri. Tears were falling from her eyes.

"What are you sorry about?"

"That I yelled at you."

"It's OK, baby." Breanna pulled her closer. "I'm sorry I missed your show. But I promise I'll be at the next one."

"It's OK if you're not. I understand."

"Hey there, little girl."

"Uncle Danny!" Teri hugged him.

"I owe you some bedtime stories, huh?" he said.

"Yes."

"All right. I'll see you soon."

The rest of the Whiplash team smiled as they passed by. None of them were married, and their closest family members lived many miles away.

"So we're on for lunch Thursday," Danny told Nuri, catching up to him. "Then we get back to work."

"Sounds good." Nuri stretched his back. He'd gotten a kink in the plane ride on the way home. "This place better be good."

"It is. Or it was two weeks ago. Senator Stockard recommended it," added Danny, pointing to Zen.

Zen had been hanging back to give his daughter and wife some space for their reunion. He pushed his wheelchair toward them.

"I don't believe we've met," Zen told the CIA officer. "I'm Bree's husband."

"Senator, it's an honor."

"Call me Zen." Zen looked at Danny. "You guys have fun?"

"Always," said Danny.

"Up for a baseball game next week? Dodgers are in town."

"I should be able to work it out. If the boss doesn't crack the whip too hard."

"I hear she runs a tight ship," said Zen.

Danny smiled, and turned back to look at Breanna. They'd given the team the next week off, but he and Nuri were heading back to work on Thursday. They'd already been debriefed by National Security and CIA staffers, but the President had asked for a personal report.

Nuri wanted to get it over with so he could join the team debriefing Tarid, who was currently at an Army base in Germany, bonding with a pair of CIA interrogators. How useful he'd be remained to be seen—with the collapse of the plot to build a secret bomb, the Iranian Revolutionary Guard was in disarray. Information about Bani Aberhadji coursed freely through the Iranian media, which was enjoying a rare period of openness as the newly emboldened president flexed his political muscles. How long this would last was anyone's guess, but at the moment relations between the U.S. and Iran were at an all-time high.

In fact, Iran was acting like a serious and responsible member of the world community for the first time since the Revolution. The country had not recognized Israel, but it had denounced a recent terror strike in the Gaza strip in unusually strong terms—an unprecedented gesture.

As for Whiplash, a great deal of work lay ahead. The team would have to be expanded. The lines of responsibility would have to be straightened out. They'd have to decide whether Hera was staying or not.

But that was in the future. Right now they'd all earned a rest. Danny was thinking baseball; Nuri was looking forward to catching up on his sleep. Flash had a few movies to catch up on. Hera was headed for a week on the sand and margaritas in Miami.

Even Breanna was going to take a few days off, as she promised her daughter when she finally released her from her hug.

"I thought we could do some girl things," Breanna told her.

"Like save the world?" said Zen, rolling close.

"That *is* a girl thing," she told him, leaning over to kiss him. "But that's not what I had in mind."

"Uh-oh," laughed Zen. "Something tells me the next few days are going to cost me a small fortune."

"Oh, no, Zen," said Breanna. "It won't be a *small* fortune at all."

"A big one," shouted Teri, hugging her father. "A real big one. Right, Mom?"